VENUS
REBORN

VENUS REBORN

Martina Devlin

POOLBEG

Published 2003
by Poolbeg Press Ltd.
123 Grange Hill, Baldoyle,
Dublin 13, Ireland
Email: poolbeg@poolbeg.com

© Martina Devlin 2003

The moral right of the author has been asserted.

Copyright for typesetting, layout, design
© Poolbeg Group Services Ltd.

1 3 5 7 9 10 8 6 4 2

A catalogue record for this book is available from the British Library.

ISBN 1-84223-152-9

About the Author

Martina Devlin was born in Omagh, Co Tyrone and now lives in Dublin. She started writing fiction after winning a Hennessy Literary Award. She has published two best-sellers, *Three Wise Men* and *Be Careful What You Wish For*, as well as a number of short stories, and works as a journalist. Her website is www.martinadevlin.com

Acknowledgements

Thanks to my father, Frank Devlin, for being the template for my lovely Dan Macken.

To my mother, Bridie Devlin, for her powerfully evocative ghost story in Chapter 27.

To my nephew, Justin Blanchard, aged twelve, for the title – the pressure's on to match it for the next book, Justin.

To my agent, Stephanie Cabot from the William Morris Agency, for her warm and unflagging support, and to her super-efficient assistant Hamish Crombie – I still can't believe he doesn't speak with a Scottish accent.

To Paula Campbell and the Poolbeg team for their enthusiasm for *Venus Reborn*; and especially to Gaye Shortland for her painstaking – but diplomatic – editing.

To Jerry and Betty Murphy, for lending me Roancarrick.

To Sarah Webb and the rest of the Irish Girls About Town crew, for wine, emails, friendship – and limericks.

To Lorraine Curran, who knows all the answers, or at least where to find them. And to David Murphy, for being my own personal cheerleader.

*For Tonia Blanchard, exactly the kind of sister
I would have chosen for myself*

Chapter One

Venus Macken took a deep breath. A ruffle of apprehension flared briefly and was flattened: fortune favours the brave, she reminded herself. Then she gripped the trolley, tilted her chin and shunted forward. The blue Nothing To Declare zone was silent and deserted, in contrast with the babble from the excitable crowd just beyond it in the arrivals' hall of Dublin Airport. Despite her reservations, the welcoming commotion buoyed her as she stepped through the automatic glass doors, and her mood lightened for the first time in weeks.

Lily, large as life and infinitely more reliable, was waiting at the front of the barrier. 'Over here, Venus,' she cried, arms flailing exuberantly, as Venus scanned the throng penned together by the inevitable building works. Almost at once, Lily's face detached itself from the amorphous mass.

'Lily,' she smiled, pleasure and relief tempering her trepidation, and she caused an obstruction as she abandoned her trolley and leaned across the metal strips to hug her friend. Their greeting was so ebullient it threatened Lily's edifice of hair, a lacquered topknot which loomed, as artful as wedding-cake icing.

Venus released Lily Dillon and grinned into her freckled face, as broad as it was long and beaming back at her with inherent sunny temperament.

'Are you a gibbering wreck?' Lily was invariably sympathetic to Venus's flying phobia.

'Made a holy show of myself. I could tell the businessman in the seat next to me was wishing he'd paid for an upgrade,' confirmed Venus, as Lily patted her caramel-streaked hair into place, knowing instinctively where its defences were breached.

'Coming through,' chimed a chorus of voices behind her. Venus glanced over her shoulder and saw they belonged to the delegation of travel agents she'd noticed on the plane from London, each with a surplus of fake tan slapped onto an even greater surfeit of bare skin. Ireland would soon goose-pimple their exposures, she thought, letting them pass. Then she wheeled the trolley to the gap in the barricade, allowing Lily to take it from her. Having single-handedly kept the plane in the air with the powers of mental concentration and her seahorse talisman, she hadn't the energy for threading around bodies or finding the carpark. Besides, these building works were so invasive, they seemed to occupy half the terminal.

Lily read her thoughts. 'It's a Government job-creation scheme. They invite in building firms on a cyclical basis – gives the industry a fillip since the slump in the economy. There's no evidence they actually do anything other than put up barriers and take them down again, but it provides employment.' She sailed along with Venus in tow, firing coins into a machine and somehow cramming all the bags into the boot of her metallic tangerine Fiat Punto. 'Did you have to pay excess luggage fees?'

'No, they took pity on me because the plane wasn't full.' Venus spoke in the glum tones of one for whom small mercies were inadequate. 'The rest is arriving next week. I have a quarter-share in a van coming across from Holloway. I saw an ad in *The Irish Post*.'

'That was lucky.' Lily's tone was encouraging.

Venus didn't bother responding. As far as she was concerned, luck had no hand in this enterprise.

'Traffic here must be as diabolical as London.' Lily flipped down her visor and inspected her teeth in its mirror as they ground to a halt on the Drumcondra Road. Then she ransacked her handbag for a packet of cigarettes.

'Don't you believe it.' Venus wasn't allowing Dublin to claim comparisons with London, where she'd lived for the past decade – even unflattering ones.

Lily lit a cigarette and prepared to wait with her customary serenity.

Meanwhile Venus cast a desultory glance out of the window at the ranks of red-brick houses: some of the front gardens had been given the feng shui treatment. Imagine finding a stone Buddha outside a terraced house in a northside street – what had they done with all those grotto recreations of Our Lady appearing to St Bernadette?

'I must say, you could have knocked me down with a feather boa when I heard you were moving back home.' Lily rolled down a window to let her cigarette-smoke drift out, but wound it up hurriedly as the wind threatened the stability of her candy-floss hair. That teased-up confection was testament to Lily's illogical nature. All through college, when she scarcely had the funds for bus fares, she would always ensure there was money for supplies of hairspray and styling mousse. 'You settled into London so easily, you seemed tailor-made for one another,' added Lily.

Venus emitted a non-committal sound, although she agreed with Lily; it felt like a penance, this resolution to move back to Ireland. Dublin would have been manageable, but she wouldn't even have the consolation of city life. She was exiling herself in the wilds of Roancarrick. North-west frontier country: remote, remoter, remotest. Where was the point in making your escape from village life if you turned round and shimmied back up the drainpipe?

'I'm going to miss having you within the sound of Bow Bells,' continued Lily.

'Nobody could hear the bells above the traffic,' muttered Venus. All the same, she didn't want to leave London – after a decade she felt entitled to squatter's rights.

Lily changed lanes and overtook on the inside. 'It was handy for weekend trips – you could be across in an hour.'

'There's always Roancarrick for a weekend retreat.'

'Ah come on, I'm a Dub. We wind up with nosebleeds if we lose sight of the Liffey. Going to London doesn't count because there's still all that filthy air and noise pollution and people jostling you on the pavements – everything to give you that home from home feeling. Anyway the country makes me nervous; it's suspiciously quiet for hours on end and then some unidentifiable animal starts up a racket.' Lily, who only smoked a couple of inhalations of each cigarette in an uneconomical economy drive to quit, stubbed it out.

'It's not the country, it's the seaside,' objected Venus.

'Still has small furry animals and no streetlights.'

'You see,' Venus addressed the dashboard, 'even my friends don't want to come to Roancarrick for a visit. And I've condemned myself to a lifetime there.'

'You might find you like it,' Lily soothed. She hesitated, debating whether to persevere. 'Sometimes you seemed a little stressed in London – you had trouble relaxing. A few months in Donegal might be just the tonic you need.'

'It's not the months that bother me, it's the idea of them stretching into years,' Venus sighed, allowing her gaze to drift aimlessly.

Yet Lily's words left her uneasy. Had she really appeared to be under pressure in London? She thrived on rushing around: work hard, play hard was the only game in town. Lily must be flagging, she decided – she was seven years older than Venus, after all, and obviously didn't understand the attractions of the metropolitan lifestyle. Dublin was only a tiddler of a city by London standards.

'I'm going to camp out permanently on your sofa bed, cramping your style with the hordes of desirable men you invite home for coffee, unless you promise to visit me in Roancarrick.' Venus's threat was delivered without even the glimmer of a smile.

Lily shrugged. 'There are no desirable men in Dublin. There seems to be a Bermuda Triangle hovering over the city which sucks them all up, sparing only pimply teenagers and balding daddies. It's a wonder the gardaí don't have a special investigation unit to check it out.'

'So you're single again,' surmised Venus. 'It didn't work out with what's his name?'

Lily lit another cigarette, radiating good humour. 'No. Thought I'd unearthed the last sane, presentable man in the country, but I discovered he was married – the smell of fabric

5

conditioner from his clothes was the clue. Then I took up with his appalling single friend, not my type at all but I was on the rebound and my selection procedures went haywire, and would you believe it, he threw me over for a divorcée with cellulite? The clincher was the couple of children she had – he fancied a readymade family. Saved him holding a screeching Valkyrie's hands during labour or having his Cartier watch flushed down the jacks by a toddler investigating the plumbing. So, Venus, I've decided to wait for the call.'

'The call to God? I don't see you in a convent.'

'The call to the Bermuda Triangle, now poised in the sky somewhere above Scotsman's Bay. The way I see it, the aliens who are creaming off all our single men must need women too. It's only a matter of time before they work their way round to me.'

Venus laughed until the tears flowed, more than Lily's banter deserved in truth, but weeks' worth of second thoughts melded to produce a giggling spasm that left her gasping for air.

Lily leaned on her horn, refusing to make space for a four-wheel-drive attempting to pull away from Connolly Station – nobody expected vibrant tangerine cars to fight their corner. 'Anyway, Venus, I have a spare room now that I've finally bought an apartment after years of procrastination unforgivable in an estate agent, so you won't be able to cramp my style. Even supposing the aliens finish their experiments and return some of our men. It's a boxroom with only a shop-rail for your clothes, but it's all yours until you can face Roancarrick.'

Roancarrick. Venus flagged as she thought of the seaside community where she'd grown up. It was scarcely more than a huddle of houses, a shop and a pub, lacking even the sub-post office that defined a village. And she was returning to live there because she felt the need to pay back a debt, although no bill had ever been presented – not even implicitly. It was one of those decisions taken because it was the right thing to do. But it tasted of ashes in her mouth.

'I have to face Roancarrick. Not much point in galloping back on an angel of mercy mission if I balk at the last leg of the journey.' Venus pushed a strand of red hair behind her ear and tried to radiate determination.

'I have a friend called Karim who's partial to angels,' remarked Lily. Then, as she swiped a pass card to access the carpark in front of her block of flats, she added, 'There's something you should remember about angels, Venus.'

Venus arched an eyebrow and waited.

'They have wings. They're supposed to spread them.'

Venus harried the inside of her teeth with her tongue while she mulled over that gem. How could retreating to the freckle of a village she called home count as spreading her wings? Her friend was spouting nonsense – all that adrenaline from negotiating Dublin's traffic jams must have overheated her brain. Imagine being dubbed both stressed out and unadventurous – they had to be mutually exclusive.

It occurred to Venus that Lily was suggesting she had settled into a groove in London. It was true she had held down the same job for the past ten years and had lived in the same Barbican apartment for the last seven of them. But she loved teaching in the Bridges Across The World language school – why switch employers for the sake of it? As for the apartment, it was a fabulous place, all blond wood and ivory walls, and she'd had the lease at a cheap rent from the school's director – it would have been folly to turn in the keys. Once a week she would buy tightly sealed cream rosebuds to match its décor, watching each day as they unfurled a shade more. *La vie en rose*, just the way she liked it.

Venus pursed her lips. She hadn't intended staying at Bridges Across The World when she'd arrived initially in London. Hadn't she meant to travel around South America? Take singing lessons? Do charity work one night a week? Instead of which she'd spent a decade walking along Vauxhall Bridge Road, with a briefcase in one hand and a takeaway cappuccino in the other, devoting herself to the school. Where it had always been touch and go whether the past pluperfect would be added to the repertoires of students who could say 'pop a chill pill, teach' but who had a problem with anything other than the present tense.

Venus swivelled her head towards her reflection in the car window – and saw her mother instead. Which was curious, she reflected later, because they bore no resemblance to each other, not even in some fold of skin or inherited mannerism. For she was adopted.

Yet Maura Macken continued to gaze at Venus. The image wasn't the usual way she was saddled with visualising her mother's face, bones jutting through paper flesh. Her clavicle, in particular, had developed a way of poking through the hollow of her neck that had made Venus catch her breath. Maura's eyes had been the most distressing to look into: Venus would never forget the film that had covered them as, glazed by drugs given to control the pain, her mother had stopped recognising people. Even Venus, unless she leaned right over the bed and spoke. 'Mam,' she'd murmur, 'don't you know me, Mam?'

'Of course, chicken,' the response would come. But

Maura had taken to calling everyone chicken to mask her failing vision.

Today, Venus saw her mother as she'd looked at her daughter's graduation. Elated, flushed with vitality. Perhaps it was a positive sign, since Maura Macken had been so proud that day. The image showed an ageing, upright woman of medium build in an aqua wool suit with cascading pleated skirt. Venus had wanted her mother to borrow her torc, to match the soft silver waves of the hairstyle Maura had never varied since the age of twenty, but the older woman had believed silver didn't count as real jewellery and had worn her gold crucifix and chain. She hadn't believed in lucky charms either, unlike Venus, who never left home without her seahorse. That cross and chain had been her mother's golden calf, however – treasured because it had been blessed by the Pope during his visit to Ireland in 1979, when Venus had been laid up with chicken-pox and too infectious to make the trip to the Phoenix Park.

Maura hadn't brought any jewellery into hospital with her, convinced she'd be robbed in her sleep. But one day she'd fretted for the cross and chain, clutching at her bare neck, and although Venus had just arrived to visit she'd driven home immediately to collect it. The image of it glinting in the sunlight would never leave her. For she associated it with those surges of atavistic fear that had mauled her as her mother's breath had hacked through her lungs – terror that had accelerated as the gaps between each soughing intake of oxygen had widened.

Venus glimpsed the cross and chain again, glittering from the car window glass. All that glisters is not gold, she thought. Then averted her eyes. The last time she'd seen that crucifix on its matching chain had been in Roancarrick six months ago, when her mother's body had been laid out. Just before the coffin lid had closed on her ravaged, beautiful, irreplaceable face.

* * *

Lily's apartment was on the quayside close to Tara Street Dart station, in a block accessed via a set of metal gates which had *Adelphi Court* worked into them in arabesques. She led Venus into the living-room, with picture windows on two sides that allowed light to flood in. They were fitted with wooden blinds and, in tandem with the polished wooden floors, lent the room a modern, spare appearance. Lily adjusted the blinds while Venus considered her surroundings. Her friend had chosen well: it was central, had a security camera in the foyer and seemed spacious by London standards, although Lily apologised that it was cramped. Venus almost envied her friend this trapping of adulthood – a mortgage signalled maturity in a way that a marriage certificate or university degree could never match.

'I like the floorboards.' Venus tapped her heels, castanet-fashion, against the honeyed wood.

'I had to have them stripped – can you believe it, they were painted black? To add insult to injury, when I moved the furniture left behind I discovered the previous owner had painted around the outlines. I was left looking at all these armchair and sofa shapes. There was even a bizarre oval on the bathroom door that can only have been the painted-around contour of a shower-cap. I thought I'd seen everything as an estate agent, but that managed to surprise me.'

Venus grinned. 'Never mind, you have a fantastic apartment now. How do you describe it in your jargon?'

'Bijou. Although my mother calls it a kennel. But she grew up on a farm with outhouses twice the size of this – it warped her expectations. She thinks everyone should have three sheds and their own supply of milk fresh from the udder.' Lily shook her head over her capable, square-fingered hands. 'Generations of farm workers have produced these fists, they're wasted in an office. I should be driving tractors to get the benefit of them.'

They debated leaving Venus's bags in the car, decided it was inviting a break-in, and went off to bump them upstairs.

'I can see the ships when they dock on the quayside – it always makes me feel as though I've looped back a couple of centuries,' chattered Lily.

Preoccupied with thoughts of the next stage of her journey, Venus rationed out a smile.

'Feel free to ring home and tell your father the eagle has landed,' offered Lily.

'Maybe later,' hedged Venus. Her father believed she wasn't arriving until the following day and she'd prefer to maintain the fiction – she wanted some time with Lily in Dublin before trekking on to Roancarrick.

Venus felt simultaneously guilty and defiant. She was up-ending her life like a snow-globe for her father, scattering the flakes helter-skelter; she was entitled to a weekend with her friend first. Then again, her father hadn't asked for anything, least of all self-sacrifice. She knew he was lonely up there, rattling about in that windy house on his own, but he always made an effort to sound busy and contented when she rang.

A conscience was a curse, as weightily invasive as an albatross dangling around the neck. Everyone knew if you were going to play truant you should at least have the sense to enjoy it. Venus's eyes skimmed towards the open doorway where she could see the telephone lead, wondering if she should own up to being in Dublin already.

Lily made the decision for her, leaning over the back of one of her corduroy armchairs with an expression of innocence so contrived it screeched guilt. And just to cement Venus's suspicions, her blinking tic went into overdrive. Lily always blinked rapidly when she was up to something.

'Venus, I've met this asylum seeker I'd like to introduce you to. His name is Karim and he's from Chechnya. I haven't known him long so a second opinion would help.'

'A second opinion on what – whether or not to employ him to paint your kitchen?'

Lily had been complaining she couldn't find a tradesman to tackle the job because it wasn't lucrative enough. They only wanted to do total refurbishments, preferably of four-storey houses.

The blinking accelerated. 'I'm thinking of marrying him so he can stay in the country. He needs citizenship, I can help him get it. Don't look so worried – it's just a marriage of convenience.'

Chapter Two

Lily stepped back to admire her housewarming present from Venus, which she insisted on placing in pole position on the living-room mantelpiece.

'It's a mermaid, Lily, shouldn't it go in the bathroom?'

'Too obvious. Besides, it's not a mermaid, it's a siren.'

'What's the difference?'

'Sirens are bold hussies, mermaids are just vain.' Lily was adamant. 'Mermaids distract sailors and wreck ships by accident, as they sit around combing their hair and flaunting themselves on rocks. Meanwhile sirens have a strategy and deliberately lure sailors to their doom.'

Venus lifted the chubby pottery mermaid, grinning mischievously rather than seductively. She wore a necklace of shells and looked as though she were romping through the surf in a glut of puppy energy, thinking about nothing more compelling than where to lay her hands on a couple of chocolate eclairs. 'If you say so, Lily.'

'Isn't there some kind of mermaid's cave in Roancarrick?'

Lily remembered peering over the fence alongside the cliff-top, steadfastly refusing to climb down to inspect the cave at close quarters – she'd twist her ankle on that squiggle of a path.

'That's right.' A twinge of nostalgia stirred as Venus thought of the cave she'd explored as a child, accessible only at low tide.

Lily stroked the pottery siren on her bulging tummy. 'You know, for a woman who couldn't wait to leave the seaside behind, you have a habit of buying beach-related trinkets.'

'Maybe there's something in it,' conceded Venus. 'I never said I didn't like the sea; I just find Roancarrick a bit limiting. London's my kind of town – everybody minds their own business and nobody knows chapter and verse on who you are and where you come from.'

Lily levelled her perceptive gaze at her friend. 'There's no shame in being adopted, Venus. It means you were wanted. And chosen.'

Weariness bled into Venus. She'd slept little the night before and had risen early to catch the tube to Paddington for the Heathrow Express. She lacked the energy to talk about family issues. 'How about a cup of coffee and we can discuss your asylum seeker, and why you think marrying him might not be on a par with paddling a cardboard canoe towards rapids? You've always been flighty, Lily, but I can't imagine why you should suddenly contemplate something so risky. Surely it's illegal for starters.'

'They have to prove it.'

'Has to be a belated attack of forty-itis then. I had misgivings that you crossed the decade divide with unreasonable self-control the other month. No tears, no tattoos, no toyboys.'

'It's obviously a delayed reaction,' agreed Lily. 'You can have me certified on suspicion of being midlife-crisis-ridden.'

She was impossible to offend. Venus smiled as Lily went into the kitchen – little more than an annex off the living-room – creating enough commotion to suggest a gourmet meal was being prepared.

However the smile dwindled while she lolled on Lily's two-seater corduroy sofa, which matched the bucket-shaped armchairs and shared their capacity to act as a fluff magnet. She closed her eyes and the back of her father's neck appeared, its ruddy skin textured with lines and more weather-beaten than the rest of him. He had a way of bending his head and plucking at his collar to expose the neck, and Venus was always struck by the vulnerability of that cracked slice of skin. As though it had suffered more than it should.

'How's your father coping?' Lily rattled through the glass-bead curtain separating the kitchen from the living-room, a tray with a coffee pot and a plate of sandwiches in her hands. She'd cut them into triangles and balanced them on their crusts, as if Venus were a visitor instead of her flatmate through three of their four college years in Dublin.

'He's eighty – he shouldn't be living on his own.'

'That's why you're coming home.' Lily was encouraging. 'I think you're being incredibly selfless.'

Venus shook her head; it wasn't a denial so much as a gesture of impatience. 'No choice.' Her voice was smothered. 'If I don't move in with him he'll have to go into a nursing home and it would kill him.'

'That's what comes of small families – not enough people for passing the buck around.' Lily lifted the top slice of bread to inspect her filling – which struck Venus as bizarre because she must know its contents already. 'Of course,' continued Lily, 'if you'd emigrated with your Tasmanian you wouldn't be in a position to do your *mater misericordiae* act and rearrange your life for your father. You'd be living on the other side of the world and moving back to Roancarrick wouldn't be an option.'

Venus thought of Andy – her bit of rough with a PhD, as she used to refer to the former London Underground ticket collector who'd studied at night and wound up a lecturer at Birkbeck College. He'd loved being called that, claiming it lent him peer-group credibility with the students. That had been back in the days when they'd been a couple and the Barbican flat had seemed to have soccer strips permanently on the radiators from his five-a-side sessions.

'Andy wasn't Tasmanian, he was English,' she said. 'He just talked about the island all the time – it tricked people into imagining that's where he came from. Anyway I could never have emigrated with him – he didn't love me enough.'

'He fetched and carried for you,' protested Lily. 'He cracked that joke about you being his own personal goddess so often it was threadbare.'

'That was only for appearances. He never truly cared.'

'How do you know?'

Venus reflected, holding a swig of coffee in her mouth before releasing the liquid. It wasn't because he'd been tight-fisted, although he had showed a certain zeal in tallying up every shared household bill to the last penny. The calibre of man, according to her father, who'd go on honeymoon and leave his wife at home to save money. But that hadn't been what had decided her against moving to Hobart with

16

him. 'Andy could never be bothered remembering how I take my coffee,' she said. 'We lived together for two years but he never worked out that I only like the least suspicion of milk to take away the black look. He'd flood the cup. I know it doesn't sound like much, but towards the end it exasperated me. Even the latest recruit to the staff-room knew how I drank my coffee after a couple of weeks in the job.'

Venus passed a hand in front of amber eyes – her Croft's Original eyes, according to the ex, aware that compliments cost less than flowers but sometimes counted as much with a woman. 'Details didn't matter to Andy, but it's from minutiae that a relationship is built. Couples shouldn't be allowed to commit to one another unless they can answer a questionnaire about their likes and dislikes. Which side of the bed the other prefers, whether they wash their hair or body first in the shower. Otherwise they're storing up trouble.'

'A questionnaire,' exclaimed Lily. 'That's what I should compile for this Karim project. There's no danger of the immigration authorities seeing it as a marriage of convenience if I know whether he prefers mustard or pickle in his cheese sandwiches.'

Venus removed the hand from her forehead and directed a look at her friend.

Lily laughed, crinkling the small crescent scar an inch below her left eye, legacy of a diving accident. You had to hunt through the mass of freckles to find it, but Lily was convinced it disfigured her. Although even that couldn't dent her happy-go-lucky nature.

'What does your family think about your plans to marry a Chechen?' asked Venus.

'I haven't told anyone yet – you're the first.'

'I'm not even 100 per cent sure I know where Chechnya is, apart from being close to Russia and formerly part of the Soviet Union.' Venus harassed tendrils of dark red hair, pushing them off her face. 'I've never taught any Chechens, which is generally how I work out how far East of Eden a country is.'

'Don't know what it's east of but it's south of Russia, north of Georgia.' Lily's response was instantaneous. 'There's huge unrest in the region, it's been dragging on for years. The Chechens call it a fight for freedom and the Russians a police action.'

'Glad we've cleared that one up. Now, Lily, about your Chechen, he must think all his birthdays have landed together –'

But Lily hadn't finished yet. 'Huge chunks of the country are lawless,' she recited by rote. 'Tens of thousands of people have been killed in massacres and counter-massacres between the army and the Islamic fundamentalists; entire villages have had their throats slit. Venus, it's a desperate place for a sensitive man to be trapped in. He's not even a practising Muslim. He says most of his countrymen had never set foot in a mosque until recently – being Muslim was just a way of differentiating themselves from the Russians.' Lily's eyes waxed saucer-shaped. 'I have to marry him, otherwise he'll be deported to Grozny, and it's a shell because it's been bombed so often.'

Venus glowered. This didn't sound like a marriage of convenience, it had the ring of a rescue mission.

'Or they might deport him to Moscow since that's where he was living and Karim says he can't work there. Nobody wants a Chechen doctor – they behave as though he has horns and a curly tail. You may find this hard to believe, Venus, but Russians think the entire Chechen race is evil. They might decide to slap him in a gulag, or worse. Karim told me they used to commit anyone who questioned the state to a lunatic asylum.' Lily's face radiated sweet reason. 'Now who could have that on their conscience?'

'A social conscience is all very well but you can't tackle the asylum seekers' situation by marrying them all,' complained Venus.

'I only want to do it for Karim. Honestly, you'll know why when you meet him, Venus. He's a doctor, but he isn't able to practise medicine here because refugees aren't allowed to work. He has nothing to do but sit around all day watching medical dramas on television.'

'I don't want to hear about his healing hands. Just tell me you haven't done anything irrevocable, Lily. Say it's only a casual meeting with Karim tomorrow and not your wedding day.'

Lily's skin flushed under the layer of freckles her make-up never managed to obliterate. 'I'm not that spontaneous. It's just a suggestion Karim has put to me and I can't think of a single reason why I should say no.'

Venus squinted at Lily. 'I can't think of a single reason why you should say yes.'

'That's because you haven't met Karim.'

Venus frowned at this capricious streak in her supremely wayward friend. No wonder Freud had suggested the Irish were the only race that couldn't be psychoanalysed since they were already such mental cases. In fairness, he'd said fanciful – but he didn't know the half of it. Lily was forty, too young to be menopausal. And too old to be whimsical.

'Is he paying you for this marriage?' asked Venus.

Lily's guileless blue eyes flashed with the first spark of anger Venus had met from her in years. 'I'm not a street-walker, I don't sell myself.' Then she relented, for her nature was too generous to bear grudges. 'I'm just considering doing him a favour, Venus, one human being to another.'

Some favour, thought Venus, biting back the retort. Lily was so rarely waspish that when she nipped, it stung. And you didn't have to be a genius to recognise that Lily felt subjective when it came to her asylum-seeker. Very subjective.

'We're lucky being born in this part of the world – we take all sorts of liberties for granted,' continued Lily. 'Freedom to work and earn a decent income, to live how and where we choose. We've already won our lottery jackpots.'

They fell silent and Venus scuffed her feet against the seagrass matting on the floor.

Traffic noises drifted up from the street, along with the sound of schoolchildren playing football. 'Over here, Anto – to me, Jacko – this way, Robbo.' Boys' names ending in o were the rule in Dublin.

Lily navigated the subject away from Karim. 'Won't you go spare without a job?' Not to mention the danger of running short of money, she added mentally.

'I'm hoping to teach some classes at Sligo's College of Further Education – we always knew it as Sligo Tech, but it's had a makeover. I've already been in touch with the college principal and we're meeting next week. Apparently there's a vacancy for a part-time Spanish teacher, which is a stroke of luck. Spanish is my best language. After English, of course.' Venus was expansive, to meet Lily halfway.

'Bit of a comedown from being the second-in-command of a language school in London.'

'I can always go back – I've only taken a year's leave of absence. I'm entitled to a sabbatical after so long in the school. I'm not doing anything that can't be undone.'

Even as she spoke the words, Venus realised she was past the point of no return. True, her job was being held open, but she realised instinctively she'd severed her links with the city that had been her home for most of her adult life.

Conscious that she hadn't taken Lily fully into her confidence, Venus risked an admission. 'I should have done something six months ago, when my mother died, but I dithered. I didn't want to leave London. I thought if I held on to my job and my salary I could pay for Dad to go into a nursing home should that time ever come. But I wasn't thinking straight. When I made that flying visit to Roancarrick two months ago I could see how failed he was growing.' Venus's eyes clouded. 'It was there in the details – like forgetting where he'd left his watch. He always sets it on the dresser beside the radio, but he turned the house upside down looking for it. Only to find it was on the dresser all along.'

Her voice rustled. It was doubly distressing to see her father wane since her mother's death: it reminded her of how utterly alone in the world she'd be when he was gone. Venus took a steadying breath and continued. 'It's not fair to have him living there on his own – it's too isolated and he's not able to drive any more. What if he took a tumble on the stairs? The neighbours are kind, but I don't want to be reliant on them. And, watching him there – pottering about his kitchen, checking the racing pages and lifting the phone to place his bets – I realised he'd wither away if I transplanted him from familiar surroundings. I can't dump him in a home; he's always been fanatical about sleeping in his own bed. The one time he was in hospital with his lame leg he discharged himself after a single night because he couldn't settle.' Venus worried at a rag-nail, then sat on her hands to remove temptation. 'So then I made enquiries about working in Dublin and commuting to Roancarrick at weekends, but I was living in a fool's paradise. It's too far and he'd still be on his own four or five nights a week. I had to face the inevitable.'

'It's the right thing to do,' Lily reassured her. 'That has to be worth something.'

It was balm, for Venus's friends in London thought she was deranged. 'Blood is thicker than water,' one of her teaching colleagues, Gary Hesketh, had remarked. 'Of course, it stains more than water too.' Compared with some of the other comments from her associates, that had been an endorsement.

'But it's a pinhead hamlet! You don't even like Rowing-whatever-it-is — those Irish place names of yours are impossible tongue-twisters. You'll go into decline.' Tamsin, the language-school director, had been aghast. Although not from purely impersonal reasons. Tamsin, a rigorously accessorised woman who matched her earrings to the clasp on a handbag, would need to find both a new deputy director and a tenant for the Barbican apartment she regarded as her pension plan. Plus she'd intended taking a month-long break in November. Tamsin had a Caribbean cruise in mind to splurge on, for the pupils paid handsomely and the teachers earned moderately. But she probably wouldn't be able to spare the time to go away now; she might have to — she quailed at the prospect — teach. Tamsin's nail-extensions were not compatible with holding chalk. Venus had objected to Tamsin's tone, although she considered her a friend. Venus was allowed to criticise Roancarrick but nobody else could.

'It's not that I mind the place,' she said now to Lily. 'It was fine to grow up in and it's grand for the odd weekend visit, but I wouldn't want to live there.'

'That's exactly what you're doing.' Lily's tortured hairstyle quivered in sympathy.

'I know.' Venus was dejected. 'The problem is I feel I owe my parents more because I'm adopted.' She forced herself to become upbeat before melancholy gripped. 'If I'm going to carry this off convincingly, I have to make my father believe I'm returning to Roancarrick because there's no place I'd prefer to be.'

'Is he that credulous?'

Venus nodded. 'He thinks Roancarrick is Xanadu. Dad's never spent longer than a few hours in any city and believes nobody would, given the choice.'

Venus's thoughts strayed to the apartment she'd rented in the Barbican. She loved everything about it – from its own Underground station to its bulbous appearance, the Sixties' strip-cartoon version of a space-age complex. There were marigolds in her window-boxes which flowered in spite of every discouragement, and over their heads she could see clear down to Blackfriars Bridge, with the Thames idling beneath it. And then there was the Barbican Centre – even if she hadn't gone to its exhibitions and plays as often as she'd meant to, it had been reassuring to know it was there. Waiting to pour culture into her as soon as she paid her admission.

Renting made it less complicated to pack up and leave. But it also left Venus wondering just how concrete her life in the English capital had been. Ten years there and all she had to show for it was some furniture in the back of a van, not even a whole load's worth, and a leaving card signed by the staff along with a silver bracelet that slid off her wrist.

She could take care of the bracelet by having a jeweller remove a few links – but what could she do about the hollow sensation reverberating in the pit of her stomach?

'We may as well make tracks.' Lily interrupted Venus's introspective wallow.

Venus's eyes were puzzled as they unglazed and focused on her friend.

'To see the car you might be buying,' Lily reminded her. 'You need wheels in the country.'

'The seaside,' Venus corrected.

'There too. The owner's a work colleague of mine. If we go now we'll miss the rush-hour traffic.'

Lily lit up a cigarette as soon as the key turned in the ignition. She seemed to associate driving and smoking – if she switched to public transport she might manage to kick the habit, Venus theorised. She wound down her window a couple of inches, crushing her inclination to complain about passive smoking. She'd lived in a city where you had to wash smut-streaks off your face if you so much as walked down the street; she could tolerate this.

'Have we far to go?' Venus breathed shallowly, trying for minimal inhalation. To distract herself, she separated out her euro from her sterling and transferred the British money to a zipped compartment in her bag. She wouldn't need pounds for the foreseeable future, but it was comforting to hold on to some. It might galvanise her back to London to spend them.

'We're going to my office – it's only twenty minutes' drive. Senan's expecting us; he has the car parked in a side street.'

Venus favoured the car that was for sale, even before she slid behind the wheel. It had been years since she'd owned one – life in central London didn't encourage it – but this car seemed ready to belong to her, a strangely reassuring state of affairs, as though ownership had to be by mutual consent.

Senan Mulqueen, a gangly twenty-year-old with an air of urgency about him, bundled the vehicle-registration document into her hands, along with a myriad of paperwork. Venus giggled: under 'colour' it read crocodile green. A crocodile-green Volkswagen Polo. The juxtaposition of this predatory image, and the reliable little runaround parked in front of her, single-handedly persuaded Venus to buy the car.

'There's five months' road tax left on the disc,' said Senan, who had an extravagance of gel on his baby-fair hair.

'Fine, I'll take it,' agreed Venus.

'I've never had a moment's problem with her, but my new car has a soft top.' Senan's expression settled into complacency.

'Hope you have off-street parking with your apartment,' said Lily. 'Soft tops and break-ins is one of those phrases that rolls off the tongue.'

It triggered a haunted look from Senan, who returned his attention to Venus. 'So is there anything you need to ask me about? Are you clear on when to use fifth gear for maximum energy efficiency?'

Venus claimed she was.

Senan could bear the non-haggling nature of the transaction no longer. 'Look, I'll knock off a few hundred euro since you're a friend of Lily's and a cash buyer,' he burst out.

'That's kind of you.' Venus flashed a full-toothed smile instead of the slivers she'd been doling out.

'A luck's penny,' expanded Senan.

'He's from the country like you.' Lily gave Senan a comradely slap on the shoulder and steered Venus away. 'Quaint customs they persist in clinging to, but they have their uses occasionally.'

The cigarette packet was produced as soon as Lily eased out into the traffic. 'All the same, that was a sound day's work,' she told Venus on the first exhalation.

'Thanks for your help.'

'I could tell he had his eye on you right from the start.'

'Who? The little lad?' Venus was too drained from events of the past few days to feel either outraged or flattered.

'Why else did he keep insisting you check out the boot size? He was gaping at your curvaceous behind. There's chemistry between you, Venus, you're in denial.' Lily licked her forefinger, held it up to the air and mimed being scorched.

Venus laughed. 'Do me a favour, Lily. I have a fairy for the top of my Christmas tree that's older than Senan Mulqueen.'

Memory floated Venus back to a Christmas shopping trip with her mother. All the way into Sligo town she'd clutched a pre-euro one-pound note with a colleen's face on its front, gripping it so tightly her fingers had nearly worn a hole in the paper. It had been a fortune to the five-year-old Venus.

She'd been promised she could spend it on anything she liked, anything at all, and after inspecting a music box that tinkled 'Santa Claus Is Coming To Town' and an inflatable reindeer, she'd fallen in love. With a ballerina fairy in a tiara, whose baby-pink tutu scintillated with spangles, and who carried a wand for sprinkling magic dust over the Christmas season. Or so her mother had claimed. She had cost more than Venus's green note – but Maura had reached her the excess without hesitation when she'd seen her daughter's mouth curve into a breathless, wordless, exclamation of adoration.

Venus had taken the fairy to London with her. Even in the years when she hadn't bothered with a Christmas tree, she'd propped her on top of a rubber plant. And she was in Venus's luggage for the return trip to Roancarrick. One of her legs was wobbly and had to be glued afresh every year and the glitter had worn off the tutu, but Venus could never have countenanced Christmas without her ballerina fairy.

It mattered that Maura had been with her when she'd found the fairy in Lyons's department store, waiting with placid detachment to be bought. Waiting for Venus, her mother had whispered. She'd lifted Venus to reach the top of the tree with her fairy that first Christmas. But her mother wouldn't be there to settle the festive season into its traditional groove this year; it would be the first without her. Those late-night phone conversations she'd taken for granted were gone too. So were the shopping trips – and the surprise packages Maura used to tuck into her bags when Venus left Roancarrick after a holiday. Home-made soda bread, maybe, or a bag of Merry Maid caramels. A vein pulsed in Venus's temple.

'We'll go back to the apartment and rest now – it's been a long day for you.' The depleted look on Venus's sharply etched features hadn't escaped Lily's notice.

Venus sank into the passenger seat, already mentally sprawled on Lily's sofa with her shoes off.

'Unless . . .'

Something in Lily's tone activated Venus's guard. 'Yes?' There was a slight spillage of hostility into that single syllable.

Lily stubbed out her cigarette and rearranged her features to disarming. 'Unless you'd like to meet Karim now instead of tomorrow. That call I took on my mobile while Senan showed you how to work the car's ventilation system was from him saying he's on his way over. There's an emergency and he's had to move out of his hostel. So he's homeless and headed our way – isn't it exciting?'

Venus's teeth enamel came under threat, so tightly did she grit them.

An undercurrent of excitement bubbled up from Lily. She turned to Venus and beamed.

'This might mean we have to fast-forward the wedding date. How do you feel about being my bridesmaid?'

Chapter Three

Back on the quayside, a stocky man with a shock of black hair, eyebrows that beetled into one another and jutting cheekbones was standing outside Lily's Adelphi Court apartment. His aura of boredom converted to one of rapt attention as he recognised the car.

'Couldn't you rescue a stray cat or something?' muttered Venus.

Lily's clear blue eyes rounded with incomprehension.

'Or do voluntary work. I mean, if you're determined to make a difference. Instead of marrying an asylum seeker. It's so . . .' Venus trailed off, not because she couldn't find the appropriate adjective but because she had trouble restricting it to just one. Extravagant. Extreme. Excessive.

Already Karim was tugging at Lily's door handle, telling her how enchanting she looked. His eyes gloated as they lingered on her face, reverential as he waited for her to speak.

'Meet my friend, Venus,' was all she said, but Karim

reacted as though he were Zebedee on a spring and bounded to Venus's side of the Fiat.

Now he was bowing over her hand and good heavens, he wasn't, he wouldn't, he just had; the man was grazing his lips against the back of her hand.

'Another beautiful Irishwoman. Good day, lady,' he pronounced in heavily accented but charming English. Or she might have found it charming if she weren't so ill-disposed towards him. His voice was cavernous and seemed to ooze up from within him.

They regarded one another for a few moments, with a tension that escaped Lily. Karim observed the mass of russet hair spilling below her shoulders and the faint vertical lines framing her mouth, where channels would indent in later years, with a flicker of his intelligent eyes. Eyes that were the colour of a three-day-old bruise. Venus saw how his Adam's apple protruded between the gap where his shirt collar lay open and that his hair looked as though he cut it himself. She guessed his age to be no more than hers, maybe even a year or so less. Yet he had the aura of a man decades older.

He saw a pale, elliptical face wearing a guarded expression and she saw an opportunist.

Lily shepherded them indoors with a clapping motion which Venus was convinced she'd copied from a nursery-school teacher. A buried memory resurfaced. She'd forgotten how casual Lily was about bringing people home with her; in the three years they'd shared a flat, Venus was always waking up to find some needy person tucked inside a sleeping bag in a corner of the living-room. Either they'd missed the last bus or they were between homes or they'd just arrived in Dublin and hadn't started searching for accommodation. That had

30

been acceptable when they were students, their days tinted with that addictive aimless quality she remembered from college years. But surely Lily couldn't still be collecting waifs and strays – life had shifted up a gear.

As he stood aside to allow Venus to precede him into the flat, Venus noticed that she and Karim were virtually the same height. She was five feet ten-and-a-half inches and had never been obliged to stretch to embrace a man. Sometimes, she'd had to bend. Her ex who'd relocated to Tasmania had been an inch shorter. Such height differentials, although inconsequential to many, always struck Venus as an unsatisfactory arrangement. The further her neck inclined, the faster passion ebbed from her kisses.

Karim smiled, Venus bristled.

'Lily tells me you've applied for asylum, Karim.'

He bowed his head and joined her on the sofa, at Lily's instigation. 'I am still waiting for my application to be processed. But I suspect it will be rejected – you do not have an open-door policy. Just a fraction of supplicants are allowed to stay.'

Venus sniffed; supplicants sounded so worthy.

He continued in that sonorous voice: 'Ireland has the third lowest recognition rate in the European Union – only Italy and Luxembourg allow in fewer asylum seekers.'

'Open-door policies tend to be abused,' Venus said.

His eyes assumed an even more wounded appearance. Resigned, too, as though he expected to be treated with suspicion.

Venus felt guilty. He was making her spew out unreconstructed opinions. Which she didn't even subscribe to; in London her friends called her a socialist-idealist. They wouldn't recognise her now. She didn't care how many refugees arrived in the country just so long as they didn't go about marrying her friends. Venus cursed softly under her breath: that made her sound racist as well as right wing. She smiled in a conciliatory way at Karim and was humbled to see how gratefully he responded.

A jangle of beads from the kitchen alerted her to Lily checking on the two of them and it stimulated Venus into trying to make conversation. She knew nothing at all about Chechnya; let's see what she could dredge up about Russia. The Romanoff Royals. The Bolshevik Revolution. Those goose-stepping May Day parades along Red Square. She seemed to have reduced a vibrant history to three facts.

'Lily tells me you speak Russian – is that instead of Chechen?' she asked.

'I speak both. Russian is the language of government and education so it's necessary for Chechens to learn it – however antagonistic they feel towards Russians. My mother was Russian and she insisted I speak a proper version of her language. She said most Chechens had an atrocious accent.'

There was an anxiety about the way his eyes slid off her face, addressing his words to a patch of air beyond her ear, that touched Venus. The man was desperate for approval.

Conversely, however, her hostility broke through. He wanted her imprimatur because he was expecting a cushioned landing via her friend. 'Why don't you want to return to your own country?'

His teeth flashed against the down-turned flesh of his lower lip. 'There is no quality of life there – it is a battlefield. After the war there is a strong chance the Islamic way of life will be imposed because the majority of the population is Sunni Muslim. *Sharia* law is not a system I wish to live under.'

'I'd have thought a doctor would want to do what he could for his country if it were ripped asunder by war.'

He spread his palms outwards, cruciform. 'Perhaps if I were a surgeon I might be of some use, or even a psychologist. But I am a general practitioner. I am also human. I want a home, a normal life. I want to put Chechnya behind me.'

Lily's arrival with tea for three and a plate of Fig Rolls interrupted their exchange.

'Have you two been getting acquainted?' Her smile was the rictus of a hostess on edge.

She must have heard every word, thought Venus, embarrassed about the tone she'd adopted. But it was only because she thought her friend's artless nature was being abused – she couldn't be allowed to swan about marrying people to save them from deportation. It was unethical.

So was dumping asylum seekers onto planes and washing your hands of the problem, pricked Venus's conscience.

She decided she couldn't become involved right now; she had enough to contend with. She should tell Lily, firmly but kindly, that she was making a mistake and hadn't considered the consequences of this madcap scheme. She'd do that tonight after Karim left. Lily would see sense and Venus would be free to turn her attention to her own affairs.

'I've been thinking.' Venus lifted a Fig Roll but didn't bite in. 'Maybe I should head up to Roancarrick sooner than I was planning. It feels wrong to be in Ireland and not be with Dad.'

'Roancarrick probably seems like a haven of peace and quiet after Dublin.' Lily passed her the milk jug; there was that knack for reading Venus's mind again.

'It just strikes me the two of you probably have a lot to discuss.' It sounded lame, even to Venus.

Karim was engrossed in ladling spoonful after spoonful of sugar into his tea. Venus thought he must intend to transfer the entire contents of the bowl to his mug. Look at him – he had his feet under the table already. Venus wished the crocodile-green Polo was hers now, not in limbo until after an AA inspection tomorrow, and that she could concertina her long legs inside it and drive off somewhere. Anywhere. Even to Roancarrick.

Lily made clucking sounds while Karim explained his predicament at the hostel. His room had been given away to a Nigerian woman with two children who was a more needy case, and although he was on an emergency list for a bed and breakfast place, the accommodation shortage meant single men weren't priorities. Meanwhile the authorities were talking about shipping him off to Kerry as part of a decentralisation programme and he didn't want to go. Karim didn't mean to sound ungrateful but it was already strange adapting to life in Ireland without being uprooted yet again. This place, Kerry, was it far? He gave that open-palmed shrug again. Several hundred miles was not a long way by Russian standards, but he'd prefer to stay in Dublin.

Venus studied Lily. The way her body angled towards Karim, the eager expression on her face – she was so intent on him she'd even stopped fidgeting with her hair. Venus wondered if Lily might be attracted to Karim. He was a courteous man, handsome she supposed, and that accent made for addictive listening. She just knew he'd say 'darling' with a k sound at the end of the word. Darlink. Like the spy who comes in from the cold in James Bond films.

Perhaps Lily was in love with her asylum seeker. The proposed humanitarian gesture might have another dimension.

'How did you two meet?' Venus asked.

'It was very romantic,' dimpled Lily, confirming her friend's misgivings. 'I'd just run out for a pint of milk when I slipped on some wet leaves in the street. It's been so windy recently, the footpaths and roads are littered with them. Karim was passing and he stopped and helped me to my feet. I must have turned the ankle as I went down because I wasn't able to put my weight on it.'

Karim sat on the edge of his seat, riveted, as though he hadn't been the one rescuing Lily and knew nothing of how the episode turned out.

'He made me sit on the doorstep of an office block while he took off my shoe and ran his fingers across the foot, checking for a sprain. Big, warm hands feeling their way across my tendons.'

Venus stole a glance at the big, warm hands. They certainly did look efficient.

'He was so caring that I didn't want to let him walk out of my life. When he insisted on giving me his arm to lean on until we reached the apartment, I invited him in for a cup of tea. Without milk, because I never did reach the shop.'

Karim and Lily laughed, at the private-jokes stage already.

'Although Chechens take their tea black with a slice of lemon, so it didn't matter,' Lily continued. 'Then he told me all about working as a doctor in Moscow – that's where he trained. There was a quota system at the university and all the former satellite states used to send students to Moscow. After qualifying, he started work as something equivalent to our general practitioners, but Chechens are hated by Russians. They say they're all racketeers. Poor

Karim lost his patients as soon as they realised he was Chechen and he couldn't make ends meet. They can tell by looking, apparently, even though his mother is Russian so he's only half-Chechen.' Lily's eyes acquired that goggling aspect Venus was starting to associate with her in relation to Karim. 'He even stopped wearing his high black Chechen hat because people reacted with so much hostility, but it made no difference – they still knew where he was from. "You Chechens don't want to work, you're all Mafia crooks," they kept telling him. He'd protest that they were biased and an entire race couldn't be gangsters – but they'd insist it wasn't prejudice but fact.'

Venus puckered her mouth. It was unfortunate for Karim that he'd been the victim of racism, but she still didn't want her friend involved in a marriage of convenience with him.

'So he caught an Aeroflot flight to Shannon,' concluded Lily. 'He thought he'd be welcome here – he'd heard the Irish were a hospitable race. Obviously he knows differently now: the *céad míle fáilte* is extremely selective.'

Karim nodded throughout Lily's account of his history, watching her with those unblinking eyes.

'That makes him an economic refugee rather than an asylum seeker.' Venus found herself addressing Lily, although Karim had textbook English.

Lily shrugged. 'Isn't that what the Irish were when they flooded into the United States? I don't see how we have the right to turn all high-handed and pump back most of our refugees through a revolving door to their point of origin, just as quickly as we can process their applications. It's not as if he expects the State to provide a feather bed for him; he wants to work and support himself. But we won't allow him to work until his application has been granted so he has to take hand-outs.'

'When will his case for asylum be heard? And doesn't he have a right of appeal if it's turned down, Lily?'

'His case should be coming up soon. But realistically he has very little chance of success – and even less hope of an appeal overturning that decision. That's why,' Lily glowed at Karim, 'we need a plan B.'

Karim spoke at last, his voice guttural with emotion. 'She is an angel.' He grasped Lily's hand and rained butterfly kisses on it, knuckles, fingertips and wrist all smothered. 'An angel sent from heaven to watch over me. My Guardian Angel.'

Venus judged Karim to have a surfeit of angels in his life. She liked them as much as the next person, but there were limits. She decided to concentrate on practicalities. 'So the plan is for a marriage in name only?' she checked.

'Of course – we haven't known each other more than a fortnight,' Lily reproved her.

Venus wondered if it might be too early to turn in for the night. It was just after seven o'clock – it would look bad. She resigned herself to an evening with Karim and Lily: her friend completely spellbound but in denial that this was anything other than altruism, and Karim obviously unable to believe his luck.

'Is your guest house far from here?' Venus asked Karim, hinting heavily. 'It might be worth double-checking with them in case another room is available.'

'There is no space in the guest house. The landlady was most regretful, but she said all her rooms were accounted for. I don't know where I'll lay my head tonight.' His eyes were fastened on Lily's.

'You'll stay here – I won't take no for an answer.' She was on her feet immediately, scandalised that he might think her so heartless as to toss him out on the street.

Venus found another rag-nail and savaged it. Just where was he supposed to sleep? Lily had already promised her the sofa bed. Surely she wouldn't share her own bed with him? This was lurching from melodrama to farce.

'I'm afraid you'll have to camp out in the living-room, Karim. It won't be terribly comfortable but it's the best I can offer.'

Karim seized Lily's hand and went into his guardian-angel routine, while she blushed in a way that was almost becoming. Watching them, Venus nagged at her rag-nail so viciously it spurted blood.

'Maybe I'll ring my father now, if you don't mind,' she told Lily.

'No problem.' Lily was scarcely able to tear her eyes away from Karim, whose lips hovered above her hand. 'Use the line in my bedroom.'

The phone pealed eight times before he answered it. Venus knew his limp had slowed him down, but the wait seemed protracted – after all, the phone was wall-mounted in the kitchen and that was the room her parents used most commonly. Her father used, she corrected herself.

His voice sounded querulous and she wondered, momentarily, if she'd misdialled.

'Hello?' she asked.

'Maura,' he exclaimed, and her pulse slowed.

'No, Dad, it's Venus.' She pitched her voice louder than normal, for he was becoming increasingly deaf but refused to wear the hearing aid he'd been fitted for – claiming it made him look like an old man. At eighty, he was worried about looking like an old man. Venus hadn't known whether to laugh or cry.

'Dad, I'm back in Ireland. I'm in Dublin, staying with Lily.'

'I thought it was your mother. Whenever I lift the phone I always imagine it's Maura calling, asking me to collect her from the shops or checking whether I want boiling bacon or chicken for dinner. It's hard to take in, that I'll never hear her voice again.'

Venus realised her father had not sounded peevish but agitated. 'Dad, I'm hoping to buy a car. If it all goes according to plan I should be able to drive to Roancarrick. I'll be home by tea-time tomorrow.'

'Tomorrow?' He was bewildered by the change of plan.

'I managed to catch an earlier flight, Dad. I'll explain everything when I see you. Till tomorrow, then, I'm looking forward to it already.'

'Drive carefully, lass, take your time on the road.' His voice gained in strength as he issued instructions. 'Remember the man that made time made plenty of it. Don't go too near anyone with those continental number plates – they take head-staggers and drift across to the wrong side. Especially coming off roundabouts.'

'Dad, we're the ones who've only just stopped allowing learner drivers out on their own, even after they've failed a test,' she protested. 'My friends in England were aghast when I told them about it.'

He disregarded her, listing all the towns she'd pass through and forecasting which ones would cause her delays.

Venus escaped at last and replaced the receiver. She'd been home only once since her mother had died; she wasn't ready to go back. She cocked her head, listening for Maura's voice – she'd want her to go back to Roancarrick, for Dan's sake. She heard the words as distinctly as if her mother were speaking.

'Live your life, Venus, don't let it live you.'

That's what her mother had always advised, down the years. But she couldn't act on it now: she had to put her life on hold. Venus sat on the edge of Lily's bed and sank her face into her hands. She luxuriated in a sense of being thwarted by fate, burdened by a dependent father for whom she would have to forfeit her own desires. Then she recollected the loneliness that had laced his voice and the tremulous timbre which was a new addition. Venus took her face out of her hands and stood up.

* * *

Karim and Lily stayed up talking and drinking tea after Venus went to bed, deciding she wasn't chaperone material. She heard their laughter collide as she lay in the spare room at the end of the hallway, fretting over her irresponsible friend.

The next morning was a flashback to the student era – which had been fine at the time, but Venus had no desire to recreate it – seeing the bundle in a corner of the living-room when she stumbled towards the kitchen.

It wasn't her place to complain – she was a visitor too. Venus brought a couple of mugs of coffee into Lily's room and complained anyway.

She waited a bare few seconds after drawing the curtains in Lily's room before launching in. Now was her best chance to hammer some sense into her naïve friend. 'Is it safe to have Karim stay over?'

Lily sipped her coffee and appeared to be considering the implications of Venus's accusation veiled as a question.

'Is it?' Venus repeated.

Lily yawned from the hollow of her oversized sleigh-bed dwarfing the room. 'Is it what? My brain hasn't woken up yet.'

'Is it safe having Karim spend the night?'

'It's too early in the day for this, Venus. Look, he's hardly likely to strangle us with the sheets and abscond with the family silver because there isn't any. You have to take people on trust.'

She stifled another gaping yawn – evidence, Venus thought darkly, of a late night in the arms of Karim. Within their vicinity anyhow. Sure that was nearly as bad; the man was always snatching at you and dripping saliva on your hands.

'Karim had an unlucky break being born in Chechnya and we had a lucky break pitching up here, Venus. I'm just doing my bit to reverse one of the inequities that exist between us. A bit of karmic realignment. Was your bed comfortable? You're the first person to sleep in it.'

'Don't change the subject; there's no knowing when I might corner you on your own again. Can't you do something a little more hands-off to right these inequities? Maybe fire off an indignant letter to the newspapers?'

Lily dragged a pillow against the bed-head to prop herself up. 'Why are you so bothered about it? I'd say you have enough to deal with in Roancarrick.'

The remark tripped up Venus. It was true – she was developing a fixation on the enormity of the mistake she felt convinced Lily was making. Maybe it was less complicated to address than her own worries.

The smell of sizzling bacon intruded, followed by a knock on the door and Karim calling that breakfast would be ready in five minutes. He even made that sound glamorous, with his heavily accented bass. Lily leapt up and reconvened her topknot, dragging a comb through caramel-streaked hair. Venus's suspicions were validated by her friend's reluctance to allow Karim to see her with her hair down – Lily's equivalent of facing the world without make-up.

At the last minute Lily wouldn't let them emerge in their dressing-gowns, hissing that Karim was old-fashioned and there was a modesty issue here. So Venus had to go next door and shuffle into last night's clothes. She emerged to find Lily in a T-shirt with *never eat more than you can lift* emblazoned across it, regarding Karim in a way that was, frankly, cannibalistic in its appreciation. Apart from his stubble Karim looked refreshed, less haggard than he'd been the previous day. Venus deemed it unnatural that anyone's eyes should glow so brazenly before noon: he was a Sacred Heart picture on legs – that gaze followed you everywhere.

'He's the only doctor I know who still allows you to fry bacon.' Lily settled down at the table beneath the side window to be waited on, motioning to Venus to sit too.

Venus obeyed grumpily. He was supposed to be a doctor; the human form could hold no mystery for him. So why would her neck-to-floor bathrobe offend Karim? She didn't like wearing last night's clothes. They smelled of airports and Lily's cigarette-smoke.

Karim carried the pan with bacon and eggs to the table, greeting Venus in his courtly fashion – 'Good day, lady' – and enquiring if she'd slept well. He knew how to fry bacon, she'd grant him that: not too much fat in the pan and he'd trimmed off the rind.

'I thought you were supposed to be Muslim,' said Venus,

as Karim tucked into his rashers. 'Isn't bacon a forbidden fruit?'

'He's a selective Muslim, the same way we're a la carte Catholics,' Lily nudged her. 'Pass the ketchup.'

Breakfast was a jolly affair, as Lily maintained a resolutely affable stream of chatter about the house viewing she was in charge of that afternoon in Mountjoy Square.

'They wouldn't let me advertise it as "high ceilings, low dive" so I'm stuck with lying to everyone about the lap-dancing club at the end of the street. It advertises itself as offering multi-layered lap-dancing – presumably it only employs contortionists. Do you think I'd get away with describing it as a gym? At least some exercise is taken there.'

Meanwhile Karim smiled incessantly, his teeth opalescent against coffee skin.

The coffee was so strong it left both women shuddering, although Karim, who had funnelled at least half a dozen spoons of sugar into his cup, sipped with equanimity.

'What happens after the wedding?' Venus asked, not pausing to consider that this liaison had subtly shifted into a case of when and not if.

'Karim is hoping to go to college here as a medical student and eventually practise,' prattled Lily, whose voice always sounded breathless as she cantered through a conversation at breakneck speed. 'It shouldn't take him as long to qualify as it did the first time in Moscow. Maybe he'll be able to skip a few years. Broken limbs are broken limbs, whatever the language.' She looked at Karim for confirmation.

'You are my Guardian Angel.' He seized her hand.

No more angels, pleaded Venus mentally. A call from the AA rescued her. There was nothing wrong with the car, apart from a dent in the passenger door which had been hammered out and a few scrapes in the paintwork which might rust. A written report would be sent on, but Venus decided to ring Senan and arrange to collect the car on the strength of the verbal summary. Anything to escape Chechens drooling over Lily's hand and calling her an angel. There was only one of Karim but, with those holy-picture eyes, the apartment seemed stuffed to capacity with him.

Yet driving away that afternoon, Venus felt a pang. Lily and Karim came downstairs to the foyer to wave her off and they looked like a couple already, standing so close that Lily's topknot tickled against Karim's earlobe. Chilled by an awareness that she was virtually alone in the world, Venus pulled over in the next street and scouted through her handbag for her seahorse totem with its iridescent tail. She dangled it from the rear-view mirror, needing the comfort of her lucky charm again.

Chapter Four

Beyond Mullingar Venus chugged along in second gear, trapped in a tractor's slipstream. A convoy of vehicles snaked in her wake and she could sense their mounting frustration that she hadn't overtaken. But one bend fed into another and she couldn't see her way clear – there was no option but to crawl. Venus drummed her fingers on the wheel, deliberately not looking into her mirror in case she caught sight of the impatient Audi driver behind. She knew he was itching to overtake both her and the tractor and Venus felt like winding down her window and shouting: 'If you want to commit suicide, do it in the privacy of your own home.'

The clamour of engines overhead distracted her and she peered at a stream of letters floating in front of her windscreen.

Try Finding Not Sacrificing Yourself.

Venus blinked, braked sharply as she realised the tractor had started climbing and was losing speed, and looked again. The sky-writing streaming behind the bi-plane read: *Try Findley's Sandwiches For Yourself.*

Nevertheless she was unnerved. Venus pulled over onto a grass kerb – ignoring the Audi's enraged horn – and switched off the ignition. This wasn't simply a case of misreading the slogan; it had to be subliminal messaging. Here she was, homeward bound to immerse herself in duty, a determination Lily called death by self-denial – but in an admiring tone – before kissing her goodbye. Duty above inclination – such a Victorian concept. So alien to the twenty-first century's preference for personal gratification. And now she'd encountered a sky-writing commentary on her decision.

The silver plane's drone faded into the distance, but Venus sat on, clutching the moulded steering wheel, a diadem of perspiration on her forehead. How was she going to acclimatise to Roancarrick after ten years in London? Tamsin, the accessory-fixated language-school director, had put it succinctly as she'd sat there in shoes with buckles repeating the silver squares of the buttons on her jacket. 'There's nothing wrong with living in a small town, darling. As long as it's not your own small town.'

From the outset, London had fitted Venus. And she had fitted into it. Her visits home had dwindled over the ten-year cycle, as metropolitan life had become more compelling at Roancarrick's expense. Of course she loved it when she was there: the purity of the air, the extravagant sweep of mountain and strand, the famine-era pier with its tethered jumble of boats. But its hold on her slackened as soon as she was back in the city. Venus had flitted from bar to restaurant to club in London, spending her salary as she earned it, and Roancarrick had become a place that was magical for two days, maybe three at a push. After that she'd start pining for noise, traffic, people. Life.

The village was a place she'd never anticipated returning to, not permanently. The world promised too much variety and adventure to settle for the familiar. Looking back, she realised she'd spent her early life there waiting for something to happen. And that something was the opportunity to leave.

'You must know there's no going back,' Tamsin had said the day she'd handed in her notice. Tamsin's perfume had been like incense and Venus's head had started to pound as Tamsin had stood over her in a parody of solicitude, as though she'd confessed to an incurable disease or suicidal impulses. Instead of a return to Ireland.

'You'll be mummified, Venus.' The director's tone had been petulant, although she had been genuinely concerned for Venus too. She couldn't imagine life outside Wimbledon, let alone London, and envisaged Roancarrick as a walled-up tomb.

Venus had sighed. So what if she were mummified for a couple of years? Bandages unravelled in time. Nevertheless she had tried to make Tamsin understand. 'If I don't go back and live with my father he'll have to enter a home. The nearest one is twelve miles away. Not only would he lose his independence, he wouldn't even be on familiar ground any more. He's past eighty, not able to cope on his own. It was different when my mother was alive – they looked out for one another. It's not just a case of seeing to it that he's fed and cared for – he needs company. Someone else's key in the lock at night.'

Tamsin had looked sceptical. 'So much for me thinking nobody locks their doors in Ireland because it's so friendly.

Come on, I've watched *Ballykissangel*. I bet neighbours are always dropping in with batches of freshly baked scones. Your father's probably suffocated with kindness.'

Venus had tried again, although the director wasn't making this easy for her. And she had an outdated view of rural Irish life. 'The year's winding down,' she'd said. 'It's nudging six months since my mother died and I stayed with him for a fortnight afterwards, but it wasn't enough. I've let him manage on his own because I wanted to believe he could. But he can't – he won't make it alone through the winter ahead. I have to go home. There is such a concept as obligation: a responsibility to your own flesh and blood.' Venus had realised she was cracking her knuckles, a habit she'd had as a teenager. Swallowing a blockage in her throat, she had hurried away from Tamsin's office, mumbling about checking the accounts from the latest batch of summer school students.

Venus shifted in her seat, reaching to adjust the car heater. Another minute and she'd pull out onto the road again. Strictly speaking, noted one of the cacophony of voices in her head, your father's not your flesh and blood.

But that makes it all the more essential you should acknowledge your debt to him, countered another voice.

'Shut up, the lot of you,' barked Venus. Imagine having a Greek chorus squatting inside your skull.

She started up the ignition and continued homeward. She tried not to think of that last fortnight in Roancarrick, during the desolate time after her mother's death, when she and her father had skirted around one another – each floundering behind a mist of grief. Instead the sky-writing began to plague her.

Try Finding Not Sacrificing Yourself.

48

She clinked the phrase around in her mind; it had serrated edges and they scratched at her.

Perhaps there was more to her decision to retrace her steps towards Roancarrick than the virtuous daughter role. Perhaps she was driving halfway across the country, not because she had a Cordelia complex, but because the village was calling her back.

It could be that Venus was compelled to revert to life there, for it was only in Roancarrick that she could quarry her life.

And as suddenly as she had decided to invert her existence, turning away from London, comprehension overtook Venus Macken. She could no longer survive without answers. Call it a postponed issue of identity or a cure for her ostrich complex, but the time had come, as the walrus said, to talk of many things.

She needed to discover the identity of her birth mother and why she had abandoned her. Venus was determined to start excavating the past.

Her identity had mattered before, in her early teens, when she'd first probed for information. Always hazily aware she'd been adopted, it had held no meaning for her until then. She'd been satisfied by the whimsical explanations given to a small girl.

You hatched from an egg, said her father.

You were sent to us by the sea, said her mother.

You're a changeling, said Birdie, their closest neighbour.

But with puberty came the urge to know.

Do I look like my mother or my father?

Which of them had red hair?

Have I any brothers or sisters?

The questions had been incessant for a time.

At first Dan Macken had appeared inclined to answer Venus, but Maura had intervened, raising her voice in reproach against her husband. A rare occurrence – he'd been dumbfounded, collecting his hat and leaving the house in silence. It had been late when he'd returned from Brennan's pub, knocking against furniture in the kitchen. Maura had gone downstairs, hushing him and leading him to bed, while Venus had strained in vain to hear her sotto-voce commentary.

After that, when Venus had tackled him, Dan would insist he knew nothing and bury his face in the newspaper, ignoring the interrogation. Venus had always tired of the pantomime before he did, but Maura had taken it to heart.

'Aren't I mother enough for you?' she'd beseech, craving reassurance. 'Do you need another one, a better one, a younger one?'

So Venus had embalmed the desire to probe her parentage. Let it hibernate during those teenage years in Roancarrick, the student years in Dublin, the working years in London.

Just once, Maura had seemed inclined to talk to Venus about the past. There had been only the two of them in the functional hospital room, with its crucifix above the bed, and Venus had been reading out snippets from court cases in the *Donegal Democrat*. Her mother had always relished the mixture of the pedestrian and the tragic that characterised district-court proceedings. Such attractions had palled as the disease had gripped, and she had listened only from courtesy – she had a tragedy of her own to grapple with. Maura's time was finite. The doctors had been candid with her mother: the cancer had taken tenacious root by the time it had been diagnosed in her stomach.

In a lull, as Venus had attempted to tame the flyaway newspaper sheets, Maura had spoken. Her voice had been tentative, as though she'd lost the habit of words. 'I know you've always wondered who your real mother is.'

Venus had looked at her face, grooved and hollowed by the cancer that was inoperable, and had laid a finger on those chapped lips. 'You're all the mother I want,' she'd whispered, and Maura's furrows had dissolved into a smile.

'*No spring nor summer beauty hath such grace/As I have seen in one autumnal face,*' murmured Venus, as she drove. But her mother was beyond being hurt by her questions now; she didn't need to protect her any longer.

An emotion akin to euphoria possessed Venus, so that she pressed her foot on the accelerator without realising it and the needle ticked upwards on her speedometer. She felt she had a purpose in life – almost a mission. She'd start by approaching Dan again, to see if she could cajole her father into telling her now what her mother had stopped him from saying years before. If he wouldn't speak, she'd hound neighbours, officials, gardaí, the adoption agency and social workers for their version of events. She'd slice through mythology and insist on facts.

As far back as she could remember she had felt like an outsider, long before she could have realised she was one. She still didn't know where she belonged – or, indeed, if it were possible for her to belong. But she hungered for the skeleton of her own history to be fleshed out. She was no longer content with the sleight-of-hand version, the borderline supernatural interpretation she'd been peddled all her life.

Until she became the archaeologist of her own past, she'd never unlock the riddle of who she was. And it mattered to her to know, she realised, dropping downhill into Sligo town. Craning for her first glimpse of Ben Bulben, her personal mountain. Traffic was light through the town and it was just a few minutes until she was on the dual carriageway leading towards Drumcliffe. She was on the pig's back now. Venus smiled. The closer she came to Roancarrick, the more her father's idiosyncratic expressions rippled to the surface. A tour bus ahead pulled over to disgorge visitors to Yeats's grave, in the country churchyard where his grandfather had preached. But it was not his poetry that threaded her consciousness, for all Venus had memorised it at school.

Try Finding Not Sacrificing Yourself.

* * *

Her first sight of the sea after an absence always winded her. There were hints of it to the left beyond the hedgerow-frilled main road as she drove, will o' the wisp glimpses that disappeared as soon as she looked for them. Venus had to wait until she reached the outskirts of the village for that first unimpeded vista. She passed an ancient stone cross set back from the roadside and then shortly before Bundoran, just inside the Donegal county border, she turned off the N15 and slowed to third gear for the next couple of miles. At times she was doubling back on herself as she drove along winding lanes. And then she was upon Roancarrick – the seal's rock, as it translated, although seals were rarely seen there nowadays.

In the late afternoon light the sea was looking-glass still and an involuntary smile irradiated her face as she gazed at it. But Venus hadn't time to savour the stretch of coastline cradling the village in a horseshoe embrace, for she knew her father would be watching out for her and she was later than intended. She pressed on to the main street, virtually the only street, with its gaudily painted shop fronts that promised more than they delivered. At one end lay O'Dea's newsagents, with a waist-high plastic ice-cream cone on the footpath outside, come winter or summer, and at the other was Nora Brennan's pub where Venus had drunk her first legal Bacardi and coke. She'd sloped into Bundoran for the illegal ones. In between was a chipshop, a self-styled gift 'emporium' – which relied on leprechaun snow-globes and Connemara marble jewellery for its grandiose claims – a coffee shop and an amusement arcade, the latter three businesses open only during June, July and August. They were vacant the rest of the year, to the annoyance of the locals, who felt they lent Roancarrick a ghost-town mien.

There was one other business on the main street. Beside O'Dea's was a restaurant, Seascape, eulogised in a guidebook on the basis of its seafood chowder. The owner, Kathleen Magee, who'd been two years ahead of Venus in the Ursuline convent in Sligo, had promptly hiked her prices, lost her regulars and been obliged to entice them back with a series of promotions including free bottles of wine. Venus remembered her as a wistful girl who'd grown into a wistful woman, as she steered her Polo uphill towards home.

And then slammed on the brakes, pitching herself forward so abruptly the seatbelt sliced at her sternum. Thank heavens the brakes were sound. But who was the idiot who'd stepped out in front of the car?

An angular man with fawn-fair curls bent before her bonnet to gather scattered sheaves of paper. Moving in a leisurely fashion, as though he had ownership of the road, he dawdled to inspect each folio for damage and then store it in a burgundy leather portfolio. Venus was exasperated: the least he could do was look sheepish, but he didn't so much as glance at her. When the final white rectangle had been retrieved she expected him to step out of her way, but he approached the car window and gestured for her to roll it down. Good, at least he had the grace to apologise.

He lowered his face to the level of the window until it was only a hand's breadth from hers. There was a hint of stubble on his chin, not the designer smattering she was accustomed to but the incipient beard of someone who had forgotten to shave. Despite his fair colouring he had the all-weather tan of a man who spent a considerable amount of time out of doors.

His mouth opened, emitting a whiff of spearmint chewing-gum. 'Could you reverse a few inches, please?'

'Sorry?'

'That's all right – you were obviously admiring the view. It tends to mesmerise strangers. But you might drive more carefully the next time you come through our village – there's always a danger children could run out.'

Venus was speechless. He was calling her a stranger. He was lecturing her on her driving. He was describing Roancarrick as his village.

He raised his eyebrows at her, arched eyebrows such as women haemorrhaged money to cultivate, and looked pointedly at the steering wheel. 'If you wouldn't mind reversing.'

She checked her rear-view mirror with a deliberate show of familiarity with the rules of the road, then eased back a yard. He bent and gathered up another sheet of paper – it appeared to be a sketch of the harbour. It was scrutinised, returned to the leather folder, and with a jerk of his hand to his forehead he set off whistling.

'Drive carefully,' he called through her open window as she passed him.

It sounded like an order, although delivered in one of those deceptively soft Northern border-county accents. Venus peeked in the mirror and saw his daddy-long-legs in their reinforced sailing trousers stride along the road. She bridled. There was something innately aggravating about that self-assured man – he'd sabotaged all her hard-earned homecoming stoicism.

Now she was almost at her journey's end and it was too late to do anything about it. She'd just have to go indoors and pretend to be glad she was back.

Chapter Five

Dan Macken had been watching for his daughter since before 3 p.m., although warned it would be teatime at the earliest before she would arrive. She'd phoned before setting off. Expect me when you see me, she'd said in that airy voice she used on him when he tried to pin her down to times, dates, plans. Just like her mother, God rest her.

He'd been afraid to walk the length of the village for butter in case she arrived while he was out of the house. Not that he was low on butter, but it never did any harm to have an extra block on standby. Imagine running out and having to take the bread dry. That daughter of his would think he was in his dotage and couldn't cope at all.

Dan settled with his *Donegal Democrat* into the armchair beside the elderly black range and turned to the court cases, scanning for names he'd recognise. A Gallagher from Tullaghan had pleaded guilty to driving with three times more than the legal maximum in his bloodstream – that must be one of the headmaster's sons. Wouldn't you think his father would have taught him better than that? He kept an ear cocked for a car engine as he digested the intricacies of a case he was already memorising, from habit, for repetition to Maura.

However, when the engine chugged into the yard he didn't hear it. Nor did he see Venus step from the car and study the square outline of the two-storey house.

She felt her heart contract at the sight of this squat building that was more home to her than her Barbican flat, however much she contrived to believe otherwise.

It was set back from the cliff and partly sheltered by a semi-circle of scrubby evergreen trees that were hectored daily by winds blustering in from the Atlantic. The house faced to the side, in the hope of evading these dogged winds, and had a pillared porch protruding from the belly of the building. There was an ostentation about that front porch and looming doorway too large for the scale of the house; it looked as though it had been tacked on long after the building was completed, as indeed was the case.

It had been an affectation of her mother's which had been humoured only so far: she'd been allowed to have her porch and 'proper front door' built, but everyone disregarded it and continued to used the back entrance. Venus had no recollection of that front door with its swirled glass circular insets ever being opened. Not even at her mother's wake.

Venus's home had neither name nor number. If it had been situated anywhere else but by the sea they might have painted its grey-bricked exterior walls: perhaps yellow, she fancied, with a glossy black door and gate. But the elements here were as powerful as they were merciless; they seized on paintwork, teasing at it until tongues of colour peeled away and the underbelly was exposed.

Her father's whistling snore was the first sound Venus heard when she opened the back door. The newspaper had fallen from his hands onto his chest and the spectacles had slipped down his nose, dangling by one leg. His head was sunk on his chest, making a concertina of the folds of skin under his chin – it always bemused her how such a scrawny man could wind up with excess skin, even if it was only at his throat.

Venus felt a nostalgic urge to murmur 'God bless all here,' just as her mother had persisted in doing when she had arrived at the apartment in the Barbican. Whatever about carrying it off – just – when she'd visited Venus in her shared student flat in Dublin, it had sounded incongruous in London. It wasn't a city that encompassed either folklore or pieties.

Once Maura had brought her a holy-water font, an understated Belleek china oval chosen with care because she had realised her daughter would shy away from anything that shrieked 'Superstitious Catholic: Buy Your Plenary Indulgences Here'. Guilt had niggled as Venus had explained it was contrary to her lease to hammer nails into the wall. But no, not even for her mother could she have a holy-water font by her front door in London.

Venus watched the newspaper rise and fall against her father's diaphragm and noticed he was wearing his Sunday trousers on a Saturday. As though she were a visitor. There was a razor-nick on his chin, which meant he'd wet-shaved instead of buzzing himself with the electric razor, another sign he was trying to look his best for her.

She felt a contraction in her throat. God bless all here, she thought. But she didn't say it. Instead she dropped her bags and coughed – she wasn't about to go native.

The noise woke her father, who scrabbled for his newspaper and denied he'd been sleeping.

'I didn't hear the car pull up, lass – it must be stormy out.' He hauled himself from the armchair, holding onto the back for support.

Venus bent to kiss his cheek, feeling a patch of bristles missed by the razor against her cheeks, and inhaled his Old Spice aftershave. He must have splashed it on for her – that was something else he tended to bother with only on Sundays, as though wet-shaving and Old Spice were designed to separate the Sabbath from the weekday. To humour him she agreed the wind was howling, but by Atlantic standards it was mild.

Dan insisted she take his seat near the range to warm herself while he bustled about brewing tea. Venus would have preferred coffee but suspected he had none. He claimed it was a foreign brew – you'd imagine tea-bushes were native to Ireland the way he carried on.

Her eyes roamed the kitchen while he chatted. Everything was exactly as always, in a furniture pattern that neither time nor fashions altered. There hung the gilt-framed Sacred Heart with its votive light above the table, disconcertingly positioned to oversee every mouthful consumed in the room. Here stood the battered tweed sofa under the window, one side piled high with newspapers and library books. Nearby was the dresser with her twin brothers' photograph among the welter of crockery, bills and household detritus including lengths of string and rubber bands, for her father suffered if he had to throw away anything.

There was a smell of burning wood from the range, overlaid by the pungent aroma of the pink cough medicine

Dan guzzled like lemonade. The room was cloaked in stillness, ruptured by no sound except the comforting metronome of a ticking alarm-clock, which her father carried up and downstairs with him daily because its numbers were the only ones he could read without glasses. This throbbing silence was the strangest to adapt to after London, with its interminable noise levels.

Venus panicked. She didn't belong in Roancarrick any more – this was going to be more laborious than she'd expected. A labour of love, in truth. But love should not be laboured. Venus drooped. She had a sensation of living within a continuum, her present, past and future fused. Then her father said her name and gave his gummy, slow-spreading smile. His overgrown infant's smile. And her spirits revived.

She could do it.

Other details started filtering in. He'd laid the table using one of her mother's linen cloths. The potatoes were already scrubbed and immersed in water in a pan on the cooker, awaiting her arrival. A vase with scarlet chrysanthemums perched on the dresser, lending the kitchen a jaunty air.

'Lovely flowers, Dad.' She rose to sniff them but they had no scent.

'Birdie left them in – I suppose she wanted to make the place more homely for you.'

Naturally they'd have come from Birdie, their nearest neighbour. Red was her favourite colour; she insisted it was lucky.

You make your own luck, thought Venus.

Dan's leg seemed to be dragging more noticeably than usual as he shuffled around the kitchen. But when she enquired about it he only shrugged. 'Sure it's been crocked for years.' Then he turned the conversation to her journey, quizzing her about exactly how long it had taken and whether she'd come through much wet weather en route. He was invariably fascinated to hear it was raining in Westmeath but not in Longford or vice versa.

He never stepped out of the house without glancing at the sky, checking for rain clouds, and the teachers at Bridges Across The World had teased Venus about the same habit. 'Child of the soil,' they'd joke.

She did it instinctively and could not buck the custom.

She looked at Dan, limping now to the table with mugs. It felt wrong to have him waiting on her but Venus held her tongue, knowing he'd want to do it on her first day at least.

The pain in her father's leg dated back a lifetime, to the days when he'd played Gaelic football as a young man, and he accepted the limb's increasing immobility without complaint. A combination of cartilage problems in his knee and a broken bone in his foot which had not been diagnosed caused his lameness. There were photographs of him in his football strip in a drawer somewhere, scowling and fierce and impossibly young. He'd played full forward for the county – the striker position in soccer. Her twin brothers had been regarded as promising players in their time too, those carefree young men she knew only from photographs. The two Christys, she'd called them as a small girl. Christy and Luke. Interchangeable faces, interchangeable names.

Dan Macken served up potatoes with butter, mushy peas from a tin and tranches of cold boiling bacon.

'I steeped the bacon to drain the salt, just like your mother always did,' he said.

'She always used the water to cook her cabbage in,'

responded Venus, wondering why they were discussing Maura Macken's cooking tips. Perhaps because she was taking her lead from her father.

'Aye, I'll not deny I'm fond of a head of cabbage,' Dan agreed. 'I should have set a lock of rows by now if I want any next year but I hadn't the heart for it.'

'I'll help you, Dad. We can do it tomorrow if it's dry.'

'There's rain forecast, lashings of it. I heard it on the shipping news.'

Dan Macken always predicted rain, even without the authority of the shipping news behind him.

He clinked his cutlery on the plate as he ate, chewing each mouthful with a ruminative air and washing it down with milk that had been sitting out on the table. He didn't like it cold from the fridge – he claimed it gave him an ache in his gut. Venus sipped tap-water and thought of the bottles of crisp white wine she kept in her Barbican fridge.

It was the first time Venus could remember Dan cooking her a meal as an adult, although she supposed he must have grilled her fish-fingers as a child. She couldn't recall how they'd managed for food in the aftermath of her mother's funeral – probably they'd lived on sandwiches or had heated up some of those meat-pies and quiches neighbours were always dropping in to them. Food as an expression of sympathy. Raining down at a time when you least felt like eating.

Venus forced herself to finish every morsel – Dan hated to see food wasted and always accused her of slimming if she left anything on her plate. She smiled: hotels were probably doling out similar meals to American tourists keen to share the authentic Irish experience. Meanwhile the bulk of the population was eating lasagne with chips.

Then she noticed her father had pushed two potatoes to the side of his plate and most of his slice of bacon. Maybe he'd filled up at lunchtime – unless he'd never regained his appetite since Maura's death?

He followed her eye-line. 'You need less food at my time of life, lass.'

Still, she felt uneasy. He was such a slight man, he couldn't afford to lose weight. A gust of wind would blow him over the cliff-top.

'I suppose you're too tired to go for a stroll.' Her father had a tendency to phrase questions as statements.

Venus was about to agree that she needed to unwind a little longer before she took the walk to the beach that she'd promised herself. But she realised in time that he wanted to step out with her into the early evening air. 'I'm stiff from the drive, it would probably do me a power of good to stretch my legs.'

His face with its shadowed semi-circles beneath each eye brightened.

'We won't go too far though, Dad – you'll tire yourself out.'

'Exercise helps you sleep.' He fumbled into his padded waterproof jacket – he called it his car coat, for reasons she had never been able to discern, for Dan Macken didn't drive any more. She held it for him while he made groping stabs at locating the sleeve. 'Anyway,' and this was an afterthought, 'you need less sleep at my time of life too. I lie for hours in the dark, waiting for morning to come.'

Venus stifled a snuffle. Dan was notorious for claiming he hadn't managed a wink of sleep when her mother could confirm he'd snored the night through. It had been a private joke between mother and daughter. Still, he looked tired. Maybe it was the weariness of outliving so many of his contemporaries. He'd be eighty-one in January, if God spared him. She realised what she'd said and slapped a hand to her forehead. What was she thinking of, lapsing into devout colloquialisms already after only an hour or so in Roancarrick?

Just as she believed they were finally ready to leave, he made a fuss about selecting a hat from a collection of identical trilbys. They were all either grey or olive and each had a discreet feather tucked into the hat-band. Dan Macken would as soon leave the house without his trousers as with his head bare. There was very little hair left on his head, apart from an iron-grey fringe that ran from ear to ear, and he said it was inviting trouble for a man to expose his scalp to the elements.

Venus's tawny eyes were tender as she watched him check the tilt of his hat in a cracked mirror that hung by the back door. She made a mental note to replace it – she wasn't ruled by superstition, but she drew the line at keeping broken mirrors in the house.

Dan made a final adjustment to his brim and turned to her. 'What's keeping you, lass?'

Chapter Six

Venus assumed they would walk towards the beach – she was looking forward to a ramble along the seafront. Instead of heading downhill towards the strand, however, Dan Macken directed their footsteps left past Birdie Ross's cottage with its ragged plume of turf-scented smoke, and they climbed along the cliff road. Venus glanced behind regretfully but didn't demur. It was still only September; there'd be light enough to return to the beach later that evening. Besides, there were still be day-trippers on the strand and she preferred it deserted.

Her father leaned on his stick, bone gleaming through knuckles. Venus heard his breath wheeze as it skirmished down into his chest, and slackened her already measured pace. The elderly had to battle for breath, Venus mused. And yet they did it, with a determination that was humbling to witness.

At the crest of the hill she realised where his steps were leading but made no comment. By an outcrop of cliff with views across Donegal Bay they stood, side by side but not touching, the old man's breathing gradually easing. The light in the sky was turning purple now, with the advent of dusk, and glow-worms appeared one by one in the dolls' houses on the far side of the bay. Beneath them they could hear seagulls squabble as they bedded down for the night in crannies along the cliff ledge. And further below, if she peered over the edge, were the irregular shadows of rocks under the surface of the water.

What did seagulls gossip about as they tucked their heads towards a wing and prepared for sleep? Venus always thought of them as the birdlife equivalent of village snoops, scavenging for morsels of news along with bread-crusts.

They were standing exactly where they had scattered Maura Macken's ashes six months previously. Dan had resisted it, for he believed a body was needed for reincarnation on Judgement Day. But Maura had insisted that she didn't want to moulder in the ground and a visit to her hospital bed from Father McGinley, designed to deter her, hadn't succeeded. 'Dust thou art and unto dust thou shalt return,' she'd quoted at him. 'What does it matter how quickly my body turns to atoms if that's what will eventually happen?'

What saddened Dan most about her decision, which he regarded as pagan, was that they would not lie side by side in the churchyard at the mouth of the village.

'But it's your people buried there, not mine,' she'd contended.

'I thought my people became yours when we married,' he'd flashed back, stung.

Dan had regarded it as a betrayal, after fifty-odd years together. A man and wife should be buried in the one grave, just as they shared the one bed. Ultimately he'd acceded to her wishes because he loved his wife and could not bring himself to thwart her. His misgivings had chiselled at him afterwards, however, and he had raised it in Confession. The priest hadn't been pleased about his dead parishioner's 'primitive urges' either, but Father McGinley had charity enough to reassure Dan Macken that cremation and scattering would not disbar his wife from heaven.

'We waited for a still day.' Dan's voice croaked and he coughed to cover it.

Venus slipped her hand into the crook of his arm.

'You need a still day for sprinkling ashes,' he elaborated, hacking subsided.

'It was a lamb of a March day,' said Venus.

'The ceremony wasn't as bad as I expected. I could almost see the point of it . . . your mortal remains being blown about by the breeze and then settling on the Atlantic to be swept out into the world.' He coughed again, into his handkerchief this time. 'She took fanciful notions from time to time, your mother. Sure the woman suggested I should be cremated too, when my time came, and then we could both become part of the ocean. Mingled together, light as air, she said. Dancing with the waves.'

'I suppose,' Venus was tentative, 'she saw it as a way of being closer to the boys.'

She thought of the photograph on the dresser of her brothers in their roll-necked fishermen's jerseys, arms wrapped around one another's shoulders. Twins but not completely identical, one sturdy and the other more slightly built and with a distant cast to his eyes. Something had ruptured when their mother had given birth to them and there had been no further children.

Dan trudged away from the headland and she followed a footfall behind him. His words pivoted towards her on a draught of air.

'You just remember, Venus, I'm to go in the family plot with my parents and grandparents when my time comes.'

'You've years ahead of you, Dad . . . don't be melancholy.' Venus hoped her father wasn't going to harp on about death and funerals; she'd prefer him to be one of those elderly people who imagined they'd live forever.

'I've more hot dinners behind me than ahead of me, that's for sure.' He smacked his lips with a certain relish.

Venus banked down her exasperation. The old fellow was enjoying this morbid streak he'd started to indulge since Maura's death.

On their way back, breathing less strained because there was no climbing, he mentioned that the captain's house was finally occupied again. Dan heard everybody's business on the nights he'd stroll down to Nora Brennan's pub for his two pints of Guinness, never more and never less. One pint wet your whistle for a second, he'd say, but take it to the third and you were left with a thirst that wouldn't be satisfied until they carried you home.

Venus was aflame with curiosity, for the captain's house was a local landmark and most of the villagers felt proprietorial about it. It was the only thatched house in Roancarrick and Venus had a sense of connection with it. She'd never even set foot inside, although she'd stood on its front stoop as a child trick or treating at Hallowe'en and singing carols at Christmas, peering into a hallway with crimson and gold flock wallpaper, a pungent smell of cat litter and a brass ship's barometer with two needles. She could still envisage the barometer: *set fair, fair, change, rain* and *stormy*, it read. Her father used to tease her that it also had a setting for moist air, that state peculiar to Ireland where it was neither wet nor dry. But Venus knew the five permutations off by heart and could not be shaken from her inventory: set fair, fair, change, rain and stormy.

The house had lain empty for a year after the captain's only child had died. Edith Ferguson had nearly reached her century and had outlived her direct heirs; it had been widely predicted by the seers in the village pub – whose powers of divination improved in direct proportion to the amount of Guinness-and-shorts they accounted for – that she'd bequeath the property to a cat sanctuary. She had been devoted to her pusses and had always kept a dozen or so.

Visitors would complain about tripping over saucers of milk every time they took a step front or back and of having to stand because the cats couldn't be budged from seats. Indeed, the furry posse had spat and unsheathed their claws in outrage when the suggestion had been put to them by word or gesture. However, the old lady had died intestate, no provision made for her pets let alone her paid companion, and a few distant cousins in Aberdeen had emerged to instruct the sale of the house. The cats' cushioned existence had come to an abrupt end.

'You can imagine the shape the house must have been in for the newcomers, between old Edie's cats and the year it was lying idle. Sure the world and his wife know you can't leave a house by the coast empty – the wear and tear is catastrophic.' Dan's rheumy eyes, still as blue as a summer sky, twinkled. 'I hear they've had to spend a fortune on it, even with bringing their labour across the border and avoiding paying VAT. They imagined they'd be in by last

December, then they hoped to move in at Easter, and now they've only just managed to take possession a matter of weeks ago. That house will be a money-pit.'

'Magnificent views, though.' There was yearning in Venus's voice.

If she were ever to buy a house in Roancarrick, an impossibility because she'd never settle permanently in the village, the captain's house would be the one she'd choose. There was sea to the left of it, sea to the front of it and sea plus blunt-nosed Ben Bulben to the right of it. Best of all, it was raised so high on a ridge of land that nobody could ever build at the end of its garden and mar its crow's-nest position.

'I suppose it's blow-ins who bought it, jacking up house prices beyond the pockets of locals,' she complained.

'A Northern family, I believe they are called Landers.' Dan corroborated. 'There are quite a few new faces in the village now between the Germans, the English and the Northerners. At least the English and the Northerners spend their money locally, unlike that shower from Frankfurt who wouldn't spend Christmas. They like a drink, sure enough, but they do it in their own homes with beer they've brought across from the Continent in the boots of the cars.'

Venus was only half-listening to her father's repetition of village pub talk. Instead she recalled the curly-haired man with the artist's portfolio under his arm and bristled. Some of the newcomers believed in making themselves right at home – she'd prefer a little Teutonic reserve. He had a nerve; she'd never laid eyes on him before so he couldn't be in Roancarrick long, and already he was calling it 'our village'.

The village was divided on the subject of weekenders. Some locals were unsettled by so many strangers encroaching on their seclusion, but those with small businesses insisted it had an invigorating effect, and anyone with property to sell did not mourn the days of a stagnant market.

'I told you about the captain's house when it sold at auction. Don't you remember? There were five or six bidders. It was bought the same week your mother went into hospital for tests.'

Venus didn't recall. If it had been the week her mother's cancer had been diagnosed in Sligo General Hospital, everything else would have evaporated.

She'd flown home for the weekend, bringing her mother a satin and lace nightdress which Maura had stroked with a hand suddenly gnarled, calling it a ballgown and not bedwear at all. Venus had found the strip of lavender material, still in its original wrapping, in one of her mother's drawers after the funeral. It was probably still there, for she'd never followed through with her plan to donate her clothes to the Cancer Research Shop in Sligo. Venus made a mental note to find a couple of black bin-bags and rectify the omission.

'I believe the new owners might be from Tyrone,' continued Dan. 'Solicitors, the pair of them, with a grand family of sons. Imagine, the wife's a solicitor too.' He was continually bemused by the existence of women lawyers and doctors, despite the increasing frequency with which he encountered them. Yet he never regarded it as unnatural that Venus should go to university or become deputy director of the Bridges Across The World Language School. She was unique. She was his daughter.

Venus tossed her wind-tousled red hair. 'Of course they're Northerners – they'd benefit from sterling's strength against the euro. It's no wonder people like myself have to clear off to England – there's nothing left for us here with all the weekenders buying every house in the village and turning them into holiday homes.'

Dan used his stick to flick a rock in the middle of the road to one side. 'That had no bearing on your reasons for leaving home. You had it in your head to swim in a bigger pond, lass.'

Despite the fact that she was a large, handsome woman whose looks in no way could be defined as girlish, he claimed a father's blinkered prerogative and always referred to her as 'lass'. She found it reassuring: there were enough people in her life treating her as a woman. She had complained about it just once, in a fit of pique, and had been mollified by his shrewd observation.

'I'm too large to be a lass,' she'd objected.

'You're statuesque, not large. Never denigrate yourself, lass – there's enough people out there willing to do it for you.'

Her father sensed Venus's dwindling spirits. 'We could both use a drop of tea. Birdie left in a ginger cake for you along with the flowers. I'll cut it when we get indoors.' He grimaced. 'What was it she told me? Ginger's for energy and healing. Sure the woman would turn your head. Still, she bakes a tasty ginger-cake – you couldn't beat it with a big stick when it comes to settling the stomach. Birdie said you were to be sure and call as soon as you were sorted.'

Venus's mind ticked over: their neighbour would certainly be worth cultivating. She'd known Birdie all her life, but she'd been her mother's friend, an adult with somewhat unconventional traits. Perhaps now they could meet on equal ground.

As a child she'd been fascinated by Birdie's tortoise – she had a succession of tortoises but called them all Jude – and by her insistence on always wearing something red for luck. She had a habit, too, of slipping a sprig of heather in her shoe 'so luck walks with me'. In those judgmental teenage years, Venus had found her peculiarities pitiful and dismissed them as attention-seeking. Later Venus's attitude towards Birdie had tended to blend indulgence with a smattering of disdain.

But at least she was an individual, Venus reasoned. It took strength of character to persist in 'combing' the atmosphere of her home with a feather to ensure balance, or hanging bells outside windows and doors to frighten evil spirits away. Most people would have dissolved before the scorn of their neighbours. Not Birdie.

She'd gladly take the parish priest's arm and advise him to burn blue candles to help him find a missing book. 'No point in relying on St Christopher, Father McGinley – they don't think he even existed at all. Bit of revisionism there. Imagine all those medals people daren't wear any more. St Anthony's your man, of course, but he must be withered from tracing missing spectacles. As for St Jude, you're not such a hopeless case as all that.' All of it said with a glimmer that was only slightly wicked.

Yes, thought Venus, Birdie should be worth cultivating. And not alone because of her peculiarities.

'Birdie was with Mam the day you carried me home, wasn't she?' Her tone was deliberately nonchalant.

'She arrived just after us.' Dan found another rock to knock sideways with his stick; although he no longer drove, he worried for the car tyres of others. 'Thirty-three years ago next month, as you know only too well yourself.'

Frown-lines indented between Venus's eyebrows. Birdie must know something of her history. She shouldn't lose sight of her goal here in Roancarrick. *Try Finding Not Sacrificing Yourself.*

She was going to go sleuthing and she'd start with Birdie. A batty old girl like her should be a pushover.

Chapter Seven

Venus strolled down to the harbour, shivering as she realised she should have pulled a coat over the cable-knit sweater she was wearing but reluctant to turn back. Donegal Septembers were climatically continents away from the London version, where she'd be sweltering in an Indian summer. She thought of all her wispy Monsoon dresses – they might get a fortnight's airing next August. Investment in a few more sweaters was essential: her London wardrobe would look ridiculous here, from the shoes upwards.

She hadn't managed a walk on her own the previous night after all, because her father had seemed loathe to allow her out of his sight – she knew now what was meant by the child being father to the man. Their roles were reversed and he was dependent on her, just as she'd hovered at Dan's knees in her time, vying for his attention.

Both had opted for an early night. She'd discovered the drive had tired her – or perhaps it had been her Damascene experience. Moments of epiphany were wearing after the euphoria faded. Before bed, Dan had laced on his boots and had gone out to the yard to inspect Venus's motor, quizzing her about how much she'd paid for it and shaking his head over the criminal cost of cars nowadays. He'd handed over fifty-eight punts for his first car, spitting on his hand to seal the bargain.

Dan had sat in the driver's seat of the Polo but had declined to take it for a spin. His confidence in his motoring abilities had faltered since his eyesight began fading.

Ironically he'd stopped driving around the time he was least able to manage walking any distance. But there had been a near-miss with a woman wheeling a buggy who'd stepped out onto a pedestrian crossing in Bundoran, and he had come home ashen, mumbling how it was only by the grace of God he wasn't a double killer. He had sold his Corsa to Nora Brennan from the pub the next day. She had wanted it as a twenty-first birthday present for her only son. Convincing herself it might help him mature.

Nora had hopes of Timmy Brennan following her into the business, but he was already developing a drink problem and was far from ideal pub-owner material. Indeed, with his daily alcohol intake he was far from ideal driver material. Nora had paid Dan a fair price for the car, knowing that with only one pub in the village he'd return the money to her sooner or later.

Dan still took an interest in cars, even if he no longer drove, and last night Venus had followed him out to the yard, hoping to win his approval for her crocodile-green Polo. 'Senan Mulqueen left me his coconut air purifier,' she'd volunteered, clutching at straws.

'Wouldn't you just roll down the window if you wanted fresh air?' he'd responded, mystified.

Venus had decided against introducing him to the climate-control principle and had retired to bed with a niggling sense of her life having taken a detour.

* * *

But the next morning dawned crisp and clear, lifting her mood. She awoke to the chime of church bells and after breakfast – she'd have to buy some coffee, tea didn't jumpstart her system – she struck out for the beach. It was one of those days when you felt you could see forever except the horizon blocked your line of vision. That was the trouble with horizons, they put boundaries on infinity.

She passed the sub-post office that no longer sold stamps – it had been converted into a weekend home by a childless couple from Wicklow who seemed never to visit. The woman's mother was from the area and she had a fondness for it, for her sake. But the husband complained about the length of drive and insisted a weekend retreat in Wexford would be more convenient. Venus had all this from Dan at breakfast. He said they'd only visited three or four times during the summer and predicted a 'for sale' board would go up in the springtime. Typical of Roancarrick, thought Venus – not only did everyone know your business, they knew what you'd do before you'd made up your own mind to it.

A car slowed and the window was rolled down; it was the man who delivered the oil for their central heating. 'Home again, Venus,' he said, as though she'd been away for a fortnight's holiday in London instead of ten years. She raised her hand and kept walking. But as she turned the bend that led into the village she stopped, awed by the panorama unscrolling before her. Every time Venus sighted the coastal strip of Roancarrick afresh after an absence, she marvelled at her ability to be away from it. Yet she always forgot about the pull it exerted on her heart when she left Roancarrick behind.

Perhaps she deliberately eradicated it.

She gazed beyond the harbour, with its tethered confetti-coloured boats, looking towards Ben Bulben with that swoop of nose. The nose under which Yeats was buried, just as he'd specified. People were often kinder to the dead than to the living, zealous in carrying out last bequests. Then her glance shifted to the strand, where the tide was out and the sea coiled, a narrow satin ribbon, at the base of the beach. Her eyes travelled back in leisurely fashion to the harbour walls, where she could discern the orange string of lobster pots piled against the granite.

In terms of sheer physical beauty, this was paradise.

Except everyone knew which creature had thrived in paradise.

Movement attracted Venus's attention. It was a man's figure, spare and moving quickly, a burgundy portfolio under his arm. The wind whipped a flurry of fawn-fair curls across his eyes and he raised a hand and brushed them away. Venus gritted her teeth. Look at him – he even moved like a snake, undulating along with the confidence of the predator.

He needn't think he could condescend to her again. She'd be polite but distant. The trick was not to stop walking – it limited conversation.

He was almost abreast of Venus before he saw her, engrossed in whatever was troubling him. It had to be something grave to engrave those worry trenches between eyes that were normally carefree, she was willing to bet. She caught herself short – that sounded too partisan. Despite his abstracted appearance, he was shrilling the same tuneless whistle she'd heard at their first meeting.

The man straightened his hunched shoulders as he drew level with her and smiled. It was a gap-toothed, captivating smile and she couldn't help but eke out some measure of response. Walk, she urged her strangely lethargic feet – if you're stationery he'll criticise your posture or complain you're on the wrong side of the road.

'It's the woman who likes looking at the sea. And she's doing it again.' His voice was one of those laughter-fuelled ones and he had a richly rounded Northern accent – a broadcaster's tones. There were sun-rays radiating out from the corners of his eyes where he crinkled them to smile. Best of all, she had to creak her neck back an inch or so to look up at him.

'You don't talk much, do you?' he commented. 'Of course, maybe you don't speak English.' He slowed down to a staccato monotone. 'On hol-i-day? You should visit the cave. Very in-ter-est-ing. Special rock there. Locals say mermaids – you know mermaids? – women with fish's tails? – used to sun themselves on it.'

There he was, treating her like a stranger again. Advising her on the tourist attractions. The man was incorrigible.

'I happen to live here,' she snapped. Then she amended it. 'Well, I used to live here, I suppose I do again.' She gathered her flayed resources and strove for clarity. 'I come from Roancarrick.'

'Lucky you.'

The sunlight reduced his pupils to needlepoints, but she still couldn't tell if his eyes were blue or green, or a shade midway between the two. Walk, she howled at her feet, and they shunted her forward.

'See you around,' he said, in that voice with its suggestion of laughter just a syllable away. Then the whistle started up.

She dug her hands into the pockets of her beige combat trousers and pretended not to hear his farewell. Anyway, shaggy-haired men weren't her type; she preferred the sleeked-back look she'd been accustomed to in London.

Besides, how dare he spoil her walk with his gratuitous references to the seal's rock, which was her special place? She'd spent months of her life there if you added up the hours – maybe even an entire year. She used to bring down a book and a clingfilm-wrapped sandwich to the rock and sit on its flat surface, whiling away the day. From a distance it looked like a dumpy capital T, with its platter roof; she always imagined the rock was guarding the entrance to the mermaid's cave because it stood by its mouth. Theirs was the closest house, only minutes' walk away. She'd been exploring that cave for decades: she and her best friend at the time, Teresa O'Dea, had scrambled through every inch of its echoing cavern. That's what the cave was famous for – its reverberations. According to local folklore, mermaids used to drape themselves on the seal's rock at the entrance to the cave – but one mermaid, caught in a storm, had ventured inside and her tail had become trapped. The echoes were her plaintive voice calling to her companions for help.

Venus's plan was to walk along the beach and collect a *Sunday Independent* for her father from Mrs O'Dea's shop on the way home. He'd gone to early mass, but the shop hadn't been open, as it usually was, on his way home.

'Mrs O'Dea must have slept in,' Dan had grumbled, dismayed by the disruption to his routine.

'Mrs O'Dea might fancy the odd lie-in,' Venus had countered.

Dan had looked at her as though she were daft. 'And lose the trade? All the O'Deas still have their First Holy Communion money.'

Venus decided to ask Mrs O'Dea about her daughter Teresa. With real interest instead of her usual cursory enquiries. She'd been best friends with Teresa during their school years, but Teresa's name had been pulled out of a lottery for Morrison visas and she had headed to Buffalo around the same time as Venus's move to London. They didn't swap so much as Christmas cards now. Venus felt a flurry of guilt at how readily she had allowed contact to dwindle away with so many school-friends – she could use some of them now. She hadn't realised at eighteen how few genuine friendships there'd be in life. Maybe she'd copy down Teresa's address in the United States, drop her a postcard. She wondered if her friend still practised kissing her reflection in the dressing-table mirror so she'd know how to do it when a boy grappled with her. Probably not, on balance. After all, she was married with a child; some kissing must have preceded it.

She couldn't pick up the newspaper for Dan until after Mass. He thought Venus was there now instead of strolling on the beach, inhaling tangy air that startled lungs accustomed to London pollution. She hadn't felt like telling him she no longer went to church every Sunday, just on the odd one when she fancied it, and even that was from sentiment rather than conviction. It would have caused ructions she wasn't girded to ward off just yet.

Anyway, where was the point in coming home to care for him if she precipitated a heart attack inside the first twenty-four hours? So Venus had kept up appearances when Dan had pointedly remarked on the time twice, alleging that seats were scarce at the 11 a.m. service. She found that difficult to believe, given the grandiose nature of the church and the meagre size of the population. However, she'd lifted her chunky oatmeal sweater, which had always been too warm for London and made her look like a Bord Fáilte commercial besides, and allowed him to believe she was on her way to church.

Full-scale confrontation was overrated, in Venus's view. Guerrilla tactics worked more effectively.

The beach was so elongated by the waning tide that the handful of other walkers disintegrated into its sandy depths. She felt she was alone and it soothed her. She gravitated to the water's edge and rested her eyes on the constantly moving surface. Something jabbed underfoot and she lifted a shaving of yellow polished glass, worn smooth by the waves' buffeting, twirling it between her fingers. Church bells pealed for the start of Mass at Our Lady of the Assumption and she smiled. She and Teresa used to call it 'Our Lady Making Assumptions', a nickname they had regarded as almost bold enough to deserve telling in Confession. Except they'd quit going by that stage – the first sacrament to bite the dust.

The mass-going crowd spilled onto the seafront, smokers reaching into pockets and handbags for cigarettes, children clamouring for change for sweets, and Venus judged it safe to approach the shop to buy Dan's Sunday newspaper. A parked car with a sedate aura flashed its indicator as she crossed the street: its driver was the shopkeeper's son, John Óg O'Dea – 'young' John, called for his father John senior. John Óg was something vital in the accountancy sphere, according to his mother. He executed the most protracted three-point turn in the history of motoring and drove off, showing more scalp than the last time they'd met. He can't have recognised her or he'd have paused to demand her business, an interrogation dressed up as a welcome.

'Long sermon?' asked Dan, as she reached him his newspaper.

Venus did a double-take. Surely he wasn't checking on her? She'd have to put a stop to this sooner rather than later. She was thirty-two, with a university degree, a bank account and a car, quite successful in her career – she didn't have to fib to her father.

'So-so,' she fibbed. 'I'm just running across to Birdie's to thank her for the flowers.'

* * *

Rather than take the longer route by the road, Venus cut across the path from the back of their house that led to Birdie Ross's cottage. It was a track flattened by feet over the years and she thought of how many times her mother must have tramped it. It comforted her, so that a half-smile illuminated her features despite damp feet from the jungle of weed-choked grass when she reached Birdie's house. It was too close to the cliff-face for comfort, but Birdie seemed impervious to the possibilities of a slither towards disaster.

'This house will be standing long after I'm not,' she'd retort, if anyone expressed reservations about her safety.

There was a half-door at the back of the house, with the top always left open unless weather conditions were hurricane. 'Anyone home?' Venus called through the door, the current of air from her voice setting a clutch of metal bells jangling.

'Lift the latch and walk in,' invited Birdie, in fairytale mode.

It took Venus's eyes a moment to adjust to the gloom, for Birdie's house had tiny square windows with panes of dense glass that seemed designed to prevent light from entering.

'If it isn't Venus Macken, home from London and rake thin. It suits you. I've always found fleshy women distasteful – no willpower.' Birdie's voice was as scratchy as gravel.

'Perhaps it has nothing to do with willpower – it could be their natures,' protested Venus.

'You're right.' The mercurial Birdie concurred unexpectedly. 'Anyway now that I look more closely at you, you're not skinny at all. It was just the way the light caught your face and lent you some bone structure. No, you'll have to wait until you're an old woman before you can enjoy cheekbones. In the meantime you may content yourself with what you've got.'

Venus wasn't convinced Birdie would be a pushover after all. She'd forgotten how sharp she was, fleet of thought and tongue. She eased her way into the cottage, little more than a single enormous room with matching rectangles sliced off at the sides for a bedroom and bathroom, her heels reverberating. Further into the room there were rugs scattered for warmth – red, naturally, Birdie was obsessed with the colour – but near the door the scrubbed flagstone was naked and as old as the house. Some two centuries old, according to Venus's guess.

She inhaled the autumnal scent of Birdie's room, neither kitchen nor sitting-room but an amalgamated space where Birdie lived and worked. Although what she worked at nobody knew. It always smelled of twilight and harvest, regardless of time or season. It had been years since she'd called into Birdie's cottage, for the older woman didn't encourage visitors, and Venus looked around now with curiosity.

The room was dominated by an exposed brick and beam fireplace from which a serpent-framed mirror was suspended, its glass mottled with age. Birdie didn't appear to have a television set, but a computer screen, its motor whirring, straddled the kitchen table alongside haphazard stacks of books. A wooden owl balanced on top of the screen, mustard-painted eyes glowing in the shadows. A state-of-the-art compact-disc player stood on shelving in a corner, with a Stan Getz CD propped against it.

'I came to thank you for the flowers,' said Venus.

Birdie's pared-down face was in shadow as she inclined her head and returned her attention to the computer keyboard, saving some text onto disk.

Venus hesitated. Then she crossed to the hearth, to where Birdie's pet tortoise was dozing in his accustomed spot alongide a basket of turf. That much she remembered. She stroked Jude's shell and his blinking eyes emerged, followed by the rest of his elongated neck. She traced her fingertip along a knobbly forefoot.

'Why Jude?' she asked.

Birdie transferred her gaze from the computer screen to Venus. She had an enigmatic way of looking at a person from that streamlined face composed entirely, Venus was convinced, of a collection of triangles. Venus had given up all expectation of an answer before Birdie spoke. '*Jude the Obscure* . . . I call him Jude because a tortoise is an obscure pet for a grown woman to have. But he's company, of sorts. The Chinese believe his four feet represent the four corners of creation. They're supposed to be divine messengers, but I can hardly persuade Jude past the first patch of grass by my path.'

Birdie tapped a final command into her computer and

left it, heading for the fridge where she rustled in the salad container. A lettuce leaf was produced and fed to Jude, who took scimitar bites.

'I suppose I should think about bedding him down for his winter hibernation but I hate to say goodbye to the old boy. Another fortnight or so and then it's five months of sleep for you, Jude.'

She watched the tortoise's fastidious chewing. 'There's always the worry he'll never wake up, that's really what's stopping me. Hibernation is so extraordinary. A biological imperative that's unavoidable, and yet it's Russian roulette. You might wake up in springtime – then again you might not. At least we have choices; we can get a grip on our biological imperatives, take them to therapy if they persist in troubling us.' Birdie's narrow slits of eyes flashed as yellow as her wooden owl's. 'But what can those male spiders do, driven to mount a female that sometimes kills the mate – and sometimes spares him? It's completely arbitrary, not even a reflection on performance, because we have no evidence that technique matters to spiders.'

Venus was dumbfounded. She'd only stopped in to be polite to Birdie, who'd shown consideration for her father these past six months. She hadn't imagined the pair of them having a cosy chat about the mating habits of murderous spiders. If she didn't need to pump Birdie about her origins she'd make her excuses and leave. She should try and respond in kind, not betray to Birdie that she found her outlandish. She stroked Jude's honeycombed shell. 'There are days when I think I'd like to sleep through the winter and waken to springtime,' murmured Venus.

Birdie had her back to Venus, rattling through a cupboard, so tiny she had to stand on tiptoes to reach her china. 'Nonsense. You'd miss Samhain, Hallowe'en I suppose you call it, then the year's equinox, followed by Christmas – for those with a sentimental bent – and finally the phoenix finale, the death and rebirth of the year.'

'Enough,' objected a rueful Venus. 'You've convinced me. Now that I think about it, hibernation may have a mythical slant but it's not particularly emancipated from the heroine's point of view. Snow White and Sleeping Beauty are always obliged to wait for a handsome prince to animate them. They're not allowed an internal alarm-clock, and there's no question of them rejecting the prince.'

'Witches are invariably wicked in fairytales.' Birdie poured mint tea into two fragile cups. 'It's pejorative – no wonder they were persecuted after propaganda like that. What are fairy godmothers but kind witches? Nobody takes that into account. Anyway, good and bad are subjective.' She reached Venus a gold-edged cup and saucer so delicate Venus feared they might disintegrate in her hand. 'For relaxation,' elaborated Birdie. 'It disperses anxiety. I grow the mint myself.'

Venus sipped the bruise-tinged liquid, its colour reminding her of Karim's eyes. Was Birdie implying that she appeared to be on edge? Such strange ideas that woman formed. She risked another mouthful. It certainly had a mellowing effect – and there was a ceremonial aspect to drinking from a porcelain cup, clinking it gently against the saucer.

In the lull that followed, Venus decided to risk a circuitous question. She knew instinctively that Birdie would bridle at direct interrogation but she was curious about how this neighbour lived. After all, she couldn't be older than her early fifties, yet she'd spent most of her life without a companion in a cottage in Roancarrick. She must have been attractive in her time, with those slanting eyes so deep-set you had to peer to discern they were hazel, and that cloud of soft, black hair.

She had it tied back with one of her habitual scarlet ribbons worn for luck. All Venus's life she remembered Birdie had looped her hair in them, the bank of fine hair contrasting with the vibrant tongue of ribbon. From behind she looked like a girl, for there was still not so much as a thread of grey. Last Christmas Venus had asked how her hair retained its colour.

'I just made up my mind not to go grey,' Birdie had responded carelessly.

There were rumours about her having a private income, about being the illegitimate daughter of a wealthy foreign politician – or sometimes it was a minor European royal – who'd left her an inheritance. Villages specialise in rumours. Most of them seemed to emanate from Nora Brennan's pub. Some even said Birdie had become a recluse after a brief flirtation with fame but she'd bolted, finding the attention too invasive to handle. It was unclear, however, whether she'd been a film star or a pop star.

Venus didn't believed any of these theories, but all she knew for a fact was that Birdie Ross had lived in Roancarrick since before Venus was born and had been friends with her mother. Her accent wasn't local – it had a trace of the Midlands, blurred after a lifetime in Donegal.

'It must be difficult –' Venus wavered, then ploughed on, 'to earn a living in Roancarrick. I mean,' she was rushing now in case Birdie took offence, 'I'm hoping to teach some classes in Sligo Tech but you wouldn't make your fortune from it – if I weren't living rent free I might feel the pinch. It's so remote here, there's little work.'

Birdie smiled, not fooled by the subterfuge. 'I manage. Computers link you to a wider world. The Internet's a particular boon. I start every day by dipping into it.'

So that was where she came by all her abstruse data about cannibal spiders. 'You must rely on your computer a lot.' Venus was still reluctant to risk a direct question.

'It's a tool, not a friend.' Birdie grew sombre. 'Machines can't replace people. Maybe I have been tapping away on my computer a lot recently – it takes me out of myself. The fact is that I miss your mother, Venus. She was a valued friend, a woman with an independent mind. Maura passed most of her life in this gasp of a village, bar those few years training as a nurse in Dublin, and yet you'd go far to meet her match for worldly wisdom.' She stretched out a child-sized hand laden down by a lump of quartz on the wedding-ring finger and caught Venus by the wrist. 'Your mother was never judgmental. You know what she said to me once? "I've come to the conclusion that the fewer conclusions people reach the better. Especially with regard to others' actions." How's that for tolerance? Great thinkers pondering all their lives couldn't reach those heights.'

Venus felt her eyes moisten at this testimonial to her mother. She'd always known her mother was exceptional – but it had appeared unexceptional to her that this should be so. It was only now she was starting to appreciate those qualities which had set her apart. She reached her free hand across to take Birdie's but the older woman appeared not to notice the gesture and moved back.

'Dad's fond of you,' Venus murmured.

'He thinks I'm only borderline sane. But he puts up with me because I was Maura's friend.'

'You connect him to her.'

Birdie shrugged. 'We forge our own connections – go-betweens don't work.' She watched a cast of shapes undulate in the turf fire – kept lit, winter and summer – until roused by a brick that tumbled, smouldering, onto the hearth. 'Your roots in Roancarrick are deeper than you realise, Venus. The transplantation to London didn't take.'

'I'm only here because Dad needs me.'

'That's why you think you're back, but it's not the real reason. Where you're from is always who you are, Venus. But knowing who you are is less important than understanding who you want to be.'

While Venus was digesting this, Birdie's tone became suddenly businesslike. 'Now then, there's something you want from me. How can I help?'

It flummoxed Venus. She'd hoped to approach the subject gradually – and yet here was a tailor-made opening. She'd seize the overture.

'I want to find out who my real parents are.'

There, it was in the open.

'Dan and Maura are your real parents.' Birdie was wearing one of her emblematic unfathomable expressions.

'My biological parents.'

'Ah, biology. So we're back to the biological imperative.'

'If you like.' Venus took a deep breath. 'This is something I must know. It's need, not curiosity.'

'But surely the point about our earlier discussion on the biological imperative is that we can overcome it. We're not like those spiders who lack foreknowledge and go blindly to their fates. We can choose which web to spin and which one to leave unspun.'

'Birdie.' Venus pinioned her with a glance. 'Out of love and respect for my mother, who became distressed whenever I raised the subject, I never investigated my parentage while she was alive. Will you help me now?'

'What about your father's feelings – aren't you worried about dislodging his foundations at a time of life when he deserves peace? When you start lifting stones and disturbing corners, there's no telling what might come crawling out.' Birdie's tiny, geometric face was austere, and it gave Venus pause.

'I'll tell him what I'm doing,' she said haltingly, 'but I don't believe it will matter so much to him. I think Dad would have told me what he knew years ago only my mother stepped in. I could go back to him now rather than come to you but he's frail, he's been through a great loss recently and I don't want to do anything to distress him. I'm trying to go about this discreetly.'

Birdie clattered her chair as she stood. She bustled about gathering teacups and Venus had the impression she was playing for time while an interior debate raged.

'I'm asking for your help, Birdie. I'm entitled to know who I am.'

Birdie's mouth, little more than a squiggle in the lower third of her face, contorted with amusement. 'If that's what you want then no-one can help you. You'll have to rely on yourself to discover who you are. And as for where that might lead you, Venus Macken, bear in mind that we all of us become what we already are.'

Venus felt mocked. She glowered at Birdie for a moment, then jumped to her feet in a flurry of copper-haired temper, slamming the door on her way out. The commotion set the silver bells suspended above the door frame jingling and their clinking followed her across the yard. Even inanimate objects were jeering at her.

Chapter Eight

Venus's feet flew towards her home, but they trailed to a halt as she realised she couldn't go in to her father in such a state of pumping agitation. She skirted around the house and started towards the beach – but as she reached the T-junction above Nora Brennan's pub, instead of following through, impulse veered her to the right. She was walking in the direction of the captain's house.

The road became noticeably steeper and she felt the pressure of the climb in her calves. However, there was diversion ahead in the long, low building clinging to its perch some yards above the road. At least these cuckoos hadn't changed the nest's colour. The house, topped by a thatch that extended onto its perimeter walls like an unruly fringe, was painted a far from nautical pink. Unless it was a reference to pink gin for which the captain had a predictable taste, according to the oldest resident in the village. Although he'd been a boy too young for pubs when the captain had died. More rumour-mongering dressed up as fact, Venus decided.

She dawdled past, searching for signs of occupation. There were cars inside the gate, both with Northern plates, one of them a four-wheel-drive. Some flabby-chested flowerpots were arranged near the door, the heads almost blown off the Black-eyed Susans skulking in them. Venus curled her lip. The house was one of the most exposed in the village – nothing but the hardiest shrubs would survive up there – a few heathers, maybe. The newcomers would soon learn that for themselves.

She noticed the ship's wheel above the front door needed a coat of varnish: they ought to do it before the winter set in. Then she shook herself. It was their house, their ship's wheel, their business.

But there was another addition, now that she inspected the house, for a weathervane was roosting alongside the chimney. She narrowed her eyes and craned, trying to detect what the newcomers had plonked on their roof.

'It's a duck,' said a male voice.

Venus looked over her shoulder. There was the helix-haired artist from the beach, complete with sketchpad.

'The webbed feet are the giveaway,' he elucidated. 'Although maybe you can't make them out from here.'

'How did you know what I was looking at?

'You were mumbling to yourself.'

The blood pumped through her translucent skin, flushing her face. He went around whistling to himself, sure that was just as bad. 'Blow-ins,' she snorted. 'Forcing property prices up beyond the reach of local people. Is it any wonder all the young ones have to leave the area? What right have these people to come flashing their cash in Roancarrick and buying my house?'

'They bought your house? I thought the owners were Scottish.'

'Well,' she amended, 'the house I might have bought. One day. Maybe to retire to, I hadn't decided.'

'Never mind, perhaps the locals will make them feel so unwelcome they'll sell up at a loss and you can seize your chance.' His eyes crinkled at her – his company had a relaxing quality when he wasn't being annoying, even more therapeutic than Birdie's mint tea.

'I just hope they don't go wrecking it on me,' she muttered. 'They might tear down interior walls or rip out features.'

'I heard they wanted to keep it exactly the way they found it, apart from sorting out the woodworm and the leaks in the roof,' said the artist.

'Well,' Venus regarded the house doubtfully, 'I suppose they have left it pink. Some people might have been tempted to tone it down a couple of shades or even change it altogether. But they can't just muscle in here and expect to belong.'

'Not everybody can be lucky enough to be born somewhere as glorious as Roancarrick – some folk have to search out a Roancarrick of their own.' The stranger had one of those faces that seemed to smile, even when his mouth was still.

Perhaps he wasn't inherently exasperating after all, despite his high-handed criticism of her driving. Venus was about to introduce herself, with the intention of inducing him to do likewise, when the front door of the captain's house opened.

A woman with fawn-fair curls called out, 'Conor, I thought it was yourself. Your father was wondering if you have his car keys – he wants to go into Bundoran.'

'Be with you in a minute, Mum,' he replied.

Venus was aghast; the day which had beckoned so promisingly was disintegrating around her. First there was the altercation with Birdie, then she criticised the new owners of the captain's house to their son's face. The man turned to her, extending his hand. He started to speak but Venus backed away, riddled with embarrassment.

'I have to be going,' she stuttered.

And decamped for the second time that day.

* * *

Her footsteps decided she'd be safer indoors, since her brain appeared incapable of choosing a direction in which to flee. Her father was settling down to watch an all-Ireland Gaelic football semi-final on television and didn't notice the commotion she made.

'Had a nice visit with Birdie, Venus? I went ahead and had my lunch without you, just a slice of cheese and a tomato between a couple of heels of bread.' He spoke above the prattle of the pre-match commentary. Without waiting for a reply, he went on, 'It's Derry versus Cork. The experts are handing the title to Cork on a plate, but I wouldn't be so quick to rule out those Derrymen. They play a robust game. They could be celebrating being through to the final in a couple of hours and who knows after that? Sam Maguire might be northward-bound this year.'

Venus perched on the edge of the sofa, which faced the portable television set on the dresser. There was a tin of toffees beside her father on one of the cushions and he looked as though life had taken a blissful turn. He passed the toffee tin to her, she shook her head, and he unwrapped one for himself.

'Of course,' his cheek was bulging, 'all those strapping

guards on the Cork side are well able to handle vigorous play, I'll grant them that. But they have nothing at midfield.'

Instead of retreating to her room, as she'd intended, Venus slid into the seat beside her father and reached for a toffee after all. It had been years since she'd watched a Gaelic football match. The camera panned to the VIP box in Croke Park, where the President and her husband were waiting for the starting whistle.

'Her husband used to play.' Dan nodded towards the President as she listened to the Artane Boys' Band.

'Do you ever miss it yourself, Dad?'

'Sure I'm only an old crock; it's years since I was on a pitch. Hold your whisht now, they're away.'

He chattered all through the first half, flaying the referee for his decisions, becoming ever more heated at his apparent habit of looking the other way at crucial junctures, and groaning over the performance of the players. He could do better himself with his one sound leg. Galway men shouldn't be let near a referee's whistle – the power went to their heads. That commentator should be taken out and shot, he was talking gibberish. He'd a good mind to turn down the sound. Meanwhile Venus was hissed into silence if she volunteered a word.

Resting there beside Dan on the battered tweed sofa, an idea occurred to her. Just because she'd been rejected by Birdie didn't mean she was beaten. She could ring all the hospitals in the vicinity and ask them to check their records for a baby girl with red hair born around October 31, 1969. There couldn't be many of them. That would give her a springboard in her search for her mother.

At half-time, with the score stalemate at one goal and

five points to eight points, Venus offered to make tea. Dan beamed, in high humour.

'Can't risk tea – I might need to use the bathroom during the match. I'll stick with the Devonshire toffees. The bladder's banjaxed as well as the leg. Shame they couldn't send me to a repairs shop.'

Venus suspected he was the only one allowed to pass such remarks.

'The teams seem fairly evenly matched,' she suggested.

'Nonsense. Cork are running away with it.'

'But you fancy Derry's chances.'

'They're not a bad side,' he allowed, 'but they missed a goal during that free kick. They haven't a prayer now, their luck's on the turn. Anyway I have a bet on with Mickey Joe and my money's riding on Cork.'

This was excellent father-daughter bonding: she should keep him talking. 'What made you gamble on Cork – are they the favourites?'

He rummaged for another toffee. 'No, the smart money's on Derry. And as an Ulsterman I shouldn't go betting on a Munster squad. But Mickey Joe offered me a decent price so I thought I'd take a punt. Whisht, now, that eejit of a referee's about to blow the whistle. Although he was very slow about using it when young Hickey was sent flying with a dirty tackle in the first half.'

She watched the rest of the game, jaw jutting with a succession of toffees, and observed how fresh-faced yet paradoxically ferocious were the teams. They seemed cut from the same black-haired, white-skinned cloth, concentrating on the holy grail of stealing the ball from their opponents. Beside her, Dan moaned 'another giveaway point' and 'that shower don't deserve to win'. One player, labelled selfish with the ball because he was grudging about passing, was earmarked for particular censure.

'Just like his father before him.' Dan shook his head. 'He wasn't a bad player, mind you, until he discovered women. That took his mind off the game entirely.'

The match ended with Cork scraping to victory by a single point scored during injury time. As the players acknowledged the crowd's applause, Venus realised that her negativity – kindled at Birdie's and reinforced by her embarrassing encounter with the artist at the captain's house – had evaporated. She'd started watching the game with Dan to humour him and wound up enjoying the companionship. Even if some of the finer points of play had bypassed her.

Her father was fairly chortling as he took a precautionary swig of cough mixture, wiping his mouth against the back of his hand, and then laced on his boots to go to Mickey Joe's. The opportunity to crow over his friend, who lived in a former shebeen near the holiday cottages, motivated Dan more than any urge to collect his winnings, for the stake was small. Venus planned to use his absence to unpack and hang up her clothes in the wardrobe that had once held her school-uniform blazer.

'Dad,' she handed him his blackthorn stick, 'there's something I meant to mention to you.'

He tested the stick against the ground, so jubilant over his win he scarcely seemed to need it.

'It's about where I come from,' she continued.

'You hatched from an egg,' said her father.

That old chestnut.

'No, I really need to know,' she insisted. 'I want you to tell me how you and Mam came to adopt me.'

His mouth scissored open and then clamped shut again. He leaned on his blackthorn, jamming his hand against its bulbous head, and a shadow swarmed across his vision.

'Dad?'

'Let sleeping dogs lie, Venus. Life's too short to go poking into all its musty corners.'

And with that he was gone, hunched over his stick, the elation sapped from him.

Chapter Nine

Monday morning. Was it really only two days since her arrival in Roancarrick? Venus opened her eyes onto the lemon-sprigged wallpaper that had hung in her bedroom since she'd been cramming for her Leaving Certificate – then she screwed them shut and imagined what it would be like if she were back in her Barbican chrysalis. She could potter out to the kitchen in her nightdress because there were no draughts in the flat, no father leaving the back door open while he went out to the yard for blocks to feed the range.

She could make herself a pot of coffee, maybe grind some beans for a treat, and slide back to bed with it. She could lie there, propped against pillows, and leaf through a magazine while the caffeine surged through her system, or she could read a chapter of whichever novel lay on the bedside table, waiting to divert her. Better still, she could flip a tape into the video recorder and fast-forward to the 'Sixteen Going On Seventeen' scene in *The Sound Of Music*. Venus hummed a snatch of the song, picturing the summerhouse and the froth of petticoats as Liesel leapt from seat to seat with the straight-backed Rolf holding her hand.

Venus stretched. Oh yes, she could have the most indulgent morning to herself if she weren't in Roancarrick. Although, she reflected, Monday mornings were always spent ploughing through the administration backlog at the language school. She threw back the duvet, making a mental note to buy a new mattress because she suspected the one on the bed was as old as herself, and reached for her bathrobe.

Padding downstairs, she decided that today was the day she'd liberate the Golden Pages from whichever drawer in the dresser it was crammed inside, and begin ringing the hospitals. Persistence would throw up a clue.

Her father was sitting by the range with his stockinged feet straddling the oven door. She told him she'd never seen a man who looked more in need of fresh air.

'You're huddled over that range, Dad. A sea breeze would do you the power of good.'

'It looks squally out.' He was doubtful.

'Wrap up warmly and it can't do you a bit of harm.'

'I suppose I could take a stroll down to Mickey Joe's. He's just had the Sky dish installed – he says there's great racing to be seen on it, from Kentucky-town and all sorts of places. Then I'll light a candle in the church. I was going to leave it until later, but maybe I should risk it now – there's showers forecast this afternoon. It's your grandmother's anniversary today. Thirty-five years dead. She was a great knitter – we never had a shop-bought sock or pullover in the house when I was growing up.'

The dead were more real to her father than the living. Venus turned brisk. 'Here's your coat and hat, Dad. I'll have a nice cup of tea and a slice of Birdie's cake ready for you when you come back.'

As soon as she was on her own Venus started phoning. It was a tedious process, between being transferred to wrong departments and holding for people who seemed not to exist, but finally she acknowledged defeat. One hospital had still to ring her back, but it seemed, for now, as though she hadn't been born in a hospital. A home birth was less easy to trace. Venus flushed with annoyance. Also with a trace of embarrassment, because it proved her parents' story of how they had come by her was true, after all. Not that she'd doubted them, exactly, but people had a way of interpreting the truth to suit themselves.

However it hadn't been a completely wasted exercise: one of the hospitals' administrative staff suggested she should contact the social services. It struck Venus that she'd make more headway talking to local people in Roancarrick than dealing with officialdom, but she scribbled a number for Donegal (South) Health Board. There had to be a file on her adoption there. Perhaps there'd be a clue in the paperwork that could throw some light on her origins. Then she glanced at the clock and realised it was time she changed out of her bathrobe because Dan would be home shortly, plus she had an appointment in Sligo that afternoon.

Venus was leafing through a tangle of photographs in a Rover's biscuit tin, found returning the Golden Pages to its place in the dresser, when Dan returned. She laid down a black and white photograph of her mother and father on honeymoon in the Burren, bashfully holding hands. 'I'm going into Sligo today, Dad, if there's anything you need.'

'Devonshire toffees,' he said promptly.

'How about food?'

He looked hazy. 'I pick up a few sausages and my porridge oats and the like in Mrs O'Dea's shop. Her husband drops up anything that's too heavy to carry, the odd sack of spuds or tins of peas if I'm stocking up. Sure we have to give Mrs O'Dea the custom or the shop would go out of business. She's handy – we'd miss her if she called it a day.'

'Don't you use a supermarket?' Venus rummaged for coffee in the press, knowing there wasn't any but unwilling to concede defeat without one final sweep.

'The odd time but they're noisy places, full of people rushing about with trolleys they have no control over and tinkling music that hurts your head. You can't find a blessed thing in them; you'd be tormented wandering the aisles like a lost soul. Mrs O'Dea gets the elbow in with her prices, but you don't go home with a headache or forget what you wanted in the first place.'

Venus could see she'd be obliged to take the cupboard supplies in hand. Her father probably wasn't eating balanced meals without her mother to keep an eye on him. He was elderly enough to be her grandfather, almost half a century her senior, and the years were no longer nipping at his heels but had overtaken him. It left her chastened now to realise that the father of her childhood, who had always seemed ancient, had been relatively fit and well. Not young, never young, but hardy.

Watching him toast his toes, wriggling them like a toddler, it seemed to Venus that he had embraced a quaint mixture of youth and age.

'Are your feet cold, Dad?'

'Sure the blood runs thin at my age.'

'What do you mean "at your age"? You're barely past your prime.'

103

'I've more hot dinners behind me than ahead of me, lass.' Delivered with that lip-smacking bogus resignation again.

She debated a stratagem and decided to chance it. 'I suppose you're right, Dad. I won't include you in my Christmas arrangements – just in case.'

Dan's jaw worked furiously, then he surrendered and snorted with laughter. 'You were always a demon for the oneupmanship, Venus Macken.'

Venus was due to meet the principal of Sligo Tech to discuss teaching Spanish there. If there weren't enough classes she could always advertise her services for one-on-one tuition. Spanish was a useful language, lots of people were keen to learn it. Knowing how to ask for a second-class return ticket to Madrid in perfect Spanish, and to check which platform it was leaving from, must appeal to some people, she reasoned – the Irish were always making a song and dance about being committed Europeans.

She mentioned the appointment to Dan.

'I thought you taught English to them foreign people in London-town,' said Dan. Everywhere was a town to him: Donegal-town, Belfast-town, even America-town.

'I did, but there aren't enough of them here – sure we're so insular we call Dubliners foreigners. Maybe in the summer I'll be able to teach English as a foreign language, but in the meantime I'm a qualified Spanish teacher. I may as well put it to use.'

Dan followed her to the door, showing a touching solicitude that she should be wrapped up against the wind. A sore throat was fiendishly hard to shift, he warned, as the wind caressed the scant hairs scattered across the top of his head. They had never been a family given to hugs and kisses – they had been rationed out, not from lack of affection but because her parents came from a generation less accustomed to casual embraces. On impulse, however, Venus bent and rested her cheek against the indented ceiling of her father's scalp that was slightly too large for his skull, as though the bone had shrunk away from the flesh.

Her tall, strong body topped his by almost a head and a protective wave washed over her, looking down at the age freckles on his pate. He had wavy brown hair springing back from his forehead in the wedding photograph that stood on a mahogany shelf-unit in the living-room they never used, but as far back as she could remember Dan had been balding. He used to tease her as a child that she had so much hair it was only fair to share some with her father. She had taken it seriously and had protested, 'But you wouldn't look like Daddy any more with red hair.'

'So you only need toffees,' she checked, grimacing at a seagull's calling card on the bonnet of her car. She scrubbed at it with a tissue, inadequate to the purpose.

'That's all, lass. Of course you wouldn't go to the supermarket without asking Birdie if she has any messages?' her father prompted.

Venus pursed her lips and climbed into the Polo. Birdie wasn't her favourite neighbour right now. Then again, this could be a way of currying favour. 'I'll stop by on my way. Expect me when you see me.'

Her seahorse totem danced on its chain attached to the rear-view mirror, encouraging her.

Birdie was engrossed in painting her gate, assiduously recreating a verdigris effect which Venus had always assumed was the result of weathering. She leaned across the car and wound down the passenger window with the engine throbbing.

'I'm on my way into town if you need anything from the shops,' she cried.

Her neighbour rested her paintbrush on the tin lid and stepped across to the car. 'Didn't catch a word of that.' Her thin brown face was level with Venus's; Birdie always looked tanned, winter and summer.

Venus repeated her offer and Birdie considered. 'Washing powder,' she said, 'but only if you're going into the supermarket anyway.'

Venus remembered that Birdie had a minor obsession with washing and loved pegging out billowing lines of it – despite the tendency towards rain in Roancarrick – so she was always running low on powder.

'I'd like the biggest size in the supermarket's own brand,' she continued. 'It comes in a box so high.' She gestured with her hand to a distance level with her knees. 'Mrs O'Dea only stocks piddling little boxes that wouldn't last you a week. She's cute enough to know when you come back for more you'll buy other things too.'

Not a word of yesterday's fraught exchange. Either Birdie was an accomplished actress or she hadn't realised how upset Venus was by the refusal to discuss her origins.

'Orange is a good colour for you,' called Birdie, as Venus put the Polo into gear.

Venus looked at her peach silk shirt visible under the suede jacket. Surely it couldn't be described as orange?

'It allows you to harvest what you sow – it's lucky,' continued Birdie. 'Except when you're driving, in which case white is the only colour to wear.'

What an inexplicable woman. Full of portents one minute and buying bargain-basement washing powder the next. For some reason which she chose not to examine,

Venus took the long way through the village, turning right at the junction instead of going straight ahead. It meant she had to pass the captain's house. Not that she could face the artist again – Conor, his mother had called him – after the free way she'd spoken to him. Mind you, he'd led her on, allowing her to believe he had no connection with the captain's house when he lived there.

The two cars were parked in the same place, but there wasn't a soul to be seen. Venus put her foot on the accelerator and told herself she wasn't in the least disappointed. It was illogical to like someone simply because they had laughter-lines around their eyes. And an easy way of conversation. Not to mention that engaging habit of leaning in towards you when you spoke, concentrating on your words. 'Tell me I'm not developing a crush on the blow-in,' groaned Venus, and the stained-glass seahorse dangling from her rear-view mirror quivered in sympathy.

He could be sketching on the beach, or messing about with boats – most weekenders came to Roancarrick for the sailing. Unless he was gone from the village until next weekend, or even several weekends' time. Venus tapped the steering wheel with bitten fingernails, thinking about that possibility. Feeling a disconcerting drumbeat of emptiness. But the cars were still parked outside the house so perhaps the artist hadn't left after all. Venus smiled. Not because she might see him again soon. Certainly not. Her humour was on the mend because she'd discovered a couple of tapes left by Senan in the car. She slid one into the cassette player and Bono's voice filled the car.

Venus sang along to 'She Moves In Mysterious Ways', pretending not to pay any attention to the thought that jabbed her. The realisation that there had been a sea-change in her attitude towards Conor Landers in the course of a couple of encounters. She'd moved from instant dislike to what struck her as an inappropriate partiality for him – neither response based on any pretext of reality because she didn't know the man.

She lectured herself as she waited for a Renault carrying a surfboard on its roof rack, which had pulled out from a slip road in front of her, to gather speed. It was pointless taking up with weekenders because their Roancarrick life wasn't real – they were only playing house when they came to the village. Still, Bono's voice streamed through her head, his lyrics telling her it was all right. Venus allowed the smile tickling her lips to spread.

* * *

Sligo was bustling. Venus leaned against her car door, watching the eddy of the crowds, enjoying the sensation of activity: on a reduced scale it reminded her of London. She remembered her first day in the capital, standing on the pavement at Tottenham Court Road by an Underground station exit – wrapping her arms around herself in a solo hug of glee. There were streets streaking in every direction, a chaotic convergence of horns, car engines and rumbling buses, men selling the *Evening Standard* and women brandishing *The Big Issue*. Even the pigeons alighting near the queue outside The Dominion theatre had struck her as confident. Cocky city birds. People had side-stepped around her without a second glance; even the ones whose feet had collided with her luggage had muttered automatic apologies without swivelling their heads in her direction. After the claustrophobia of village life, she'd exulted in it.

Venus roused herself and headed for an Internet Café

just off Wine Street, where she paid for half an hour's time on-line and keyed in Chechnya, printing out some information about the country. Venus didn't plan to take Karim on trust, even if Lily were innately credulous. She folded up the sheets and stored them in her bag, planning to study them later.

Her next stop was the college where she had an appointment with the principal. Benedict Archer kept her waiting for fifteen minutes and when he arrived his eyes – the colour of minestrone soup, but without so many foreign objects floating in them – continually slid to the wall-clock behind her. She stifled her objections and chased out an alert expression.

He'd lost her application letter and curriculum vitae but remembered their telephone conversation from London. At least he claimed to recall it, at Venus's nudging. In any case she'd brought a back-up copy of her CV and he flicked through it as she sat there.

'My secretary's off sick,' he said, sensing her frustration behind the mask of civility. 'I'll be much more organised when she's back.' He leaned forward, a disconsolate expression in those soup-sad eyes. 'Trouble with her Fallopian tubes. Tricky things.'

Was he referring to women or Fallopian tubes? Venus decided it was safer simply to nod.

Despite its unpromising opening, and his insistence on calling her Venice instead of Venus, the interview was a success. A new series of night classes had started already, but the Spanish conversation teacher would be willing to hand over his lessons to her, Benedict Archer predicted. He was quite certain of it. Could she relieve him from next week? It was only three hours twice a week, beginners on Tuesdays and intermediate level on Thursdays. Venus said she could do it and asked how far the students had progressed.

'Early days. Very early days. They all know their names and occupations in Spanish in the beginners' class. That's about it,' he said. 'The intermediates are further along, obviously – they're having a look at the literature of the country.' Then he confided, 'Actually, I'm the Spanish teacher. I should never have taken it on – too much on my plate, Venice.'

Benedict Archer's aura of dejection magnified as the interview progressed, although the news he imparted was positive from her perspective. In the New Year he thought it possible Venus might be slotted into a temporary position on the day staff. One of the teachers was due to take maternity leave – something he'd mentioned to her on the phone already when she'd rung from London. He was all but snivelling as he checked she was qualified to teach French as well as Spanish.

'And your Fallopian tubes, how are they?' he enquired, in a breathtaking non-sequitur.

'Fine, not a bother on them,' she reassured him. But only because of the torment in his eyes. He'd never be allowed to get away with a question like that in London.

He needs a deputy, Venus surmised, as she strolled towards her car. Her London boss, Tamsin, had never looked downcast – she'd simply offloaded her problems onto Venus. Benedict Archer had to learn the art of delegation.

Buoyed by the prospect of work, she paused alongside scrolls of rainbow ribbons at a pavement stall. There were buttons, too, embossed and pearlised and flauntingly gilt – but it was the ribbons that drew her eyes and she bought a length of wine-dark velvet for Birdie as a peace offering. And possibly as a bribe.

As she paid for it her eye landed on some intricate white

lace looped around a cardboard holder. It reminded her of the petticoat she had worn under her First Holy Communion dress as a seven-year-old. Her mother had unpicked the lace from her own wedding gown and stitched it to the ruched hem of the little girl's petticoat – a garment Venus had never owned before or since. Maura had insisted that a Holy Communion frock required a petticoat to lend substance to its outline, and a petticoat needed lace or it was downgraded to a slip. Venus had mourned the fact that the lace wasn't visible beneath the dress.

'But we know it's there,' her mother had smiled. 'It's our secret.'

Still, Venus had hitched her dress inside her sash so that the lace peeked from under it. She'd wanted other people to know too.

The stall-holder noticed her lingering admiration at the lace and unwound it so the pattern could be appreciated. 'Perfect for a bride,' he sang out – whereupon Lily Dillon popped into her mind.

Venus scanned the street and saw a pay phone at one end of it. She left the lace but stored the red ribbon in her bag, extricating a fistful of change along with her address book for Lily's mobile.

Lily answered on the third ring, her voice trickling into the receiver in that throaty way she had. Nicotine-fuelled huskiness.

'Look at your hands. Are you wearing a wedding ring?' demanded Venus, not bothering to identify herself.

'Not yet.' Lily sucked on a pen in lieu of a cigarette in her non-smoking office.

'Is Karim still occupying the sofa bed or has he wheedled his way into the sleigh-bed?'

111

Lily laughed, not in the least offended. 'Yes, he's still staying with me. No, he's sleeping in the spare room. Of course the wedding plans are still on, why wouldn't they be? I've attempted to tell someone called the Registrar of Civil Marriages in my district that I'd like to apply for a licence. I was hoping it might be a straightforward procedure and the licence would arrive in the post in the next couple of weeks so we could have a Hallowe'en wedding.' She chuckled all the louder at Venus's gasp. 'Which wouldn't mean you'll be allowed to wear black and a long face to match it. But it's not going to happen so quickly because apparently you need to give three months' written notice and make an appointment with the registrar, at which you produce all your documentation. Birth certificate, passport, proof of residency, a mountain of paperwork. Which could be a problem for Karim but we'll cross that bridge a little further down the track. In the meantime I'm waiting for a form to fill out, something awesomely official called Notification Of Intention To Marry.'

'This sounds precipitate to me,' objected Venus. 'And I don't see how you're going to circumvent the proof of residency clause. I see illegality looming.'

'Doom and gloom,' warbled Lily. 'Of course he's resident. He's been living in Dublin since May. Citizenship isn't a marriage condition – I checked. Now, your wedding present to me can be a visit to Dublin for the occasion because I have enough cutlery and dinner services already. That is, I have one set of each which is as much as anyone could want.'

Venus heard muffled sounds and then Lily's voice again. 'Senan wonders if he left some tapes in the car.'

'U2 and some country and western outfit,' confirmed Venus. 'He can have them back.'

More mutters.

'He said the only one he'd keen to have returned is the country and western tape – apparently it's his brother's band.'

'They're desperate. They should be exterminated in some particularly painful fashion,' said Venus.

'His brother committed suicide shortly after recording it.' Reproach oozed from Lily.

Venus groaned. 'I'm the one who should be exterminated. I'll buy a padded envelope and post it off to him before I drive back to Roancarrick. I presume the office address is OK?'

'That's grand. By the way, I invented the brother's suicide to teach you a lesson.'

'Ouch! Listen, if you're determined to go through with this wedding, I presume at least you'll have the sense to make out a pre-nuptial agreement – you could be fleeced.'

'Don't be silly, I trust Karim,' said Lily. 'He wouldn't try to take advantage of me. He knows this is only a way of giving him a European Union passport – it's not a real marriage. Besides, our health service is crying out for doctors. I'm doing the nation a favour.'

'Maybe you should lobby all your friends to marry asylum seekers with medical qualifications,' suggested Venus. 'The Department of Health might give you a grant to cover expenses.'

Lily was immune to sarcasm. 'You trot out the most bizarre ideas, Venus Macken. Do you think I should have a hen party even though it's only a marriage of convenience?'

'I think you should have the hen party and scrap the wedding.' Venus noticed a teenager's face pressed close to the glass of the green telephone booth, indicating a customer who felt she'd monopolised the only working kiosk long enough. 'I have to go now – promise you won't do anything rash without talking to me first.'

The teenager flounced past Venus into the kiosk. 'Buy yourself a mobile and start texting people,' she snarled.

'Pots look ridiculous calling kettles black,' retorted Venus. Anyway, she was useless at texting, all fingers and thumbs. She and Lily had tried it before and her messages never made any sense, with extraneous asterisks and stray letters dotted everywhere, and she always pressed the 'send' button too soon. All the Bridges Across The World teachers had textitis, but Venus was too clumsy.

In a simmering rustle of fury, she returned to the ribbons and buttons stall and bought several metres of the lace. If Lily were determined to have a wedding day there'd have to be lace involved. At least it would bring a genuine bridal touch, even if the marriage should be a sham.

'The world is becoming more artificial by the day,' she announced to the stall-holder.

He looked at the russet-haired woman with the high colour in her cheeks and admired her discernment. 'There's nothing artificial about this lace,' he reassured her. 'It's handmade by Belgian nuns.'

Venus, sceptical about the nuns' addendum, attempted to pay with sterling instead of euro in her indignation at Lily, Karim, phone booths and stall-holders making false claims on behalf of their wares. She dropped her purse, then Birdie's ribbon and worked herself into a lather.

114

Chapter Ten

Venus sat in the passenger seat of her car, where there was more space, and concentrated on slow, steadying breaths. She pacified herself with positive imagery: she had secured work already, her father was thrilled to have her at home with him – their relationship was entering a new phase – and she had the opportunity now to ferret out the details of her adoption.

Try Finding Not Sacrificing Yourself.

An image from her leaving do in the Snakes and Ladders pub materialised, when everyone had wanted to take to the karaoke machine and sing female empowerment songs. Especially the men. It was of Gary Hesketh cornering her, while Tamsin sang 'These Boots Are Meant For Walking', to tell her statistics showed people spent two weeks of their lives kissing. His eyes had been bulging from their sockets as he'd relayed the data. At the time it had struck Venus as pathetic. 'Gary, you're an anachronism,' she'd chided him. 'But am I an anachronism you want to get all hot and bothered with?' he'd asked. She'd lacked the heart to remonstrate with him – busy being the spectre at her own feast. Now, however, Venus forgot her exasperation and found it endearing.

Gary had taken a shine to Lily when she'd visited Venus in London; his eyes had lit up so radiantly when he'd met her, Venus had been convinced someone had plugged him into the electricity mains. Later he'd approached Venus to establish whether Lily was single.

'That's putting the cart before the horse – you've already asked her out,' Venus had objected.

'Only because you keep rebuffing me. Anyway she didn't say no.' His brown eyes had been wounded behind the oblong tinted spectacles that pinched the bridge of his nose.

'She didn't say yes either. That's Irish for no – we just don't like using the word. You know how the Eskimos have dozens of different words for snow? We have endless permutations for no – and none of them use the negative.'

If it weren't for his undeniable skill in the classroom Venus would have ensured that his contract was not renewed. However Gary was a gifted teacher, so able that she always allocated him the beginners' groups. Sloppy habits learned there were the toughest to shift so it was essential not to give their misplaced pronouns a chance to take root. He was even able to reconcile the orderly Japanese to the disorderliness of irregular verbs. A man who was good at his job couldn't be completely written off, reflected Venus.

Stop, scrap that thought, shrieked some last vestige of sanity in her brain. It's panic-induced. Last month Gary Hesketh had been a cliché, now he was a character. London was becoming so rosy she'd have to spray it for aphids.

Eager for distraction, Venus rooted through her bag for the printouts on Chechnya from the Internet site. Lily seemed to regard ignorance as bliss, but she should have

116

some inkling of what she was becoming involved in. This starry-eyed indifference to pitfalls was vexing. It meant Venus had to intervene when she should be researching her own family history, not investigating Chechnya.

She produced a biro and started highlighting the salient passages – underlining 'human rights violations' twice, as well as 'the area is a potential tinderbox'. She not only underlined 'Neither side recognises non-combatant status' but also added an asterisk. Somebody was quoted about the 'pervasive corruption at all levels which does not augur well for the economy's reconstruction' and Venus was sorry she didn't have her phosphorescent felt-tipped pen to hand.

She'd photocopy these passages, enlarge them and shove under Lily's nose. If she wasn't careful she could have hordes of Chechen relatives on her doorstep. What if one of them should turn out to be a warlord? The Internet printout had a disturbing section on warlord trials. Lily might find herself playing host to outlaw inlaws.

At least, Venus consoled herself, Karim didn't want to whisk her friend back to Chechnya. He showed zero desire to go there himself. Lily would know all about it if he became homesick and cajoled her into emigrating, with no hairspray in the shops to keep her topknot in place. And she certainly wouldn't be showing two-storey over basement houses oozing potential to prospective buyers because they'd be too busy looking for properties with bomb shelters.

Her qualms intensified when she read there were many fundamentalist elements fighting in the Chechen forces keen to extend strict Muslim law to the region. Venus's hyperactive imagination leapfrogged ahead: Lily would be trapped in Grozny, forced to cover up from nose to toe, unable to work at all. Or use contraception or drink alcohol or wear high heels or leave the house without a male relative in tow.

Venus gasped at a potential scenario in which this marriage was a trap to trick Lily into becoming a captive Islamic bride in Chechnya. In her fevered state she completely overlooked Karim's lack of interest in the Muslim religion and patent unwillingness to remain in his homeland. Not to mention the fact he'd applied for asylum in Ireland, which indicated a preference to live there.

The more she read about the banditry in Chechnya, the more convinced she became that Lily must be saved from herself. There was nothing else for it but to head to Dublin this weekend and interfere in Lily's life.

Venus decided to abandon that day's planned shopping expedition for essentials which her father didn't view as essential – ground coffee, cheese that didn't come ready-sliced in squares, fresh pasta – and collect a few standbys. There was also Birdie's washing powder to buy but she should be able to squeeze that through the five items or less counter. Especially if she cheated. She'd blitzkrieg her way through the aisles another time.

Driving back through Roancarrick, she parked her car by the seafront, restless for some fresh air. Lily's rush of blood to the head was distracting her from her own mission to find herself. Come to think of it, Lily needed a sky-writing jolt too – *Finders Keepers Doesn't Apply To Asylum Seekers* should fit the bill.

She walked down to the beach, nose and earlobes rouged by the breeze. Her ankle-strapped interview shoes had slight heels which sank into the sand and she moved closer to the water's frilled edge, where the compacted sand made progress easier. She was wearing a cream linen trouser suit and the wind whistled through the warp-weft of the thread – she invariably wore trousers, not because she disliked the shape of her legs but because the length of them offended her. Venus believed skirts should be teamed with heels and a heel horrified her; she rationalised it as pandering to male fantasies, but it was simply that in heels she felt even more Amazonian than was already the case.

To balance the perceived manliness of the trousers she favoured, although they were often velvet or shot silk and far from masculine, she tended to plump for lace blouses and chokers, pearl strands wound round the alabaster length of her neck, or black ribbons from which dangled cameos. Jackets were always neat and box-shaped with cinched-in waists, and she had an extensive collection of dangling earrings in semi-precious gems such as moonstone. Today, because she'd wanted to look businesslike, she'd avoided jewellery apart from tiger's eye oval studs in her ears.

By a sand-dune some yards further up the beach, Venus saw the outline of a man with a sketchpad. He was sitting on a tartan blanket and his back was turned to her, as one hand moved busily and the other arm curled to protect his pages from the breeze riffling his fawn-fair hair. The wind blew the faint strains of a whistle towards her.

She was tempted to approach and peep at his sketchpad, but hesitated to intrude because he seemed so engrossed. She wouldn't appreciate a passer-by listening in during one of her classes, so why should he want her to gawk at his work in progress? She tracked Conor's eye-line to see what he was drawing with impatient movements of his left hand. It must be Ben Bulben – most artists who stayed in the area reproduced their impressions of the mountain sooner or later. Its multiple personae were addictive.

She passed him, keeping her distance down by the water-line, but moving slowly as she studied the latticework pattern left in the sand by an earlier tide. He didn't raise his eyes from his work.

Venus couldn't imagine why she felt so disappointed.

All right then, she could.

* * *

For dinner she served her father a steak pie from the butcher's in Sligo, instead of his preferred Fray Bentos tinned variety. He was dubious but ate it anyway, noting he could always regurgitate it later if it disagreed with him.

'You mean throw it up?' she checked, aghast.

He nodded. 'I always bring up anything I have trouble digesting – it's the safest course.'

Venus sank her face into her hands: a bulimic eighty-year-old father, that was all she needed. Suspicion flared. 'How often do you weigh yourself, Dad?'

'Never, the scales are crocked.' He chewed the pie, still with the circumspect air of a man taking a culinary risk.

Over dessert, which he insisted on taking with a cup of tea, she mentioned she might make a trip to Dublin.

His response clutched at her.

'How long are you planning to stay away?' Anxiety contorted his features. Already he was becoming accustomed to her company and the prospect of being left alone again unnerved him. Terrified him, in truth.

'Just two nights at the weekend,' Venus reassured him. 'You'll hardly feel it till I'm back. I'll bring you some of those Marks & Spencer toffees you like.' She bribed him as she would a child.

His dignity was offended, for he deciphered her tone. 'I can buy my own sweets in Mrs O'Dea's.' Then he relented. 'Just take it easy on the road – they drive as though they're hurtling straight to kingdom come these days.' He patted her hand across the table. 'It must be dull for you here after London-town. I dare say you miss company of your own age, lass.'

'I'd miss you more,' she smiled into sky-blue eyes which gleamed back.

* * *

Venus rang Lily the following evening to book the spare room. She was quite capable of having Karim's entire family camped out in it if Venus weren't careful. The sooner her laptop arrived from London in the vanload the better; then she could email Lily. That had been their preferred way of keeping in touch during the London years.

'I know why you're coming – it's a sabotage mission and it won't work,' said Lily.

'We'll see about that. Is the bed free or not?'

'It's yours whenever you want it, Venus. Besides, young Senan will be thrilled. He was making enquiries about you the other day after you rang.'

'He's a child,' exclaimed Venus. 'What sort of enquiries?'

'The sort of enquiries a man makes about a woman when he wants to establish her availability.'

'I'm not available. At least not to urchins. What would I want with a twenty-year-old?'

'Nothing – but it's empowering to know he wants you.'

'I don't see anything too empowering about it. Tedious, more like. You'd have to lead him every step of the way – it wouldn't be worth the effort.'

'Don't bank on it,' contradicted Lily. 'Remember he comes from Limerick? We don't call him "the Shannon

Stopover" for nothing. He's had more one-night stands than I've had gin and tonics.'

'And that's supposed to be an inducement?' interjected Venus, but she was ignored.

'His boyish innocence conceals a serial lecher. It might only be one night – but you'd have the time of your life. Of course that's only Senan Mulqueen's version of events.'

'So he kisses and tells too,' complained Venus. 'Selling me his car is one thing, trying to palm himself off on me isn't part of the deal. The only bodywork of Senan's I'm interested in belongs to his Polo.'

'Your loss. See you Saturday. We'll have to stay home because there's a rugby match in the afternoon so the city centre will have turned into a barbarian's stronghold by teatime. But I dare say we'll be able to make our own fun. Until then, be good. Ish. No point in going to extremes.'

She was a fine one to talk, thought Venus. Lily was always buffeting from one ill-advised extreme to another. Especially when it came to asylum-seekers with brooding eyes and an angel fixation.

* * *

Venus pushed a torn envelope between the pages to mark her place and stood for a spine-cracking stretch. That was enough of flicking through dog-eared text books to refresh herself on Spanish conversation. Some of it was too esoteric – her students wouldn't need to know phrases for interviewing prospective parlour maids; they'd want vocabulary to take them though holidays on one of the Costas.

Is there a hotel nearby? *¿Hay un hotel cerca de aqui?* Could I have breakfast in my room? *¿Pueden subirme el desayuno a la habitacion?*

She'd re-think the lessons if they were business people keen to be taught something more technical – profit and loss and gross annual turnover phrases. But that shouldn't be a problem. Meanwhile she definitely wasn't pandering to anyone who wanted to tell a Spanish man or woman they had liquid eyes that refreshed the soul. They could check the dictionary and work it out for themselves.

A few years ago Venus had been obliged to wade through a sulky minefield, with a group of label-fixated Spanish sixteen-year-old boys on a summer crammer course. All they'd wanted to learn was how to tell girls they were hot. They had known the basics already from watching MTV but had regarded it as her job to supply additional adjectives.

Venus stretched again and wandered downstairs from her bedroom to the kitchen. She still hadn't contacted the social services to establish what they knew about her adoption – she should put a call in, she scolded herself. Roancarrick was having an insidious effect on her: there was all in the time in the world here and yet you still ran short at the end of the day.

The house was quiet. Dan was at Confession, although what an eighty-year-old man had to confess she couldn't fathom: 'Thought-crimes again this week, Father'. She was alone in the house and, unexpectedly, it seemed too empty. She decided to go for a stroll because she never felt solitary out of doors.

Venus gravitated to the harbour and leaned against the granite wall surrounding it, watching the boats bob on the end of their moorings. She fancied they were straining against detention and would prefer to be floating out to sea. A car pulled up beside her and hooted its horn, interrupting her reverie – it was John Óg O'Dea, her old school-friend,

Teresa's hugely important accountant brother. According to his mother.

He wound down the window of his Volvo and called out in a magisterial tone. 'Venus Macken, if I'm not mistaken. What brings you to these parts? Return of the prodigal?'

'If it is, I haven't noticed any fatted calves being slaughtered,' she responded.

John Óg was a cadaverous version of the chubby lad a couple of years older than her who used to complain to Mrs O'Dea if she or Teresa touched his collection of Marvel comics. He was still reading them in his late teens – using surgical gloves and tweezers to turn the pages, according to Teresa.

'The weight has peeled off you since I saw you last, John Óg,' Venus continued. 'You must have great willpower.'

Or worms, she added mentally.

John Óg exuded gratification, in addition to the complacency he seemed to have sprayed on with his aftershave. He leaned out of the car window in a move that accentuated his unhealthy pallor, pale grey eyes with their curly girl's lashes alight with zeal. He had the air of a man about to unburden himself of a universal truth.

'I weigh everything I eat, Venus. I'm scrupulous about it. It's reached the stage where I can estimate the weight of a potato to within a few grams, just from the look of it.'

She could tell he was prepared to discuss his dietary habits endlessly. And the car was blocking her so she was a captive audience. 'How's Teresa?' That should change the subject.

'Heavy. Very heavy.' A sorrowful expression settled on his face. 'She never shifted the weight after the baby was born. Myself and the Mammy went over to Buffalo for the christening last year and I watched how she added butter or sauce to every morsel that crossed her lips.' He shuddered. 'I bought her a set of kitchen scales before I left, but I don't believe she's using them.' His eyes skittered across Venus's frame. 'They're on special offer in Dunnes Stores – you might think about investing in some.'

Outrage bloomed in Venus and she opened her mouth for a tart response, except John Óg pre-empted her.

'Not that you need them. Yet. But it's a good habit to acquire. Anyway, mustn't idle about here gabbing all day, I have clients to attend to. I dropped in to see the Mammy while I was in the neighbourhood.' He switched on the ignition. 'I don't live at home any more. I have a house of my own. A town house on an executive development in one of the more refined parts of Sligo.'

And with a wink that was more nervous than salacious, he roared away, changing gear before the engine was ready for it.

Venus didn't know if she felt more disdain for the teenage John Óg hoarding his comics or the adult John Óg dispensing dietary advice. No wonder Teresa had deserted to Buffalo. But mention of his mammy prompted her to call in and see Mrs O'Dea in the shop – she knew everyone's business, there was a chance she might have the inside track on Venus's.

She'd been rebuffed by Birdie and her father but she should be able to wheedle something out of the village shopkeeper. Mrs O'Dea had been presiding over that counter for all of Venus's life: her origins can't have escaped the woman's attention. Or interest.

A bubble of optimism buoyed Venus as she crossed the street.

Chapter Eleven

Venus reminded herself not to interrogate Mrs O'Dea as she made her way towards Roancarrick's general store. She'd have to quiz her in a roundabout way because Mrs O'Dea didn't respond well to direct questions. Nobody did in these parts. It was regarded as unmannerly to be too direct. The two German men who were involved in textbook translation and living in one of the bungalows beyond the church were always being criticised for this behind their backs. The English couple who ran the fishing-tackle business beside the harbour, however, had adapted easily to the village's code of conduct. Another decade or so and they might be accepted.

A somewhat stealthy approach was the only way forward, but it generally worked because everyone knew the rules. Ask a direct question and you'd be answered with a question. Approach a subject obliquely and you could discover all sorts.

The more she thought about it, the more astounded

Venus grew that the circumstances of her adoption had
never been discussed with her. She didn't see why it had to
be treated in such a mysterious fashion. Obviously some
poor girl with no husband or an absconding boyfriend had
become pregnant, and had handed her over. It was simply
a case of establishing the girl's identity and it was possible
someone in the village might know it. Roancarrick was too
insular for secrets to go undetected.

The odd globule of information must have come Mrs
O'Dea's way over the years. And it shouldn't take too long
to siphon it out because Venus had been in to Mrs O'Dea's
shop several times since her return, so her novelty value had
been eroded. Which meant she wouldn't be badgered with
queries tricked out as solicitous observations about why she
was back in Roancarrick. She'd already dealt with those.
Quashing, in the process, speculation that she'd been made
redundant, jilted at the altar and had suffered a nervous
breakdown. Actually, the jury was still out on the jilting,
because Timmy Brennan maintained she had the shell-
shocked countenance of the publicly humiliated.

Venus walked past Nora Brennan's black and white pub,
which always had a neglected air during the early part of the
day. Her glance grazed the empty businesses and she
thought it a shame they couldn't be occupied by potters or
jewellers. Surely there must be grants available. The
chipshop had a queue for takeaways, but when she peered
through Seascape's plate-glass window she noticed only two
tables were occupied. She checked her watch: it was 3 p.m.
– the lunch rush would have died down.

Kathleen Magee looked up from clearing a table and
waved to Venus, who thought that the restaurateur, who
always looked slightly out of focus, seemed more blurred

127

than usual. Maybe there hadn't been a lunch rush. The day-trippers and holiday-lets were all but gone now and wouldn't be back until the Easter weekend, apart from a few hardy souls for Christmas, Hallowe'en and St Patrick's Day.

It struck Venus that most of the businesses in Roancarrick were operated by women: the shop, the pub and the restaurant. Even the chipshop, although nominally owned by a pair of brothers, was managed by their wives.

She reached the shop and twisted back her head as she read the sign. Fitzgerald's, it proclaimed, the owner three generations back – the O'Deas had never bothered to change it. They claimed it would bring about a change of luck, but others in the village suggested they didn't want the expense of hiring a sign-writer.

Despite the traces of peeling paint on the window-frames, always a problem for the seafront properties because of the Atlantic weather which harried them, the shop had a well-kept appearance belying the charges of penny-pinching. The colour scheme was exuberant: green and purple, edged with a band of blue in a shade to which Mrs O'Dea always referred – most insistently – as celestial.

Above the shop name, old metal cigarette signs for brands that no longer existed jostled for space alongside gaudy new advertisements for fizzy drinks. Craning to read them, Venus took an involuntary step backwards and collided with the plastic ice-cream cone on the pavement. The villagers were forever complaining because you had to step out onto the road to pass it. Mrs O'Dea would always shrug helplessly and agree it was a nuisance, as though it belonged to some other sweetshop – when there wasn't one for miles.

The bell tinkled, in a sound catapulting Venus back to

childhood: she could almost taste the ice-cream wafers cut from the open block of HB raspberry ripple. Mrs O'Dea was leaning on the counter, one elbow nudging a stack of tricolour sticks of rock, engrossed in a phone-in radio show about bouncers in nightclubs. Instead of serving Venus she gestured urgently towards the window-seat, holding her finger to her lips but somehow conveying a determination that she should listen too.

Venus settled herself, as a teenager's mother complained her boy had come home from a club needing stitches after an altercation with the security staff a few weeks previously. 'They're animals,' she shuddered. 'I was up half the night with worry the next time he went out.'

Mrs O'Dea, a thickset woman, sucked on her teeth and pulled her cardigan, the colour and texture of a used teabag, around her body until its edges overlapped.

Another caller suggested the nightclub clientele were the animals and the doormen were hard-pressed to keep the peace. 'My son worked for a security firm for two years and he clocked up a couple of fractured ribs, a broken thumb and I've lost count of how many black eyes,' she said.

Mrs O'Dea's teeth were subjected to some concentrated sucking that threatened their stability in her gums.

Venus's attention wandered. She looked out towards the coastline and daydreamed. It struck her that in London every hour had seemed accounted for and her life had been suffused with a White Rabbit's headlong pelt to make up for lost time. But in all her frantic socialising and racing around, she'd only skimmed the surface of people's lives. How many true friends had she left behind? Tamsin had been her closest, but they'd probably end up keeping in touch via Christmas cards and maybe the odd email when one of them felt guilt-twinges. Venus perceived, with a clarity that had her shifting in her window-seat, that she'd embraced an out-of-sight out-of-mind society.

She had kicked up her heels in the Snakes and Ladders pub with the other language-school teachers, had drunk coffee with them, had attended the odd show or art exhibition with them. But there had been a distance between people. Come so close and no closer. Her place in the set would be filled and it would be as if she'd never taught at Bridges Across The World. Her footprints would be washed away by an incoming tide. And she'd espoused that culture – welcomed the barricades people erected to safeguard their privacy. Her fortifications had been among the highest.

There was a cleaning lady in the school who'd worked there longer than Venus; sometimes she'd pause by Venus's desk, plucking at her Marigold gloves and hacking her smoker's cough, and try to strike up a conversation about her grandchildren. One of them was in university in Leeds and the other was on the dole. Venus had begrudged the mournful-faced Sadie the minutes she had eaten into her day, sitting there with a fixed smile until she'd take the hint and lift her bucket to move on.

Even Gary Hesketh, whom she'd consigned to the rubbish-bin, was an individual. He was in his mid-twenties – he was supposed to hit on women, it was genetic programming. Had she ever troubled to see what lay beneath the braggadocio?

Venus realised, to her shame, that she'd bought her morning latte from the same coffee-stall a few paces away from Vauxhall Bridge Underground station for four years and had never once enquired the name of the reserved

Chinese woman who served her. Her English had been patchy initially, but that was no excuse. As for the family in the 24-hour shop near the Barbican where she had stopped in for groceries and the odd onion bhaji – what did she know about them? She couldn't even tell if they were Pakistani or Indian. She hadn't troubled to learn anything about them, although they'd made it their business to remember she liked packets of Kimberley biscuits and had stocked them especially for her.

Perhaps Lily had been right when she'd predicted that Roancarrick might be healthy for Venus. She'd seen safety in numbers, but there was isolation within their ranks as well. Meanwhile here she was in O'Dea's, twiddling her fingers while the owner, who had probably never set foot in a nightclub let alone tangled with a bouncer, stood entranced by a radio programme about clubland violence. She'd never have given her custom to such a shop in London; she'd have turned on her heel and gone next door. But in Roancarrick there was no shop next door. Besides, there was always time enough to spare for waiting.

She glanced towards the shopkeeper and hadn't the heart to intrude. The woollen cardigan with twice turned-up sleeves was being mauled in sympathy, as its owner listened to a nightclub owner describe the impossibility of recruiting responsible staff who could keep a drink-saturated clientele in order without pounding them to a pulp.

Venus tiptoed towards the door – she'd return later.

'Venus Macken.'

Mrs O'Dea stopped her in her tracks. Venus hadn't a notion of the shopkeeper's Christian name. She'd never heard anyone address her by it. Her husband and children called her 'the Mammy' and to everyone else she was Mrs

O'Dea. Venus turned. It was a tone of voice that said 'come back here and spend money'.

'Come back here and let me serve you.' The shopkeeper shouted to be heard above the radio.

'Just a litre of milk, please, Mrs O'Dea.'

The self-service concept had not yet reached Roancarrick and Mrs O'Dea pitter-pattered towards the back of the counter to a fridge. She had a way of walking quickly with short steps that lent her the semblance of rushing.

'Shocking places, nightclubs.' Mrs O'Dea held the milk without passing it over to Venus. Her brown hair was bolted into her scalp with an inflexibility Lily would have admired.

'Shocking,' agreed Venus, when she realised Mrs O'Dea was waiting for a response.

'You wouldn't know what class of person you'd meet in them,' continued the shopkeeper, reaching to a shelf beneath the counter and taking an absentminded bite from a cream puff sitting there. Mrs O'Dea always had a half-eaten cream puff on the go. 'Mind you,' she continued, 'I met Mr O'Dea in a nightclub, only we called them dance-halls in those days. The Stellar Ballroom, it was. It's a video games arcade now.'

Opportunity glimmered. 'Did you ever go dancing with my mother when you were all young together, Mrs O'Dea?'

'Maura was considerably older than me so she'd stopped going to the Stellar by the time I started running around.' Mrs O'Dea wasn't pleased to have six years added to her age. 'Considerably older,' she repeated for effect. 'But she was a great one for the dances and light as a feather on her feet by all accounts. Of course, she gave it up when she married your father because of his leg.'

'And were my brothers keen dancers?'

Mrs O'Dea rang in the price of the milk on the till and reflected. 'There was one who'd céilí the night away and one who was always slow to stand up, but I can never remember which way round it was. Sure God love them, they were taken so young neither had much chance to enjoy their dancing days. They can't have been more than twenty-one.'

Venus thought of the brothers she would never know, one a dancer and the other too shy to dance. Maybe he was afraid of rejection. They never seemed real to her, these two Christys dead before she was born, no matter how often people spoke of them.

She affected a casual tone. 'I'm fond of dancing myself. I used to go to tango classes in London – it was all the rage. But of course I can't have inherited it from my mother since I'm adopted. I wonder if my real mother went dancing?'

She handed over a five-euro note, hoping Mrs O'Dea would be distracted by counting out change.

'I wouldn't know, dear.' Mrs O'Dea's face was bent towards the coins in the till.

Venus took a chance. 'Didn't you know my mother? I understood she was local.'

'It was always Birdie who –' began Mrs O'Dea, before she glanced up, registered Venus's avid expression and hesitated.

'It was Birdie who . . .' hinted Venus.

Mrs O'Dea clanked shut the till and jingled the coins in her hand. Venus had never seen her look so displaced.

'My goodness, Venus, I hadn't realised it was so late. I'll have to get Mr O'Dea out to help me unpack some tins of soup – there's only cream of leek on the shelves.' Her eyes betrayed embarrassment as they met Venus's. Unless it was trepidation?

Venus held her gaze. 'You were saying something about Birdie.'

'Only that she and your mother were very great. I must switch off this radio, that presenter's yapping is giving me a migraine. Mr O'Dea!' This was yelled over her shoulder towards an open door that led to the living quarters. 'Mr O'Dea! There's work to be done here and I only have one pair of hands.'

'Coming, Mammy,' responded the sleepy voice of a bear of a man. Seconds after, Mr O'Dea's tiny frame emerged from the doorway, button eyes snapping with inherent high humour.

Venus didn't stop walking until she reached the harbour wall, legs pumping and milk gripped so tightly the container was in danger of being pierced by her nails.

Birdie, she thought. Why had she never considered her before? It was so flauntingly obvious it taunted Venus.

She'd found her mother sooner than she foreseen. Closer to home than she'd expected, too.

It was Birdie.

Chapter Twelve

Calling on Birdie to force an admission from her seemed the obvious course of action. She'd go straight up to her house as soon as she caught her breath – but for some reason Venus was having trouble controlling it. It felt as though tiny wings were attached to her heart and it was fluttering behind her sternum, its beating as frenzied as an insect's.

It made perfect sense, now that it was dangling under nose. It explained the close interest Birdie had always taken in her, the responsibility she seemed to feel for Dan, the friendship with Maura, the seamless way she had fitted into their family. It also accounted for Birdie's tendency to know what Venus was thinking before Venus realised it herself.

She should call to Birdie's house and challenge her about it.

Except Venus needed time to adjust – her heart was still aping an agitated moth.

She struck out for home, feet flying, hands jammed in the pockets of her velvet trousers with the worn patches on the seat and knees. She wouldn't dream of setting foot outside her Barbican apartment in them, even though her chances of running into an acquaintance let alone a friend were remote. But in Roancarrick, where everybody knew her, she couldn't be bothered worrying about her appearance. Passing the harbour, a clanking sound floated towards her ears, as the boats' shrouds chivvied their masts, but Venus was in a tearing hurry and did not pause, as she usually would, to listen to their discordant clamour.

Barely had she reached the fork in the road when feet pounded behind her and a voice called out her name. It was the artist – she hadn't realised he knew her name. Venus found herself flushing, to her horror – blushes were sub-adolescent.

'Venus, you left your milk after you.' Conor brandished the carton.

She looked at it as though she'd never laid eyes on it before. An irrational impulse to deny ownership gripped her, because forgetting a carton of milk seemed so pedestrian.

'What makes you imagine it's mine?'

'I saw you come out of Mrs O'Dea's shop with it and set it on the harbour wall beside you.' There was ink smeared on his chin and some of it had transferred to the green and orange carton. 'It was a surveillance operation.'

Under different circumstances the flattery would have gratified her, but she'd just learned her mother's identity; her attention was elsewhere. Nevertheless Venus's sherry eyes glimmered faintly as she asked, 'Why were you doing a surveillance operation on me?'

'I wasn't. I was studying the shopfronts. I'm thinking of moving on to them for my next theme. I don't want to do trees any more and I don't have the gravitas for mountains. So it might be shopfronts – then again it might be caves. I'm still weighing my options.'

A strand of hair floated into her eyes, directed there by a wayward breeze, and Venus was too listless to dislodge it. Conor looked at her in a way that set the blood drumming in her ears and then leaned forward, lifted the tendril and tucked it behind her ear. The intimacy of the gesture startled Venus.

'Shopfronts are a revelation,' Conor went on. 'I'd always believed they were essentially static but observing Mrs O'Dea's for a couple of hours shows me how wrong I was. They're full of movement and vitality, with endless comings and goings. I have to admit I feel a bit hesitant to tackle them because the picture-postcard market has monopolised shopfronts, but maybe it's time to reclaim them.'

He fell into step beside Venus and she was consumed by an urge to confide in him. To tell him she'd just this moment discovered her mother's identity and didn't know what impact the knowledge would have on the tilt of her universe. Which struck her as untoward, she reflected later, because she was generally slow to share secrets with people. Her friendships were gradual constructs.

At the junction, with its fuchsia-spiked boundaries, where his way went left and hers straight on, he paused and shaded his eyes towards the sky. 'There's rain coming,' he observed.

'Spoken like a true countryman,' Venus responded. 'It was one of the things I noticed in London – nobody ever checked the sky for a weather report. They always read it from the newspaper or heard it on the radio.'

'I'm only practising at the rural stuff; it doesn't come naturally yet. See you around.'

Venus raised her hand in farewell.

'Wait,' he called after her. 'What did you want to be when you grew up?'

Venus swivelled on her heel, remembering. 'An Olympic swimmer. I wanted to stand on a podium with a gold medal around my neck and hear the crowd roar my name. The joke of it is I can barely swim. Put me in water and all I do is splash a lot. What about you, what did you want to be?'

'I fancied a more sedentary career. I'd set my heart on being a snowman.'

'So we're both sunk,' she chuckled.

'Looks like it,' he dimpled back, before heading for home with that perennial whistle on his lips.

There's daggers in men's smiles, fluttered a random thought. But she was still smiling to herself as she reached the house. And that whistle of his was growing on her.

Her father was on the phone to O'Hara's, his bookies; he covered its mouthpiece to tell her there was tea in the pot and returned to dictating his bet. It was the highlight of his day and although Dan never exceeded a small predetermined amount, he gave his selection as much consideration as if a fortune were riding on it.

Venus considered telling him what she'd learned from Mrs O'Dea, but decided to wait until after she'd spoken to Birdie.

'Birdie called while you were out.' Dan replaced the receiver.

Venus set down her tea untasted.

'She's gone to Belfast-town for a few days. You know how she heads up there from time to time on business she won't

138

discuss. She wanted a word with you before she left but said it would keep until Monday when you're back.'

A gush of disappointment deposited an acrid sediment in Venus's mouth. Common sense reminded her she'd waited thirtysomething years to learn her mother's identity – a few more days before final confirmation wouldn't matter.

Although it did, in truth.

* * *

Her father insisted on checking the oil in the car before she set off for Dublin, and she had to open her glove-compartment to show him she had a map, in case there were detours and she was sent down country boreens.

He stood in the yard and waved her off. Her throat constricted as she saw the windblown figure in her wing mirror and she reversed the green Polo a few yards to lean out of the window and speak to him again. 'I'll ring as soon as I reach Lily's. You won't forget to defrost the chicken for your dinner tomorrow, will you? I've cooked it in gravy the way you like it. No skin.'

'Go on, lass, you need to get some of the road under your belt,' he said. 'You enjoy yourself in Dublin-town – I've no doubt Roancarrick seems dull to you. It has no night life for young people.'

It chafed at her, as she drove off, how brittle his frame was growing. Venus fretted, and then, because she couldn't drive and angst, she listened to Lyric FM. Gradually it placated her.

* * *

The traffic was heavy in the city centre, as ever, but she reached Lily's apartment on schedule, swinging through the gates past the elaborate Adelphi Court sign with its intertwined lettering, and parking beside Lily's metallic orange Fiat. All they needed was a white car sandwiched between them and they'd look like the national flag.

Lily buzzed in Venus and was waiting with a hug by the front door.

'Country air agrees with you, Venus.' She squeezed her into a second embrace.

'Sea air.' Venus lifted one of Lily's hands.

'What are you doing?'

'Checking for wedding bands.'

'Of course I'm not married yet; I want you as my witness. And it takes three months, remember? Spontaneous marriages aren't allowed here.'

Some laws made sense, thought Venus, who decided to wait until after she caught her breath from the journey before remonstrating with Lily. Even though that was precisely why she was in Dublin.

Lily was the person she cared most for in the world, after Dan. Despite the age gap between them – one they'd never particularly noticed – Lily and Venus had met as first years at Dublin City University. Venus had been reading applied languages, while Lily had enrolled as a mature student after a succession of low-paid jobs, signing up for business studies because she fancied the ring of it. Her last job had been in telephone sales. 'It was too stressful – I only stayed until I got down to my ideal body weight,' she'd told Venus.

They had shared no classes in common but both had enjoyed sitting in the nearby Botanic Gardens, and repetition had led to recognition. They used to warm themselves in the tropical greenhouses in the winter and moved outside to benches in the spring, swapping secrets and sandwiches.

'Senan may be dropping in.' Lily's voice drifted through the glass-bead curtain separating living-room and kitchen.

'That's nice.' Venus's response was automatic.

Lily's face poked through the cobalt beads. 'Do you really mean that?'

'Sure,' shrugged Venus, 'it's no odds to me either way. Have you work matters to discuss?'

'No, stupid, he's coming to see you. You know he has a crush on you.'

'Oh come on, I'm nearly twice his age. If I ask him where he's been all my life he'll have to say "in school".'

Lily carried in a bag of miniature Twix bars and two mugs of hot chocolate, insisting the latter would revive Venus after her journey better than tea or coffee. 'I've told you before, Senan's interest is empowering. You don't have to want him – it's enough to know that he wants you.'

'I haven't the energy for this.' Venus unwrapped a fun-sized Twix and bit in. 'You're setting this up deliberately to deflect attention from your own dangerous liaison.'

'Of course,' agreed Lily.

They settled comfortably beside one another, Lily pushing a cushion under Venus's heels on the coffee table, as she pointed out that Senan had potential. He was a supportive colleague, working her Saturday stint today – she'd cover for him next week.

'Even as we speak he's on sentry duty in Clontarf, on crowd control as the hordes pour in for an open viewing of a house I've had on my books twice in the space of as many years,' said Lily. 'Hopefully they'll be pouring in, anyhow. I've awarded the blurb my ridiculous phrase of the week: "sumptuous yet minimalist". I didn't write it – we can thank Garret for that flight of fancy. He wants to break into advertising – estate agency isn't to his taste. He maintains,' she peeled off the wrapper on a second chocolate bar, 'it doesn't satisfy his creative urges.'

'Is he responsible for all those unrealistically blue skies in the photographs of houses you're trying to sell?' asked Venus. 'The sort of hallucinogenic blue that makes you think of chlorinated water?'

'All estate agents have those,' mumbled Lily, still chewing. 'It's called artistic licence.'

They caught up on each other's news, switched from hot chocolate to coffee, and Venus gave her the bottle of gin she'd brought, along with some Roancarrick honey. At least it claimed to be local honey; her father denied there were any beekeepers in the area. Lily told her Karim would be joining them for dinner. Indeed, he was cooking it.

'Why is he still living here?' Venus couldn't help it: her upper lip curled around the query.

'He has nowhere else to go.' Lily was busy with her topknot, which needed some pinning to safeguard its frivolity, and didn't react to the scornful lip. She turned and offered her trusting smile. 'He's gone for a walk this afternoon so that you and I can have time privately together. Isn't he thoughtful? He even changed the sheets on your bed before he left – he's been sleeping there. But he says he doesn't mind a bit moving out to the living-room for a couple of nights.'

Why should he? thought Venus. It was still better than bed and breakfast accommodation.

'He's so useful to have about the place, Venus. He's cleaned out my kitchen cupboards – he says he doesn't know how I can live in such squalor.' Lily beamed as though it was the height of flattery. 'And he's going shopping with me to help pick out some rugs because he thinks the apartment is a little bare-looking. He has a contact who can get me cost price on oriental carpets.'

'But I like your apartment's wooden floors with only that seagrass matting on them – and more importantly, so do you.'

Lily shrugged. 'Coloured rugs would be more homely, Karim finds the wood stark.'

Venus realised it was time to embark on her lecture warning against the dangers of misguided philanthropy, especially when it involved something as semi-permanent as marriage. Lily deftly headed her off. Instead, Venus found herself being examined on life in Roancarrick.

Lily was delighted to hear about the teaching stint lined up at Sligo Tech but somehow formed the idea that Benedict Archer was an alpha male just waiting for Venus to transform his life, or vice versa. And it could only be a matter of time before she became deputy principal there too, in Lily's relentlessly roseate view of life.

'He insists on calling me Venice. I'm sure he does it deliberately to provoke me,' she objected.

'Maybe he just pronounces it strangely,' suggested Lily.

'Hmm.' Venus pushed her hair behind her ears. 'If it was anyone else I'd say he was being droll, teasing me because Venice was named for Venus, but I don't think Benedict Archer has a playful bone in his body.'

'Never mind – a sense of humour is a bonus but it's not essential. Now, have you considered the possibility of male students? If you're teaching night classes your pupils must be grown-ups – potential boyfriends – instead of teenagers with no potential whatsoever.' And she was off, speculating furiously.

Venus didn't dare mention her artist in case Lily started choosing honeymoon destinations for them. She was on an unreconstructed couples' binge.

'Quick, describe Mount Ararat,' she ordered Lily.

'I haven't a clue what you're talking about – I'm an estate agent not a travel agent.' Lily fidgeted with her hair-clips.

'I thought you must have discovered you were Mrs Noah in a previous life, you're so possessed by the urge to have us all marching two-by-two.'

Lily laughed. 'It's the natural state – "only" rhymes with "lonely" for a reason. Now, let's see if I'm clear on how life has been treating you in Roancarrick: it's worse than you expected and not as dire as you imagined – is that a fair summary?'

Venus nodded and watched the light filter through the blinds on Lily's windows. The light was different in Ireland – it had a more diffused quality than in England.

'But it's not a life sentence,' said Lily. 'Without being indelicate, your father isn't going to need you forever. A few years at most.'

Privately Venus agreed, but her attachment to Dan Macken had strengthened since her homecoming. Her freedom from responsibility could only come with her father's death – it was as bleak as that. Besides, was lack of responsibility really freedom? She said nothing.

A veined-marble clock on the mantelpiece that had been someone's grandmother's – but not Lily's because she'd bought it in a saleroom – chimed the hour.

Lily leapt to her feet. 'Must change; Karim will be home soon. He's cooking us his speciality: borsch, that's beetroot soup to you and me, served with rye bread, followed by some kind of meat stew he's been marinating all day and a cabbage salad that's stinking the fridge.'

'My father would like that – he thinks there's nothing like cabbage,' said Venus.

'Doubt if he'd be so keen on the ice-cold vodka from the freezer we'll be drinking. We're having it from these little shot-glasses Karim brought from Moscow. No mixing with tonic or white lemonade allowed – apparently that's sacrilege.' Lily rummaged in her pocket for extra hair grips, blue eyes misting over with affection. 'He was trying to lay his hands on some Soviet *shampanskoye*, but he couldn't track it down. Probably just as well because I tried their champagne once and it's so sweet you'd imagine someone emptied a bag of sugar into your glass while you were looking the other way.'

'What was it that you mentioned about dressing for dinner?' Venus was incredulous.

Lily became flustered. 'I'm just taking off the jeans – you don't have to change if you're comfortable as you are. Karim prefers me in a skirt: he says it's more feminine.'

Fury swelled in Venus. 'Since when have you cared about looking feminine? I can see what's happening here – he'll have you covered up from scalp to ankle in one of those *chador* robes next.'

Lily scalded her with a look that stopped Venus in her tracks. 'I think you ought to be careful what you say. We've been friends a long time, but Karim's my friend too. You shouldn't bandy accusations about.'

An internal warning-bell deterred Venus and she subsided, mumbling an apology. But she had the suspicion that Karim was starting to reshape Lily into his version of womanhood. That didn't strike her as the behaviour of a man who was planning to exit stage left as soon as he had his passport secured.

She had the distinct impression Karim planned to stay

on the stage. And start shifting scenery until he had it arranged the way he liked it.

She trailed into the bedroom after Lily and watched her pull out an ankle-length crushed-velvet dress in a mulberry colour. Lily dragged her socks off and Venus saw, to her relief, that at least she was still wearing her toe-ring. If Karim decided toe-rings were less than feminine she didn't rate its survival chances.

'Do you wear it winter and summer?' Venus indicated the silver ring with its filigree tracing.

'Of course.'

'But you can't see it in the winter. Nobody wears open-toed sandals once October comes.'

'It's the feel-good factor – if you feel desirable it radiates out. It's like wearing sexy underwear, Venus – even if nobody else sees it you feel wonderful.'

Venus analysed this while Lily fussed with her appearance, applying Vaseline to her mouth, then lipstick over it, blotting and re-applying it. She ran her finger along her teeth, checking for lipstick stains, and popped a breath mint into her mouth. Next she sprayed Oscar de la Renta's Volupté and closed her eyes, stepping into the cloud. Finally she pencilled on a beauty spot to cover the sickle-shaped scar from her diving accident.

Venus's temper stamped furrows into her forehead. This was date mode: it didn't augur well.

Chapter Thirteen

A key turned in the lock and Karim's footsteps sounded in the apartment. It made sense for him to have his own key, but Venus was perturbed by that too. He might never leave, divorce or no divorce. And that was another hurdle: it took four years before you were allowed to apply for a divorce, so even if it were a counterfeit marriage they couldn't end it in a hurry.

'Karim's here.'

Lily's tone was pointed so Venus stomped out to meet him, feeling like a recalcitrant teenager. He laid down a paper bag with a box of Lily O'Brien chocolates protruding from it – chosen deliberately for their name – and she noticed he'd had a professional haircut, a huge improvement.

'Good day, lady.'

Karim gave her the full hand-drenching treatment and she had to admit that, under different circumstances, she might enjoy having her hand kissed. Once it stopped tickling it was quite flattering.

Still, all that chivalry had to be contrived. Chechnya was a war zone, according to her Internet search. People didn't have time for social niceties in war zones. The trouble with Karim was he had delusions of adequacy.

Despite her reservations, the meal was a success. Karim moved the table and chairs into the centre of the sitting-room, where there was more space. Then he bustled in and out of the kitchen like a whirling dervish with advanced culinary skills. He swirled cream into borsch, baked the bread himself and for dessert produced little almond cakes with a layer of jam in the middle. They teased him about baking those too, but he confessed to buying them in Bewley's -- although he was quick to point out they were similar to pastries eaten in Chechnya.

He showed them how to drink a mouthful of vodka and take a bite of rye bread immediately afterwards – the flavours complemented each other and he said it also kept a person breathing.

'Some people are unaccustomed to the effect of neat vodka – the bread is good for the respiratory system.' Karim tapped his chest, sending a tremor through his bass tones. 'I learned to drink it this way as a medical student in Moscow.'

He ensured their glasses were constantly topped up – chalices of vodka, he called them; every so often his English had an antiquated ring. But he'd grasped the tenses superbly, thought the teacher in Venus. She was surprised to discover Karim had a dry sense of humour, and he had them gasping with merriment as he described his first time delivering a baby. He had been so terrified he had hardly known which end of the woman to approach – fortunately, as a mother of five, she had proved experienced enough for both of them.

'She called him Alexei after my middle name,' he said.

'Karim was too Chechen for her taste. But it was an undeserved compliment. The porter was more use to her than I was in delivering that baby – and he wasn't even in the room.'

Venus caught a glimpse of Lily's face as Karim told his story and it troubled her. She was gazing at Karim as though she'd like to reduce him down to fit inside one of those little shot-glasses he kept refilling and then guzzle him whole. It was obscene. This was infatuation – and juvenile crushes at the age of forty had a pulverising tendency. On the person with the crush.

'Karim,' said Lily, 'The meal was *precrasna*.'

'Magnificent.' He clapped her on the shoulder and left his hand there for a few heartbeats after it might have been appropriate to remove it.

Lily flashed a triumphant beam in Venus's direction. 'That's Russian for "excellent". Karim thinks it might be a more useful language for me to pick up than Chechen.'

This was at a more advanced stage than Venus had anticipated. Not so much devotion as addiction.

'And now,' said Karim, sensing her sombre mood, 'let me pour you both another chalice of vodka. Don't worry, it's only the third half-bottle. Of course we must open it – God loves the Trinity.' He smiled. 'I know you are wondering why a Muslim should talk about the Holy Trinity, but I learned that from my student days too.'

Venus observed that he didn't empty his own glass as often as he exhorted them to lift theirs. She mistrusted people who did that. She also realised he was speaking with a slight Dublin intonation; much more of this and he'd be saying 'howrya?' native-style when he met her, instead of his baroque 'good day, lady'.

The phone rang and Lily went to take the call, brushing past Karim. Deliberately so, it appeared to Venus. She glowered at Karim while Lily chattered on the line. Unaware of her scrutiny, his face settled into pensive folds: his natural expression was melancholy – even those rare smiles which transformed his face couldn't shift it.

Venus felt obliged to make some minuscule effort at conversation. 'Have you left family behind in Chechnya, Karim?'

The smile with which he had begun to attend to her question dimmed. 'There is my father, his wife, my stepmother, and I also have three young half-brothers – my father's second family – I do not truly know them. They live in Grozny, our capital. At eighteen I went to Moscow against my father's wishes. I do not know when I will see him again. Perhaps never. He disapproved of my choice of university, but I wanted to go there for my mother's sake. The marriage was not a happy one – the gulf was too wide between them. He believes that like should gravitate towards like.' Karim nursed the bridge of his nose. 'My mother died long before the war, but she always dreamed I would go to the university in Moscow and I wanted what she wanted. Except the city is beautiful but cold. Everything was new and exciting and for a time I was happy there, but . . .' His voice ground to a halt and he gazed into middle distance.

Venus felt she was intruding on a private grief.

Just as the silence began to shriek, he spoke again. 'My father lent me the money to escape. It is unlikely I will be able to repay him for many years. He sold a part-share in a mineral-water plant to raise the money – it was closed because of the war and earning him nothing anyway. Then I had to convert the money on the black market to

American dollars for my air ticket. The exchange rate was not in my favour. Air tickets seem cheap to you – I know that already from living here – but with us they cost large sums.' He looked troubled. 'I hope my father has enough saved to keep the family fed. In the city there are near-famine conditions because of the air raids. At least in the rural areas they can grow vegetables. My father told me "God will provide", but God has many to provide for and my brothers are still boys, too young to work.'

Venus reflected that Karim's father sounded as though he had much in common with her own. Different religion, same conviction there was a benign divine plan.

'Doesn't he want you to go back to Chechnya?' she asked.

'No. He says there is nothing there for me, it is better to move on. We are an ancient culture, fiercely proud of our individuality. We are not Russian and never will be; we want our independence. But I am half-Chechen and half-Russian; I feel at home in neither country. I want to live somewhere free of conflict.'

He's come to the wrong country then, thought Venus. Hadn't he heard of Northern Ireland?

Karim swallowed, Adam's apple bobbing. 'There has been fighting in Chechnya for so long, the country is destroyed and the economy is in pieces. We have rich reserves – oil, gas, petroleum, mineral water. That is partly why Russia wants to retain control of us. The routes of pipelines which bring oil from the Caspian Sea to Russia run through my country. It will be many years after the war is finished before there is stability. And I cannot live in Moscow because my patients say to me "all you people understand is making trouble, you cannot make anybody better". It is difficult for a man to be despised automatically because of his race. It is best for me,' his shoulders slumped, 'to start again.'

Venus nibbled a thumb-nail. She felt some sympathy for the man, but she still didn't think it was fair of him to attach himself to Lily.

Karim acknowledged some understanding of the antagonism churning inside her. 'You must believe that I truly appreciate Lily's trusting, open nature,' he said. 'She is a most unusual woman, not just because she is willing to marry me but for the way she has taken me into her home. Of course I make some contribution – your country gives me social security while it decides my fate – but she does it from no other motive than kindness.'

Venus inclined her head, hearing him out.

'In the bed and breakfast place where I stayed in Stoneybatter,' he continued, 'we had to be out of the house by eleven each morning and our return was barred until evening. All day long I wandered the streets. A person takes the small things in life for granted, until he no longer has access to them. Being able to make yourself a pot of tea or having – how do you say it? – a lie-in, these are not huge matters, but they are significant. Lily has given me back that independence. She is my –'

'Guardian Angel,' Venus finished his sentence for him. 'Let's hope she doesn't live to repent her generosity.' She would have said more but Lily bounced back into the room.

'That was Senan Mulqueen,' announced Lily. 'He can't call by tonight after all – he's fallen into company and says he's involved in an extended rounds' system. But he specifically asked me to pass on his apologies to you, Venus.

Anyway he wants us to drop by his place tomorrow. I haven't much choice because I have the keys to a townhouse he needs to show somebody. He struck up a conversation with one of the punters this afternoon at the Clontarf open viewing and he thinks this other place by the Financial Services Sector would be ideal for him. Bit of an operator, our Senan.' She looked thoughtful as she touched her pencilled-on beauty spot, testing it hadn't faded. 'Good job I'm not competitive. The interested party's a software programmer commuting between Edinburgh and Dublin – he's very keen to find somewhere permanent. Senan thinks this maisonette affair I have the keys for is a guaranteed sale.'

'He's industrious,' Karim noted with approval. 'He has much energy. I too wish to earn my living – a man should be active in the workplace.' He sighed and drank some vodka, automatically following it up with a morsel of bread.

'It's madness that they won't let asylum seekers work.' Lily radiated loyalty. 'By the way, Venus, I think Senan's sorry he sold his car to you. Joyriders keep trying to break into his new motor because it's so flashy. The neighbours are always complaining about his car alarm.'

'He can't have the Polo back – he cashed my cheque.'

Lily lifted a couple of clips from the mantelpiece, her extrasensory perception warning her they needed wedging into her hair. Her round blue eyes in the freckled face were artless – then the blinking tic sprang up. 'The property market is vibrant in the north-west at the moment, Venus – we're thinking of sending an agent up there to check it out. Senan Mulqueen was the first to volunteer. He might have to stay in a hotel for a few nights. I'm sure he'd be glad of some company.'

'Senan's not old enough to be allowed away from home on sleepovers. Stop foisting a child on me, life is complicated enough already.'

Lily laughed. 'Watch out you don't iron your life so smooth there's no room for a man in it at all, Venus. The perfect relationship doesn't exist.' With that, she rattled through the beads in the kitchen doorway to fetch the chocolates Karim had forgotten to serve.

Karim watched their exchange with glinting eyes that missed nothing. Now he glanced speculatively at Venus and she realised he was assessing her. Probably discounting her as a sour, man-hating harpy.

'Do you ever miss Chechnya?' she asked quickly.

Karim's gaze clouded. 'Yes.' His manner was almost brusque.

'Would you ever hope to return there under a different regime?'

He didn't answer immediately. Instead he lifted the vodka bottle with its distinctive black and gold label, an onion-domed church below Cyrillic lettering, and refilled their glasses. He flicked his wrist at the end of the manoeuvre so as not to spill any vodka. 'Bodka,' he pronounced it. As he placed it on the table, Karim's bruised eyes met Venus's watchful ones.

'A man carries his homeland inside his heart.'

Lily chose that moment to return, humming contentedly. As she stacked plates, Karim added, 'But if circumstances improved I would want my sons to know Chechnya. In an ideal world I would wish them to grow up in the city of their father's fathers.' His eyes slid away from Venus to rest on Lily.

Illuminating, thought Venus. He plans to have children

154

and he'd like to raise them in some Stone Age collection of huts in Grozny, where the local Mafia were the puppeteers who controlled everyone's strings.

For Lily's sake, Venus knew she had to break them up.

Chapter Fourteen

Voices woke Venus and she lay in the dark, confused to hear a man's rumble interwoven with a woman's lighter timbre. Then she realised she was in Lily's apartment and the noises were coming from her friend's room.

There was a giggle, a gasp, then silence. But not quiet silence. This was a sighing, creaking one – the noisy silence of two bodies sharing a bed. Venus lay awake and fretted. There was monkey business next door and she had no choice but to play the 'see no evil, hear no evil, speak no evil' game.

She must have fallen asleep at some stage because when she stumbled out to the kitchen for coffee, there was only Lily. Karim had gone to visit a Ukrainian friend whose application for asylum was at the appeal stage. Lily stretched, sleek and contented, leaving Venus feeling even more drawn.

'Karim is very considerate about tidying away his bed so the living-room isn't cluttered up,' Venus blurted out.

Lily exuded even more feline qualities and said nothing.

Venus felt like a desiccated maiden aunt.

Her spirits improved after coffee – Lily always kept beans in the freezer and ground them fresh – and provided Karim didn't reach the coffee pot first she could be sure of a decent cup.

Venus decided she would interfere in Lily's life later that day. First she was entitled to some quality time with her friend.

They were planning to go to the National Museum to admire the *lunalí*, a collection of gold jewellery from the Celtic period that proved their predecessors were anything but half-hearted about personal ornamentation. Ostentation wasn't a lifestyle choice, it was a religion in pagan times. Christianity had obviously operated as a taste-control mechanism, paring down the excesses.

Lily said they should call over to Senan's place first so she could drop in those keys for the private viewing he'd arranged. Venus was reluctant to go in with her after Lily's teasing, and suggested she should wait in the car.

'It's only for a few minutes,' cajoled Lily. 'He has a flat on the South Circular Road so we'll whizz over and then back to Kildare Street. If you behave yourself and don't pull nasty faces at Senan, I'll buy you a sticky bun in the museum café.'

They took Lily's Fiat from the Adelphi Court carpark in case Senan became sentimental at the sight of the Polo. Lily flopped into the driver's seat and switched on the ignition, but instead of lighting up a cigarette she produced a packet from the well beside the gear-stick, popped a pellet from the foil and her jaw started moving.

Venus lifted the box of Nicorettes. 'Trying to quit?'

Lily nodded and pulled out onto the main road.

'I'm proud of you, Lily Dillon.'

She sloped a sideways smile at Venus. 'Karim says he's worried about my smoking. These have enough nicotine in them to help me deal with driving but I won't die screaming of lung cancer. That's what Karim said when he recommended them. I didn't think they'd be any good but they're the business.' Her jaw worked and a vein bloomed in one temple. 'You can get patches, too, on prescription. Of course I have to make sure I don't end up hooked on the cure because Karim says women shouldn't be like cattle chewing the cud. It's undignified.'

Karim says. Venus was ready to spontaneously combust if she heard another 'Karim says'. He was the Oracle at Adelphi – it was a wonder Lily didn't sell tickets so the public at large could benefit from his wisdom. She drove her thumb-nail through the foil in the Nicorettes pack.

'Stop frowning and keep an eye out for the guards while I ring ahead on the mobile and warn Senan we're on our way – I can't afford another fine if I'm caught,' ordered Lily.

Senan's hallway was jammed with crates of empty Ritz bottles and they had to shuffle sideways in single file to bypass them. Lily said the obstruction reminded her of her student days, when she would deliberately annex a table in her local near the passageway leading to the men's toilets, so they had to squeeze past and chat to her. Senan looked at her as though he'd never heard anything more pathetic in his life.

'A man who throws a party and accidentally-on-purpose forgets to tell his workmates has no grounds for looking superior,' Lily objected.

'What do you mean?' Senan scratched his stomach.

She indicated the crates.

'Oh that. Just having a clear-out. My flatmate's joined the Greens and keeps harping on about the environment so I'm bringing these to a bottle bank.' He stifled a yawn. 'Hello, Venus, hope the car's running like clockwork.'

'No problems so far, touch wood.' Venus tapped the dado rail in the hallway, trying not to pant after climbing three flights of stairs to the flat.

'Nobody has so many crates of Ritz unless they've had a party,' Lily challenged him.

'I do.' Senan ran his fingers over his stubble, delighted to find it bristly after only two days' growth. 'I like a Ritz after work. I put up my feet, watch back-to-back episodes *of The Simpsons* and sink a bottle or two. It relaxes me. It stands to reason, Lily, if I'd held a party there'd be more than just empty Ritz bottles.'

They followed him through to the living-room, inexplicably furnished with dentist's chairs in cracked brown leather. One of the chairs even had a shelf-table attached for the glass of bubblegum-coloured water every dentist supplied, although Senan's held an empty bottle of Ritz. Curtains were hung at the window in shades of lime and yellow so garish they sent Catherine-wheels spinning across Venus's field of vision. Lily opened them and Senan winced, then she threw herself into one of the chairs and studied the curtains which were covered by a colony of surfers. She eyed up one of them.

'He's cute, but it'd never work,' Lily sighed. 'He's only a few inches tall. This is one of those moments when size really does matter.' She lifted the empty Ritz bottle alongside her chair and shook its dregs. 'I think you ought to kick the addiction, Senan. Ordering bottles of Ritz at those trendy city-centre nightspots you queue to get into can't enhance your pulling power. Don't people ever question your proclivities on the strength of it?'

Senan shrugged and attacked his stubble again. 'Just like the way it tastes. Girls can drink pints of Guinness so I don't see why I shouldn't enjoy my Ritz. Anyway, I don't feel the need to do macho things to prove my heterosexuality. I'm not a detective in a 1970s TV series.'

Venus felt a stirring of interest. Obviously he was way too young for her, but there was a certain independence at work here. 'If I were standing at a bar counter and there was a man with a pint of Guinness on one side and another with a bottle of Ritz on the other, I know which I'd prefer to talk to.'

'Which?' Senan was wary.

'The man with the Ritz, of course. It's unconventional.'

'See?' He gloated as he turned to Lily. 'Now, can I offer you ladies some refreshment? A bottle of Ritz, perhaps?'

'I'd prefer a glass of red wine,' said Lily.

'I only have Ritz. The great advantage it has over red wine is that it doesn't need to breathe.'

'I find wine can breathe all it likes in my stomach.' Lily swivelled the dentist's chair in a circle, feet extended, then hauled herself off. 'It's probably too early for wine anyway, especially after all the vodka we packed away last night. Know what the Russian is for "cheers"? *Dosvidaniya*.'

'I thought that was goodbye,' protested Venus. 'Not that I was trying to learn Russian but' – and she mumbled this last bit under her breath – 'it was rammed down our throats.'

Lily ignored her. 'We're off for some culture. Here are the keys to Bull Alley, Senan – stress that the owner has gone abroad so it's vacant and there's no chain. Your commuter can take possession as quickly as his solicitor is able to process the paperwork.'

'Good to meet you again, Venus.' He made eye contact as she shimmied past the crates.

She smiled as she caught him yawning again, neutering that urgent air of his. 'Likewise, Senan.'

In the car she flicked a sardonic eyebrow at Lily. 'Thought he was supposed to be wild about me.'

Now that it was clear he wasn't, she felt cheated of an admirer.

'He is, he couldn't keep his eyes off you,' Lily persisted.

'He couldn't keep his eyes open, let alone look at either of us. It must have been some session he was up to his oxters in last night. He reeked of drink and cigarette-smoke – you don't need a crystal ball to divine your man and his bed made minimal contact.'

'I haven't the stamina for that any more,' admitted Lily. 'One night out and I'm wiped for a week.'

'Me too.'

'You know what the trouble with the younger generation is?'

'Remind me.'

'We don't belong to it any more.'

* * *

They parked in St Stephen's Green, a short walk away from the museum, and rummaged in their purses for change to feed the insatiable metre.

'You can commit murder in this town but you daren't park illegally.' Lily clinked coins as she sorted through them.

At the museum they loitered over the zodiac mosaic in the hallway. 'I wish I were the archer or the twins instead of Scorpio,' complained Venus. 'Scorpions always look so threatening.'

161

'You should worry.' Lily was firing pins into her unravelling topknot, fingers doubling as eyes. 'Imagine what it's like for me, born under a star sign that kills more people than Aids.'

An involuntary shudder passed through Venus: her mother had been one of the victims. Lily realised what she'd said and became garrulous, to cover the awkward pause.

'Someone told me about reading a book in which all the star signs were changed to something that had more relevance nowadays. So instead of archers and goats you had, I don't know, corporate-asset strippers and boy bands. You could replace the scales with a calculator and the Gemini twins would become quadruplets because of modern fertility treatments. Virgo would have to be scrapped because virginity has lost its value as currency, and Pisces would be shown with two heads and no fins because of North Sea pollution.'

Venus nodded absently: she was thinking about Birdie, who was her biological mother. She felt inclined to talk to Lily about her discovery – but decided against it. She should explore this development with the other half of the relationship first.

'You look miles away.' Lily nudged her.

Venus shook off her pensiveness. There was no point in dwelling on Birdie's role in her life right now. Her questions would be answered soon enough, when she let Birdie know her secret had been plumbed. In the meantime there was bank upon bank of Celtic gold in glass cases to bewitch her.

They pored over a display case, breath fogging the glass.

'Saint-seducing gold,' quoted Lily, imagining herself in a torc that curveted from collar-bone to navel. 'Not many opportunities to wear it, granted, but you'd certainly shine on the odd occasion you decided to play it glamorous.'

'Let's go upstairs and admire the tapestries,' suggested Venus.

'You look a little ragged around the edges. Let's go to the café and admire the cakes,' countermanded Lily. 'It has the advantage of not being restricted to the theoretical.'

They had chocolate-dusted cappuccinos and a slice of carrot cake apiece.

'Aren't you worried about Karim becoming more attracted to the fundamentalist aspects of Islam? He may not be a practising Muslim now but it could sweep over him at some stage,' warned Venus.

'No.' Lily chewed, irredeemably placid. 'I'm a Catholic, not a particularly committed one, but the early training means we're comfortable with fundamentalism.'

'It's just that I hear alarm-bells when you tell me Karim thinks smoking is unladylike, and it sounds suspiciously strict if he doesn't even like you wearing trousers.' Venus produced her Internet printouts from her handbag. 'I downloaded this for you, so you can see for yourself what it's like out there. Chechnya looks like a really dangerous place – they advise people who have to travel there to bring bodyguards.'

Lily took the pages. 'I'm still only doing this to get Karim a passport, Venus – nothing's changed.' She clattered her fork against her empty plate and smiled without a hint of rancour. 'And I don't know why you think I'll be going to Chechnya. The way Senan's flogging houses it's not safe to take a weekend off let alone a holiday – I'd come back to find he'd overrun the office and my desk had been moved to the back yard. "Sorry, madam, it's by order of the Personal Republic of Senan Mulqueen."' She flicked through the Internet printout while Venus toyed with her food, wondering what it was about Lily that made her so determined to have the world's poor and huddled masses sent to her doorstep.

'Why are you so irredeemably nice all the time, Lily?' she demanded. 'It's unnatural.'

Lily laid down the printout and looked at Venus oddly; there was a distance in her periwinkle eyes that unnerved Venus and immediately she felt apologetic. 'Listen, sorry, forget I spoke. I'm a little tense.'

Twin orbs flared in Lily's cheeks. 'I know you think I'm a goody-two-shoes, Venus – you've always made that plain. Maybe I am. But when I was eight years old my grandmother took me by the hand and told me something I've never forgotten. She said, "Lily, there are two classes of women in life – those that are pretty and those that are kind. We can't all choose to be pretty but we can all make a conscious effort to be kind. And you'll find, my dear, as you make your way, that kindness lasts longer than looks." If I had a daughter, which I suppose is unlikely now, I'd say as much to her.'

Venus was silenced; shamed, too. For the first time she perceived that her friend's decent nature might be acquired rather than innate, and it seemed all the more worthy for it. She felt she owed Lily an explanation for her uncharitable outburst and, casting around in her mind, came up against the impassable obstruction of the true reason. 'I think I know who my real mother is,' Venus blurted out, pushing aside her cake.

Lily was intrigued. Venus hadn't told her about her sky-writing epiphany and although she knew her friend was adopted, she had no idea Venus was on a mission to track down her mother. She struggled to keep pace as Venus galloped through an outline of how the adoption wasn't something Maura and Dan had ever discussed in detail, and how she'd dropped the subject for Maura's sake but felt free to pursue it now.

'A person needs to know where they come from,' said Venus.

'Surely it's where you're going to that counts.' Lily chose her words with circumspection. 'The past can be a burden as much as an asset.'

'But I still have a past,' objected Venus. 'It's there even if it's hidden from me. I have a right to know who I am and why I was given away.'

Lily rocked on the legs of her chair. There was an evangelical cast to Venus's features that left her wary.

'You haven't asked me who my mother is,' Venus prompted.

Lily landed her chair legs with a bump on the tiles. 'Who is she?'

'Birdie, our nearest neighbour.'

Lily had met her at the funeral. 'The witch-woman with the girlish red ribbons. She told me to find a spider and whisper my financial needs to it, then release it outdoors. I hadn't even told her about my overdraft. The mad part of it is that I did as she suggested and three days later a cheque arrived in the post – I'd been overpaying my tax. Is Birdie old enough to be your mother?'

'Just about. She was probably twenty or so when she gave me away. Except by having my parents adopt me she could still be part of my life. It makes perfect sense.'

Lily's blinking tic emerged as her mind raced. 'You've known Birdie all your life – why are you suddenly now convinced she's your mother? You couldn't look less alike – isn't she a little dark creature?'

'I could take after my father,' Venus pointed out. 'You

don't look like your mother either. I don't know for sure it's Birdie – but it seems to add up. She's always been exceptionally interested in me, what I do and where I go.'

'You'll just have to ask her. But she may not admit it, even if it's true.'

'She has nothing to gain by hiding the truth now. My mother's dead so she doesn't have to spare her feelings.' Venus reached across the table and grabbed Lily's hands in her own, face colouring with excitement. 'Don't you see, Lily, this is my chance to find myself.'

Lily squeezed her friend's hands. 'I hope it works out for you, Venus, truly I do. But finding yourself is one thing, liking what you find is another.'

'I'll know everything by tomorrow, one way or another,' said Venus.

'Tomorrow,' repeated Lily. It seemed to her that she could sense Venus's excitement course through her fingertips. And it struck Lily that Venus was over-stimulated, banking on this encounter with Birdie to solder together every fissure and set at ease every uncertainty she'd ever experienced in her life.

She wanted to warn Venus against raising her hopes too high. But Lily didn't know how to say it without striking a negative note, so she mustered a plastic smile to mimic confidence. 'Tomorrow,' she said again.

Venus's eyes were luminous as she looked at Lily. 'I've lost one mother and found another this year. It's as though Mam is intervening to give Birdie and me a second chance.'

Chapter Fifteen

That evening, Venus scanned the Sunday newspapers while Lily caught up on her ironing. When she'd re-read the same paragraph three times without making sense of it, she realised something was awry.

She missed Roancarrick. And she missed her father. She asked Lily if she could use her phone to ring home.

His voice sounded meagre, stripped of its outer layer, but at least he didn't call her Maura – an occasional mistake which continued to wrench her.

'Are you still coming home tomorrow, lass?' He didn't manage to strike the casual note he'd been aiming for.

'Straight after breakfast, Dad.'

'What's that?'

His hearing seemed to deteriorate on the phone – perhaps he partly lip-read, it occurred to her, but he still refused to wear his hearing-aid. Venus pitched her voice a little louder. 'I'll be heading for home straight after breakfast. Lily has to go to work so I'll probably leave with her.'

'Right so, see you then. Drive carefully and remember the school-runs clog up the traffic in those Midlands towns.'

'Wait, Dad.' He was about to hang up and she'd hardly spoken to him. It was always difficult to make conversation with her father on the phone; he didn't believe in small talk while Eircom was clocking up the bill. 'How have you been managing? Did you remember to defrost the chicken for today's dinner?'

'Certainly I did. I opened a tin of mushy peas to go with it. I've the pan steeping but the rest of the dishes are washed and dried. Nobody can accuse me of keeping an untidy kitchen.'

'Birdie hasn't been in to see you today, has she?'

'I've laid eyes on neither chick nor child since after Mass. It was Father McGinley instead of the young fellow from Bundoran. He's getting doddery, Venus – he lost his place twice. Sure the poor old fellow must be at the heel-end of his seventies.'

Venus smiled and poked her index finger into the tightly curled telephone lead.

Dan continued, 'Birdie would normally stop by on a Sunday but she must be in Belfast-town on business still. Not that she ever tells you what her business is; she likes to keep it mysterious. Sure that's women for you – they'd never want to be straightforward when they can go all round the houses.'

'Any other scandal?' She was hungry for news from Roancarrick.

'No news, it's always quiet in these parts. Wait a minute,' an afterthought struck him. 'That artist neighbour of ours, the Landers fellow, landed himself in a spot of bother. He put out to sea in a rowboat last evening and had to be rescued when the gales blew up. The coastguard was called out and they thought they'd have to do whatever it is they do with the search and rescue helicopter – poach it or something.'

'Scramble it, Dad.' She was too anxious to laugh.

'That's right. Anyway he was found before the helicopter crew were up in the air. And do you know what the eejit said when they reeled him in? He was trying to see the back view of the mountain for a three-dimensional drawing he's working on. Can you credit that class of stupidity? Going out to sea without even checking the weather forecast. Some people shouldn't be let off dry land.'

'But he's all right, Dad – he hasn't been hurt?' Venus held her breath and listened to the static on the telephone line, willing her father to provide reassurance. Quickly.

'No,' he allowed, 'he hasn't been hurt, bar a drenching which serves him right. He has that mother of his to thank for it. She was watching the storm-clouds gather and rang the coast guard the minute she thought there was any danger. She invited all the rescue team in and sat them down at the kitchen table and made them hot whiskeys and ham sandwiches. Turned into a bit of a *céilí*. That Landers woman has a fine singing voice for a solicitor – she gave them the first and last verse of "She Moves Through The Fair" and there's not many can manage that without botching it.'

He broke off, under attack from a coughing fit, and Venus's anxiety was transferred to him. She wanted to race home and make sure he was wearing his thermal vest. He drank cough mixture like lemonade – obviously its potency had worn thin.

Dan sounded wheezy when his voice piped down the

line again. 'Mickey Joe's son Michael said there was some money spent on that kitchen in the captain's house. Granite worktops everywhere, and a clatter of shiny copper saucepans that looked as if they never saw service from the day they left the shop – they were hanging from a pulley gadget above the cooker. They spoiled it with a big brute of a Belfast sink, though. We threw ours out years ago and bought a metal one. Your mother grew herbs in it at the bottom of the garden, if you remember. I suppose there's still parsley and what not there.'

'And where was Conor Landers when all this revelry was going on?' Venus realised her father's fascination with the Landers' extravagant kitchen fittings made it unlikely he'd give her a condition check unprompted.

'Someone ran him a bath and he took to his bed. I heard his mother brought him up a hot whiskey when she made a batch for the lifeboat crew but he was sound asleep. There's nothing like a drenching at sea for leaving you bone-weary. I dare say he's learned his lesson. Artist types are airy-fairy but he'll have to learn to keep his feet on the ground. There's more experienced folk than him have fallen foul of the sea, as we know only too well in our family.'

Venus wondered at her father's ability to talk about his twin sons' deaths by drowning with such composure. Perhaps old age and the passage of time brought acceptance. Her mother had grieved to the end, however: she didn't belong to a generation that yearned to have their ashes scattered at sea.

She rang off and sat on the edge of Lily's bed in a state of some distress. But it wasn't due to her father's hacking spasm – and it wasn't because Conor Landers's near-miss turned her thoughts towards the brothers who were never more than a photograph to her. She couldn't imagine what was gnawing at her. Unless it was that Conor Landers had nearly died.

Which made no sense at all because she scarcely knew the man.

It had to be the waste. He was too young to fling away his life in such a foolhardy fashion. There'd been one death close to her this year already – she didn't want another.

'Any news?' Lily unplugged the iron.

'Bit of a drama involving one of the blow-ins, but all's well that ends well.' Venus took care not to look at her friend in case she noticed she was more perturbed by the drama than she had any right to be.

Lily crashed onto the sofa. 'You know who I ran into on the street the other day? That girl from Athy who was in college with us. Remember Barbara Rafferty? She used to wear drawers with nursery rhymes embroidered on them to cheer herself up when she went to the loo. Except she was always saying she wished whoever designed them would write them upside down because she was developing a crick in her neck.'

Venus collapsed beside her, rocking with laughter. Good old Lily, she had a knack for bouncing her out of the doldrums. 'Of course I remember Barbara Rafferty. Whatever happened to her?'

'She has a radio show on RTÉ – it's very popular.'

'A sketch programme?'

'No, heavy duty political punditry. Wonder if she still wears her nursery-rhyme drawers to interview the party leaders? "Incey Wincey Spider" was her favourite.'

'I don't know how you remember these things, Lily. I suppose you mentioned the underwear when you bumped into her.'

'Give me credit for some taste and decency, Venus Macken.'

'So that's a yes then.'

They were chortling so hard they didn't hear Karim's key turn in the lock.

'Share the joke,' he said.

They looked at one another and giggled all the louder.

When they subsided he smiled at Lily in that lingering way he had. 'Have you told your friend of my good fortune, Lily?'

She straightened. 'Not yet.'

Venus was alert as Lily turned to her. There was something dubious afoot. 'Told me what good fortune?'

'Karim has been in touch with University College Dublin's medical faculty and they're prepared to accept him as a student,' said Lily. 'So I'll be keeping him on as my lodger, after we're married. Just until he finds his feet.'

He's already found his feet, thought Venus.

Lily, who could read Venus's responses as clearly as if they were spewing out of her ear on tickertape, flicked her topknot defiantly. 'Now, who's for a cup of tea? I have a tin of Danish cookies pressed on me by a grateful client. For services not only rendered but billed with VAT at 21 per cent included. Still, if it made her happy to give me a tin of biscuits, who am I to complain?' She disappeared through the bead curtain with a deliberate swagger.

Venus released a look in Karim's direction as he took a seat opposite her. He folded one hand over the over and said nothing. She raised one eyebrow, then another, heaving them into the silence. He cracked.

'She is an angel sent from heaven to watch over me,' he said.

Not the angel routine again.

'I think she's taking a fairly hefty gamble.' Her voice was steely. 'There may be laws against this sort of undertaking. Are you really prepared to allow someone as decent as Lily to risk prosecution?'

'What choice do I have?' His expressive eyes overflowed into Venus's. 'I cannot go back to Grozny and I will not go back to Moscow. All I want to do is to work as a doctor and heal people – is that so wrong? Whatever small amount of harm I am doing now, I will repay by working in your health service. Ireland needs doctors; I am a good one. This will benefit everyone.'

Venus was surly. It was a riposte she had no ammunition against.

The beads parted and Lily's honest, freckled face appeared through the blue glass. 'Everybody happy? I'm making herbal tea to counteract the sugar injection from the biscuits.'

That won't stop Karim relocating half the sugar-bowl to his mug, thought Venus.

She should grasp this opportunity to find out if it were really a marriage of convenience to be followed swiftly by severance – or whether he planned to freeload off Lily indefinitely. After all, if he intended returning to medical school he could do worse than live rent-free in Adelphi Court – Venus's faith in human nature wasn't as trusting as Lily's. If this Chechen doctor with the bruised eyes were simply using her, then Lily could wind up tossed on the scrapheap.

She could find herself in trouble with the law too.

Chapter Sixteen

'Nice visit to Dublin-town?' Dan beamed his gummy infant's smile, relieved to have Venus home again – the two days had seemed interminable without her company. 'It's been a fine, soft day for your drive. I'm sure you're ready for a sup of tea.' Not waiting for an answer, he lifted the kettle, already bubbling on a back plate on the range, and splashed water into the teapot to scald it. 'Unless you'd rather some of that coffee you drink?' He hesitated, with the caddy opened and the spoon for the loose tea in his hand.

'Tea's grand,' Venus reassured him.

She felt a swelling of affection for this crumpled old man. 'You're looking a little worn, Dad. Maybe you overdid it in the garden yesterday.'

'Maybe I did, lass. But your mother was proud of what small bit of garden we can grow here by the sea and I wanted to bed it down for the winter. The flower-beds needed happing with fallen leaves to protect them from the frost and the grass was ready for one last cutting.'

'I could have managed the grass, Dad.'

'I'm sure you could, there's plenty of meat on your bones, but the mower's a contrary beast and I know the workings of her. Anyway the exercise does me good: a man should work up a sweat every once in a while. Get the blood pumping.'

He drank his weak, milky tea while Venus sipped hers almost black, wincing at the loose leaves. By Christmas she intended to convert him to teabags.

'You'll have to take it easy for a couple of days,' she insisted, and unexpectedly he agreed.

'My bones are stiff.'

She was on her feet instantly, adding more water to the kettle to fill two hot-water bottles – one for his feet and one for between his shoulder blades. Dan pretended to object to the fussing but she could see he delighted in being pampered. Just a little. He settled down on the sofa, ready for a chat.

However, priorities had to be addressed first. 'Does your friend live near a church? What Mass did the two of you go to below in the city?' he asked.

'I didn't go to Mass,' said Venus.

'I'm surprised at you, Venus, missing your Sunday obligation. What class of a Catholic did we rear at all?' His face was bewildered, the hot-water bottles thrust to one side.

Their parting of the ways on the religious front was upon her sooner than Venus would have chosen but she might as well deal with it now. 'No class of a one, for I don't believe,' she replied.

'Don't believe in God?' he pressed her, incredulity rearranging his features.

'Not as defined by the Holy Roman and Apostolic

175

Church, no.' Goaded, her pitch sharpened. 'I believe in a life force and the power of good, but not the self-serving male hegemony we've been saddled with for a religion. Come on, Dad, it's not so long ago women had to be churched before they were allowed back in after childbirth. Justify that if you can. We're labelled the fount of original sin, with Eve leading the virtuous Adam astray and paradise squandered as a result. We're sinners by dint of gender. Sinners if we regulate our reproduction. Sinners if we don't maintain our purity. Virgin motherhood is brandished at us as our ideal, a virgin of virgins conceived without original sin is supposed to be our role model.' Venus tossed back long red hair from her heated face. Ensnared by her own verbosity, she was unconscious of its devastating effect on Dan, whose devotion was unequivocal. 'We're not worthy to be accepted into the priesthood but we can decorate the altar and clean the church. Thanks, but no thanks. Why on earth would I want to subscribe to a religion that persists in treating me like a second-class citizen, at a time when equality laws regulate virtually every other institution? The joke of it is that the men who've run the Catholic Church for the past two thousand years aren't exactly trailing clouds of glory – it's one scandal after another. It's safe to say the Catholic Church and myself have come to the end of the road.'

She realised, finally, from her father's frozen expression that her objections had been spelled out too explicitly. Venus spoke gently now, hoping to mitigate the body-blows she'd pounded him with. 'Here's the credo according to Venus Macken, Dad: lead an honourable life, then when you're old you can look back and enjoy it a second time. Some of the best Catholics I know are the worst Christians – licking the shine off the altar-rails one minute and spreading scandal the next.'

Silence was suspended between them like a prayer.

'It's a mercy your mother didn't live to see this day,' he mumbled, but his heart wasn't in the rebuke.

Later she apologised, not because she'd changed her mind but because there was no mileage in bad blood with an eighty-year-old man. She could be consigning herself to a lifetime of regret. Venus searched him out, sitting, as she knew he'd be, on the low drystone wall overlooking the harbour, watching a sea mist creep across from Ben Bulben and swirl around the bay.

'I'm still your daughter and you're still my father. We should let nothing come between us. We only have each other.'

He nodded, and although still shocked to the core by their exchange, consented to be led home.

* * *

It wasn't as easy as Venus had anticipated. You couldn't just look someone in the eye and say: 'Are you my mother and why did you give me away when I was a baby?'

Particularly not when that someone was Birdie, with her narrow, knowing eyes and her pseudo-calm air. At least it struck Venus as pseudo-calm, sitting opposite her in the cottage. She'd imagined the scenario endlessly – occasionally confrontational, possibly emotional, but never tranquil. Now she stroked Jude's shell and debated how to approach Birdie.

'I see you still haven't put him down for hibernation,' Venus remarked.

Jude's nostrils, followed by his eyes, then his neck emerged from the shell, and she traced a whorled fingertip along the top of his head. His neck reminded her of her father's.

177

'Not yet.' Birdie had acquired some half-moon spectacles in Belfast and they roosted on the bridge of her nose, heightening her a resemblance to the wooden owl she kept by her computer. 'I'll do it soon.'

Venus struggled for a conversational gambit. Preferably one that would lead on naturally to a question about identity. She abandoned the effort and asked, 'How was Belfast?'

'The usual.' Birdie was monosyllabic today; her trip to the city seemed to have tired her. She hopped about the kitchen, more jerky than usual, melting chocolate and pouring it into heart-shaped moulds.

'I don't know what the usual is,' said Venus.

'Busy after Roancarrick. People in a hurry. Jostling people not in a hurry. Money being spent like it's going out of fashion. Tense, despite the peace process.' She darted a glance at Venus and became less staccato, to set her at her ease. 'I'm stirring this clockwise for positive energy.'

'Are you making chocolate hearts as a present for someone?'

'For myself, to incite self-love. Cities always leave me feeling drained – of everything, including any sense of who I am.'

It struck Venus that Birdie had enough self-love to propagate a new species.

Stop it right there. This was her mother she was criticising. Probably. Only one way to find out.

Venus drew courage from the realisation that the ruby ribbon in Birdie's smoke-dark hair was the length she'd bought for her in Sligo.

'Birdie.' She ground to a halt.

Birdie raised those all-seeing eyes to Venus's desperate ones.

'There's something you want to ask me,' she prompted Venus.

'Are you my mother?' It slid out in a single downward breath, without preamble.

She should have rehearsed what to say. Instead of which she'd inadequately framed the most important question she was ever likely to ask anyone in her life.

Are you my mother? It was too bald. It would panic Birdie; it would alarm anybody.

Birdie's tiny frame was rocked by an internal spasm, and some of the chocolate she was doling out slopped over the edge of a heart mould, pooling on the counter. The jolt forced out a whoosh of air, followed – to Venus's astonishment – by a howl of laughter. Birdie surrendered herself to the luxury of mirth for a minute, shoulders shaking and blood flooding her face beneath the tanned skin. As the attack faded to hiccuping tremors her eyes, still damp from laughter, seemed to fasten on a drawer in the kitchen table on which her computer rested. Her gaze darted back towards Venus, its expression suddenly regretful, until a veil was whisked over her eyes. She seemed to steel herself to finish sharing out the chocolate between moulds, even dipping her finger automatically in the spillage.

Venus watched her, perplexed. Finally Birdie joined her by the fireside.

'Forgive me,' she gasped, uncharacteristically breathless. 'I was expecting a hundred and one questions but that's the hundred and second and it caught me unawares. Where on earth, Venus, did you come by that far-fetched notion?'

'Mrs O'Dea,' muttered Venus.

'Mrs O'Dea told you I was your mother?'

'Not exactly,' Venus allowed.

'And since when did you pay a blind bit of attention to the likes of Mrs O'Dea? Sure the woman is too busy nagging her husband, mollycoddling her son and decimating cream cakes to add two and two. I'm surprised at you, Venus, treating idle speculation as fact.'

Venus squirmed.

Birdie folded her arms. Eventually she took pity and turned away, opening the fridge door to store the chocolate hearts. It was a vast red oblong unit, with a Coca-Cola-bottle-shaped handle, completely at odds with this centuries-old cottage. If she'd kept pints of milk in a bucket of cold water in her back larder, as Venus remembered some of the older village residents doing, that would have seemed more apt.

'I take it you're not my mother then.' Venus was on her dignity, icy in her hostility. She resented Birdie for making her assemble the words and Mrs O'Dea for having planted them there. And herself most of all for having leaped to conclusions. The wrong ones.

'No.' Birdie was back in monosyllabic mode.

'And do you know who is?'

'Yes.'

Venus inhaled deeply. 'Would you be kind enough to share it with me?'

Birdie straightened, hand massaging her back. She looked withered, in that moment; Venus had never thought of her neighbour in terms of age before.

'Your mother was Maura,' said Birdie.

Venus sighed. They'd been down that road already. She wasn't going to hack down Birdie's reserves so she may as well have that walk on the beach she'd promised herself. Even Jude had retreated into his shell. She gave one of his honeycombs a farewell tap and stood up.

'Maura loved you so much,' murmured Birdie, oblivious to Venus's preparations to leave. 'She said you made sense of her loss . . . the sea, which had taken her sons, had repaid the debt with you. That supremely merciless force of nature had shown some compassion after all.'

Venus sat down as unobtrusively as possible, apprehensive that noise might fragment Birdie's flow.

'She often spoke to me of the day your father brought you home, skyclad, not a scrap of clothing on you. He'd taken off his shirt and wrapped you in that for fear the tweed of his jacket would rasp your skin. I called in to see Maura just after your arrival. You were only a few days' old but as self-possessed as a grown woman. We gave you warm milk with a spoonful of honey in it, then we bathed you in the washing-up basin, and put you to sleep in Maura and Dan's bed – all hemmed in with pillows on either side in case you toppled out.'

Birdie's voice was cobweb-fine, caressing Venus with her memories.

'You never cried, that first day. Not once. You just settled in here as though you were born to it.' Birdie directed a searing glance at Venus. 'I'll admit that once or twice I wondered what would have happened if I'd found you instead of Dan. If I'd brought you home to my cottage and looked out for you here. But you were meant to be with Maura and Dan, that's why they were the ones to find you – and that's why they kept you too. Everything happens for a reason, nothing in life is truly random. Never forget it, Venus Macken.'

Birdie turned abruptly and crossed to the computer, switching it on, and Venus could tell there'd be no further retrospection from her. She straggled outside, her brain whirling with contradictions, and trudged towards the shore.

John Óg was parked by the harbour. He stepped out of his Volvo when he saw Venus and leaned against the bonnet, trying not to smear dirt on his smart grey Crombie overcoat. She wanted to be alone to weigh her impressions and hoped a nod would be adequate, but John Óg fell into step beside her.

Churlish that privacy seemed an impossibility in Roancarrick, she sniffed. 'You spend a considerable amount of time in the village for a man who doesn't live at home.'

'Sure the Mammy loves to see me – it brightens up her day.'

Venus cast a covert glance at the unexceptional figure with a girl's eyelashes who could do that for Mrs O'Dea. Motherhood had much to answer for.

'Anyway, I told you, I have a client here. It's Nora Brennan in the pub. There's a lot of accountancy work attached to running a licensed premises. But I can't tell you any more – client confidentiality.'

Venus nodded, not in the least interested.

'It would be unethical of me to breathe a word of her business,' he added.

Venus combined another nod with a shrug.

'Well, seeing as it's yourself, she has big plans for the place. Expansion plans. But you won't tease another word out of me, you minx.' He tapped the side of his nose.

John Óg was having difficulty matching his strides to her pumping ones; Venus noticed his patent shoes were flecked with sand and acquiring a smudgy patina, and wondered at him risking them, for he took pride in his appearance. She sniggered at a stray memory of John Óg using tweezers to turn the pages of his Marvel comics. Fast-forward twenty years and he probably folded his trousers into their creases and positioned them over the back of a chair before making love to a woman.

'Share the joke,' he invited.

'Just wondering if you still read those comics you used to collect,' she lied fluently.

Not only did he still read them, he had every copy from his schooldays, stored in boxes in the spare room. Of his detached house in Sligo, he added meaningfully, in case she'd forgotten he was Roancarrick's most eligible bachelor. Venus noticed his tonsure of scalp and decided that troublesome and all as it was being a woman, men had it tougher. At least women generally held on to their hair.

She gazed towards the horizon, dominated by Ben Bulben's purple outline, and paid minimal attention to John Óg O'Dea. The sea-swell filled her ears – there was always noise by the shore, with its rushing and fretting.

So Birdie wasn't her mother after all: and yet she'd swear her neighbour knew more than she was willing to reveal. Well, the man that made time made plenty of it, Venus thought, and then clapped her hand to her forehead. She was at it again, repeating her father's phrases.

'Have you a headache?' John Óg's wan face with its acne-pitted chin was inches from hers.

'No, I'm grand,' she assured him. 'I just have a few matters churning away in my mind.'

He seemed to have something on his mind, too, and opened his mouth twice, before volunteering, 'You know that name of yours, Venus.'

'I do, John Óg.'

'Is it some kind of pagan goddess of love reference?'

'Not at all, John Óg, it's a goddess of chastity one. The Romans had loads of goddesses called Venus – I'm named after the Venus their respectable matrons worshipped. You didn't doubt me there, did you?'

He checked her face trying to assess whether she was toying with him; it wasn't clear one way or the other. 'I have to turn back.' John Óg felt a little out of his depth with Venus Macken. 'I didn't realise we'd walked so far.' He checked his shoes, mouth puckered with distaste. 'Not to worry, I always carry polish in the car. My mother taught me that no well-dressed man would be seen in public with mucky shoes.'

Venus thought of Mrs O'Dea's father, who used to sit in the shop with a pipe that was forever going out, after he'd handed over the farm to his eldest son. He'd never worn anything but hobnailed boots.

As John Óg turned away he reached something to her: he'd been carrying it all along only Venus hadn't noticed.

'I brought you a present,' he announced.

She raised thunderstruck eyes to his light grey ones which skated off her face, reconsidered and crept back on. 'Why?'

'Just,' he shuffled.

She opened the plastic bag and took out a set of weighing scales.

'For weighing your food,' he explained. 'It's a great habit to get into.'

'Thank you,' said Venus. 'I'll, ah, start weighing then.'

John Óg exuded self-satisfaction. 'I'm going to tell you something, Venus, that I wouldn't share with everyone. Always weigh with the wrappers and stalks on – that way you'll fool your body into believing it's getting more to eat.

Now, what do you think of that for a tip? Don't try to thank me, just use those scales. And I'll be seeing you very soon.' With that, he turned away, his steps mirroring the pitter-patter of his mother. He paused, wheeled around and returned to her side. 'There's one other thing, Venus. Cream puffs are the divil. Stay away from them at all costs.'

Venus watched him, bobbing along close to the sand-dunes. She wondered if she were imagining it, berated herself for being conceited, and finally conceded it might be so.

John Óg O'Dea was courting her.

Chapter Seventeen

The fractious wind nipped at Venus, despite her waist-length quilted jacket. When would she learn to dress for Roancarrick? She needed layers – lots of them. But she couldn't turn back just yet. John Óg was still slip-sliding in his gripless Italian shoes towards his Volvo. He'd imagine she was pursuing him. Venus took refuge in a sand-dune, crouching among the flattened grass, and tried to formulate a plan in her search for her mother. *Try Finding Not Sacrificing Yourself.*

If only she had a real birth certificate she might be in with a chance, but she didn't. She had something *called* a birth certificate, but it was an adoption one, incomplete. Only Dan and Maura's names were on it, so that was no use. They didn't know where she was born, let alone the date. Maybe there was a genuine birth certificate somewhere, with her true date and place of birth, and her mother's name, at least, if not her father's. Except how would she go about finding it? It may well exist, filed away in the office of some government building or other. But she had no identity beyond that of Venus Macken: tracking down a sheet of paper to prove she was someone else would be impossible.

Venus savaged her lower lip, trying to circumvent the obstacles. It might be worth tackling her father again, now that Maura wasn't around to be hurt by questions. There had to be more to the story than she'd been told as a child.

A whistling tune alerted her to company.

'Skulking?' asked a male voice.

At least it may have been a question; it could also have been an accusation.

Venus looked up from her sand-locked retreat to find Conor Landers looming over her. Looking hale and hearty and not in the least half-drowned. Venus scrabbled to her feet, uncomfortable with being found with her elbows in the sand and a length of reed in her mouth. She could look extremely glamorous, given half a day to prepare herself.

For some reason, she felt like being candid with this man. 'I suppose I'm trying to make sense of my life,' admitted Venus.

'A tall order. I'm just trying to make it to the end of the week.'

That's what she got for opening up to a stranger. Venus's voice was clipped. 'I heard they had to scramble the search and rescue helicopter for you.'

'And I still didn't see Ben Bulben from the other angle – they rescued me too soon.'

He sneezed and it blew away her irritation.

'Bless you. You should still be indoors if you took a soaking. My mother always said the Atlantic takes no prisoners.'

'I probably should,' he agreed, 'but I was bored in the

house on my own. The rest of the family went back to their jobs last night – I'm the only layabout without a permanent nine-to-five. But they'll be here again at the weekend; they can't get enough of the place. My older brother is planning to bring his girlfriend, and the younger one, who travels in a pack, is trying to figure out how to fit thirty of his closest friends into the spare bedroom. We're all besotted by Roancarrick.'

That's because the captain's house and the village is still a toy to them, thought Venus. It's hardly out of its pristine wrapper. But she wouldn't spoil the moment: Conor had been right when he'd pointed out that some people had to search out their own Roancarrick in life.

They ambled back towards the harbour, Conor with his inevitable claret portfolio under his arm. Venus noticed their strides were equally matched. Another sidelong peek revealed that his angular face could belong to someone aged between twenty and fifty – but the curls were those of a child. The sum of the parts added up to an intriguing whole. She cast her eye along the beach and estimated it would take them twenty minutes to reach the harbour: plenty of time to improve their acquaintance.

'There's something I've always wondered,' she began.

He looked encouraging.

'There used to be a barometer in the captain's house when I was a little girl. It fascinated me. It was made of brass and had two needles – I couldn't imagine why it needed both – and it read: set fair, fair, change, rain, stormy. Is it still hanging in the hallway?'

'No – I wonder where it can have vanished to? Maybe the captain's Scottish relatives took a shine to it.'

'That's a shame. It was a wonderful old piece.' A tickle of

188

disappointment that the barometer wasn't in its appointed place tiptoed through Venus.

They walked a little further, Venus mourning the barometer which hadn't belonged to her in the first place.

'I'm always taken aback by your eyes,' said Conor. 'There you are, a sister to that young Venetian woman in Durer's painting, the one who's smiling furtively despite her mourning ribbon, obviously planning some flighty escapade. Her lips, hair and gown are all an identical shade of dense amber. Exactly the same as your hair. When I look at you I always expect to see dark brown eyes, like my Venetian. But yours are golden.'

'Oh no,' she gasped.

'It's not as bad as all that,' he reassured her. 'It's feline.'

'No, you don't understand – I left my weighing scales by the sand-dunes.'

'Do you always bring your weighing scales to the sand-dunes with you?'

'They're a present, for weighing food before you eat it. I left them where I was sitting. It's a long story – you wouldn't be interested.'

Honestly, he was making her feel daft, wearing that mild, non-judgmental expression when he clearly thought she was deranged. Not to mention one of these diet-fixated women. The kind who think emaciation and emancipation are interchangeable.

'I'll have to run back for them, I can't litter the beach,' snapped Venus.

'I'll wait if you like,' offered Conor.

'No, I might be some time. One sand-dune looks a lot like another.'

'Unless there's a set of weighing scales beside it.' Conor's gaze was serious, but Venus could swear humour lurked behind it. At her expense. He had a nerve, the blow-in who had the emergency services out scouring the place for him because he wanted to see what the back of a mountain looked like.

'I have to go.' She turned on her heel and struck out towards the dune where she'd sheltered from the wind, feeling plagued by the John Ógs and Conors of this world.

* * *

Venus took the well-trodden path looping around to the back door and luxuriated in the blast of hot air as she opened the door straight onto the kitchen. Dan Macken laid aside his paper. Already he'd forgiven her the anti-Church explosion. He didn't bear grudges and besides, he'd started a novena to propel her back into the fold. Dan's faith in the power of prayer promised him his daughter's atheist days were numbered.

'Enjoy your walk, lass?'

'Bracing,' Venus lied. Back in the warmth, her nose started to stream and she rooted in her pocket for a tissue. Her father reached her one of his hankies – he was the only person she knew who still used linen handkerchiefs. In the winter he dipped them in Vicks for his sinuses. She sniffed: no Vicks yet – it mustn't count as winter, although the chill in her bones from the beach walk told a different story.

She sat back, waiting for the creeping warmth from the range to work its restoration, cradling the mug of tea her father had reached her. She didn't want to drink it, but there was comfort in its presence.

'Aye, well, there's news,' said Dan. 'Your furniture arrived in a van from London while you were out.'

It hadn't been due for a week; Venus perked up. 'Where is it?'

'I had them unload it all into the shed outside, apart from that lapdog thing you're always going on about. That's over there on the table.'

Venus noticed her laptop and stood to stroke its plastic surface, welcoming an old friend. She'd be able to send emails now. And she could access the Internet from home instead of going into town. She raced outside and peered into the shed, where her boxes of books, videos and china were stacked. A couple of plants, towering expanses of foliage in the Barbican, seemed to have shrunk. The rubber plant in particular only had five or six leaves instead of three times the amount.

She stomped back indoors. 'What happened my plants?'

'The lad driving the van said they hadn't thrived in his warehouse. He gave them the odd saucer of water, but it didn't make much difference. They've been having a bit of a heat wave in London-town, did you not see it on the news?'

Venus, who was shivering after charging outside without a coat, felt doubly aggrieved.

Still, at least she had her own belongings now. She could move some of the books and ornaments upstairs to her bedroom, maybe even cover that sprigged wallpaper with a couple of layers of cream paint. And she'd hook up the video recorder there so she could watch her favourite films under the duvet.

She went back outside again and rooted around in a box until she found *The Sound of Music*, with its cover of Julie Andrews skipping along and swinging a hefty carpetbag as though it weighed nothing. Venus sat down by the range to warm herself, nursing the video.

'What are you doing with a new set of weighing scales?' asked Dan, who had used her absence to peek inside Venus's plastic bag. 'Are you thinking of taking up baking?' His eyes shone – he missed Maura's soda bread.

'Present from an admirer.' Venus was still grieving over her plants. She'd give them some tomato feed and see if that didn't rouse them. Although from the looks of these fellows, it was Lazarus feed they needed.

'Who's your admirer?'

'John Óg O'Dea.' Venus remained distracted, wondering if the china she'd packed was in one piece but afraid to check. Surely she hadn't committed her life's possessions to a couple of cowboys?

'I wouldn't have thought he was your type at all. Granted, he's not short of the readies. I'd say when we converted to euro John Óg had cash stashed under every floorboard in the house to change.' Dan chuckled. 'His mother's people are a rare bunch. They're from down about Mohill way. I'm not calling them crooks, but they'd have the eyes from a corpse's head and go back for the eyelashes. Mind you, John Óg's father is a civil soul – I can't say a word against John senior.'

Venus, who had been paying attention to none of this, dragged her hands through her heavy coils of hair and felt swamped by a need for definition. In the last couple of days she'd worked out her mother's identity, only to have that certainty snatched away. It could be anybody. She could live anywhere. She might never find her mother.

She looked at her father, rocking with laughter as he trotted out some ancient grudge story about a family in the area for two generations instead of twenty like any self-respecting Roancarrick native, and channelled all her pent-up frustration and misery into a plea.

'Tell me about myself, Dad,' she begged. 'Tell me who I am.'

His mouth opened slackly and he looked at her in a way she couldn't quite fathom. There was a rustle as he folded up the *Donegal Democrat* and laid his calloused hands on his knees.

'All right so,' he said. 'I'll neither add nor subtract, lass. I'll tell you everything I know.'

Chapter Eighteen

'It was Maura who named you Venus.' Dan cleared his throat and warmed to his story. 'She'd lived in Dublin, like yourself, when she was training for the nursing. But she came back to Donegal in the heel of the hunt.' He nodded his approval. 'She saw some sights in her time, but she said there was no sight to gladden the heart like the coastline around Roancarrick. We were engaged before she went off to Dublin, to Holles Street Hospital – it has another name on it now, but that's what we always called it. I knew her all her life, your mother. I was five years older than her and I remember her as a little girl. She had an older brother I used to knock about with – your Uncle Liam. He joined the British Army because he didn't think he'd see much of the world with the Irish Army. He was always mad for the road, Liam. He only made it as far as France. He's buried in Normandy. Maura and I used to talk about going there and finding his grave, but we never did.' Dan's leg troubled him, and he massaged it above the knee. 'I remember the day

Liam came to school and told me he had a new sister. He was disgusted, for he wanted a brother. It was never mentioned in those days, but I think Maura's mother lost babies nearly every year. Only Liam, your Aunt Betty that's godmother to you, and Maura survived.'

Unobtrusively, Venus brought him a cup of milk to the table, hearing his voice begin to croak. Then she sat opposite him, elbows on the table. Dan paused to drain the cup – he didn't like the way milk tasted from a glass – and nodded his thanks.

'I always had an eye for Maura,' he admitted. 'I never saw such a sweet-faced lass and none of the other girls in the village could hold a candle to her. She had a grave, steady way about her and a man knew instinctively he could trust her with his life. I started courting her as soon as she turned fifteen. The things she would turn round and say to you – I never knew where she came by them. Once I brought her a length of timber with Greek lettering on it that had washed up on the shore, all the way from Cyprus it was, and she told me Cyprus was the birthplace of Venus. "The world is a never-ending cross-reference, Daniel," Maura said. She kept that strip of wood until it rotted into the ground.'

His eyes shone as they came to rest on Venus's face and she thought how, if circumstances were different, he might tell her at this point that she had her mother's upturned mouth. But she was adopted and he could never offer her these comforts – nor could her physical presence return them to him.

'I sometimes wondered if the village might be too claustrophobic for Maura afterwards,' mused Dan. 'After the nursing training was finished. I feared I might not be educated enough to hold her attention. How could I compete with all those clever folk she'd have met below in Dublin? But she came back to me, just as she promised, and we were married as soon as she qualified. She used to say, "I'm where my heart wants to be, Daniel, and the heart has reasons reason knows not of." Isn't that a fine thing? Then she'd lay her hand on top of mine. No-one but Maura and my own mother ever called me Daniel.'

He lifted one hand off his knee and stretched it across to the other to pat it, unconsciously mimicking his wife's gesture.

'This old leg would never have had a chance to get so crocked if Maura had been around. She'd have made me go for an X-ray and it would have been sorted in jig-speed time. But we didn't see much of each other while she trained. The matron was strict and people didn't travel as much as they do now. Dublin seemed light years away from Roancarrick.'

It still does, thought Venus.

Dan smiled at his daughter, saying her name. It was odd to hear it on his lips, for she was always lass to him.

'Venus . . . your mother told me about a painting she'd seen in a book, Venus. It was by an Italian man – he was long dead by then, but the picture stayed with her. It showed a Roman goddess with hair that reached beneath her knees, being carried ashore on a scallop shell because she was born from the foam, or so they said. A silly piece of nonsense, but Maura had a fondness for it. The girl's name was Venus, she told me, and so should yours be. An uncommon enough name, but it grew on me.' He chuckled, a rasping sound akin to a cough that had Venus jumping to her feet to refill his glass of milk. 'Father McGinley didn't like it one bit. He said it was a heathen handle to attach to a Christian child, but Maura stood her ground. So that's what you were

196

baptised below there in Our Lady of the Assumption. Venus Mary Macken. Our lucky star.'

Venus had heard the story before, but it contented her, for a while. It lent her an identity of sorts.

Then she remembered the sky-writing and Birdie's refusal to tell what she knew of her origins. 'But where do I come from, Dad? I didn't spring from the waves like that other Venus.'

He seemed not to hear, lost in contemplation of the pock-marked wooden table where Venus was seated. Maura's father had made it as a wedding present for the couple. It felt warm to the touch, almost animate, and Maura had done everything there: chopped vegetables, written letters, washed their sons and later Venus in a tin bath Dan used to carry in from under the stairs. He'd never wanted his wife to lift weights, sturdy though she was; it had struck him as inappropriate. Sometimes when he looked towards the kitchen table he fancied Maura's form was bent over it still, rolling out dough.

But his vision cleared and it was Venus he saw there now – the impatient, clever daughter Maura had loved from the day he'd carried her into their home. Loved with a ferocity that had alarmed him. He'd been afraid they wouldn't be allowed to keep this infant and her sorrow would implode and swallow her whole.

He hadn't wanted his wife to experience loss again, not after the death of their sons. But Maura had shown herself inflexible about Venus. 'She's ours,' she'd insisted. 'There's no-one can take her from us.' And Birdie had backed her to the hilt. Birdie had told them if they gave they'd receive – she was forever spouting that class of nonsense. Maura had always humoured her, and in the early days he'd gone along with it for her sake. Now he was accustomed to Birdie's semi-heathen ways. Her heart's in the right place, he'd remind himself, whenever she trotted out some of her superstition dressed up as wisdom.

Venus leaned his blackthorn stick against a table-leg in case he needed it and watched her father move about the kitchen, exercising the pins and needles in his injured leg.

'The size of you, lass, even as a baby,' Dan marvelled. 'You were walking at nine months, talking at sixteen. Maura and I never knew a child to grow so quickly. You'd outstripped me by your mid-teens and your mother long before that. You're a sapling, Venus, with your height grazing the clouds and your hair the colour of autumn leaves.'

'You make me sound like a princess under an evil enchantress's spell, the heroine who couldn't stop growing,' she laughed.

They formed an unlikely pair, for she was all Renaissance curves and he exuded scrawny desiccation.

'I sound like a vaguely ominous fairytale figure,' added Venus, 'a walking, talking copper beech. When I'd really prefer to be Snow White.'

'Not a bit of it, you wouldn't. You didn't even like the film when Maura and I brought you to see it for your sixth birthday. "Too thoppy, Daddy," you lisped.'

Venus smiled. 'I think even at that age I realised marriage to the prince was probably more of a living death than the glass-casket fate. I don't see how it can be called a rescue when as soon as he wakens her he takes her away from her home and her seven best friends and dumps her in another palace. And we all know what a nasty time she had in the last one. That fairytale never struck me as plausible – it simply wasn't far-fetched enough.' She shot a meaningful glance at her father. 'Only the truth should be improbable. Like my story.'

This was his cue to tell her the frayed but perennially beguiling tale of how Maura and Dan Macken had come to adopt a red-haired baby girl almost thirty-three years ago. Perhaps in the repetition she'd seize on some clue about her identity. Or maybe the story would career off its grooves and take her somewhere new. However, Dan had wearied of the *seanchaí* role, and those reminiscences of his dead wife grieved him, for his loss remained thin-scabbed.

'I'm spent, Venus. I think maybe I'll go above to the bedroom and rest my eyes for an hour before tea-time. It'll give you peace and quiet to prepare your lesson for the technical college tomorrow night. You'll be wanting to make a good impression on your first day.' He frowned, red-rimmed eyes almost disappearing into wrinkled folds. 'I don't know who this Benedict Archer character is that's got the principal's job there. We never had any Archers about these parts.'

'Maybe they gave the post to an outsider, Dad. Someone from beyond the county border – Leitrim, say, or Monaghan,' Venus teased.

'Could be so.' Dan eased himself with tentative movements towards the hallway, leaning on furniture for support, forgetting already that his daughter had laid by his blackthorn stick for him. 'Sure there's shenanigans of all sorts going on these days – Mickey Joe tells me a Listowel man is taking over the big doctors' surgery in Bundoran.'

Venus's lips twitched; Ireland operated on a parochial level and people made no apologies for it.

Alone in the kitchen, she opened her green Oxford University Press oral Spanish textbook. She should be marking out useful phrases. I have missed my train. *He perdido el tren.* How long until the next train? *¿Cuanto falta para el proximo tren?* Instead she fretted about her father going to bed in the afternoon – it was unprecedented. But the way he had shuffled from chair to table, as though willpower alone propelled him along, was even more disturbing.

She hated it when he became an old man. Telling stories, he was ageless.

A kernel of trepidation tapped against her chest cavity.

She needed to do something to distract herself. It felt vaguely disloyal to Dan, but Venus opened her bag and took out the number for Donegal (South) Health Board she'd copied down earlier and rang, asking to speak to the department handling adoptions. Maybe the officials who'd dealt with the adoption would tell her more than her parents about the circumstances. Some detail which had seemed unimportant to Dan and Maura, but which might make all the difference in her search. It was even possible they'd discovered her mother's identity – but had never told her for some reason. Perhaps to protect her. Even if the staff members who'd dealt with her case were retired by now, they must have left notes and files.

A woman who elided her r's could find no record of Venus's case. But she didn't seem unduly surprised, for she told Venus that many adoptions had been handled by orphanages run by nuns years ago, and documentation varied from one religious order to another. They might have kept it, then again they might not.

'But I know the health board handled the adoption, not nuns,' protested Venus. 'I may not know much about who I am or where I come from, but that much I'm certain of – my parents told me. Please check again.'

The woman left her dangling for what seemed an age, but when she returned she was conciliatory. 'Forgive me, there is file on you, Miss Macken. You were formally adopted in 1970 by Daniel and Maura Macken, of Roancarrick, Co Donegal. My goodness, the way they came upon you was unusual, to say the least –'

'Does it give my mother's name on the file?' Venus interrupted.

'You have a legal right to your mother's identity, if it's known, although not your father's.' The woman scanned the lines of type. 'Of course, I can't just give it to you over the phone, you'll have to make an appointment – oh, I'm sorry, it says *mother unknown.*'

Venus sighed. A dead end. So her parents hadn't been hiding her birth mother's identity, they really hadn't known.

However, she learned that an Adoption Board had been set up in Dublin and it might give her a lead. It was only an outside chance, but the board might have some additional nugget it could pass on to her. For all she knew, her mother might have repented of losing her and left a message for Venus through the board. *'Red-haired baby girl abandoned in Roancarrick on October 31, 1969. Mother urgently wishes to make contact.'* She was probably clutching at straws, but it had to be worth a try.

Venus confided in the woman who couldn't pronounce her r's that she should have made efforts to trace her birth mother years ago.

'You mightn't have had much success, I'm afraid,' came the reply. 'We only introduced rights about being entitled to the mother's name in 1999 – we're years behind the North and Britain. And they're years behind Scotland, which gave adopted people the right to their original birth certificate as far back as 1930.'

Nevertheless Venus felt she'd made some progress. She had an address for the Adoption Board and could write to it. It was a long shot that anything would come of it, but if she didn't ask she'd never find out. She opened her Spanish textbook to prepare her class but couldn't settle: her father was causing her anxiety. There was nothing obviously wrong with him, other than old age.

'It's not just the leg that's crocked, the whole body's falling to pieces as well,' he'd quipped only the other morning. 'I'm getting on in life, lass, no two ways about it.'

She'd deposited a kiss on the crown of his head, laughing, 'I grow old, I grow old, I shall wear the bottoms of my trousers rolled,' not taking him seriously.

Now, however, Venus went out to the car and unlooped the seahorse totem from the rear-view mirror. Indoors, she traced her fingers across the glass outline, then clutched it in the palm of her hand so that the corners bit into flesh. Spring seemed so far away, and winter was a burden for the elderly. Especially on an eighty-year-old man who missed his wife and maybe – she swallowed – maybe didn't feel he had enough left to live for.

The apprehension that had troubled Venus before making her phone call fluttered again.

Chapter Nineteen

Benedict Archer was all but clucking as he led Venus into the classroom. 'You're on your own after tonight, but I thought it best to introduce you and sit in for the first while. We have twelve students enrolled for Spanish For Beginners, but there's usually a tailing off after the first week or two. Good intentions and all that – sure you know yourself.' His minestrone eyes were jaded. 'Ideally it would have been better if you'd taken the class from week one, but ideal circumstances rarely prevail.'

'How are your secretary's Fallopian tubes?' She was breezy, determined to head off an incipient anxiety attack.

He blinked. 'Getting back to normal, thanks. At least I think they are. Can Fallopian tubes ever do that? Anyway she's due back to work the week after next.' Fervour glazed Benedict Archer's features. 'And I thank God for it, Venice.'

'Venus,' she corrected him gently.

'That's right, Venice,' he agreed.

All except three of the students were women. Benedict called out '*Buenas tardes*' as he entered the room and they chorused '*Hola*' back at him. Venus wasn't enamoured of his plan to sit in on her lesson – she felt it implied he might not have full confidence in her abilities – but curbed her resentment.

She began by asking the students why they wanted to learn Spanish and answers ranged from business opportunities to the cliché about broadening the mind.

'Very worthy,' said Venus. 'I first experienced a passion to learn the language when I fell in love with a Spaniard who came to my village on a surfing holiday. I can't have been more than fifteen and he hardly knew I existed.'

A couple of the younger women nudged one another and erupted into giggles.

'Our boyfriends are Spaniards,' explained the blonde one, who was about twenty-five and worked alongside the other girl in a solicitor's office. 'The lads have a restaurant business in town. They'd work every hour God sends if we weren't around to distract them. They speak good English, but we want to beat them at their own game. We'd like to know what they're saying when they launch into that wild babble we can't make head or tail of – forewarned is forearmed.'

The confession lightened the atmosphere and it emerged that half of the students had Spanish boyfriends or girlfriends. Venus smiled to herself: Spain was doing a fine job of spreading its language and culture by sending out a crack troop of its most attractive specimens. Missionaries with a secular motive. She saw Benedict Archer pursing his mouth at the back and ignored him. They were her pupils, not his. And they were grown-ups, here by consent on a wet

September night after a day's work. They couldn't be treated like schoolchildren.

She produced her emerald-green *!Bravo! Spanish for the Oral Exam* and opened it at the page where she'd used an envelope as a marker. 'Here's a useful phrase for when you're conversing in Spanish. The trouble with speaking a foreign language is that native speakers go too fast, so never be afraid to ask them to slow down and repeat what they've just said. Here we go. *Por favor* – everyone knows that, it's please – *por favor repetirme*. Could you repeat it please. And let's do exactly that. All together now: *Por favor repetirme*.'

Midway through the class Venus noticed Benedict Archer had pulled the parachute string. She supposed his absence must be a vote of confidence, despite the foreboding in his soupy eyes as she'd begun the class.

Towards the end of the lesson she told her students they'd be doing some role-playing next week, which meant learning the relevant vocabulary for conversation.

'We'll make it birthdays,' she said. 'So useful words to learn might include *felicidades*, happy birthday, *la sorpresa*, surprise, *celebrar*, to celebrate. As well as eating *una tarta*, a cake, young people in Spain can expect to have their ears pulled on their birthday – one tug for each year.'

Venus felt an adrenaline rush at the end of the class. It had been years since she'd taught Spanish, although she'd kept her language skills honed with regular visits to the country, and she often took Spaniards for their English classes at the Bridges Across The World language school. Wall-to-wall designer gear facing her from the desks: she always felt under-dressed. And they said the French were style-conscious.

Tonight had gone well. Her students wanted to learn –

and they seemed a lively bunch. The blonde girl, the first to admit she was learning Spanish for the sake of her Antonio, had recommended his restaurant. 'Tortillas like his *madre* makes,' she said. 'You should call in and taste them. Tell him I sent you and there'll be a glass of *vino* on the house.'

* * *

Her father was leaning with his hands on a chair and his back to the open oven door of the range, toasting his bottom, as she walked into the kitchen. He closed up the oven with a clatter and sat down when he saw her, guilty as a child with his hand in the biscuit tin. Venus affected not to see; she couldn't care less if he crawled into the oven, but the community nurse who'd visited during her mother's illness had been forever warning him against it. He'd wind up with piles, she used to say, hands on her hips.

'How was the class?' He pretended she hadn't spotted him at the range.

'It went well. It was the beginners tonight, a dozen students. I have the intermediate crowd on Thursday – we're supposed to be looking at *Chronicle Of A Death Foretold* in Spanish. I thought it would be easier than *Love In The Time Of Cholera*. That's easier as in shorter. I'll have to flick through my notes tomorrow, stay ahead of the posse.'

'That's the place to be. Now, take the weight off your feet, lass, I'll put the kettle on.'

Venus and Dan sat on either side of the range, licking marmalade from their fingers from the toast he'd made, and batting conversation back and forth. Inconsequential exchanges of information about the people Dan had bumped into on his walk to the village and how his friend

Mickey Joe had won money on the Leopardstown races but lost it on the Shelbourne dogs. In return Venus described her students, telling him about the girls with boyfriends running a Spanish restaurant, and gaped to learn her father knew the difference between a *tortilla* and a *burrito*. Although he'd no desire to taste either.

'They chop potatoes through one and wrap up their food in the other,' he said, with the authority of one who watched travel programmes.

Venus realised she was slipping into her mother's shoes, in this new role as companion to her father. They felt comfortable on her feet.

'Will we say the rosary?' He rattled his beads in his trouser pocket.

'I'll say my own in bed,' she lied, to avoid an altercation.

'The family that prays together stays together.'

He repeated the mantra she remembered from childhood. All her life she recalled him saying it as he reached beads to her mother and herself; visitors, too, if they should be staying overnight.

Dan looked at her, thinking of his novena which should surely be making some impact on the lass by now, but didn't press her. Instead he popped out his teeth and slipped them into a beaker reserved for them on the windowsill. Without his dentures he had only three or four teeth. 'It's bedtime for me, so.' His voice lisped without its full complement of teeth. Self-conscious, even after years upon years of wearing dentures, he touched his nose with his hand to hide his mouth.

He felt his way along the table towards the door leading to the staircase. 'Birdie called, looking for you.' He paused in the doorway, holding onto the handle for support. 'You wouldn't have been long gone, maybe three-quarters of an hour at most.'

Venus, who'd been debating sending an email to Lily in Dublin and another to Tamsin in London, now that she had her laptop computer, hesitated. Maybe Birdie had something to tell her after all, some clue which might help in her search.

'Is it too late for me to drop by her house, Dad?'

'She keeps strange hours. I'd say she's still up.' Dan scrolled the brown wooden beads, worn from a lifetime of handling, through his fingers. 'But she told me to give you a message, that was all. You're to remember your birthday is due in a matter of weeks. And if you make a wish with a hopeful heart on your birthday, it will be looked upon kindly. Desperate drivel that woman spouts.' He gathered the beads in the palm of his hand. 'Mind you, she bakes a fine cake – she left in a madeira.'

Make a wish with a hopeful heart on your birthday. Her father was right, it was desperate drivel. Still, it had to be worth a try.

Chapter Twenty

'Venus,' cried Dan, as she came through the back door, 'you have a visitor. A good friend of yours has come all the way from Dublin-town to see you.'

It had to be Lily, here to surprise her. Her smile blossomed: Lily must realise Venus felt isolated in Roancarrick.

'We've been having a drop of tea and a grand chat, haven't we, Senan?' Her father chattered, not noticing Venus's expression slide towards dismay.

Senan Mulqueen, who'd been tucked in the corner on the tweed sofa out of her line of vision, stood up.

'I'm working in this area for a few days. Sorry I didn't phone in advance, Venus.' He skimmed her cheek with his lips, exuding savoir-faire as only a twenty-year-old can who's convinced he's going places.

Kissing her – he scarcely knew her. Venus folded her arms and sulked.

'Lily gave me your address – she told me I should just drop in unannounced,' he continued.

'Good for Lily.'

'She's a champion,' agreed Senan. 'Was that exceptionally fine granite pier I noticed driving through the village a famine-relief project, Mr Macken?'

'Indeed it was.' Dan settled down, all but rubbing his hands in glee, to describe how the men who built the pier were paid in the Queen's soup. It was either hew rock or starve, and some did both.

Venus realised how much he relished an audience, as he listed all his relatives on his mother's side who'd helped break stones for the pier. Wait until he discovered Senan had sold her the Volkswagen, he'd be in his element quizzing him on the car's history. She supposed she should be gracious and treat Senan's visit as occupational therapy for her father. She'd wanted to prepare a Spanish lesson but there was no urgency – she could do it later.

Presently Senan, who'd listened with admirable patience to Dan's stories, admitted he hadn't come to Roancarrick only to visit Venus. Which was more annoying again than confessing he'd come to the village specifically to see her. He was investigating seafront properties in an advisory capacity for a client and had been directed to a man in Ballyshannon, who owned a number of them in Roancarrick. Apparently some of the leases were due for renewal and the owner couldn't decide whether to renew or sell. The properties had been in his family for generations, but business was business.

Venus remembered Kathleen Magee from Seascape mentioning that her lease was about to expire, when she'd dropped in for a coffee the other morning. Kathleen hadn't seemed bothered by it and certainly hadn't mentioned anything about a developer – which was what Senan's client had to be. Kathleen definitely wouldn't want the business she had taken pains to build up torn down and replaced by, well, what exactly?

'What sort of development does your client have in mind?' asked Venus.

'A luxury hotel. One of those get-away-from-it-all jobs.' Senan waved his arms about as he outlined his vision, trademark aura of urgency intensifying. 'The views are sensational and that strand is one of the finest in Ireland. The party we're negotiating with owns the entire seafront strip, bar a grimy little pub at one end and some kind of huckster's shop at the other. But we'd make them an offer they couldn't refuse. We'd have to knock everything down and start again – the architecture isn't worth preserving. I'm being a tiny bit indiscreet talking to you about this, but I thought you could give me a few pointers about the people we may have to buy out. Knowledge is power in business.'

Senan had been heavy-handed with the hair gel that morning and Venus flirted with the idea of leaning forward and snapping off a spike or two. Instead she snorted, 'What about the locals? You'd be taking away their only shop.'

'I expect there'll be a shop in the hotel.' Senan seemed to sense his fringe was under threat and touched it nervously.

'Not one selling tins of beans and loaves of sliced pan. And I can't see my father enjoying his pint of Guinness in a plastic hotel bar when he's supped all his life in Nora Brennan's. Which may not be one of your smart city establishments, but which certainly isn't a grimy little pub.'

At this, Dan Macken regarded Senan as though he'd invited a viper into his home. Speechless with indignation as Senan had outlined his brave new world, he was galvanised now. 'Nora Brennan would never sell her pub and Mrs O'Dea will have to be carried out of that shop feet first,' he insisted. But a worm of doubt was already working its tiny maws. The O'Deas had a regard for money that was legendary. And Nora might decide to remove temptation from Timmy Brennan's sight and sell up before he supped away his inheritance.

Meanwhile Senan was genuinely surprised to meet opposition. This was a wonderful scheme. How could anyone object to it? 'Think how it would benefit Roancarrick – remember all the employment it would bring to the area,' he urged. 'Half the main street seems to trade only in the summer – that couldn't put jam on the table for long. Your young people have to go away to the cities to work. You had to leave yourself, Venus.'

Venus twined a coil of red hair around her forefinger, immersed in thought. He was right that Roancarrick would profit from a hotel. In some ways. But what he was proposing would change the village irrevocably. Everything from its appearance to the calibre of visitor it attracted would be altered. Roancarrick was secluded, that was an integral part of its charm, whereas large hotels meant traffic and bustle.

There was a human cost here, too. What of Kathleen Magee and the other lease-holders? At least Mrs O'Dea and Nora Brennan could accept or refuse this offer, but Kathleen had no such luxury.

Realisation flooded through Venus: she cared about what happened to Roancarrick.

* * *

After her first surge of interest, when Dan had passed on Birdie's message about wishing with a hopeful heart, Venus had hesitated. It was all such mumbo-jumbo. Imagine what her London friends would think if they heard about her making birthday wishes on the stroke of midnight on a deserted beach. They'd tell her to stick to a tried and trusted tradition, blowing out the candles on her cake.

But on the night before her birthday, as Venus sat watching a cowboy film with Dan – westerns were the only films he could tolerate – she suddenly decided to give it a whirl. She had nothing to lose. She needed to try something, for she was getting nowhere sleuthing among the old folk in the village. Either the entire village was complicit in the plot to keep Venus in ignorance, or else people in Roancarrick genuinely didn't know who her mother was. She'd just have to wait for a reply to her letter to the Adoption Board: Venus was watching out for it on a daily basis, remote though the chances were that it might provide the answers she craved.

She pulled on her winter white cashmere coat, so sophisticated in London, so inappropriate in Roancarrick, and prepared to walk to the beach.

'Are you going out at this hour?' her father looked up from an Indian massacre, slack-jawed.

'I need to stretch my legs.'

'Aye, young people have energy that needs burning off. Watch your step near the cliffs, lass.'

Passing Nora Brennan's, she heard the hub of voices which signalled a lock-in. Licensing hours were at the discretion of the landlady in Roancarrick and Nora obviously had the inclination for a late night tonight. It was the last Friday in the month, and customers' bank accounts would have that temporary bulge which always swayed her.

She had a head for business, Nora Brennan. All the

women in the family did. And the more efficient the women were, the more ineffectual their men became. Timmy Brennan was a case in point, drinking his mother's profits the instant her back was turned and handing out free drink to his friends to act the big fellow.

She was passing the harbour now, where hardly any boats hovered, although the season didn't end officially until after the October bank-holiday. It hadn't been a vintage year for business. Kathleen Magee had been despondent as she'd taken a break from cleaning Seascape's windows the other day. The flighty summer weather had affected the number of day-trippers, while the families renting out the holiday homes in Jim Kearney's meadow had tended to cater for themselves or drive into the towns abutting Roancarrick. They drew in people with their Indian restaurants and pizza parlours – there was even a new Spanish restaurant that had received a glowing review in the local paper, she'd reported.

Kathleen was still opening from 10 a.m. with breakfasts and morning coffees, working into the wee small hours when there were dinner customers, in the hopes of making enough to tide her through the winter. But it would be tight this year.

Venus felt a needle of guilt: little did Kathleen know what Senan's developer had in mind for the business to which she was devoted. Bulldozers and wrecking-balls. There was nothing she could do, Venus told her unquiet conscience. She'd convinced her father it was all fancy talk, to set his mind at rest, but she suspected Roancarrick was ripe for the plucking. Venus sighed. All right, maybe she'd email Lily and check what Senan Mulqueen was up to – in the meantime, she had her a project of her own under way.

The pinprick of light from her torch skirted the beach,

hovering above remnants strewn along the high-tide mark. She crunched sand underfoot, rummaging for a flawless shell. What she wanted had to balance sweetly in her hand – just large enough and no larger to cup a copper coin. That was for luck. A lucky repository within a lucky repository. She picked her steps along the shoreline, stooping to consider and discard in arch moonlight that showed itself one minute and retreated behind tendrils of cloud the next. She intended to make her wish on the stroke of midnight, her porthole into hope fulfilment – straddling the cusp of one year and the next. After midnight came tomorrow and tomorrow brought her birthday.

That is, the day she celebrated as her birthday.

Her hands were becoming too cold to grip the torch. Then her eye fell on a shell with a distinctive tortoiseshell pattern, like Jude's. An omen. It was as though Birdie were helping her endeavour. She lifted the shell's calcified body to her ear, where it whispered of waves, then she blew sand from its grooves, dropped in an old penny and balanced them on her palm. A perfect fit.

She walked through loose sand, hit a straggle of seaweed and finally reached wet sand, for the tide was well out. She walked right to the water's edge, as close as she dared before the waves would rustle up to nuzzle her toes, and strained her eyes towards the horizon. She could just distinguish the lighthouse flashing twice before turning 180 degrees, and she watched for its rotation.

It was time now. Her fingers closed over the shell, heavy with the weight of the coin. She bounced it once in her palm and then inhaled deeply: make a wish with a hopeful heart. Hope was left clinging to the base of Pandora's box when she released everything else that was discordant and mischievous into the ether. Hope, the gods' gift to mankind. Venus was seeking a gift of her own.

She willed a sense of optimism to well up inside her before firing her missive into the Atlantic. Trying to forget that someone had once described hope as a feeling you have that the feeling you have isn't permanent.

'Show me who I belong to.'

She was unsure if she'd said the words aloud, but they rang in her head as she listened for the shell to strike water. Venus glanced upwards at the moon, watching serenely but not indifferently, she fancied. Then she turned homewards, away from the raw silk shimmer of the sea. She half-expected to feel ridiculous, but instead there was a tumescent sense of promise.

She'd made her wish with a hopeful heart. Now let's see what it brought her.

Chapter Twenty-one

Venus picked up her stride, keen to be toasting herself by the kitchen range. She thought of Conor Landers, whom she hadn't seen in weeks – nobody knew where he'd gone. The family still visited at weekends, but there was no sign of him. Venus felt a ruffle of loss; there was nobody else in the village to compare her to a Venetian painting.

Their last encounter had been on the strand, when she'd catapulted back to the sand-dune to retrieve John Óg O'Dea's weighing scales. She should have left them there. Conor had probably dismissed her as neurotic and was avoiding her.

Meanwhile Venus was seeing more of John Óg O'Dea than she'd have chosen – the man seemed to dog her footsteps. If she didn't know better she'd suspect he'd moved back in with the Mammy and was watching for her from the window of his old bedroom facing the beach. Furthermore, he seemed to regard these walks, when he accompanied her without so much as a by your leave, as dates. She'd have to take that situation in hand.

Venus ruminated on her latest email from Lily as she walked. She must be picking up snippets of Russian from Karim still: she'd signed off with *dosvidaniya* and put goodbye in brackets afterwards. Which showed the crush on Karim remained constant. Venus tutted to herself.

Birdie was loitering by the crossroads as Venus approached home. She loomed from the darkness, in so far as such a petite woman was capable of looming, and caught Venus loosely by the wrist.

'I saw you go out. I had a notion you'd not be away long. Will you step inside for a minute? I have a birthday gift for you.' Her voice was the mock-sensual timbre of a chain smoker, yet Birdie was so health-conscious she wouldn't touch caffeine let alone nicotine.

Venus fell into step beside the older woman, shortening her pace to avoid outstripping her companion – the rainbow-striped wellies Birdie invariably wore didn't make for quick progress. Birdie had worn rainbow wellies as far back as Venus could recall, all year long except for the summer months. And even then there were turbulent days when she'd root them out.

They walked in congenial silence. Anyone else would have queried her movements, abroad so late, but Birdie had a capacity for accepting others' vagaries.

Inside the cottage flickered bank upon bank of candles. Candles in sconces, in minute earthenware pots, in wooden and metal candlesticks and in the necks of wine bottles. A pair of votive lights were positioned to send reflected gleams from her elliptical fish-eye mirror, fashioned from a coiling silver serpent. Suspended on the chimney breast, it was too high to be used for preening, but sometimes the sea scintillated across it. Venus looked towards the mirror, attracted by the flickering candlelight it reflected.

'Snakes signify wisdom,' said Birdie. 'Perhaps that's why we fear them.'

Venus swallowed, more fearful of Birdie's habit of leaving candles burning everywhere – she foresaw a wall of flame and her neighbour trapped behind it, unable to reach the door. Even if Birdie weren't mutilated or killed she could find herself homeless.

Venus knew better than to protest, however: she remembered her mother recounting how she'd remonstrated with Birdie about leaving candles burning. Birdie had responded with an astringency that Maura had found difficult to stomach and she'd complained to Venus. 'That one's a law unto herself,' Venus had responded. 'You either take her or leave her, but there's no changing her.'

The association between Venus and Birdie was being subtly remoulded. For all of Venus's life, Birdie had been her mother's friend and she had viewed the older woman as a kindly-disposed neighbour – interesting but eccentric. Birdie had not been one of those adults who fobbed children off, no matter how long their inventory of whys. Questions had always received answers, even if sometimes Venus couldn't fathom them. Now, with a lacquer of maturity coating her, a different rapport was building in incremental stages between them. Nearly a friendship, she fancied, despite some two decades' disparity in their ages.

Venus inhaled the harvest scent of Birdie's room and looked towards the CD player, where Django Reinhardt was playing. She was becoming familiar with Birdie's habits and knew she started the day by delving into the Internet and finished it by listening to jazz.

She crossed to the hearth, but Jude was no longer snoozing there. 'Hibernation?'

Birdie nodded as she rummaged in a press, producing a bottle of saffron liquid and two tiny crystal glasses with midnight-blue stems.

'To you, on your birthday, my dear.' She handed Venus a brimming liqueur glass.

'It's kind of you to remember.' The endearment was rare from Birdie and it warmed Venus as much as the honeyed drink which trickled down her throat.

Birdie squinted at her, eyes little more than slits under a surfeit of skin between brow and orb. 'How could I not remember? I arrived to see your mother just after Dan landed in with you. And on that day above all days. It was . . .' she reflected, 'an augury.'

Venus touched her lips to the glass again and sank into one of the weathered Chesterfield wing-backed armchairs ranged either side of the fireplace. Perhaps Birdie was in an expansive mood and might shed some light on the puzzle of her arrival in Roancarrick. 'Did nobody ever own to me?' she asked.

'Nobody,' confirmed Birdie.

'A changeling, so.'

Birdie did not contradict her and rancour pulsed through Venus. Birdie sensed it but made no comment as she placed a plate of shoe-shaped sugar cookies on the arm of Venus's chair. Birdie only laboured over the square heels and pointed toes of these distinctive biscuits to mark exceptional occasions.

She watched her guest nibble and waited for the hostility to subside; Birdie knew that nobody could eat these cookies and harbour a grudge for long – shoes were lucky. Additionally, she'd made them with cochineal to turn the dough a blush colour.

'I baked you ruby slippers,' she told Venus, who paused and regarded her biscuit with renewed interest.

'Click the heels together three times and you'll always find your way home,' murmured Venus, the resentment draining from her. She finished the cookie and reached for another. 'Wherever home is,' she added, with a final sting before her annoyance ebbed.

'Homes are invented.' Birdie tutored a bright but wayward pupil.

Venus frowned, eyelids hooding her golden-brown eyes.

'I invented this home, after all.' Birdie unclasped her thin hands and flung her arms outward to indicate the cottage. Or perhaps the entire village. 'I imagined it and made it real and yet it's no less my home.'

Venus inclined her head cautiously, boomeranged back to childhood when she'd struggled to decipher Birdie's cryptic utterances. Was she telling her that she came from Roancarrick? Or that it didn't matter where she came from, it was where she was now that counted? Perhaps she could invent her own reality. Venus shook her head; too many thoughts were ricocheting, tripping her up.

Birdie filled her glass again and Venus sipped, mellowed by the fortified wine. Logs crackled on the fire and she let her glance float across to the owl, whose inscrutable eyes were fixed on her. She could sit anywhere in this room and that wooden owl would be watching her. Sacred Heart pictures didn't have a monopoly on staring.

But there was someone else scrutinising her too. The pupils of Birdie's eyes glittered in the firelight and Venus felt filleted by their gaze. One side of her face flushed with a prickly heat that was uncomfortable – she must be sitting too close to the fire and yet she was too lethargic to adjust her position. Her father had a saying for that class of conundrum. What was it? She chafed at the sluggish pace of her thoughts and brought the glass to her mouth again. He'd tell her she was like a dog sitting on a thistle that couldn't be bothered to jump off.

'In numerology this counts as a special birthday.' Birdie perched on the edge of the other wing-backed armchair. 'Three radiates with fortunate energy: it denotes harmony, balance and purpose.'

Purpose: Venus could use some of that.

'And you're thirty-three, three and three again, the fulfilment and completion number,' continued Birdie. 'This is a most auspicious combination, Venus. Whatever you set your mind to this year you'll achieve.'

Venus was tempted to tell her where she'd been at midnight and to what purpose. But Birdie was still speaking and she was loath to interrupt, anticipating a clue might be fumbled about her past.

'It was a tumultuous evening when Dan found you, in that glimmering sliver of time before the last light fades, and the bully-boy wind was howling so that people feared for loved ones at sea. That is what your mother was thinking of that night – your brothers were never far from her mind. Maura longed to turn the clock back and forbid them to join the fishing trawler. But the boys were young, the money was generous and they had no fear. Fear is something they never grew old enough to learn. Their confidence was contagious. "They thought they were immortal, Birdie," Maura said, "and so did I."'

Birdie's contemplation of the flames was so prolonged that Venus became concerned she might have said her piece. After a while the older woman smiled. 'I didn't see

Dan bring you in, but Maura told me about it often. She said she was sitting there, reminiscing about your brothers, when the door crashed open and in came Dan. With a naked girl-child, a skyclad daughter cradled inside his shirt to keep her warm.' Birdie's voice rose and fell with a rhythmic cadence, lulling Venus as a rocking crib soothes a fractious child. 'Maura and Dan were bewitched by you, Venus. You alchemised their lives into something worthwhile. It was an act of mercy that sent you to them thirty-three years ago.'

'But I don't even know if I'm celebrating my birthday *on* my birthday,' protested Venus. 'It's my foundling day, not my birthday.'

'What odds?' Birdie drained her glass and snapped to her feet. 'I celebrate my birthday on April 30th rather than in February because I like the Eve of Beltane connection. And because it keeps me younger for an extra handful of weeks. Birthdays were never meant to be taken literally. Now, where did I leave your present?'

'How old are you?' Venus asked, greatly daring.

'Old enough. A woman that will tell you her age will tell you anything.' Birdie rummaged on the kitchen table, a repository not just for her computer but for the detritus of her life. Eventually she located a lozenge-shaped package in a scarlet covering. She smiled as she reached it to Venus, the gesture softening her peaked face with its little spike of a nose. Every year without fail Birdie remembered Venus's birthday; packages had followed her to Dublin and London, once even to Andalucia.

'May I open it?' Venus fingered the bright tissue paper.

'It's your birthday now. It's well past the witching hour.'

It was wrapped Christmas-cracker tyle and Venus

untwisted each end, peeling it apart to reveal a dream-catcher. The feathers fluttered as Venus admired it by candlelight.

Birdie watched her with an expression that might strike the onlooker as maternal. 'It's my belief that birthdays should always pave the way for a new experience in the coming year. Everyone should learn to sing a song through to the end, or travel to a new destination, even if it's only to the imagination's outer reaches. We should all of us, Venus, have the courage to dream at least one dream.'

'You've never spoken of your own dreams.' Venus caressed the fronds of her dream-catcher, threaded with shells and beads.

'Of course I have dreams. It's the essence of human nature to spin webs of fantasy.' Birdie's secretive smile didn't falter. 'But anyone can weave a dream – it takes another quality altogether to pursue that dream, to walk in its shadow until you overtake it.'

Venus eyelids were growing heavy, a combination of the mead and the hour, and she stood to leave. 'You'll come by tomorrow night for some barmbrack, won't you?' She stooped to press her lips against Birdie's cherry-scented cheek.

'I always do. I can't go breaking with tradition at this stage. Maura loved this time of year, so Dan enjoys it for her sake.'

Venus thought of her mother presiding over the Hallowe'en games – apple in the water, apple on a string – always knowing which slice of apple tart to cut so that Venus would find the foil-wrapped coin inside. The memory was poignant and she was engrossed in it still as she dangled the dream-catcher from her wooden bed head. She'd never dreamed of her mother since her return to Ireland, which struck her as peculiar because she had flitted through her slumbers in London.

Maura Macken was less in her thoughts, Venus acknowledged, with a pang. She saw it as another loosening of the tie between them, a process set in train irrevocably when she'd moved to Dublin at eighteen to begin her studies. Maura's need for Venus had exceeded Venus's for her, and yet she had never tried to block her daughter's ambitions when they had taken her away from Roancarrick. 'Live your life, Venus, don't let it live you.' That had been her watchword.

When she had been in Dublin, Maura would visit the city regularly on shopping expeditions, especially at Christmas, because she had loved the decorated shop windows. Above all, her mother had marvelled at the towering tree topped by a star at the mouth of Grafton Street. 'A Christmas tree can never be too tall or too tasteless,' she'd insist.

She had followed Venus to London a few times but never with the frequency that she would visit Venus in Dublin. It was more effort, with the extra distance, and her strength had begun failing her. Venus had first remarked this, without realising its cause, when she'd noticed her mother had stopped plucking her eyebrows. The exertion of even this minor vanity had become too strenuous, but Maura had claimed it was due to a tremor in her hand and Venus had let it pass.

She didn't dream of her mother that night either. Instead Venus saw a shoal of flashing fish raining down on her, tangling in her hair and sliding down the back of her neck. She held out her arms for them, but, try as she might, she couldn't maintain a grip and they slithered to the ground and wriggled at her feet.

For some reason this distressed her, for it seemed crucial that she keep at least one of the silver-scaled creatures. She awoke the next morning with the same sense of loss she'd felt on the morning after her mother's death, a sensation of something ominous just beyond her consciousness.

Except it was her birthday, or so they said. And surely she was entitled to something positive on this one day at least.

Chapter Twenty-two

'Happy Birthday and Happy Hallowe'en, lass.'

Venus's father laid down his *Racing Post* as she walked into the kitchen, where *Highland Radio* chattered in the background. The table alongside the range was laid for breakfast and a lilac envelope waited for her on the side plate. As she slit the flap with a knife he said, 'I put money into it – sure I've no idea what to buy a young woman. Your mother took care of that side of the business.'

'Thanks a million, Dad – it's far too much.'

'I had a win on the horses.'

'I'll put it towards a new winter coat – something with a tog rating instead of fashion details.' Venus tucked the notes into her towelling robe's pocket and hugged her father, before setting the embossed floral card on the dresser alongside the radio. It was emblazoned with the word daughter: he always bought cards which specified his relationship with the recipient. Also waiting to be opened were cards from Lily, Tamsin, her godmother from

Lisdoonvarna and a group one from the Bridges Across The World staff room. She was touched that the crew had remembered – the camaraderie in her old job had been a bonus that had almost compensated for the measly salary. Nevertheless, she felt vaguely discontented as she looked at the five pastel envelopes. She had few enough people in her life. Birthday well-wishers you could count on one hand.

Aunt Betty's was predictable: two embossed bunny rabbits with linked paws. Her aunt always treated her as though she were a schoolgirl. Even when they'd met again at Maura's funeral, Aunt Betty had seemed to think she was a student in London instead of a teacher there.

Tamsin's card was a sophisticated black and silver affair; Venus had hoped for a letter but there was just a scrawl, 'It's frenetic here, we must catch up soon for a proper chat, dashing to a first night at the ENO.' She sighed. The other teachers had all scribbled messages such as 'have a drink on us' and 'we've formed an escape committee in your honour' on their balloon-shaped card – apart from Gary Hesketh, who'd decorated the back with his mobile-phone number inside a heart, adding, 'Just in case absence really does makes the heart grow fonder.' It transformed her pout into a smile, which widened to a grin when she opened Lily's card, a cowboy hat inside which she'd written 'no going native in the wild (north) west'. Also inside, encased in electric-blue tissue and bubble wrap, was a pair of diamanté drop earrings. Trust Lily to be so casual about postage – anything could have happened to the earrings in transit. She held one up to the window, admiring the scintillating rainbow that appeared within its waterfall.

All of a sudden it disturbed Venus how easily her entire adult life until a few months ago was being blotted out – the incoming tide of Roancarrick's daily routine levelling her sandcastles. No matter how elaborate the edifice, with crenellations and a moat and a shell-encrusted turret, when the waves rushed in it subsided.

Those London years appeared increasingly to have no more substance than a dream. Had she really had a lecturer boyfriend called Andy who'd asked her to emigrate to Tasmania – but had gone on his own when she'd declined? A circle of friends who'd taken it in turns to operate the First Sunday brunch club once a month? Had she gone to Pamplona specifically to run with the bulls but lost her nerve? Did she help chaperone a party of fourteen-year-olds from Seville, meant to be studying Shakespeare, on a weekend trip to Stratford-on-Avon – ageing twenty years overnight when two of them were discovered missing from their bedrooms? Maybe it had been some other Venus Macken who'd led that life. Only Roancarrick was real to her now.

There was a predictability to life here that alienated her some days, seduced her on others. Her father needed routine; his day was calibrated and Venus slotted into his pattern. She checked the wheaten bread on his plate: sure enough, it was spread with marmalade, the rindless variety because the peel lodged in his dentures. She either bought her own personal pot of marmalade or acceded to his tastes.

Venus looked at her father as he drank his milky tea – taken without sugar, although he had a sweet tooth, because he believed sugar was harmful. The man had nearly as many thumbs as he had teeth – what difference could sugar make now? He compensated for the sugarless tea by having cake or biscuits or even bread and jam at a push with every mug.

Of course she loved him, but that didn't mean she

wanted to live with him. Not day in, day out. Trouble was, she was damned if she did and damned if she didn't.

Dan laid a paper bag landed alongside her mug. 'I bought you this as well. An extra little birthday present.' He beamed his gummy infant's smile, delighted with himself.

Venus extracted a box of Milk Tray, the brand he had always given his wife for anniversaries and birthdays. Shame for having resented her father's reliance on her welled through her body, coming to rest on her tongue, where it tasted of sour milk.

'I asked Mrs O'Dea to order in the largest size for me – she doesn't usually stock them,' he elaborated, congratulating himself on his resourcefulness.

'I'll save them for tonight.' Venus rustled over to the fridge with the chocolates, to hide her emotion.

What would happen when he was gone? She'd be on her own. Savagely, utterly alone. There was the London life, of course, but already she was uncertain about her ability to recreate it. Ten years of her life reduced to an insubstantial memory. One whose trajectory she couldn't even trust.

Dan Macken scattered her gloomy reflections. 'Your mother loved this day. It wasn't just your birthday, it was a re-birth day for us. You gave us a reason to live, Venus, particularly Maura, who was never the same after the boys disappeared. I suppose it's harder to recover from blows when you're that bit older. I was at the back end of my forties and Maura was a handful of years behind when you came along. By then there had been almost a year of waiting and praying and hope slipping away like water through a sieve.' His voice hoarsened. 'That's what we were condemned to, trying to store hope in a sieve. I gave up long before your mother did. Until the day she died I don't think she ever reconciled herself to losing her sons.'

Venus thought of the Daughters of Danaus, who stabbed their husbands on their wedding nights and were condemned to eternity in Hades carrying water endlessly in leaky jars. She gave herself a shake: this was mutating into a morbid birthday – then again, it was the first since her mother had died. It was only natural. But natural was overrated, protested her alter ego. She cast around for a way of reclaiming this birthday for herself. 'Tell me the story, Dad.' She smiled to conceal how abraded she was already feeling, so early in the day. He seemed not to hear, adding wood to the fire, and she adopted a wheedling demeanour. 'Tell it to me again,' she coaxed.

Dan Macken swallowed some of his candy-pink cough bottle, to ease his throat, and shuffled on his blackthorn stick to a sugán chair beside the range. He lifted his leg with the knee that wouldn't bend onto a footrest and began at the beginning which was, he always reminded her, the best place to start any story.

'It was Hallowe'en and as blustery an evening as we'd known that year – I was in two minds about stepping outside in case the leg wouldn't hold me. The winds were blasting in from the west and a man was hard pressed to stand upright with the force. But your mother was in agony with one of her headaches that couldn't be shifted and she needed tablets. There were none in the house and there was nothing for it but to chance the walk to Mrs O'Dea's shop, since the car was off the road with head-gasket trouble. I didn't like going out in that storm, I'll not deny it, for I've never forgotten a favourite saying of my father's, that the day of the big wind is no time to be doing the thatching.

'Birdie had just called in to check on Maura, who'd turned a bit introverted after the boys were taken from us.

231

I thought maybe she would sit with Maura to keep her company, but Birdie said she had business of her own to attend to and couldn't delay. I intended going the long way to the shop, on the road leading away from the cliffs, where at least there'd be shelter from the houses. But before she went Birdie persuaded me to take the coast road. She said the wind sounded more boisterous than it was and that I'd be back all the quicker. I'm ashamed to say I cursed her as I walked, for there was no let-up in the storm at all, and I was in mortal fear of a gust pushing me over the edge of the cliff. Still, I took Birdie's advice and chose that road. Maybe you could call it fate.'

He paused, images jostling in his mind's eye, and Venus prompted him.

'As you were picking your way along, hunched over against the gale, you heard a noise, and noticed a flash of white in the rock pools beneath you by the mermaid's cave.'

'Indeed and I did,' he nodded. 'Something attracted my attention and I stopped. Then I heard a cry and saw the flash of white. At first I dismissed it as a seagull, for I wasn't inclined to do anything other than concentrate on reaching Mrs O'Dea's in one piece. Except the patch of colour moved, and it wasn't only white like a seagull's wing but blood-orange too, and I thought the sound I heard could be a child's cry. High-pitched, caught by the wind and juggled through the air. If it had been later at night I'd have dismissed it as the banshee's wail and kept my eyes forward, for it never benefits a man to come face to face with a banshee. She'd stop the heart beating in you with no more than a glance.' He massaged his leg just above the knee, stroking away a muscle spasm. 'Your grandfather, my father, had a glimpse of a banshee once, on another Hallowe'en it was, long before you were thought of. That's one of the times the veil between our world and the other one is lifted. She was a fearful sight, he said. Tangled black hair streaming over a hooded grey cloak and the eyes sunken in her face, red raw from weeping. He near sobbed himself to witness it.' Dan ran a tongue over his lips. 'Bring me a sup of something, Venus, to wet my throat.'

Venus sighed as she poured him half a cup of milk. He never seemed to tell a story straight through any more – the deviations were becoming more convoluted.

Dan waited until he had drained the milk, Adam's apple bobbing, before continuing. 'He said it was a sound you'd never forget, a sound to waken you out of the deepest sleep and to cut through the fiercest gale. That was the wail of her keening. She's a messenger of death, the banshee, and your grandfather knew it could only mean bad news. Sure enough, he heard the next day that his youngest sister in Tipperary had been found dead in her bed.'

'There was no banshee when Mam died,' objected Venus.

'She wasn't born a Macken. There wasn't a banshee attached to her family that I ever heard tell of – but the Mackens always have their deaths foretold.'

Venus felt like reminding him the time for banshee stories was after dark with a roaring fire and the door shut tight against the elements, but she humoured him. Dan Macken had his own way of telling a story and if she interrupted him again he'd lose his thread.

His eyes blurred with concentration, an intensity she associated with him working at his hobby, whittling at a strip of wood until a pipe emerged. It had always struck her as somehow miraculous to see the shape emerge. Almost as peculiar as his knack for making pipes when he didn't smoke himself. If the humour were on him he could churn them out, and although he gave away so many he was virtually doling them out to strangers, every drawer in the house was jammed.

Her father had stopped making pipes during her mother's illness. Sometimes he handled the knife still, testing the blade, but he never lifted a strip of wood. Venus suspected he'd lost the heart for it. For his own part, he said the habit had left his fingers.

Dan picked up his story again. 'So there I was, going along the road above the mermaid's cave, when I heard the cry and saw the flash of white below. There was something in the sound that could not be ignored. I scrambled down the slipway, easier said than done for a man in my physical shape, even thirty-odd years ago, and as I drew near I saw a small girl, naked as a flower. Perfect as a flower too. She was laughing, not crying at all, lying in a sheltered hollow beside the seal's rock at the entrance to the cave.'

'The seal's rock that gives Roancarrick its name,' corrected Venus, who discouraged any variation in the familiar litany.

'As you say, lass,' her father acquiesced. 'The rock is what kept her safe because it formed a canopy over her. This small girl turned her face towards me and held her hands out to be lifted. And when I did she nestled into the base of my neck and fell fast asleep. Right there by the seal's rock.'

Dan's arms mimed holding a child and he gazed down towards his right elbow, seeing the slumbering form cradled there.

'Not much more than a day or two old, she was. A quare pair we made, with me none too steady on my feet and her not able to walk at all. I nursed her, with the waves lapping at my boot soles, and I marvelled at the temperature of her

Chapter Twenty-three

Venus imagined her father's tear-bright eyes were due to a resurgence of the emotion that had fired him on finding an infant daughter. She squeezed his hand and went into the bathroom to shower. In fact, Dan Macken was missing his wife. He felt a sense of loss for Maura always, but some days it gaped within him more than others.

He still reached for her in bed at night, wanting to wrap his arms around her stomach and nuzzle between her shoulder blades, inhaling her vanilla scent. Until the illness they'd slept apart only twice in all the years they were married: once when Maura went into hospital to have their sons, and once again when Dan had undergone an operation on his leg that came too late to halt its deteriorating mobility.

When he had been with her he had always considered himself as a man in his prime, despite the lame leg which pained him more with each passing year and the submerged grief over their sons. He lifted the photograph of their sons from the dresser. Christy was the happy-go-lucky one – he played the tin whistle and spent his money as he earned it; his twin, Luke, wore his cautious nature like a weight.

They'd worked on a fishing trawler based in Killybegs. It had been lost at sea in the year before Venus had come along, during a storm that had catapulted Maura onto her knees all night long, crystal rosary between fingers too paralysed to tell the beads. Their bodies had never been recovered and for that reason the wound would not heal for Maura. Nothing to bury, no grave to tend. The sea was ungenerous about returning her dead. After their boys' deaths Dan had realised age had begun to claim him, for he could see it in the gaunt ridges of his wife's face.

Dan set down the photograph and went outside for wood for the already well-stocked range; no point in dwelling on what couldn't be changed. He'd stop by Our Lady of the Assumption later and light a candle for the twins.

* * *

Venus thought of the painting her mother had named her for, as she rubbed tangy apple shower-gel along her arms. Maura had bought her daughter a postcard showing Botticelli's sloping-shouldered Venus, with her swan's neck and profusion of gilded hair only partly cloaking the high-breasted white body. Venus had envied her namesake her tranquil beauty, although consoled by the gangling height evident in the reproduction – at fourteen she was already taller than her mother and on eye-level with her father. Dan's tree references, although meant admiringly, grated. She didn't want to be a strapping lass or a fine figure of a woman or any of the other labels under which girls on the large side laboured.

The sea, she sometimes imagined, was smirking at her. Instead of delivering a water nymph, frothy as the petticoats on a wave, it had deposited a tree branch. Planted on terra firma, she had started growing and never stopped. Even now Venus suspected she hadn't finished expanding. Outwards if not upwards: her bosom swelling, her stomach curving, her body moulding into lush womanhood.

'Handsome is as handsome does,' her mother used to sniff.

Handsome does what? As it likes, Venus guessed.

She returned to the kitchen in a bath-robe to position her cards on the dresser.

'May as well make my selection.' Her father, having fed the range, was ensconced on the tweed sofa under the window and immersed in the racing pages, ticking off possibilities. Venus decided she needed to generate a little birthday excitement in her life and retreated upstairs to her bedroom, wondering how best to mark the day.

In London she had always taken the afternoon off and gone shopping for something esoteric: maybe a beaded evening bag she could use only once a year, or one of those crystal scent bottles with pregnant-bellied stoppers that couldn't be trusted to store perfume because of evaporation. In the evening, the staff room would decamp en masse to the Snakes and Ladders, where Gary Hesketh would demand a birthday kiss as a feudal right and everyone would explain it was only on his birthday that he was entitled to kisses.

When she'd spent her birthday with Lily in Dublin, or if Lily had come to London to be with her, they'd always shopped. Then they would detour off somewhere smart for coffee – the Ritz in London, the Merrion in Dublin – and

Lily would force a cake on her in honour of the day. Something that oozed stickiness.

Venus considered her options as she towelled dry her hair. She pulled on a pearlescent silk shirt bought for her last birthday by Tamsin – although she had to add a T-shirt under it because of the west-coast chill factor.

And that's when she decided there was nothing to stop her having a London birthday in Roancarrick. She could go shopping for something luxurious in its superfluity, even if it were only a jewelled hairgrip.

As Venus straightened the duvet her hand touched the dream-catcher on the bed-head; she unhooked it and tapped the shells, wrinkling her nose at their dull, clunking sound. She always imagined shells should emit the same tinkling shiver as cymbals. Venus dangled her birthday present from the window latch in her bedroom until she could find a hook in her father's toolbox to suspend it from the ceiling.

She emailed Lily to thank her for the birthday earrings. She tapped in the additional information that she had an admirer in the unprepossessing shape of John Óg O'Dea, imagining how her friend would laugh about the weighing scales' love token. Lily loved hearing about smitten men, and it might deter her from coupling Venus with Benedict Archer. Or Senan, worse again. Which reminded her – she should investigate his plans for Roancarrick. Venus added a postscript that was longer than the original email.

I'm very concerned about this hotel development Senan is working on in Roancarrick, she wrote. *I know business is business and the owner is entitled to sell to the highest bidder but a thumping big hotel would not be in the best interests of the village. Our community would be obliterated. Is your firm involved in the deal? How far advanced is it? I haven't mentioned it to anyone yet because I appreciate Senan told me as much as he did in confidence. Even if he was trying to pick my brains about the owners of properties who could block the complex. But I can't stay quiet indefinitely – there's a public interest issue here. I'm very disturbed by this, Lily. Please email me straight back.*

Love, Venus

She read it over, noticed her reference to 'our community', but left it in, and pressed the send button. Then she started a new email for Tamsin. No point in telling her about John Óg – she'd think him pathetic and Venus even more pitiful for not threatening to slap a sexual harassment suit on him if he didn't clear off. She'd just keep it light and ask about all the team at Bridges Across The World.

Just before sending it she checked her email and discovered a four-day-old one from Tamsin, telling her about a session to mark Gary Hesketh's temporary appointment as deputy director. Tamsin rarely joined the staff room excursions to the Snakes and Ladders and Venus wondered how her friends had liked having the boss with them to cramp their style.

She read a little further and saw it had made zero difference to Gary Hesketh – who was now barred from the pub for a month. Apparently he had become over-excited between his promotion and a special offer on tequila shots and had gone around volunteering to lick women's elbows. 'You can't do it yourself, it's impossible – try,' he'd urged them. His colleagues had ignored him, but by the time he had extended the offer to every female in the pub, regardless of age or personal circumstances, tensions had surfaced. Blithely indifferent, he had backed a new teacher against the cigarette-machine for a snog that had come as close to impregnating her as a kiss could. Tamsin was now wondering if she had made a mistake giving Gary Venus's job and wanted reassurance.

Venus tapped in a postscript to her Tamsin email reminding her that nobody could conjugate irregular verbs like Gary. Also, he never chatted up the pupils, which showed some strength of character. She prepared to close down her laptop with a virtuous flourish.

Lily must have been working on her computer because a response flashed in before Venus logged off.

Greetings to the birthday girl, she wrote. *Love the sound of your new beau. Accountants have pots of money. Make him take you out to dinner tonight – provided he leaves the weighing scales at home.*

Karim and I have been to see the Registrar of Marriages at Sir Patrick Duns Hospital – imagine a former hospital being a place where you get married now. Part of the complex still has a geriatric ward. We had to do something terribly formal called serving notice in person of our intention to marry. I had goose bumps going in! But the staff were lovely and didn't make us feel in the least furtive. They said they'd married masses of asylum seekers and they weren't obliged to inform the Department of Justice, which was Karim's major worry. He imagines some official or other can block the whole undertaking with a sweep of his pen. I keep telling him this isn't a Soviet state, but you know how he frets, poor lamb.

We had to bring all sorts of papers with us as proof of age and identity. Birth certificate, passport, exam results, driver's licence. I don't think you needed all of them – actually, I made up the part about exam results – but Karim said we shouldn't take any chances and made me bring everything that looked in any way official. I even had my original job offer letter from the estate agent's. Karim had to produce his asylum seeker's photo identity card, but he didn't have a passport because that was confiscated when he arrived in the country. They asked for translations of his documents and he's so clever, Venus, he'd realised in advance they'd want that and had organised it already. We should have had a letter from his community welfare officer confirming that he lives in Dublin, but we can send that on.

Isn't it exciting? All we have to do now is agree a date. The earliest it can be is twenty-two days after they complete their paperwork. So Operation Wedding Bells will be in the run-up to Christmas. Looks like I'll have an unpronounceable new surname before the end of the year. How exotic does Mrs Azarbayev sound to you? Makes Dillon seem paltry.

Come and see us soon. I need your help deciding what to wear, and Karim gets a little depressed about not being able to work – he says it's demeaning to be on social security. It's wonderful for me – I come home to hot meals and a tidy apartment – but time lies heavy on his hands. A visit from you would be a great distraction for the pair of us.

Love, Lily.

P.S. Haven't a notion about the boy Senan's empire-building schemes but will conduct enquiries. He'll either wind up behind the Taoiseach's desk or in a prison cell by the time he's thirty.

Venus read the email twice to digest its contents. At least Lily would make some effort on behalf of Roancarrick – the more she thought about it, the more determined Venus grew that her father should continue having his two pints of Guinness in Nora Brennan's pub in peace. As for her vague hope that Lily might eventually turn lukewarm on this marriage – that was well and truly torpedoed. Venus's bolthole in Dublin had a cuckoo in the nest. A Chechen cuckoo. It didn't even seem to be illegal to marry Karim.

The country was going to the dogs. But she couldn't reply now – it would strike a sour note, both on her birthday and on Lily's transparent happiness. She grabbed a scrunchie and a comb and tramped downstairs.

'I'll have to see about clearing out the shed as a makeshift garage – the car mightn't start on frosty mornings,' she told her father, braiding her sheaf of hair by the range.

He looked up from his racing pages and admired the deft movement of her fingers through flaming coils, although they were tamed for no more than a few moments before tendrils began escaping their confines.

'It never gets too frosty here, one of the benefits of living by the sea. Surely you can't have forgotten already,' he reminded her.

Venus was nonplussed – he was right. 'Still, I might convert the shed into a garage anyway, it's wide enough,' she persisted, to cover her mistake.

Venus's upper arms ached as she held them at an ungainly angle to complete her braiding. They never seemed to become inured to the manoeuvre. Nearly done. Her fingers stilled as her father spoke again, so softly that she had to strain to hear the words:

'"He whistled a tune to the window, and who should be waiting there

But the landlord's black-eyed daughter,

Bess, the landlord's daughter,

Plaiting a dark red love-knot into her long black hair."

I always loved that poem at school, we had a teacher who used to read it aloud to us, tapping his hand to the highwayman's hoofbeats – the lines had a trotting horse's rhythm too.'

A swell of affection washed over Venus; nobody could

dredge into their memory banks and reproduce a swathe of poetry with the unconscious ease of her father. And he was reaching back across seventy years to do it. But ask him what he had for dinner yesterday and he'd be stumped, for his short-term memory was in tatters. Then it occurred to Venus that she knew somebody else who could whistle a tune to the window – except Conor Landers didn't seem to be around any more to do it.

'What is a love-knot anyway?' She fastened the ends of her plait with a velvet scrunchie.

'Sure I haven't a notion,' admitted Dan, 'but it sounds poetic.'

'Birdie is partial to knots. She says they have a fastening magic.'

'Knots can save lives,' agreed Dan, thinking of fishermen. He had taught Christy and Luke how to tie knots, until the day came when they had outstripped their instructor. It still hadn't saved them. He shook himself. 'Never mind Birdie and all her supernatural nonsense.'

Venus smiled: the man who'd reminisced about the Macken family banshee had no business bandying accusations at anyone else.

She rinsed the dishes, leaving them to dry on the rack, and chatted to Dan while she worked, telling him she planned to drive into Sligo and wander about the shops. Maybe spend some of his birthday money. It was already close to lunch-time, and he was anxious in case she'd forgotten about Birdie calling over for barmbrack in the evening, but she reassured him she'd be back in time.

'Besides, I have to go into town to buy the food, Dad, and I ought to pick up a few sweets for the trick or treaters.'

'All they want is money now,' he sniffed.

245

'They can want all they like. I'm handing out bars of chocolate.'

Venus made a mental note to pick up a couple of bags of bull's-eyes, for Dan had a weakness for them in addition to his Devonshire toffees. He preferred to buy them from Mrs O'Dea's shop, to give her the business, but the supplier had disappointed her and there had been none on the shelves the last few times he'd called.

'Would you not try a few clove rock?' Mrs O'Dea had wheedled, and he'd taken a packet of the spicy red and white sweets but couldn't finish them.

'They upset my stomach,' he'd complained.

On impulse, Venus went back upstairs and changed her amber stud earrings for Lily's gift. She slid the wire through her earlobes, knowing glittering drop-earrings were incongruous with her canvas jeans and ankle boots. Roancarrick wasn't the place to wear diamanté earrings that dangled below chin level. She'd be certified.

But she'd risk it anyway, as a salute to the birthday spirit.

'What will you do with yourself for the afternoon, Dad?' She admired the earrings in the cracked glass by the back door. She still hadn't replaced it – the Roancarrick thief of time again.

'I'll ring through to O'Hara's and place my wee bet, then I'll maybe stretch my legs as far as Mickey Joe's and watch the racing with him.' Dan was engrossed again in the newspaper, chewing the end of his pencil.

'Don't forget there's corned beef in the fridge for a sandwich if you're hungry,' she reminded him, but he didn't lift his head from the tipsters' forecasts. Venus sighed – it was becoming increasingly difficult to tempt his appetite.

She slid a thumb and forefinger into the pocket of her

tartan waistcoat and encountered the studs she'd just removed from her ears. Amber was a particular jewellery favourite of hers, since it mated so precisely with her hair when the sunshine dappled it. At least that's what Andy used to tell her, before he went to Tasmania. He'd also teased her mercilessly about her goddess of love name. 'Does this mean I have to worship you?' he'd ask. 'Naturally,' would come her laughing response. But he hadn't lodged her on a pedestal – he hadn't so much as altered his plans for her.

In fact, now that she thought about it, one of the objections Venus had raised against Andy was that he had never told her she looked well except when she was naked. It might have been agreeable to receive the odd compliment when she was fully clothed for a change. Still, mustn't bear grudges – she'd probably send him his usual Christmas card again this year. Just so long as he didn't insist, in his return card, that she check his website for the wedding photographs posted there. For Andy had found a woman in Hobart who didn't object to being complimented exclusively in the nude.

It was fairly sad, she reflected, that she had taken to thinking about Andy to compensate for the lack of men in her life. There was John Óg, of course, but it would be even more deplorable if she counted him. Conor Landers sneaked into her mind, and Venus wondered why she was wasting her time even considering a man who seemed to have vanished off the face of the earth. It was outrageous behaviour, flattering her prodigally about her resemblance to a Venetian beauty, then disappearing.

He was probably a figment of her imagination. She was so bored and lonely in Roancarrick she'd taken to inventing attractive artists. If she checked again she'd discover the captain's house was home to a colony of German environmentalists.

Venus tried some positive imagery: it was her birthday and she was going into Sligo where she'd buy a desirable object that would make her feel complete – even if only for an hour. There, that wasn't so difficult. She walked across the kitchen and balanced, one hand on either side of the armchair, swooping to kiss her father. She embraced Dan whenever she left him now, even for a couple of hours. She half-expected him to resist her hugs, for he had never been a tactile man, but he didn't ward her off.

Dan stood at the open door and Venus noticed the scoop of his vest through his shirt – he wore a vest all year round, careful about chills. He stayed in the doorway and waved as the Volkswagen pulled away, despite the cold that sliced at his chest, watching until the car was an indistinct blur. And then watching the empty space where it had last been.

Passing through the gate Venus made a mental note to buy window-boxes filled with sturdy heather: she'd left her own, bought from the Columbia Road flower market, behind in London. The house needed some external sign that it was loved, as all homes did. It had acquired an unkempt air since Maura's death, although Venus was at a loss to describe exactly how this neglect manifested itself. Window-boxes would help reverse the decline, even if it would be spring before she could plant them.

She'd given Maura an earthenware window-box for Mother's Day once, filled with coral geraniums – but even these hardy plants had quailed before the ravages of wind and rain that lashed this stretch of north-west coast. Birdie had rescued the flowers, all but moribund, and managed to revive them – she had a wooden shelter at one end of her cottage which afforded some protection, and it was here she grew herbs and a few flowers. Not many blooms, only ones that could earn their keep, she said. Geraniums passed the test because they foretold the arrival of guests and deterred insects, according to Birdie. Venus didn't repeat such remarks to her father, for she knew he'd dismiss it as paganism run amok. But she suspected her mother had known of Birdie's eccentricities and had been entertained by them.

Venus drove through the main street of the village, trying not to think about the properties under threat from Senan's developer. At the junction for the dual carriageway, instead of angling her car to the right for Sligo, Venus turned left for Bundoran. Now what on earth had possessed her? She wanted to go to Sligo, not Bundoran.

She thought about turning, but with her seahorse charm dancing encouragement, she decided Bundoran might do just as well as Sligo. Perhaps better than Sligo, now that she gave the matter some consideration, for it had amusement arcades. No reason why she couldn't give the one-armed bandits a whirl on her birthday. She was supposed to be indulging herself, after all. Venus winked at her seahorse, which jiggled conspiratorially.

Chapter Twenty-four

She crawled in second gear along the main street, past a succession of guesthouses with the Bord Fáilte shamrock logo and signs for vacancies in their windows. Bundoran's seaside tawdriness seemed more acceptable out of season. Indeed, it struck Venus as courageous; a small-town Beauty Queen well past her prime but puckering up for another slick of lipstick on chapped lips. An old fellow was standing outside a pub, saluting the cars as they passed. She waved automatically and his ruddy countryman's face crinkled with pleasure.

Breathing in the salt air, commingled with a smack of decaying vegetation indivisible from the season, she debated whether to go into an amusement arcade first or do her shopping. Venus lingered by a shop window decorated with false faces – the traditional witches, vampires and Frankensteins were augmented by more recent additions to the roll-call of villains, including a character from *Lord of the Rings* whose name eluded her.

Monkey-nuts were scattered on the floor of the display, toffee-apples aped flowers in vases and a string of spectral fairy-lights girdled the contours of the window. It struck her as unsatisfactory that ghostly apparitions were, by common consent, denoted by floating bedsheets. Glow-in-the-dark Ku Klux Klansmen.

Pleasures were always better deferred, so she left the slot-machines to the end. She wasn't a regular gambler, like her father, but every once in a while Venus treated herself to a session at a one-armed bandit. Whenever she felt stifled, it allowed her the luxury of the mindless cocoon: slide in some coins and tug the lever. Slide-tug-slide-tug, wait for the jingle of music and the jangle of metal that heralded a win.

She cast a promise-fuelled glance in the direction of the amusement arcade and instead stepped into the shop; its doorbell pealed lugubriously, organ music from the crypt. The interior was cramped, every surface covered with intriguing pieces of plastic whose function she couldn't begin to comprehend, and it appeared to be swarming with children on a mission to spend. But not until they were convinced they'd considered every alternative to their eventual purchases.

Closer inspection revealed there were just four children and an adult with nominal charge of at least two of them. They dithered over treasures, a coffin-shaped gravedigger's lantern holding particular allure. Venus ducked from a bat which whizzed overhead, attached by elastic to the ceiling, and chose some candles for her almost-a-birthday cake. They were miniature black cats with arching tails and lime-green eyes and she bought a baker's dozen for the cake. Not that they'd all fit, but it seemed the appropriate number.

Then, for no other reason than that she made her smile, which seemed the best motive of all, Venus added a witch straddling her broomstick to the tally. It was a wooden pencil-sharpener and the witch was lavishly warted, with patches on her clothes – so casting spells can't have been profitable. Her pointed hat with its silver buckle above the brim was angled backwards, as though she was sailing through a howling gale, and her knuckles were visible as she clutched the broomstick. Imagine, a witch terrified of broomstick locomotion but constrained by the weight of tradition to climb aboard anyway.

Venus paid for her haul while the children continued to anguish over how best to invest their pocket money, congratulating herself on applying the Lily principle of self-undulgence to her birthday in Lily's absence. She pictured her friend's response: 'My work is done,' she'd say. Then Karim elbowed his way into the image and Venus clicked shut her purse and wheeled out into fey sunlight.

Nevertheless she was gratified with her purchases. She walked along the main street, pausing at a fruit and vegetable shop, attracted by a wheelbarrow of plump pumpkins near the doorway. It was the American influence percolating through, for pumpkins had no place in the Hallowe'en traditions of her childhood. Still, pumpkins carried off the transition from new world to old with aplomb. She always remembered the upwardly mobile Ichabod Crane when she saw pumpkins, for *The Legend of Sleepy Hollow* had been one of her favourite stories as a child. She made a mental note to unearth and re-read it.

The amusements were just a few steps away, but she passed by with her gaze averted. Venus was beguiled by the cacophony of noise and the aura of anything being possible that seeped from the arcade. But she also knew if she looked in she wouldn't want to walk on. Pumping with self-denial, and a shadow of regret, she made her way to the supermarket, then called to the nearby bakery converted from a disused church for barmbrack and apple-tart.

The blast of hot air when she stepped in persuaded Venus, after making her purchases, to take a seat in the café at the back of the shop and dawdle over a coffee and slice of sugar-dusted apple-tart. Lily would expect no less of her. The tart was served with a blob of cream that melted where it touched the cake and she watched its slithering progress towards the plate with more interest than it deserved.

For something to do, she loaded her fork and shovelled in an enormous helping.

'Mind if I join you?'

Why did people always address you just as speech was impossible – unless you wanted to pepper them with crumbs?

She nodded, swallowing semi-chewed tart, feeling its lumpen progress down her throat.

It was Conor Landers.

Chapter Twenty-five

Conor sat opposite Venus, also with some apple-tart, whistling under his breath as he unloaded his tray.

He wasn't aware that he whistled, Venus realised; it seemed to be as natural as breathing to him.

'Don't suppose there'll be a coin in this like the tarts my mother bakes at Hallowe'en,' he guessed.

'Unlikely,' she agreed.

Where had he gone for weeks on end and how had he managed to come back on her birthday, almost as though he'd timed it that way? She couldn't ask him where he'd been, it would betray an interest.

He stirred his coffee and remarked, 'I've missed Roancarrick. I only arrived back last night. Ages ago I promised to help a friend start up a new course in watercolours at the adult learning centre in Omagh and I couldn't back out of it. But it's good to be near the ocean again – I don't like being landlocked. I always think the horizon should be met by sea, not a ploughed field.'

He paused and tasted a mouthful of the tart. 'There's cinnamon in it.' His expression was so aggrieved that Venus couldn't help but laugh. 'You might have warned me,' he added, injured.

'Some people like cinnamon,' she suggested.

'Some people have no sense of what's proper.'

'How can it be improper to add cinnamon to apple-tart?'

'It's gilding the lily.' He arched an eyebrow at her and she wondered at lashes and brows so sooty, when his curls were dark blond.

Venus tried not to think about how much gilding had gone into the presentation of her face to the world when she'd lived in London. She'd let it slide since returning to Roancarrick. Now she plaited her fingers around the belly of her mug and shot the newcomer a whimsical look. 'A little enhancement never went amiss.'

He seemed to ponder this, poking a finger into one of his curl spirals. Meanwhile Venus was enjoying this encounter with the first attractive man she'd met since quitting London – and whatever you said about London, it had a stockpile of presentable men. New recruits were always teeming in. When he wasn't commenting on her driving or treating her like a blow-in, Conor had a certain crooked charm.

'Our neighbour, Birdie,' she continued, 'swears by cinnamon. She was rhapsodising about it only the other day – she downloaded some information about it from the Internet. Apparently the Egyptians used it as part of their embalming lotions and the Chinese left it as food for the dead. In the Middle Ages it was an ingredient in love potions and the Romans believed – well, never mind what the Romans believed.'

She couldn't tell him they used it as a passion stimulant.

'Goodness,' he said, 'aren't you a fount of arcane data.' But his glance had a sweetness that salved any sting.

'I have a solution. A radical one, perhaps,' she suggested, as he scowled at his apple-tart. 'The cinnamon might be only sprinkled on top. You could always try scraping it off.'

'Why didn't I think of that?' He flashed a gap-toothed smile and carefully dismembered the pastry. He tasted with caution and approved the pared-down cake. 'You've saved my Hallowe'en. I'm very particular about apple-tart.'

Venus noticed the cream to accompany the dessert was served separately on a saucer, into which he dipped his fork after first eating a mouthful of tart. Cake first, chew and swallow, then cream.

'Are you always so precise?' she asked.

'Only about the things that matter.'

'And apple-tart matters?'

'More than morality, less than friendship.' Totally at ease, he popped in a mouthful of cream.

She played with her own apple-tart and considered her acquaintance. He was showing the early-warning signs of being a maverick. Mind you, she shouldn't impose unrealistically high standards; for such a sparse community Roancarrick had its share of, er, characters. Timmy Brennan, the pub landlady's hard-drinking son, for one. He still took a soother to bed with him at night, according to village gossip. The less said about him the better. And then there was John Óg O'Dea with his scales. Kitchen appliances as a courtship prop – the poets were banjaxed if they ever caught on as a replacement for roses.

Venus drained her coffee, noticing Conor seemed content to sit there in silence opposite her, eating his tart.

She found it restful. He licked his lips as a blob of cream clung to the lower one. Bitten lips, she observed, as though the conversational tightrope act he practised disguised his share of crash landings. Her eyes dropped to the hand holding the fork. He had mashed nails too, gnawed to the quick. Venus studied her own nails, ravaged when she'd arrived in Roancarrick, smooth ovals now. There was something to be said for low-voltage village life.

That feeling she had first experienced of being sequestered here had faded. John Óg was entertaining, even if he was odd, and Kathleen from the restaurant always went out of her way to strike up a conversation when they met, or made time to sit with Venus for a few minutes when she dropped into Seascape for coffee. Venus decided to ask her if she wanted to take a trip into town to see a film: she should be more pro-active in forging friendships. For now, Kathleen was concentrating on mopping up the last of the tourists – and Venus knew she was planning a trip to Boston after that, because she hadn't taken off so much as a weekend since Easter. But when Kathleen returned she would make an effort.

And here was another opportunity sitting in front of her. Which she was wasting. She reached a hand across the table. 'Venus Macken is my name.'

'I know. Finally she shakes my hand. I haven't forgotten you fled from it the first time I offered it to you. I'm Conor Landers. It was Philanders at school, a nickname I never discouraged because I rather gloried in it. Especially as it was completely unearned.'

Venus felt slightly breathless under the commentary's barrage.

'How do you know my name?'

'There aren't many people under the age of fifty in Roancarrick. I made it my business to find out. I've seen you go for mournful walks on the beach, gazing out to sea like the French Lieutenant's Woman. I decided we should become friends: firstly, because it's unhealthy for attractive females to be too much on their own; and secondly, because I could use a friend in Roancarrick. My entire family is compulsive about sailing and frankly, my bundle, I can take it or leave it.'

Venus lowered her chin onto her palm. 'Your bundle of what?'

'Gorgeousness, of course. Don't worry – I'm allowed to lavish compliments upon you, it's part of the pact.'

She considered asking him which pact he had in mind, but decided instead to accept the flattery. It seemed there was a Conor Landers in her life.

'Of course,' he was still talking – this man didn't come up for air once he started – 'I didn't have to relocate to Roancarrick. I could have stayed at home. But I didn't much fancy it since I'm persona non grata there at the moment. Local opinion vacillates between organising a whip-round to buy me a one-way ticket to Outer Mongolia and casting any veneer of civilisation to the wind and having me castrated.'

Conor's lower lip was caught between his teeth and mauled, so that Venus flinched in sympathy with the crescent of pink flesh.

'You must have caused some rumpus there,' she said, more to give his lip respite than because she wanted to pump him. There was only so much information you needed about a new acquaintance and anything surplus overloaded the systems. They obviously had a different take on what constituted the need-to-know basis – Venus believed in drip-feed.

Conor regarded her defiantly. 'Low standards.'

'Yours or the town's?'

'Killyclogher's not a town, it's a village. Or it used to be – to all intents and purposes it's a suburb of Omagh now. Except don't let anyone from Killyclogher hear you saying that.'

'Omagh. Isn't that the place where –'

'Yes.' His interruption was brusque. 'Bombed to hell and back. Let's not go there.'

She subsided, chilled by the mottled expression that darkened his face. Embarrassed, too, by her clumsiness. Everyone from the Tyrone town must be tormented by the same inescapable questions. Were you there that day? Did you lose anyone close to you?

'I didn't mean to offend you.' Venus was tentative, careful not to look at him.

'You didn't offend me. But what happened in Omagh isn't conversational furniture, for tossing out between where do you come from and what do you do? It has its own space, and a savage, echoing cavern it is.'

Venus stared out the window, at a plastic bag struggling to escape from the telegraph wires that held it firm. She felt a little trapped herself, wincing at her insensitivity.

'Anyway,' Conor deliberately lightened his tone, to end the impasse, 'I can't believe I'm still living at home at my age. I'm thirty-five. Halfway to seventy, but I console myself that since I plan to live to be a hundred and one it doesn't signify. As long as I move out before I'm genuinely middle-aged I'll be grand.'

He had a languid way of speaking which appealed to Venus.

'The problem is,' he went on, 'artists don't tend to have

a regular income and starving in a garret has never held much allure for me. Whereas my parents have a Victorian heap that's big enough to fit all of us without friction – I even have a studio in the basement. They have an admirable work ethic whereas I'm shaping up to be a wastrel. My output, never copious at the best of times, has slumped. Left to me, it would be rags to rags in one generation.' He flicked at stray crumbs on his plate with the fork. 'Take my parents: both born in council houses, but they worked their fingers to the bone and built up a thriving law practice between the pair of them, what with clients making wills and selling houses and even the odd divorce settlement – although Killyclogher's not convinced divorce is the answer to marital collapse. People prefer the tried and trusted method of living under the same roof but only communicating via notes propped on the mantelpiece. An old school-friend's parents have been doing that for the past seventeen years. I think people must take vows to love, honour and keep up appearances as long as they both shall live.' Conor leaned his elbows on the table. 'But I was telling you about my parents. They bought the house of their dreams twenty years ago – they couldn't afford the grounds as well but nobody's entitled to everything. Come to think of it, nobody's entitled to anything.'

He was savaging his lip again. Venus wondered at his peaks and troughs of emotion. He seemed so thin-skinned, as though everything stung or enchanted him to excess. Must be the artistic temperament.

'Anyway.' He smiled at her, dismissing unsettling visions. 'I'm going to winter in Roancarrick and see if the change of scene is conducive to my work. Plus it will give the dust a chance to settle in Killyclogher.'

'I'm sure it must inspire you.' She injected an over-enthusiastic nuance into her tone, although she couldn't help feeling a blast of curiosity about what he'd done to upset the citizens of Killyclogher. She ploughed on. 'The mountains, the strand, the sea . . . painters love the combination. An English artist spent all last winter here, painting the same seascape over and over. I can't recall his name, but apparently he's highly regarded. One of his paintings hangs in the White House.'

'I'm not a painter.'

She was flummoxed. For some reason she'd been convinced those tapered fingers with their telltale nails handled oils. Mussed up splodges of paint coaxed from tubes onto a palette and then transferred stroke by stroke to canvas. Besides, she'd seen him with his portfolio. 'What do you do then?'

'Inks. It used to be trees; before that it was church spires. I'm still hunting for my next theme. Shopfronts were considered for a time, if you remember. I was intrigued by that picturesque one on the seafront in Roancarrick, run by the old dear in the cardigan who's always eating cream puffs. She could sell fur coats in Florida, that one. I felt like giving her my credit card and telling her to deduct whatever she thought was fair, just to escape from her. Her son's the mayor of Sligo, isn't he? She told me he runs the town.'

Venus stifled a giggle and spluttered, 'As good as.'

'Anyway, shopfronts proved to be a mini-theme. If I could turn my hand to faces I'd do that shopkeeper woman. But I can't. I find mouths too hard to capture – and eyes harder again.'

Venus became conscious that the café was closing and the staff, no doubt keen to go home and prepare for their

Hallowe'en celebrations, were glancing in their direction. Not ready to expel them yet but wanting them gone.

'You could use your womanly wiles to persuade the manager to let us stay on a little longer.' Conor indicated a man in a short-sleeved shirt with his name-tag on the breast pocket.

'It's been so long since I've needed them, I've forgotten where they are.'

'What about your goddess-like wiles then?'

'You don't give up, do you?' She grasped her shopping bags in a flurry of departure. 'There's no goddess joke you could crack or line you could quote that I haven't heard a thousand times already. Guys who want to fill you with their immortal longings, find your feet of clay, become the answer to your prayers or let you answer theirs. Anyway, I have to be going, I can't believe the time.' Venus paused, as a thought struck her. 'I've just realised I forgot to buy Birdie's washing-powder when I was in the supermarket but it's too late now, the shop will be closed.' She didn't mention the slot-machines – he might suspect she was a gambling addict.

'Can't you pick up some washing-powder in a Spar? Or what about O'Dea's?'

Conor was bemused by her distress.

'They don't stock the mammoth family-of-twelve box that Birdie wants. The afternoon's flown.' She was clucking now, disappointed at the evaporation of her Saturday earmarked for indulgence. She'd wanted to do something with it, not loiter in a coffee shop until the light faded. The slot-machines were still open, but she'd run out of time to play them, and she just knew she'd have won a rivulet of clattering coins – it was her birthday after all.

'But that's a positive sign, isn't it?' Conor unobtrusively relieved her of her bags and followed her out onto the pavement, as the staff locked the door behind them.

A rocket soared overhead and exploded in a cloudburst. The fireworks were starting early. She dragged her eyes back from the sky, darkening again in the aftermath of the explosion, and nodded.

'I mean,' he pressed on, 'what better way to spend a Saturday afternoon than gossiping with a friend and eating apple-tart?'

She nodded again, more energetically than before. It was a little presumptuous of him to describe their relationship as a friendship, and yet the potential was there. It was promising, as only beginnings can be.

She felt a pang walking past the amusement arcade, hearing its tinny, enticing music. At least she could go home with a Lotto ticket. There was a newsagent's on the far side of the street and Venus waited for a gap in the traffic and ducked across, followed by Conor.

'Aren't you coming in for one?'

He rested his bottom on the ledge outside the shop. 'Never bother with lotteries. I know I won't win.'

'How can you know?' She was scandalised.

'I don't have the right kind of luck. I have another sort.'

She mulled this over as she made her selections, buying two tickets – one for her and one for Dan. 'I'm feeling lucky, whatever about you,' she muttered, back on the street.

'*Good luck and fortune to the girls of Gortin, not forgetting the maids from the Plum,*' he chanted.

She flickered an eyebrow.

'Plum as in Plumbridge.'

'That's not what I meant.'

'My mother has a stock of these, she had them from her father.'

'My father's every bit as bad. What's even more worrying, they're seeping into me.'

Conor laughed. 'Tell me about it.'

They reached her Polo and Venus reclaimed her shopping bags. 'Would you like a lift back to Roancarrick or have you brought your own car?'

'I don't have a car, so a lift would be welcome – otherwise I'll have to ring home and persuade one of the brothers to swing by for me. My mother left me into Bundoran to go fireworks-shopping, but I didn't want her to wait. I thought I'd have a glorious rummage among the toffee-apples and jelly Dracula's teeth.'

Conor transferred his bags to one hand and reached into a pocket, as Venus's nose began to pinch with the cold. Another flurry of fireworks whizzed into the sky, trailing kaleidoscope sparks, and she tensed in anticipation of the howitzer bang. In its aftermath, the seaside smell was overlaid with gunpowder.

'What do you think?' Conor's voice recalled her and she looked at his extended hand: a witch sharpener on her white-knuckle broomstick ride was resting on his palm.

Venus opened the passenger door and then searched her bags for her own Hallowe'en haul. 'Snap.' She showed off her sharpener.

'Told you we ought to be friends.' He settled himself beside Venus, saluting her seahorse charm as though greeting another passenger.

As she pulled up at the captain's house, where a pumpkin lantern had appeared in the front window, Venus decided to take him up on his offer of friendship. He was planning to winter in Roancarrick, after all – he wasn't as transient as the other blow-ins. So in a diffident tone, looking at her fingers curved around the steering wheel rather than his eyes which were neither blue nor green but a shade that blended both, she invited him to that evening's get-together. He could call by later for some barmbrack and her father's speciality Hallowe'en punch if he wasn't doing anything more pressing, but it was all the same to her, really, she was just being neighbourly. And it was probably too short notice in any case. His Saturday-night plans were already made, more than likely – in fact, she didn't know why she'd mentioned it.

Impervious to her bumbling, Conor blossomed at the mention of punch and quizzed her about its contents. Venus was hazy. It had red lemonade for colour, she knew, sliced oranges for taste, poitín for effect, and she hadn't a notion what else, although it slid down the throat easily. Dan Macken guarded the recipe jealously and watch as she might, she always missed some vital stage of the procedure. They agreed on nine thirty to give Conor time to eat and set off his fireworks – which Venus would be able to see if she stepped out into her yard. Birdie was due to call half an hour earlier, but her grasp on punctuality was less than sound so Venus assumed they'd arrive more or less together.

Parking in the back yard, where her father had left on the outside light for her, Venus wondered how well developed Conor's investigative skills were. Perhaps she could persuade him to help with her search for her roots. Two heads were better than one – especially if one of the heads was covered in fawn-fair choirboy curls.

She'd made little headway so far on her own, but instinct whispered that her luck was finally on the turn.

Chapter Twenty-six

Venus forgot about Conor's fireworks, although she glimpsed the tail-end by accident when she answered the door to trick or treaters. It was the Doherty brothers dressed as a skeleton and a gravedigger, along with the smallest Campbell child, who wore neon face paint with an other-worldly quality that jolted Venus when she materialised out of the gloom. There were no street-lights at this outer fringe of the village.

Venus knew the small, silent spectre had to be the Campbell girl, born at least a decade after the others in her family, because her teenage sister was hovering by the gate. As she turned away to grab a handful of chocolate bars from the bowl left ready in the vestibule, she heard the high-pitched travelling squeal of a firework and five heads turned in unison to track its path above the captain's house. The night sky was illuminated by nameless whirling objects and a fanfare of flaunting rockets; children and adults alike sighed when the show ended.

'Who was it?' asked her father, whose leg was paining him too much to hobble to the door.

'Campbells and Dohertys. Decent of those two boys to take a little girl out trick or treating with them.'

'Aye, well, you see that's because they'd be second cousins through their mothers who are full first cousins on the Halloran side.' Her father was intimate with the closely conjoined bloodlines of the village.

She wished she'd thought to bring the trick or treaters into the kitchen for him to admire their costumes, and decided the next lot wouldn't have their bribe until they agreed to step inside.

In the end it was a rush to be ready on time, for she was busy listening to her father, who needed an audience after his afternoon alone, and in cajoling him to eat. He couldn't remember if he'd had anything since lunch-time and his face creased in exasperation as he struggled to recall. They checked the sink but there were no dishes in it to provide a clue. Then again, he was becoming compulsive about washing up as soon as he'd emptied a teacup.

Dan said he wasn't hungry and he'd wait for the birthday supper, but Venus coaxed him into joining her for a bowl of soup, with potatoes left over from the previous day's dinner chopped through it – she didn't want him drinking his punch on an empty stomach.

After their meal Venus sat in front of the triptych mirror on her dressing-table, attempting to ease a comb through her wavy hair. Hair which she despaired of and others envied. She buttoned up a copper-coloured Chinese silk tunic that ended at her hips, and teamed it with black ankle-cropped linen trousers. Then she rolled her hair into a pleat, securing it with tortoiseshell combs, so that Lily's earrings would not be subsumed by the fiery masses.

The bedroom had a few additions now from her London

life: some framed cinema posters bought in a Soho shop and a marble washstand on which she stood her video recorder and television set. They covered the Art Deco tiling on the washstand, but she had nowhere else for them. Beauty should be functional, she told herself; the deco disciples would have approved of that precept.

She returned her attention to her appearance. It seemed ridiculous to dress up for a new neighbour, an old one and an elderly father who took scant interest in anyone's appearance. But it was her birthday and she wanted to be admired. She'd have liked longer to sit in front of the age-freckled three-way mirrors, which reflected back someone unlike her mental perception of herself. They showed someone captivating, perhaps a little challenging. It must be the Hallowe'en influence.

Dan nodded without comment when Venus mentioned she'd invited an additional guest to their celebration. He drew his own conclusions from the lipstick and hairstyle but had the sense not to air them. Besides, he'd like Venus to have a boyfriend; she was too young to be interred in Roancarrick. He only hoped the extra guest wasn't John Óg O'Dea. As far as Dan was concerned, the O'Deas had never made the transition from money to class. Then again, pickings were slim in Roanncarrick; even an eighty-year-old widower could see that. He knew in his heart he should pack his daughter back to that job she seemed so keen on, to lead her own life. But he was more dependent on her than he cared to admit.

He tasted the Hallowe'en punch he'd spent the past hour concocting. 'May you live all the days of your life,' Dan murmured, reprising the toast his best man had proposed at his wedding. He'd lived his days to the full with Maura. But

Venus was being hampered from living hers. Roancarrick will be better for the lass in the long run than London-town, he reassured himself – cities chewed up people.

They switched on the portable television set in the kitchen to hear the Lotto numbers rather than move into the uninviting living-room. Venus had no matching numbers in either of her selections – so much for the Midas touch on her birthday. They turned off the television, tuning the radio to Lyric FM instead, and Maria Callas's voice soared through the room.

Venus fussed with the barmbrack, positioning her black cat candles on it – with just seven in place the fruit loaf was already crowded so she dotted the remaining half-dozen candles around the kitchen. Then she made sandwiches interleaved with ham off the bone and lay smoked salmon slices onto buttered wheaten bread, curving her body away from the food in case she stained her dry-clean-only blouse.

The supper would also include the inevitable apple-tart without which no meal could be served at this time of year, and she placed a cake-slice alongside it, ready for cutting. Finally she fetched two bowls from the dresser and poured monkey-nuts into one, while into its mate she emptied miniature mint-chocolate ghosts wrapped in silver and white tinfoil, bought from the same shop as the candles.

'Your mother would love this.' Dan's eyes moistened as they trailed Venus moving about the kitchen.

She crossed to where he was sitting near the range, hands curled around the metal towel-rail, and pressed her soft cheek against his sagging one. His bristles rasped as she rubbed her face gently against his. 'I can only guess at how much you miss her, Dad.'

His voice croaked. 'She was the Sunday in every week.'

When she emerged from their embrace, her father produced a white handkerchief bracketed with blue stripes and blew his nose while Venus pretended to alter the arrangement of the bowls.

'You haven't forgotten the punch, Dad?' she asked, to distract him. She knew full well he'd been tweaking it while she'd been primping in the bedroom.

He pressed his forefinger to his mouth. 'No point in fishing for clues, lass. You'll have my punch recipe when I'm willing to give it to you and not a day sooner.' He nodded towards the vestibule at the back of the kitchen, where a scarred and rickety table stood, wellington boots and umbrellas between its legs. 'It's ready and waiting over beyond.'

Not the safest place. Venus scurried to carry the bowl to the sturdier kitchen table. She inhaled as she walked, wondering how the drink always smelled densely rich and caramelised. Even ladling it out was a glooping exercise.

'Any luck on the horses?' Venus surveyed her preparations and decided the kitchen was too bright. She lit the standard lamp behind her father's armchair and turned off the overhead light, then flicked the switch on another lamp that squatted on the dresser. Its buttered radiance lent the room an intimate glow.

'Aye, I did. I had a place but the odds were poor.'

'Better than losing, surely.'

'Better than losing,' he agreed.

A knock on the door signalled Conor's arrival for, while Birdie tapped, she never waited but always opened the back door immediately afterwards.

'That'll be your boyfriend,' said Dan.

Venus rolled her eyes but hadn't time to correct him.

Conor wondered at her heightened colour as she

answered the door, assuming she must have been sitting too close to the fire. 'You look like the baroness from *The Sound Of Music* with your hair rolled up like that.' The gap between his front teeth materialised as he smiled.

'Is that good or bad?'

'Good, very good. I was in love with the baroness until only last year. I never could understand why the captain preferred the governess. Not that I had anything against her, but the baroness was a class act.'

He watched *The Sound Of Music*. Venus experienced that glimmer of recognition which came from encountering a kindred spirit.

'You're letting in all the night air,' Dan complained, feeling left out.

It sparked a flurry of introductions, welcomes and handshakes. Conor had a bottle of whiskey under his arm, which he presented to Dan. The older man covertly checked the label and nodded his approval when he saw it was Black Bush.

'I'll only be offering this to people if I'm sure they're teetotallers,' he quipped.

Conor looked relieved; he hadn't known what to bring, but thought whiskey was a safe bet.

'I wasn't sure if you'd use the front or back door so I left both porch lights on,' said Venus.

'Back doors are friendlier,' he responded.

Also easier to open, she thought. The front door would probably never open again without a fistful of spanners.

Meanwhile Dan, who'd levered himself to his feet to welcome their guest, limped towards the table using furniture for balance. He hated having to rely on his stick in front of strangers.

'Try that and tell me if it isn't the best punch you've ever tasted.' He pressed a brimming tumbler on Conor.

Conor inhaled, sipped and choked. Dan thumped him on the back and Venus rushed for a glass of water.

'It's powerful stuff,' spluttered Conor, tear-ducts overflowing.

'Indeed it is.' Dan was complacent. 'There's many's a one in these parts would love to get their hands on the recipe, but it was passed down to me by my father and he had it from his father-in-law who had it from his father before him.'

This was one of those Abraham begat Isaac who begat Jacob litanies, thought Conor, charmed.

Of course,' Dan was ruminative as he took a mouthful from his own glass, 'each of us modifies according to our specifications. My father, now, swore by a handful of blackberries added to the mix at the end, but I've phased them out.' He pottered over to his punch and stirred it.

Conor made eye contact with Venus, who whispered that he could switch to another drink after his first glass. And if he really couldn't manage so much as a glass he was to slip it to her and she'd dispose of it without Dan noticing. Conor pretended to stiffen with resolve, risked another sip and remarked that although he thought of himself as a lager man, the punch was growing on him.

'Why wouldn't it?' demanded Dan, whose hearing could sometimes surprise Venus. 'Isn't there the best of Mickey Joe's poitín in it.'

He quizzed Conor about 'his people' as he referred to his family, while Venus watched him indulgently. Her father loved company and was a gregarious creature. Venus could tell Conor was about to be subjected to some of Dan's stories from the gleam in his blue eyes. She had heard them all countless times and only lent half an ear as he began to speak, although she noticed Conor pumping him about the history of the captain's house and its previous occupants.

'My parents will be dying to meet you. They're very taken with the place, and the estate agent who sold it to them didn't seem to know much about its past,' he said.

Venus registered Dan's delight at the thought of these well-to-do lawyers soliciting him for information.

'Old Edie, that's Edith Ferguson, the captain's daughter, was fierce partial to cats,' he said. 'She fed them skinless chicken breast and saucers of cream, and they slept in her bed, those that wanted – although they had a four-poster bed of their own foreby.' He sipped from his tumbler, thrilled with his captive audience. 'She probably had Captain Ferguson spinning in his grave, for he wouldn't allow an animal in the house when he was alive. He was a packet-boat captain – used to do the Belfast-Liverpool run. Although,' and Dan lowered his voice for effect, 'word has it that's not how the bold captain made his money.'

He paused, obliging Conor to pose the relevant question.

Dan swilled his punch around in the glass, prolonging the suspense. If he spills that poitín on the rug it'll burn a hole clear through to the tiles, thought Venus.

'Some say the captain invested wisely,' said Dan, 'others say he inherited property. But them that's in the know point to one thing and one thing only: smuggling. And I'm not talking about French brandy.' He checked Conor's expression to establish it was appropriately impressed.

'You don't mean . . .?' Conor didn't really have much of a clue what the captain could have been transporting, but it seemed the safest response.

'Gun-running,' confirmed Dan. 'They say he stored them in the cellar of his house until the interested parties arrived to collect them. Volunteers for the cause, thugs with no cause but their own – he didn't care who bought them, as long as they paid cash.'

'We do have an exceptionally large, water-tight cellar. It was the one room in the house that had no damp.'

'I rest my case. Let me top you up there, lad.'

While he chattered about the captain, Venus's thoughts meandered back to the last Hallowe'en she'd been home for the holiday weekend. It was only two years ago, but, with memory's sleight of hand, it appeared much longer. Maura had been the one buttering wheaten bread and shopping for barmbrack, her silver hair helmeted into place by its weekly wash and set. Meanwhile Venus, hoping this weekend visit would let her off the hook for Christmas, had idled about the house painting her nails. She had been considering the ultimatum from Andy, the boyfriend who had wanted her to emigrate with him, and had been tempted to confide in Maura. Something had deterred her, however; maybe the careful way her mother had carried herself, slightly hunched forward, as though nursing a nest of eggs.

Venus had asked if there was anything wrong, but Maura had denied it, changing the subject. Venus hadn't persisted because, she supposed now with the benefit of hindsight, she had received the answer that suited her. 'Yes, dear, I'm dying of cancer' wouldn't have fitted the bill at all. Not what she would have wanted to hear, cloistered in her dilemma about how to respond to the boyfriend whose face was today dwindling from her memory.

She was roused from thoughts which were not conducive

to birthday celebrations by Dan, back straddling his hobby horse.

'I suppose you're speculating on how people with a name like Macken wound up in Roancarrick,' he nudged Conor.

His visitor, wondering nothing of the sort, nodded. Dan launched into an explanation about it being a Munster name but his grandfather had walked all the way from Tipperary, some several hundred miles, mind, to work in the stables at Lissadell House.

'You know, the Big House where Yeats used to visit when he was staying with his mother's people in Sligo.' He looked expectantly at Conor, who was starting to give off the scent of one in need of rescuing from Dan's undivided attention. Venus made a mental promise to step in shortly – but her father thrived on a new audience and she hadn't the heart to deprive him just yet.

'"*Two girls in silk kimonos, one a gazelle*",' quoted Dan. 'That was Yeats on the Gore-Booth girls from Lissadell. The one who wasn't a gazelle became a countess instead, and more besides. Countess Markievicz – you'll know all about her, I'm sure, from your history lessons. A grand woman. I wouldn't be surprised if she was one of the captain's customers for his guns. Anyway, my grandfather met my grandmother at the seafront here in Roancarrick and married her within three months. So he never went back to Tipperary. It broke his mother's heart.' He swigged punch, cheerful in the face of his grandmother's heartbreak.

Birdie's knock, followed immediately by the door opening, reprieved Conor.

'We were just about to raise a search party,' Venus sang out.

'Sure I lost track of the time.' Birdie's eyes homed in on

Conor as he stood to greet her. 'You must be one of the Landers people from the captain's house – you're welcome to Roancarrick.' She pumped his hand energetically.

'No such thing as anonymity in a village, is there?' His expression was wry.

'Blow-ins have to expect to be measured and assessed,' said Venus.

Conor raised an eyebrow in her direction, for he detected the undercurrent of malice beneath her light-hearted tone, but said nothing. Venus felt contrite. She shouldn't punish Conor over the sudden pang of loneliness for her mother that swamped her. She was so busy ensuring her father was coping that she tended to overlook her own sense of loss. She frothed into compensation overdrive and described Conor as a talented artist on the threshold of discovery, who was looking towards Roancarrick for inspiration.

Birdie and Dan quizzed him about his paintings – 'drawings,' insisted Conor, but they continued to call them paintings – and he good-naturedly talked about his trees, his church spires and his attempts to settle on a new theme. He was currently considering mountains.

'Tortoises are always worth painting,' suggested Birdie.

Conor looked doubtful. 'But you have to feel an affinity with the object – I've never been a tortoise person.'

'Faces,' said Dan. 'I've always preferred pictures with people in them. A bit of scenery isn't bad either, but I can't be doing with those still-life concoctions. A few apples and a jug – sure where's the art in that?'

Conor laughed and didn't demur when Dan refilled his glass. The punch must be winning him over.

'Did you know,' remarked Birdie, 'that three-quarters of all life forms on earth are sea cucumbers?'

Venus hadn't time to explain to the bemused Conor about Birdie's love affair with the Internet. She decided it was time for the barmbrack and turned out the lamps while she lit the remaining candles, the ones on her nearly-a-birthday cake: seven for a secret never to be told.

'Is it someone's birthday?' asked Conor.

'My lass's,' replied Dan.

Conor was flustered. 'You should have told me. I have no present for you, Venus.'

She gazed at him across the barmbrack, her face transfigured by candlelight. 'None necessary. Besides, it's only a guesstimate birthday.'

There was no opportunity for him to probe further, for she inhaled extravagantly, blew out her candles and lowered her eyelids. Making her wish. The same wish again as last night. *Show me who I belong to.* Plates were produced and slices cut and buttered and Conor was surprised by how well the fruit bread was complemented by the punch.

'We always have barmbrack with tea in my house,' he said.

'Deprivation,' Venus commiserated.

Conor smiled into her eyes, in that intimate way he had. 'I thought I'd be late arriving for your party – we kept getting distracted by vampires at the door. Also ghosties and ghoulies and long-legged beasties. I had no idea Roancarrick was so abundantly stocked with things that go bump in the night.'

'I love the trick or treaters.' Venus licked butter from her wrist.

'In my day we called them the Hallowe'en beggars,' interjected her father.

'Except,' continued Venus, 'I do feel they should be

obliged to recite a verse or sing a song, even dance a phantom jig, before we hand over the loot.'

'Did you see the little girl with the fluorescent face and the tutu?' Conor had to set down his glass as a fit of laughter choked him. 'She looked like the Sugarplum Fairy on a bad day. Obviously couldn't bring herself to throw on an old cloak and be a witch like the other girls. She was even wearing a tiara.' He bit into a slice of barmbrack and, under cover of passing the plate to Venus, whispered, 'This is our first supper – here's hoping it's not our last.'

A hum of pleasure came from Birdie, who held up a circular object wrapped in greaseproof paper. 'I found the ring. It's in my slice.'

'That'll be lucky for you so,' said Dan, whose plate was abandoned by the side of his armchair with only a bite scalloped from the corner of the brack.

Birdie unwrapped the greaseproof paper and the ring, a scaled-down curtain ring, was revealed. She tried it on all her fingers but it was too large and finally she slid it on her thumb.

'Rings refer to cycles.' Birdie was thoughtful. 'This must mean one cycle is ending and a new one beginning.' She took off the ring and bounced it in her hand, contemplating Venus.

The scrutiny from this angular face with its deep-set eyes left Venus feeling vaguely unsettled. Birdie had seemed distant during the evening. She was late even by her standards and had not changed from her old woollen tunic, as she normally would, or tidied the slipping scarlet ribbon in her hair.

'Have you been dreaming about fish lately?' she quizzed Venus.

Venus started. She saw again the shoal of silver fish raining down on her, tangling in her hair and sliding down the back of her neck. Fish she'd longed to catch but which had foiled her attempts, wriggling at her feet.

'Last night,' she admitted.

'Were you swimming with them?' Birdie leaned forward, voice harsh.

'No, trying to catch them. And failing. Does it mean something?'

'Only if you want it to.' Birdie settled back into her seat, fidgeting with her scarlet bow.

She really was the most irritating woman, thought Venus.

Obviously dreaming about fish had something to do with her search, but Birdie wouldn't give her the satisfaction of admitting it. That woman took loyalty to Maura Macken to extremes. How about some loyalty to the living?

Chapter Twenty-seven

Venus raked over her grievances, unnoticed. Then the splutter of a candle caught in a draft of air retrieved her and she clapped her hands. 'Time for the ghost stories.' She moved around the room with a taper, so that all thirteen birthday candles were lit and dotted on window sills and other surfaces. The lamps she left extinguished still. 'You start, Dad.'

'Ah no,' he protested, from politeness rather than reluctance, volunteering Birdie in his place.

'Nonsense, Dan, you're the *seanchaí*.'

He quibbled a little longer, then conceded with grace. 'But first a round of drinks for one and all.' He hauled himself across to the kitchen table again, his left leg dragging but his manner borderline skittish.

'Love the jewels. Very understated.' Conor leaned close to Venus and tapped one of Lily's diamanté earrings with his forefinger, so that it quivered in a disjointed dance.

Dan attended to his guests, then settled himself with his drink and smacked his lips over a steadying gulp. 'It took place like this, no word of a lie. I'll neither add nor subtract but tell you my story exactly as it happened.' His voice settled into the rhythmic cadence of the natural storyteller and although Venus had heard it many times before, she waited with an expectation equal to the others.

'I was nothing but a lad, only twelve years of age, and I'd been loaned out to a farm of land beyond Ballyshannon. It was my first job and I was sorry to leave school, but my parents couldn't afford to keep me on. The farm work wasn't hard, in truth I was wanted for the company more than for my labour, but it meant a few shillings for my parents and one less mouth to feed. I'm sure whatever pay they had for me was little enough, given the times.

'The farm was owned by a family by the name of Sweeney. Pat Sweeney worked like a Trojan during the day, but at night he liked to go along to Hackett's pub for a bottle of Guinness. He lived with his sister Josie and she objected to being left sitting on her own in the house, which is how I came to be hired. She'd have preferred a girl to sit with her, but Pat put the foot down and said if he had to be out of pocket he may as well have someone who'd lend him a hand with the work on the land. The Sweeneys were always fond of money. So night after night I'd sit with Josie Sweeney, and she wasn't the worst – she'd wet the tea and throw some turf on the fire and it was cosy, indeed it was. Sometimes she'd cut me a slice of sweet cake and once she had a box of fancy shop-bought fudge that she shared with me.'

Conor noticed how still it was in the room as Dan spoke; not a clock ticked, not a breath stirred, not a window-pane rattled, although the wind had been gusty as he'd walked along the roadside to their house.

Dan shifted position in the chair, seeking to ease the cramp in the leg he called his crocked one, and continued. 'Then one night I was left on my own because Josie and Pat had a cousin in the next parish back from America-town and there was a *céilí* in his honour. I waited in the kitchen on my own, keeping the fire burning, and late into the night I heard a man's footsteps coming down the cobbled path towards the door. Hobnailed boots, they were, and they rang on the stones. They walked right up to the door and stopped. I stood to lift the bar and let him in, thinking it must be Pat. I wasn't scared, just glad he'd come home sooner than expected, for the evening was long for a twelve-year-boy on his own. But when I came within a foot of the door my hand froze in mid-air and I wasn't capable of lifting that latch. I could go neither forward nor back, and it seemed to me that my heart stopped pumping inside of me, and the blood congealed in my veins.

'Then I heard the footsteps head round to the side of the house, and all at once my body jerked back into life. The sweat streamed off me and I began to shake. I found my wits and went back and sat in the corner, the heart pounding inside me like a cornered animal's, and I was too frightened even to pray – although I hardly knew what it was I feared, to tell you the truth. The footsteps circled the house three, maybe four times. They didn't hurry and they didn't pause, just kept walking steadily like a man surveying his property.'

Dan massaged his leg and stared into one of the candles, reliving his story. 'Pat and Josie Sweeney came home together well into the wee small hours and they had to hammer on the door and call my name before I would let them in. I said to

Pat, "Were you down at the house earlier?" and he said he wasn't. But he looked at his sister and she looked back at him and I knew from their faces there was something they were hiding from me. They said nothing, but I refused to sit on my own in the house again.

'It was nearly a week later before I went home, for I was only allowed a couple of hours off on a Sunday afternoon, and I related this story to my mother and father. They met each other's eyes in much the same way Josie had looked at Pat, and though they made no comment, I knew they had information they weren't letting on to me. Their faces gave them away, indeed they did. I said I wouldn't go back and they said I must, for they needed the money with five mouths behind me and my father only working as a stable-hand, for all his gift for training horses. But as I was leaving my mother reached me a lemonade bottle three-quarters filled with holy water and told me I was to bless myself with it morning and night and sprinkle it at the door and window of my bedroom.

'I finished out the term that was agreed with the Sweeneys, and I never heard those hobnailed boots again. But my parents didn't hire me out to them for a second six-month term, for in May my father said he'd found me a new position at the shipyard in Killybegs, and glad I was to go, although the Sweeneys promised me the moon if I'd stay.'

Dan's voice had hoarsened as he spoke and he paused now to sip from his tumbler. No-one else moved, waiting for the conclusion of his story. 'In later years my mother told me the truth of it. About the strange lights in the middle of the night that were seen on that farm, with horses bolting from the stable. And about the cause of it. Pat Sweeney knew his father had made a will leaving the farm to his mother. She was a drinker, like her two sisters who lived just up the road from them, and Pat was afeared between the three of them, with one leading and the other pushing, the inheritance would be supped away. The farm would come to him in time, but how much would be left of it?

'So he sat up with his father the night he was dying. And when he breathed his last, Pat Sweeney lifted his dead father's hand, with the corpse still warm, and signed his name to a new will leaving everything to himself and Josie. The story came out on account of a neighbour, who arrived to wash the body. She saw what Pat Sweeney was after doing, with his sister's help, and they persuaded the woman to witness the signature. She was paid handsomely for it, but her conscience got the better of her and she told her husband, and so word got out. Pat Sweeney's father never rested easy in his grave on account of the wrong that was done to him. The dead can't be silenced.'

The hush was absolute as Dan's voice, mesmeric in its cadences, suddenly ceased. Even the wind outside had abated. He emptied his glass of punch and sat back in the chair, closing his eyes, wearied by the strain of reaching across so many years.

Conor turned towards Venus, dazed by the experience. He had begun listening in an attitude of indulgence, prepared for some gossamer superstition, but what he heard strangled his instinct towards incredulity. Venus nodded imperceptibly, gleaning some sense of his response. She had heard her father's tale innumerable times but it never lost its power to touch her.

'Whatever happened to the Sweeneys?' asked Conor.

Dan's eyelids fluttered, but he kept them shut. 'No luck came to them. Pat married a girl from Enniskillen direction.

She brought money to the match and the farm was expanded, but every child she birthed lived no more than a few hours. Josie was engaged to a second cousin by the name of O'Donnell, but he broke it off and married the serving-girl in the house. A pretty creature she was, the serving girl, there was never a cross word passed her lips. So then O'Donnell's younger brother volunteered to have Josie if he'd be given the house and land that should have gone to the older one and the parents agreed, for they felt shamed by the broken match. It was an arranged marriage, in truth. I can't say if she was happy or unhappy, but, like Pat Sweeney, she had neither chick nor child. The house O'Donnell married her for was burned to the ground a few years after the match was made, but neither of them was hurt. Josie died about fifteen years ago – she's buried in the churchyard in Ballyshannon.'

'And dead faces laugh.' Birdie lanced the silence, her expression oblique.

Conor risked a laugh too, to puncture the tension. 'It's reassuring to see villains punished. Venus, could I ever take you up on that offer of a beer? The punch is magnificent stuff but it has me beaten.'

'No problem – would you like it in a glass or straight from the can?'

'A can will be fine. Although I need you to serve up some Dutch courage with it if I'm to risk the walk home on my own. Your father's story has put the wind up me.'

Dan smiled grimly. 'There's more things in heaven and earth, lad.'

Conor joined her at the far end of the kitchen, where Venus was rattling out cans of beer from their plastic mooring. 'It's years since anyone called me a lad – I'm thirty-five,' he whispered. 'Someone should record your father's stories; it's a vanishing part of our folklore. Do you think he really believes the Sweeneys were punished for forging their father's signature?'

Venus reached him his drink. 'Certainly he does. My father believes in celestial lightning bolts to blast the blasphemous into charred ashes. Hellfire's lined up for hardened sinners and the rest of us have purgatory to look forward to. He doesn't hold with ecumenism, he thinks it's diluting the formula. He says he wouldn't water down his whiskey so why would he water down his religion? Try him.'

Conor glanced over his shoulder at Dan, who was engrossed in conversation with Birdie. Birdie was advising Dan to wear a blue scarf if he wanted to avoid a cold that winter. And Dan, although he thought little of Birdie's herbal remedies and superstitions, decided it couldn't do any harm – he'd never been one for scarves, they tickled, but his chest was feeling sensitive. It might as well be pampered with a blue scarf as a grey one.

'I thought people like him didn't exist any more outside of John Huston films,' murmured Conor.

'Dan Macken's an original.' Pride washed over Venus. 'Dad,' she called, 'will I rustle you up a whiskey and water? I saw you shiver earlier – I'm afraid you might have caught a chill from the door opening and shutting to so many trick or treaters.'

'Water's for boiling to make tea, not adding to whiskey,' he responded, returning seamlessly to his pet subject: the clergy should be allowed to marry as a last resort if it kept women from taking holy orders. He'd had enough of blue scarves.

'See?' Venus whispered to Conor. 'That's an answer straight out of *The Quiet Man*. She wrestled the ice-cube tray from the freezer and extracted a frozen lemon slice to add to the vodka and white she was preparing for herself. Venus never touched her father's punch, no more than Maura would before her.

Conor radiated admiration. 'Frozen lemon slices, brilliant wheeze.'

'Spotted it in a readers' tips section of a magazine. Saves you having to throw out dried-up lemon that's only been half-used. Dad nabs them for his home-made honey and lemon drinks to keep winter chills at bay. Not exactly the purpose I had in mind but we mustn't be purist.'

They made eye contact with one another, a gaze that lengthened to a stare, and Venus felt a rustle of attraction. Their hands hadn't so much as brushed, everything this far could be construed as neighbourliness, but she felt a partisan interest in him. And he must like her or he wouldn't be here.

Venus clanked her glass against his beer can, feeling more cheerful than at any time since her return to Roancarrick. A little light-hearted coquetry was so therapeutic it should be available on prescription.

She recalled a conversation with Tamsin, in which Tamsin had insisted flirting was communication between the sexes in its highest form. It promised everything but was obliged to deliver nothing. It released all those addictive endorphins into the bloodstream without the bother of engaging in a relationship – which had a fair chance of going wrong.

'Cynic,' Venus had reprimanded her.

'Survivor,' Tamsin had shot back.

'Two-play's fun but I still prefer foreplay,' Venus had joked.

'Come and rescue me,' beseeched Birdie, 'your father is trying to persuade me that paying the nuns to light the sacristy lamp for a person's intentions is money well spent.'

'You either have faith or you don't,' said Dan, 'but you're never too old to acquire it.'

'Chivalrous of you, Dad,' scolded Venus as she topped up his glass and checked Birdie's. 'You know very well Birdie is ageless. I'm serving the supper now. Does anyone want tea with it or are you all happy with alcohol?'

They were all happy with alcohol.

As they ate, Conor asked Birdie if she were the lady with the mad-coloured door.

'Depends on your interpretation of insanity.'

'I meant mad as is in wild, funky, happening,' he amended. 'I'm interested in doors – I used to draw nothing but them until I switched to trees. They're so rich with possibilities: entrances, exits, alternative lives.'

'I've always had mine violet,' volunteered Birdie. 'Violets protect. They're also known as heartsease.'

'Heartsease,' repeated Conor, spellbound.

'Just so. They alleviate the pain that springs from love going awry. I can't grow violets, the climate's against me, so I make do with a violet door. I paint it afresh every spring.'

'Violet.' He flicked a fawn-fair curl on his forehead. Venus almost expected to hear it peal, bell-like. 'Or heliotrope. Grey mixed with blue. I must buy some violet ink and see where it leads me.'

The party broke up after everyone had eaten and Venus was astonished when Dan said it was close on two in the morning. She smiled as she unhooked Lily's earrings. At the door, Conor had turned to her and whispered in her ear, so close that one of his curls had stroked her temple. '*Good night, sweet prince, and flights of angels sing thee to thy rest.*'

This was one man she didn't mind harping on about angels.

Chapter Twenty-eight

The next morning Venus sent an email to Lily in response to yesterday's, congratulating her on the wedding preparations going so smoothly. It felt a little hypocritical – well, all right, a lot – but she might as well be gracious about this liaison since nobody cared that they were making an enormous mistake. Not even the Registrar of Marriages. You'd imagine that office, at least, would treat marriages between asylum seekers and citizens with some degree of suspicion. But no – she checked the text of Lily's email again – the registrar apparently didn't consider it any of his or her business. She promised to visit soon for a wedding outfit shopping expedition and even added an insincere 'regards to Karim'.

Then, in an excess of duty, she went to Mass with her father, whose balance was more unsteady than usual after the previous evening's punch – even when he leaned on his blackthorn stick. She caught his arm as they went up the path to Our Lady of the Assumption, fearful that some of the crooked paving-slabs might trip him. 'Don't be linking me and making an old man out of me,' he hissed, shrugging her off because his friend Mickey Joe was watching.

After the service she checked her email. Lily had replied already, wedding-obsessed and airily wondering whether she should wear a ballet or floor-length gown. Also mentioning, as an afterthought, that Senan was being clandestine about his deal but had let it slip that the commission would buy him a Ferrari. Venus decided there was nothing she could do about it, short of organising a protest group, and she had enough on her shoulders. Still, it irked her to think of Roancarrick's main street being redesigned to buy Senan Mulqueen a status-symbol sportscar. May some gouger's key scratch the length of it, the self-same day he drove it out of the garage.

Venus headed for the beach, trying to convince herself not to square up to Senan's developers. Tracking down her mother had to be her priority. Conor must have been watching for her, because she was joined by him almost as soon as she set foot on the beach. In his hand was a blush-coloured manila folder and he reached it to her self-consciously, fiddling with the cuff on his coat while he waited for her to inspect it.

'What is it?' she asked.

'A birthday gift.' He was still on cuff duty.

Inside was a drawing of a leafless tree, elegiac in its skeletal state.

'There was no need,' she protested, entranced by the pen and ink's stark simplicity.

'It's my philosophy to practise random acts of kindness and senseless acts of beauty. Many happy returns, Venus.'

'It's exquisite,' she said. 'I'd love to see some of your other drawings.'

He was embarrassed. 'I don't like showing them to people – I want to hoard them like a miser. I suppose I'm afraid of criticism.'

'I'll be kind,' she promised, resting her hand briefly on the nub of his elbow.

'Maybe,' he said, which she interpreted as a rebuff. Coming from Conor, it was akin to a promise.

He spoke to fill the awkwardness that yawned between them. 'Thank you for last night. It felt like a Hallowe'en from decades ago, as though we were following in some seamless tradition. My family, by comparison, all goggle at chainsaw massacres on TV as soon as the barmbrack's sliced. Ghost stories by candlelight are infinitely preferable.' He flashed his gap-toothed grin and she smiled back. 'My parents are seriously jealous. They're also desperate to meet your father and hear some of the history of the captain's house, as well as more adventures of the bucaneering captain.'

'I expect that can be arranged.' But Venus registered ambivalence about Dan and the Landers meeting formally, for she didn't want the families to become intertwined before she'd quantified her feelings for Conor. It was putting the cart before the horse and distorting her sense of order.

'Don't suppose he made any of his crew walk the plank, our captain?' asked Conor.

'Only passengers who evaded their fares.' Venus was aiming for a frivolity she didn't feel.

Nevertheless they walked along the strand in companionable silence. Seagulls sailed overhead, their unmusical squawking cutting across the ever-present whoosh of the waves.

Venus debated frames for her drawing, inclined towards

a narrow black one with a generous cream mount. Perhaps she should check with Conor, since artists tended to have definite views on how their work should be presented.

'You called yesterday your not-really-a-birthday.' Conor looked across at her and Venus realised he must be at least two inches taller. She felt like raising her face to the sky and dancing a jig.

'That's right.' She managed to keep her voice non-committal.

'You don't believe in giving too much away.' His mouth curved, eyes that were neither blue nor green glinting. 'Is it a secret?'

'It's not much of a secret since the entire village knows it. I'm adopted and we don't exactly know my date of birth.'

'Don't you have a birth certificate?'

'Yes and no. I have a special one for adopted people. Everybody agreed on October 31 as my birthday because that's the day my parents came by me. Since I wasn't old enough to speak, let alone express an opinion, it was decided on my behalf.'

Venus slanted a glance at Conor and thought he seemed intent on mapping Ben Bulben's squared-off outline, so closely was he scrutinising it. He gave the appearance of being unfazed by her disclosure – although her cropped version wasn't much of a revelation. It struck her again, as it had the previous evening, that perhaps she could enlist Conor's help in her search for her identity.

'And when would you prefer to celebrate your birthday?' he enquired.

She paused. Given the choice she'd opt for July. She fancied birthday picnics with strawberries and cream instead of trick or treaters, and a sqidgy gateau replacing barmbrack. She could wear romantic summer dresses as the birthday girl and press chilled bottles of wine to the base of her neck to ward off heat-rashes. Venus always felt she'd mislaid her birthday among the Hallowe'en traditions; imagine how short-changed she'd feel if she were a Christmas baby.

'July 1.' She plucked a day from the ether. 'That's when I'd like my birthday to fall.'

Conor blanched. 'That's an unfortunate date. I wouldn't recommend it.'

'Why?'

'It's . . . complicated.' His voice crackled and died.

Venus wondered but said nothing. She was a believer in partial disclosure herself – although the previous day he'd shown a tendency to volunteer a surplus of information. Of course, this was exactly what she proposed doing now, implicating him in her own search, but necessity demanded it. Sleuthing partners required something in the way of facts – Sherlock Holmes didn't go round keeping Dr Watson in the dark. 'One of my resolutions for the year ahead is to find out who my real parents are,' she admitted.

It roused Conor from the torpor into which her random date seemed to have plunged him – he abandoned scuffing the sand with his beige and navy boat shoes and turned towards her. 'Is that so difficult nowadays? I thought a child had the right to be supplied with its mother's details after a certain age.'

'Nobody knows who my mother is. I'm a foundling.' Venus was partial to its Dickensian ring, although the reality was less appealing.

Encouraged by Conor's unblinking attention, she recounted as much of her story as she knew. He was instantly keen to speed over to the seal's rock and view the spot where Dan had found her gurgling among the rock pools.

'It's so wonderfully improbable,' he gushed. 'Here you are, looking all prim and self-contained – who could conceive what lies beneath the surface?'

Venus wasn't enamoured of the description but felt mollified by his gust of interest.

'We must check the library for newspaper reports of the time and read the advertisements your parents placed, Venus.'

Excellent, he wanted to take charge. An admirable trait in men, on occasion.

'And we should interview the older villagers, see if any of them have suspicions about who the mother might be.' Conor ransacked his hair. 'Your one in the pub sounds a promising starting-point to me, also Mrs O'Dea in the shop – it is Mrs O'Dea, isn't it? I know it's not a word we're supposed to use any more but she has a most spinster-like demeanour. I can't help wondering if there's a Mr O'Dea.'

'There is,' Venus assured him. 'Although he doesn't figure highly in Mrs O'Dea's priorities. She's as near to being a virgin as possible for a woman who's given birth to two children. But I've already tried Mrs O'Dea and she steered me off course. I think she just doesn't like to admit she's out of the loop on this morsel of gossip.'

Venus pondered whether Conor should approach Birdie – just because she'd had no luck with her neighbour didn't stop him from sounding her out. Birdie might be less guarded with him, less anxious to protect Maura, who had been her friend. Venus decided against it, for now. Birdie might complain to Dan and upset him, and she didn't want her father distressed.

At Conor's insistence they retraced their steps along the beach and started for the mermaid's cave, while he probed her about her childhood. He was less interested in her time in England than she expected – after all, her London decade defined her, in Venus's view. But when she mentioned Lily he perked up, chuckling at the hairstyle which could only be described as a tribute to Pebbles from *The Flintstones*, and looking pensive when she mentioned Karim.

For one unhinged moment Venus thought about introducing Conor to Lily as a way of luring her away from Karim but decided against it. Ostensibly because she felt Lily would see through the ploy, but in a selfish little fold of her psyche she wanted to keep him for herself. Lily could meet tons of men in Dublin – even allowing for her Bermuda Triangle theory – whereas Roancarrick's selection was inevitably more limited. Anyway, Lily was too immersed in her wedding plans to be sidetracked now. She was determined to procure a passport for Karim and a fine head of hair, no matter how curly, wouldn't deter her.

'Will you be staying all winter in Roancarrick?' She kept pace with Conor's strides without difficulty.

'Looks like it,' he glowered. Then he flashed that boyish grin again and she wondered if she had imagined the ill-temper. 'It's a magnificent place to find yourself, particularly for an artist. How could I not be inspired here?'

Venus felt fairness demanded Conor should tell her why he had to give Killyclogher a wide berth, since she'd opened up about her adoption, but she couldn't come right out and say so. He should simply understand it was the quid pro quo of social interaction.

'Is Killyclogher pretty?' She adopted a lateral tack.

'There's not a lot to it, but what there is has its attractions. It grows on you. Most people have an affection for their birthplace. I don't think of it as the Garden of Eden, but it's no purgatory either.'

'I suppose you're attached to the Victorian pile you mentioned – the captain's house must cramp you after so much space.'

'It's not bad – to be honest I preferred our first house, the one I was born in. Sometimes we seem to rattle around in the stately heap – you can go all day without bumping into anyone unless you camp out in the kitchen. Cosiness has much to recommend it. Unless you hog the fire you're never really warm in those large houses.' He shivered now, zipping up his leather jacket, as they picked their way down the path that led to the cave.

The wind was less hostile in the sheltered enclave.

'Show me where Dan found you.'

Obediently Venus roosted on the planed surface of the seal's rock, a little ungainly as she clung with one hand to its outcrop, holding on to her birthday present with the other. 'Right there, in the hollow by the base of the rock.' She leaned over and pointed down, trying to imagine herself as a new-born baby, kicking her feet and crowing as she waited to be found. Had her mother kissed her as she'd left her there? Had she hesitated, watching to see who'd find her, or had she walked away without a backwards glance? How could any mother leave a naked infant in such a place on such a night? Did she care if she lived or died? There were so many questions she wanted to ask her mother and yet they could all be reduced to one word. Why?

Pinioned by her lack of answers, Venus put a hand to her plait and pulled out the band securing it, loosening it so that the sea breeze whipped through her hair. Craving distraction, she launched into speech. 'Did you know there's a school of thought that suggests mermaids were really seals? They claim sailors mistook their bright eyes and glistening bodies for those of women, as they frolicked in the water. Maybe that's why the seal's rock is at the mouth of the cave – it was probably seals that sheltered in there and not mermaids at all.'

Conor wasn't listening. No great harm, thought Venus – she preferred the mermaid version of events; explanations, however rational, were two-dimensional compared with myths.

'It's a peculiar place to abandon a child.' He looked about. 'What were the chances of anyone finding her before she froze to death or was swept out to sea? Obviously the T-shape of the rock would protect a baby tucked beneath its canopy for a short while. But you'd imagine it would have made more sense to leave her in the village where more people would be passing by. Unless' – he wrinkled his snub nose – 'unless Dan was meant to find you. Only your family and Birdie live at this end of the village, right? And I think you said you were still warm so you can't have been lying long before he happened upon you. Did someone send your father out that day? Did he receive a phone call or did he always walk above the mermaid's cave at a particular time?'

Venus reflected, disconcerted to consider she might have been placed deliberately with Dan and Maura, rather than ending up with them by chance. 'My mother had a headache and he went out for pills. He was on his way to the shop in the village when he found me. But I don't see how whoever left me here could have planned my mother's migraine.'

Conor smiled and shrugged, the light from the watery sunlight reducing his pupils to pinpricks.

'Curiouser and curiouser,' he said. Then he peered at her, bending so close she imagined for one delirious moment he was about to kiss her, and flicked at her cheek. 'You had some kind of an insect climbing all over you.'

Venus felt something somersault inside her – not her heart but some other organ lower down. Was this how it felt to fall in love? Or were her antennae warped by the boredom of Roancarrick?

As these conflicting thoughts hummed inside her, accompanied by the lulling lap of waves, Conor was gazing into her eyes. She stared back, discerning two minuscule Venuses in his pupils. Or were they Venusi?

'You look . . .' he murmured.

Yes? What? Like a mermaid? Better still, a siren. Venus sensed he was on the brink of invading her personal space – she would not be marshalling a resistance movement.

'You look frozen to the core. Your nose has turned a delicate shade of raspberry.' He stretched out a hand to take the folder containing her birthday present so she wouldn't drop it in the water. Then he reached her his other hand to help her off the rock, but, piqued, she pretended not to see and jumped off unaided.

Anyway his nose was too small, Venus consoled herself. A snub nose on a man struck an inappropriate note. A man needed a strong, sweeping nose. Romanesque or patrician.

As they parted at the crossroads, he reached her the manila folder. 'Don't forget your tree,' he smiled, wrinkling his minute nose.

And that was another thing. What man who cared about impressing a woman gave her something in a pink folder?

He was obviously gay. Or in denial of his inclinations. That must be why he had to vacate Killyclogher; perhaps he'd propositioned young male neighbours. Pretending he wanted to make life sketches and then taking advantage of their naivety to seduce them.

Although a gay boyfriend would be pleasant, she conceded, in a final paradoxical twist. They dressed well, bought their own beauty products instead of pinching yours and wouldn't always be badgering you for sex. Except that restraint might pall eventually.

Looking at Conor's receding back, common sense reasserted itself. Her vanity was a shade pitted, no more; every man who declined to fall for her wasn't automatically homosexual, tempting though it might be to believe that.

As though sensing her reappraisal, Conor turned and waved. He cupped his hand to his mouth and called to her, but she couldn't discern the words. She shrugged and he tried again. Wafted to her on the wind came a brace of sentences that had her grinning so broadly her father, minutes later, remarked her ears were in danger of being dislodged.

'You looked like a nereid down there, coiled on the rock,' Conor had called. 'There you were, all ethereal, shimmering in the dappled light – if it didn't sound so hackneyed, I'd admit I was tempted to sketch you.'

Fulsome flattery was your only man.

What was a nereid exactly?

Chapter Twenty-nine

'It's always as well to get these details out into the open from the start if you're going to be friends with someone,' began Conor.

Venus wished he wouldn't keep hammering on about friendship.

'It's as plain as your chin,' continued Conor.

Venus winced. She was sensitive about her chin, which threatened to go forth and multiply in later life but for now was merely rounded. Its decisive conclusion to the end of her face contrasted with her eyebrows, which vaulted delicately at the top, feather-fine wisps that disappeared into the jungle of her hair.

She scrutinised him, as they sat opposite one another in the shack that called itself the Carrick Chipper. He'd phoned her – and she hadn't even given him her number, although she supposed they were in the directory – and invited her there for a 'second supper', a few days after their walk to the seal's rock. The remains of their cod and chips littered the plates and she lifted a stray chip now and munched. She wondered if he'd deliberately highlighted the feature she was most self-conscious of, after her height, but decided she was behaving like a conspiracy theorist.

'I'm listening.' She pushed aside the plate and made prayer-peaks of her hands so he'd realise she was treating this with gravity.

'The reason I had to leave Killyclogher was –'

She nodded encouragingly, prepared for some crazy high jinks inspired by artistic temperament, now that she'd convinced herself he was heterosexual and interested in her. Even if he were currently in denial about the attraction and had rationalised it as friendship.

Conor exhaled so precipitately that she felt his warm breath on her hands. Who had said expelled air was wasted air? She suspected it had been her Tasmanian ex. Spouting theories had been one of his vices. Conor's expelled air connected her to him as surely as if he had reached out and caressed her face.

Along with the air came a gush of words. 'I left because I helped someone commit suicide last summer. Euthanasia, mercy killing, homicide, murder – take your pick. It was meant to be handled discreetly, but it leaked out and I wouldn't lie about it, and people became angry with me. Still are, I imagine. There was a question of criminal charges being pressed if the authorities were informed. "He asked me to do it" is no defence. It seems we don't have the right to help someone to die, even if they're in unbearable pain and plead with you to intervene.' Conor wasn't looking at Venus but at the empty chair beside her. He spoke rapidly, in a monotone. 'My parents had to make a generous donation to charity to avert a criminal

301

prosecution. It was money they couldn't spare, since they'd just bought the captain's house, so they weren't best pleased with me – over and above any free-floating moral issues. Relations are still lukewarm.'

Venus's prayer-peaks collapsed. She couldn't even frame a question. Conor continued with his machine-gun delivery.

'That's partly why I'm across the border in the Republic, in a different jurisdiction. Keeping my head down, in the best tradition of discretion and how it relates to valour. In case someone in the North decides to turn whistle-blower and the authorities have no choice but to take a case against me. All it needs is for one lawyer in the Director of Public Prosecution's office, out to make a name for him or herself, to get wind of this and I could be crucified.'

This was all too much to digest. Venus's syrup eyes clouded to treacle, and she could hardly bring herself to look at Conor. Instead, she inspected her right hand, noticing afresh the clump of three tiny freckles near the flap of skin between thumb and forefinger, her mind numb.

Conor's tone changed, his delivery lightened. 'It was an old teacher I was friendly with from school. Donal Flynn was his name. He lived on his own in a bungalow with the loudest carpets you've ever seen in your life – I used to visit Donal there sometimes. Not often. We become immersed in our own lives. But I was always glad when I did go. I used to put on my sunglasses for a joke when I'd first walk in. Donal took it in the right spirit – he'd bought the bungalow with fixtures and fittings included and never bothered to change them. The living-room was the worst – I could swear it had an alphabet-spaghetti pattern.'

Conor's expression softened and Venus saw that he'd been fond of Donal, whatever had happened between them.

'Donal was my art teacher at the Christian Brothers' School in Omagh. He worked there all his life until they made him retire. He never married or even had a girlfriend, to the best of my knowledge. I think maybe he was one of those perennial bachelors who are gay but they never acknowledge it, even to themselves. Nowadays he'd probably be outed and forced to have a sex life, whether he wanted one or not, but back then it wasn't on the agenda. Donal organised school trips to art galleries and museums when the other teachers wanted to take us to GAA matches. He taught me about the Impressionists, about perspective, about light and shade, about learning the rules thoroughly so you'd be all the better at flouting them. If I have any trace of talent at all, it was nurtured by him.'

Venus found her voice at last. 'Was he all alone in the world?'

'He was the last of his family, apart from some nephews in Canada. And he never heard from them from one end of the year to the next. I don't believe they ever met. You'd think after teaching in Omagh for the guts of four decades there'd have been more of his pupils to keep him company in the lean years, but that wasn't the case. Hardly any of us saw him regularly.' Conor rammed his knuckles into his eyes, hurting them. Glad to hurt them.

'You're not responsible for someone else's loneliness,' said Venus.

He lifted his hands away and locked eyes with her. The silence was knife-edge until he bridged it. 'Donal had bowel cancer. Towards the end he lost control of his bowels. Can you imagine the indignity of it? He was afraid to go out in case it happened to him. Look, I'm sorry if this is unseemly, but I'm telling it like it was for the man. He told me once

303

he went to a reunion dinner at the school and just as he reached the main door he felt faeces shooting down inside his trouser legs. He turned round and went home again and threw the suit in the dustbin. He couldn't even bring himself to send the trousers to the dry-cleaners because of the stench. And then he locked himself in the bathroom and sat on the toilet-seat and wept. This was a man who loved art, music, the theatre. A man who played Vivaldi in the background as we sketched and covered the classroom walls in posters by Van Gogh and Gaugin – so a bunch of schoolboy louts with testosterone-overload would be exposed to as much culture as he could trick into them.'

Venus felt tears well up in her eyes. She thought of her mother, who'd also suffered from cancer. At least she hadn't had her dignity undermined too. Small mercies were better than none at all. The Campbell teenager who'd taken her sister trick or treating cleared away their plates and Conor watched Venus, wondering how much more to tell her. The story was nearly through – he might as well take it to its culmination.

'Donal had been depressed and in pain for months. He was virtually housebound – in the end he wouldn't even get out of bed to answer the door to me, but I had a key and I used to let myself in. He had a home help and she took care of the shopping and whatever cleaning was needed, but he was isolated – desperate for company. And then he began to plead with me to put him out of his misery. The painkillers weren't working any more, but there were no hospital places for him. They admitted him for monitoring, but after a while they said he was better at home. Better for whom? The health service, not for Donal.' Bitterness permeated his voice and Venus had the urge to take his hand, but hesitated to touch him.

Conor continued, 'I went away for four weeks to teach at a sketching school in West Cork. I needed the money – I don't sell many of my paintings and when I do the gallery's commission is crippling. When I returned there was a deterioration. Poor Donal had seen nobody but the home help and the district nurse during the entire month. He said he'd used the time to think and he'd marshalled all the arguments, wrestled with his conscience, and was convinced that he wanted to end his own life while he still had some shreds of self-respect. Otherwise, he claimed, he'd die in his own squalor. But he couldn't do it alone and he begged me to help him.'

Now that his story was nearly told, Conor faltered. He supported his chin with his hand and memorised the blank wall beyond Venus. They were the only ones in the chipshop. She watched him reliving those last days with Donal while the Campbell girl who'd served them chatted on the pay phone, animated for the first time since their arrival.

When he spoke again his voice was ragged. 'Donal beseeched me to put him out of his misery. "You'd do as much for a dog," he argued, and eventually I agreed. I agreed because that's what I would have chosen for myself, in his position. I agreed because I cared about him. There was no cure, the pain relief wasn't working, it was only a matter of time. I agreed, although agreeing was intolerable, because to disagree would have been more intolerable again.'

'How did you do it?' Venus was mesmerised.

'Pills. I went from chemist to chemist buying Nurofen – did you know they sell them in foil containers now as a suicide deterrent? You have to pop them through the foil so it makes it that little bit harder to access the pills. A bottle was too easy to up-end. Fifteen are enough to kill you, or at least cause you serious liver damage. So I poured us both a glass of Lanson, his favourite champagne, and I held his glass to his lips because he hadn't the strength to grasp the stem, and we drank to friendship, which Donal said made life worth living. He said true friendship was more than time could taint. Then he swallowed the pills for as long as I held them to his mouth, washing them down with champagne. I held his hand when he couldn't swallow any more and then I laid him back on the pillows.'

Venus knew Conor couldn't see her now, although his gaze rested on her.

'After a while I worried about him starting to vomit and choking, and the vestiges of dignity he'd tried to win back for himself being eroded, so I moved him into the recovery position, still holding him by the hand.' He looked down at his own hands. 'His grip was strong, right to the end. Even if I'd wanted to, I don't think I could have prised his fingers off mine. I tried to drink my own wine but it burned my throat. Then I remembered being told by someone that your hearing is the last sense to go. So I talked to Donal – probably long after he lost consciousness. Inane chatter, about the school trips we'd taken and the boys he'd taught and where they were now. And then there was a rattle in his throat and I checked his pulse and found nothing. So I turned him onto his back again and phoned the doctor.'

Into the throbbing well of silence, Venus spoke. 'And how did he know this was a case of euthanasia?'

'I hadn't the sense to clear away the debris. I was thorough about all the advance preparations, but I hadn't thought past the moment of death, or what my own reaction to it would be. It . . . emptied me. I just sat there with Donal until the knock came at the door and I let the doctor in. He saw the champagne bottle and the packets of Nurofen and he knew Donal wouldn't have had the strength to keep popping them. I suppose he could have had them lined up ready for swallowing. Anyway the doctor took in the scene and he checked Donal over and then he turned to me and asked, "Did you have a hand in this?" And I answered – I don't know what I answered. I was told later I nodded. Then the doctor said he would go out of the room and come back in and I was to use those few seconds to jam my pockets full of the pill-packets.'

'That was decent of him,' interjected Venus.

'It was. I went to school with his younger brother. It's one of the benefits of small town life – there's a certain amount of looking out for each other.'

'But how did your part in the teacher's death leak out?'

'The doctor told his wife and she told her sister and word reached the parish priest. He came to see me and asked if it was true and I didn't lie. My parents hushed it up with a charity donation but it's out there.' He shrugged and ran a hand through his hair, sending the curls flying. 'In most people's eyes I've committed a crime. And in the law's view there's no doubt about it: euthanasia is illegal.'

'How do you feel about it now, in hindsight?' Venus was awed by how much she knew about this man she scarcely knew.

Conor nibbled at the ball of his thumb. 'I'd do it again. It was what Donal wanted and I was the only person he trusted enough to ask for help.'

'So your conscience is clear?'

'I wouldn't say that.' He barked out a laugh that was no

laugh at all. 'Of course his death is on my conscience. Donal left a suicide note which let me off the hook, but people still talked about me – there were whispers of forgery. I can't blame them.' His eyes were as bleak as the ocean in January. 'I read up on euthanasia before I did what Donal asked me to do and I'm still researching it. Just because it's illegal doesn't mean it's wrong in certain circumstances. The Dutch have accepted the euthanasia principle and laid it down in law. Other countries may follow their example: Italy, France and Britain have strong pro-mercy-killing lobbies.'

'I thought Australia had it briefly but then reversed it because of the storm of protest.' Venus remembered this because there had been an Australian teacher on the staff at the Bridges Across The World language school at the time who'd followed the debate.

'It was legalised in the Northern Territory in the mid-nineties, but the federal parliament overturned their decision.' Conor had it off pat.

Venus meditated. How would she have responded if her mother had pleaded with her to take away the pain? But Maura would never have done that; she believed suffering in this life helped prepare someone for the next. *All for Thee, Oh Sacred Heart of Jesus, All for Thee.*

'I think I'd have tried other avenues before I did what you did. Maybe stronger painkillers or – something . . .' She tailed off.

His vision blurred and then refocused, a fierce light firing his eyes. 'You don't think I tried that first? You don't think I wrestled with every alternative? I looked at the Dutch legislation too, to make sure Donal fitted their description of a candidate for euthanasia. They're a civilised people – they're not making a case for dumping the old and infirm.' His expression curdled, daring Venus to disagree. 'Under their laws a patient must have an incurable illness, which he did, be experiencing unbearable suffering, which he was, and must have given consent. Not only did he consent, he was on his knees to me to do it. The patient also has to be aware of other medical options, but there weren't any, and have been offered a second opinion by another doctor. Donal received third and fourth opinions.'

A crease emerged between Venus's eyebrows. She remembered reading that legalisation of euthanasia would put vulnerable groups such as the elderly and disabled under severe pressure. Or maybe it was the Australian teacher at the London school who'd told her this. But she didn't feel like raising it with Conor – he looked so harsh.

He sighed, pre-empting her. 'I'm not in favour of widespread euthanasia. I'd never thought about it particularly before Donal forced me to become an instant expert. He insisted it was an issue of personal autonomy and I said that must be balanced with the needs of society as a whole – the possibilities of abuse were endless. Backwards and forwards we used to debate it, but in the end I gave him what he wanted because I hadn't the heart to deny him. He died on July 1 – that's why I froze when you mentioned it as the date you'd like for your birthday. It has connotations for me I doubt I'll ever escape. Have you ever watched someone you love die, Venus?'

Maura filled her vision, shrunken to half her size, her body scarcely disturbing the smooth contours of the hospital blanket. She remembered how only her work-roughened knuckle had saved her wedding ring from sliding off her finger. To Venus's horror, tears spilled down her cheeks.

Conor was across to her in a heartbeat, fingers splayed around her skull, guiding her head to his shoulder. The Campbell girl was so riveted she hung up the phone.

'Let's get you out of here,' whispered Conor.

Instead of walking her home he steered her towards the strand. He slipped off his leather jacket and rested it on her shoulders; then they paced the sand, down near the lapping edge of the waves where it was damp and easier to tread. His hand nestled against the small of her back and he was silent while she went from snivelling, to shuddering, then nothing. Not even thinking.

After a while she became conscious of her surroundings. The sea was crystalline; it made a shivering sound and its continual noise was soporific. A random memory drifted into Venus's mind, of a puppet show she'd gone to see with her mother during those student years in Dublin. The Lambert Puppet Theatre in Monkstown had been showing Sinbad the Sailor and on impulse Venus had booked tickets for them, although they had been the only people in the audience not trailing children.

It had been an Arabian Nights extravaganza, complete with bejewelled princess, evil hypnotist with eyes that flashed on and off like Christmas-tree lights and his pet, a crocodile called Snapper. And of course there was Sinbad: as handsome and daring a hero as any pantomime spectator could hope for. In her Christmas stocking that year, the nineteen-year-old Venus had found a Sinbad glove-puppet.

The memory precipitated a smile. Conor sensed her mood-swing and moved his hand from the small of her back to her shoulder. He turned her gently to face him and for one panic-stricken moment Venus thought he intended to kiss her. Not tonight, not yet, she wanted to protest. His eyes glittered in the moonlight and his face had a silvered glow.

But all he did was secure his jacket more firmly around her and then strike out for home. He walked her to the gate, as lost in thought as she, and their parting was monosyllabic.

It hit her with something of a jolt, feeling her way through the kitchen because she didn't want to turn on the light, to realise that this was the first time she'd been with Conor Landers that there hadn't been a whistle out of him. Not so much as a cheep. She missed his whistling – it was part of the man.

Dan was already in bed and Venus slipped upstairs, lying without sleeping, her mind a-whirl, as she watched the moonbeams slink into her room through a gap in the curtains.

Just before turning away, Conor had stretched out a hand, solemn in the moonlight, to that wayward strand of hair which had a tendency to flop into her eyes. He'd tucked it behind an ear, his hand brushing her cheek. 'A *bracelet of bright hair about the bone,*' he'd murmured.

And in that moment she hadn't cared that he had helped someone to die. Venus wasn't afraid of doing something she'd regret with Conor Landers – but of something she might never regret.

Chapter Thirty

It was Monday lunch-time, more than a week after her birthday, and Venus had heard no more from Lily despite sending her a couple of emails. She was probably too wrapped up in wedding preparations. Venus felt sidelined. However, she was inquisitive enough about her friend's plans to ring – except she didn't want Karim listening to their conversation so she phoned Lily at the office.

'I'll ring you straight back,' promised Lily, 'I have to give my sandwich order to Senan – he's doing a run to O'Brien's.'

Venus brooded while she waited for the call. She hardly ever spoke to people on the phone any more, whereas while she lived in London she'd been surgically attached to her mobile phone. The one or two friends she kept in touch with from London emailed her rather than rang. It was depressing, reflected Venus, how few possessions and even fewer friends she'd built up. She couldn't even attribute it to a peripatetic life because she'd had six addresses in total: some of the teachers at Bridges Across The World had managed as many in the space of a year. After only a couple of months back in Ireland, she was starting to think she didn't have much to show for her thirty-three years.

Why was it that none of her friendships in London had put down roots? She'd been a popular staff member, her social life had been active; as cogs in the metropolitan wheel went, her progress had been well-oiled. But turn your back on London and people assumed you were turning your back on life.

Venus frowned. The school had been a train station, with teachers forever arriving and departing – she had been the longest-serving member of staff apart from Tamsin. The teachers had been companions for one another, but there had always been a sense of flux, easy come, easy go – it hadn't been conducive to anything more than superficial friendship. Perhaps genuine fellowships came dropping slow, like the gradual intimacy that had been fostered with Lily. It could be that one true connection with another human being was all that anyone could aspire to in life.

Venus shook herself out of her introspection and decided to have Conor's tree sketch framed the next time she was in Sligo. She could do it on Thursday before her intermediate-level Spanish class. She'd hang it on the hook near her bedroom door, which had held a wooden plaque shaped like priest's hands, a Confirmation present from her Aunt Betty. On her second night back in Roancarrick, she'd shuddered, taken it down, and pushed it to the back of a drawer.

The phone rang, a welcome diversion.

'Sorry about the delay,' Lily was breathless. 'I got caught by the client from hell – he keeps hounding me to know why his house hasn't sold yet. I've told him it's because it's overpriced, and at his insistence. A more competitive price would soon shift it. But he whinges on about the money he's spent on imported Italian bathroom fittings. I had to be blunt with him, Venus. "Mr Carty," I said, "there are two other houses in your street at fifty thousand euro less than your property – it's a buyers' market and you aren't doing yourself any favours by refusing to be realistic. What you lose on this sale you'll make on your new purchase." Did he listen?'

'Did he?' Venus was bored enough to be interested.

'Not a chance. If Senan hadn't arrived with my chicken and roast peppers on ciabatta and pretended to be another client with an appointment to view in Pearse Street, I'd be on the phone to him yet, hearing about how much he's out of pocket on his garden decking. By the way, Senan said to say "Hi, hot momma". His exact words.'

Venus rolled her eyes.

'Although I should warn you that I think he has a girlfriend. Don't be disappointed – it's only because he complained you were very touchy when he saw you in Roancarrick.'

'I'm not disappointed,' Venus assured her.

But Lily still had Mr Carty in her system. 'Nobody asked him to install decking, Venus – nobody promised him it would transform his home into a palace. Or if they did, more fool him for believing the decking salespeople. But he seems convinced it's my life's mission to inflate the price of his house so he gets back every cent he's ever spent on it.'

'You sound stressed,' said Venus.

'Do I?' Lily was rattled: she didn't like it when work nibbled at her equilibrium. She always maintained no job was worth it. 'Mr Carty would try the patience of a saint. Now, never mind him. Tell me all about your birthday. I rang you during the afternoon, but your father said you were out shopping. We had a cosy tête-à-tête – he was telling me how well you'd settled into Roancarrick and how much he enjoys your company. He thought you were looking failed when you first came back from London, but you're much improved now, thanks to all the walks you take by the sea. The roses are back in your cheeks, he says.'

Venus glowed: so much for her uneasy suspicion she was more of a crown of thorns than a consolation to her father. He hadn't mentioned Lily's call, however – his short-term memory was in free-fall.

'So what's new in no-streetlights territory?' Lily unwrapped her sandwich.

Venus told her about the Hallowe'en party, trying to elide the number of guests. But Lily scented the omission and harried her until Venus reluctantly admitted that a neighbour called Conor had been there. Naturally this precipitated an inquisition, followed by a scolding session for Venus's previous failure to alert Lily to his existence. Followed by a breathtaking leap of imagination involving orange blossom, pregnancy and godmother's duties to be carried out by Lily.

'A love interest in Roancarrick,' she crowed, splattering roast pepper across her notepad. 'Imagine spending ten years in London and then falling for the first man you meet back home in the middle of nowhere.'

'He wasn't the first man I met.' Venus bridled. 'What about John Óg O'Dea?'

Mention of another man pulled Lily up short. 'Of course, the weighing-scales suitor. Roancarrick must be bursting at the seams with men. No wonder the roses are back in your cheeks.'

Venus manoeuvred the subject away from Roancarrick's imaginary excess of men and onto Lily's man. At the mention of Karim's name, Lily's cheerful demeanour ratcheted into overdrive. He was still cooking her blinis and teaching her Russian; he'd even fixed her collapsing magazine rack. And she'd always said the man who could tackle that magazine rack was the one for her. It was her glass-slipper test. Of course she'd only been joking, but . . .

'I was hoping to persuade you to come to Roancarrick for a weekend,' interrupted Venus.

But Lily didn't want to leave Karim behind. And Venus didn't want to invite Karim, not right now.

'You could always come and see us,' suggested Lily.

Venus said she'd consider it.

'*Precrasna*,' burbled Lily. 'Did I tell you that means "excellent"?' She wanted to discuss wedding arrangements with Venus. The registry office at Sir Patrick Duns Hospital held sixty, but her instinct was to keep it as low-key as possible. She was tempted towards a mid-January wedding, to enliven the winter, except that meant delaying everything by a few weeks and Karim was ultra-keen to see a ring on her finger. How did Venus feel about a Christmas marriage celebration?

Venus knew she'd have trouble rustling up any hosannas but had developed cunning.

'Sensational idea,' she gushed. 'There's a call holding on the line – talk to you soon.'

Venus felt riddled with temper as she whisked out of the house for a walk before her father could quiz her. Of course Karim was on tenterhooks to have her friend wearing his ring – it would mean he was home and dry. Lily was behaving as though he were eager to marry her because he

316

loved her – she had a well-honed delusional streak. Lily Dillon was in for quite a shock after the honeymoon.

Good God. She ground to a halt. Were they planning a honeymoon too? An evil thought struck her: it would have to be spent in Ireland because Karim couldn't take the chance of being refused re-admission. Besides, his passport had been confiscated.

She met John Óg O'Dea by the seafront. He might as well move back in with the Mammy, with the amount of time he spent in Roancarrick.

'Just dropping off your laundry?' she asked.

He was mystified, but launched into a description of his new top-of-the-range washer-dryer, and her frayed temper mended itself before he managed to decode the insult. Repentant, she stayed on the concrete walkway instead of plunging down towards the shoreline, in deference to his patent slip-ons.

They paced in silence, John Óg chivvying his brain cells for a conversational nugget and Venus smouldering over Lily's impending mistake.

'Our Teresa was asking after you. She wondered how come you never married?'

'Nobody asked me,' snarled Venus.

'I've often thought a man in my position should take a wife,' remarked John Óg, 'to set an example.'

'Who do you want to set this example to?' Venus's forehead wrinkled, floundering in her efforts to grasp his rationale.

'To those who need guidance – who look to people such as myself for a role model.' John Óg laced his hands behind his back, for all the world like a curate. Even with his patent shoes.

Venus battled with her giggles and, against the odds,

banked them down. This must mean he'd transferred his attentions elsewhere because he hadn't so much as held her hand, let alone reached the stage where he might ask for it in marriage. 'When you put it like that, John Óg, I can see the logic,' she managed gravely. It was something of a relief to discover John Óg O'Dea had an eye for another woman besides herself.

'But someone's against me marrying,' he continued.

Aha, surmised Venus, Mrs O'Dea doesn't want to share her little boy. Typical Oedipal-complex-inducing Irish Mammy. They should be surgically detached from their male offspring when the boys hit puberty.

'Who might that be?' She prepared herself for diversion.

'My partner in the accountancy firm.' John Óg was glum. 'Shay Smith is a great man for the ladies, but he's too partial to them altogether to commit himself to just one. He's threatening to dissolve the partnership if I attach myself. He says a rolling stone gathers no moss and an unmarried accountant can work evenings and weekends coming up to the end of the tax year without having to ask for anyone else's say-so.' He heaved a tremulous sigh. 'The Mammy isn't one bit pleased – I was up above just now discussing it with her and she's mad keen for me to set a date. She's determined to have grandchildren this side of the Atlantic. Teresa's wee one is wasted on her in Buffalo.'

'Well, why don't you call Shay Smith's bluff and dissolve the partnership?' Venus couldn't understand why John Óg was making such a palaver out of it. 'If you love her enough there shouldn't be any hesitation.'

John Óg was puffing slightly as he tried to keep pace with Venus, and he unbuttoned his overcoat to reveal a sober grey three-piece suit.

A beer stain on the waistcoat would work wonders for it, thought Venus.

'Love who?' he asked.

'This woman you're intending to marry, naturally.'

'There is no woman.' John Óg removed one of his leather gloves to straighten his discreet tie.

Now that she looked a little closer, it wasn't a curate he resembled at all – it was an undertaker.

Venus halted without warning and leaned against the flaking railings separating the pavement from the shore. Either she'd missed out on some vital part of this conversation or John Óg O'Dea was planning to wed without having any clear idea of whom he'd propose marriage to; she decided to test the theory.

'Have you a girlfriend, John Óg, if you don't mind such a personal question?'

'There's nobody special.' He couldn't lean against the railings in case he ended up with rust on his coat, and he couldn't put his hands in his pockets because they'd spoil the line of it, so he stood with his arms folded in front of her.

'Have you anyone in mind for the vacancy?' she persisted.

'There'd be one or two girls I have my eye on, all right,' he conceded. 'I'm quite a catch in these parts, Venus Macken.' He tossed his head, a faint colour lifting the pallor on his cheeks. 'Don't I have my own house and a partnership in an accountancy firm? And then there's the shop – that'll come to me in time. No wife of mine would have to work if it didn't agree with her, but she could always take over the running of the shop premises, if she chose. Turn it into a delicatessen or something of that nature, if she had notions. I wouldn't stand in her way.'

It struck Venus that a delicatessen had as much chance of survival in Roancarrick as a sushi bar. 'So I take it you have your eye on one or two contenders, John Óg. Anyone I'd know?'

'Well,' he allowed, 'you might know the receptionist in our office, Wendy Toner. Her older sister went to school with yourself and Teresa. The family are from out about Drumcliffe direction. She's a fine sturdy lass, a bit on the young side, maybe, but steady. Very willing to please. Always listens carefully to whatever you tell her.' He smoothed back his sparse hair, swelling with confidence.

If he mentioned Wendy had child-bearing hips, Venus knew she'd laugh in his face.

John Óg continued, impervious. 'Then there's a woman who works in the Ulster Bank in Sligo – she handles the mortgages. Responsible position. She's maybe a handful of years older than I'd like, but she has a nice ladylike way about her. Her name is Una McAteer – she lives four houses down from me, and I don't mind telling you she's always delighted if we run into one another. She invited me in for coffee once to see her attic conversion. Not a stick of furniture out of place – you can tell a lot from a person by the way they keep their home. I don't believe she's seeing anybody – I've never noticed anyone coming or going.' He frowned. 'Her family background isn't known to me, which is a disadvantage – she's not from these parts, you see. But with the equity in our two houses and the joint mortgage we could command, we'd be able to buy a substantial property between the pair of us.'

Venus realised she was airbrushed out of the picture and was swamped with relief. She was forever running into John Óg; their future encounters would be thorny if he felt spurned by her. However, she allowed herself the luxury of teasing him. 'I'm devastated, you heartbreaker. I imagined I might be in with a chance.'

'I did consider you, Venus.' He tapped the side of his nose with a gloved finger. 'I don't hand out weighing scales to just anybody. There was a time when I thought you might fit the bill. But I don't think we'd be compatible. You have that London experience under your belt and I'm man of the world enough to know it might be in your blood still. I don't believe you're ready to settle down. And, no offence, but red-haired women can be a bit of a handful – they have an unbiddable streak. There's a limit to how much excitement a man wants in his life, especially when he has a certain status in the community to maintain. Anyway,' his expression dimmed, 'unless Shay Smith reconsiders his threat about the partnership, my plans may have to be deferred. I don't want the responsibility of striking out on my own and I haven't the money to buy out his share.'

Venus, flattered at the idea of being perceived as unbiddable, felt indignant on John Óg's behalf. 'This is nonsense,' she protested. 'He can't prevent you from marrying.'

'Oh, but he can,' John Óg corrected her. 'There's a clause in the partnership agreement which allows him to do exactly that. It stipulates that neither partner can take the plunge without the other's consent. So I'm stranded.' He trickled out a narrow smile.

Venus started walking again, reflecting on his dilemma. Finally she suggested, 'Why don't you start courting whichever one of those women you like the look of best? Then if it comes to the crunch and you decide to marry, think about the bachelor clause again. Sure anything could happen. Shay Smith could meet the woman of his dreams tomorrow and beg you to release him from the clause. Or you and the receptionist or the mortgage broker or whoever you're stepping out with might decide you're not meant for one another. It occurs to me, John Óg,' and she touched his elbow to stress her point, 'that you're jumping the gun.'

'Do you really think so?' He looked dubious, thin-lidded eyes with their visible veins fluttering.

'I know so.'

'And which of the women do you think would be best suited to me, Venus?'

'I'll leave you to be the judge of that.'

John Óg was pensive as he said goodbye and turned back towards his car. In the driver's seat, she saw him hunch to one side, produce a coin from his pocket and flip it.

Chapter Thirty-one

Imagine being wooed by a man who tossed a coin before asking you out. Venus watched the Volvo drive off, John Óg clunking through the gears with a steely determination, and decided it was time to be grateful again for small mercies. She'd been weighed in his scales and found wanting. Meanwhile, there was too much marriage malarkey around, between John Óg and Lily; she'd call in to see Birdie, who had never wed nor expressed any inclination to do so. Birdie had been quiet at the Hallowe'en birthday party; she should check on her.

Birdie was working on her back garden, arranging smooth, oval grey stones banded by a pale stripe along the edges of a flower-bed. She was kneeling on a heat-pad especially designed for gardeners as she worked.

'I saw it on the Internet and sent away for it,' she told Venus. 'I prefer to buy my own gardening equipment. A friend gave me secateurs once and I forgot to cross her palm with silver – of course they sliced through the friendship and we lost contact.'

She finished her job, with Venus helping her to select stones from a bucket, and sat back on her heels, sniffing the air.

'It has a New Year feel to it,' she remarked.

'There's two more months to go,' said Venus.

Birdie's deep-set eyes sparked. 'Samhain marks the arrival of the Celtic New Year. Surely a Hallowe'en child like yourself should know that.'

They went into the cottage for tea, Venus wondering if she could eke out any more information about her origins from the older woman. It had to be worth a try; Birdie couldn't have her guard erected permanently.

She sat by the fireside in a red Chesterfield armchair, missing Jude in his customary spot near the turf basket, while Birdie made orange pekoe tea 'to decrease anxiety'. I'm not anxious, thought Venus. And immediately felt agitated.

Birdie pulled a stool close to where Venus was sitting and looked up at her, triangular face shrewd. 'You want to talk to me about something, Venus.'

She shifted in her place and avoided Birdie's gaze. 'Nothing in particular – I just didn't have much of a chance to chat to you at the party. What did you make of the Landers fellow?'

'A runaway,' said Birdie, in her crisp way. 'I had the impression he's run away to Roancarrick to escape something. But there's no escaping yourself.'

It's even harder to find yourself, thought Venus, on a surge of bile.

But she lingered by the fireside, noticing how Birdie's quartz ring was lit from beneath by the glow – a ring that was unwieldy on such a small hand.

'Maura was a woman who knew what she wanted.' Birdie

frowned at wavering figures in the flames. 'I never knew a woman so determined.'

Venus registered surprise, for her mother had been imbued with many qualities but determination had not appeared to be a predominant one.

'She wanted you with a ferocity I've never encountered before or since.' Birdie's gravelly voice mellowed. 'Dan would have given you up to the authorities, if they'd insisted, but Maura was a tigress. Once she held you in her arms that first day, with your little fists bunched and your heels kicking, she never wanted to let you go again. Even as you grew up, she needed you by her. When you went away to Dublin to college I thought she'd never settle. But she was proud of you too. She'd come racing in to me if you phoned, to tell me all your news word for word. If it weren't for Dan, I swear she'd have moved to Dublin to be close to you for those four years. And when you took it into your head to go to London, she climbed into bed and didn't come out from under the covers for forty-eight hours.'

'She never breathed a word.' The younger woman was dazed. 'She always said "live your life, Venus, don't let it live you".'

'She loved you. She wanted what was best for you.' Birdie was brusque, but there was a moist shine in her eyes caused by more than the firelight.

Venus realised she and Dan were not the only ones who missed Maura. She touched Birdie on the hand. 'My mother was lucky – she had a loyal friend in you. Perhaps you'll be a friend to me, for her sake.'

'Friendship has to be given for its own sake alone.' Birdie stood, wiping down her trousers with a flurry of movements. 'I've sat too long; there's work to be done.'

Venus found herself in the back lane on her way home, with a vague sense that she'd offended Birdie. Without even trying. And an even more uneasy sense that she hadn't truly known her adoptive mother – so how could she hope to know her birth one?

* * *

A cream envelope with her name on it in backward slanting handwriting lay on Venus's desk at Sligo Tech when she arrived for her Spanish for Beginners class. Navy-blue ink. It almost looked as though it had been written by quill, so antiquated was the script.

'*¿Hola, que tal?*' she called out to the students, as she opened it. It was from Benedict Archer, who wanted her to call to his office at the end of the lesson.

Venus thought it odd that he should be working so late, but quickly forgot about him as she concentrated on the homework role play, a hospital visit. She divided the students into groups of three: a patient, a doctor and a visitor. She still had all twelve of her students, despite Benedict Archer's prediction that first evening of an inevitable reduction.

She was proud that she hadn't lost any of her class, especially with at least one of the romances that had prompted Spanish lessons hitting a rut on the *autopista* to love. One of the two girls with boyfriends running a Spanish restaurant had broken up with her Pedro.

'I still like the language, Venus,' the legal secretary had explained last week, 'even if some of the men who speak it can't be trusted as far as you could throw them. Which isn't any great distance at all because Spanish men run to fat.'

Her blonde companion, still in triumphant possession of

a Spanish boyfriend, had turned defensive. 'Irish men cheat on their girlfriends as well,' she had objected. 'And the ones who don't two-time them with other women are conducting love affairs with their pints of Guinness.'

Girl number one had looked sulky, at which point Venus had intervened to suggest that before the end of term they'd do a role play to cover cheating boyfriends. They could learn the Spanish phrases for 'love-rat' and 'give me back my CD collection'. The student had perked up, envisaging her arrival at the restaurant when it was stuffed to capacity, bawling him out in his native tongue. Perhaps wearing those clickety flamenco shoes for stamping her feet imperiously.

Benedict Archer was walloping a broken photocopier, without improving the situation any, when Venus arrived just after 10 p.m. Watching his inept efforts to pummel the machine into submission, Gary Hesketh flashed through her mind. He claimed that one in four photocopier faults was caused by people sitting on them to make prints of their buttocks. Venus couldn't imagine Benedict Archer doing that, drunk or sober. Anyway, Gary had probably sent the statistics askew by unzipping himself for every photocopying machine he had access to.

'Venice,' exclaimed the principal, surprised to see her.

Venus waited.

'What can I do for you?' he inquired.

'You asked me to call in to you.' If he were one of her students, Venus would relegate him to the dunce's corner.

His minestrone eyes regarded her doubtfully. 'So I did.' He gave the photocopier one last thump, more regretful than truculent, and sat at his desk. 'It's about the maternity block starting in January. One of my permanent staff is

327

going to be off having a baby. Her third.' He sniffed, as though three sessions of maternity leave was beyond excessive. 'It means I have a temporary vacancy. Five days a week, generous salary. I'm pleased to offer it to you. Naturally there's been stiff competition for the position, but we've been very impressed by your work these past few months, Venice.' He paused, while Venus wondered who the 'we' referred to; then she realised she was supposed to respond in suitably grateful fashion.

'Thank you.' She inclined her head.

Not grateful enough. Benedict Archer's broth-brown gaze cooled. 'I appreciate you were the deputy head of a school in London, but a language school teaching foreigners cannot compare with a college of further education. This may only be a temporary post, but it's an opportunity for you to show your mettle – it could lead to greater opportunities.'

'I'm absolutely delighted and looking forward to the challenge,' Venus over-compensated, but it was too late.

Benedict Archer, overworked and still under-secretaried, wound himself up to a sense of grievance. He was stuck here at 10.15 p.m. on a Tuesday night, with three more days to work until the weekend and only the prospect of a reheated dinner to look forward to when he reached home, where his children wouldn't bother lifting their heads from the television set to greet him. His wife would hardly have the dinner slapped down in front of him before she'd start complaining about redecorating the hall and landing, when he'd already explained to her they couldn't afford it so close to Christmas.

Now here he was offering work to this young teacher with the untameable hair and ridiculous name – who in their right minds would call their daughter after a city, and an Italian one to boot? – an elongated spaghetti-stick of a girl who spoke better Spanish than he did, and instead of appreciation he was met with indifference. Just because she'd worked away from home, whereas he'd never been further afield than Killarney. Resentment against these bright young things who swanned off abroad and then returned to make Benedict Archer feel parochial threatened to choke him. He should have given the maternity block to Raymond Barry instead. Sound man. Fond of fly fishing. But he taught German and Italian, not Spanish and French, so it had to be the Macken chit.

Venus was puzzled by the hostility she felt emanating from him. All he did was sit there drumming his fingers, but she sensed Benedict Archer was encased in a stress-balloon that could explode at any moment. Of course. Her brow cleared. He was overreacting because he'd been in this office since 9 a.m., without so much as a secretary to field his calls. He probably hadn't eaten anything except sandwiches and she guessed he'd overdosed on caffeine which was irritating his stomach-lining. In the long term he needed an assistant – but right now a hot meal and a gin and tonic would sort him out.

She could be very soothing when she chose. Venus treated him like one of the students from Bridges Across The World when they turned over-excitable, which happened occasionally. Usually under the affluence of incohol. She guided Benedict into his coat, out of the office and into the carpark, even persuading him to nibble a couple of squares of chocolate she found in her pocket – immediately improving his mood. Exactly as she suspected – the man was run-down and starving. He'd probably eat a wooden stool if she chopped it up for him.

'Why don't you take tomorrow morning off and have a rest?' she suggested. 'You've been working very hard.'

He wavered. 'A lie-in would be lovely.'

'Go on,' urged Venus. 'Have breakfast in bed. Get newsprint all over the sheets. You deserve it.'

Benedict had a yearning vision of a tray with boiled eggs, buttered toast soldiers and the morning papers. Maybe a pot of Earl Grey instead of all that coffee he'd been drinking lately.

Venus handed him his briefcase. 'Think about it. The sky won't fall in without you propping it up.'

She'd worded it too strongly: he recoiled.

'I have important meetings that cannot be cancelled, Venice. But thank you for your concern.'

Driving home, she reflected that Roancarrick was hooking its tentacles into her ever more tightly. Here she was with a five-days-a-week job, albeit a temporary post, instead of her two nights of Spanish conversation. She had an offer of a Saturday night on the razzle with the two girls from her class who worked in a solicitor's office. And she'd discovered she didn't want Roancarrick to have a multi-storey hotel slapped on its seafront – she appreciated its down-at-heel grace. The village of her childhood she thought she despised had seduced her, after all.

Best of all, she was developing an increasing intimacy with her father. When her mother had been alive they had tended to form a female phalanx that had occasionally excluded Dan. Petticoat Power huddling together to reinforce the gender divide. She wondered if her father had been aware of it and whether it had vexed him. Or maybe hurt him. Now it was just Dan and Venus, father and daughter.

It had been too late to express many of the sentiments she'd wanted to tell her mother. Thank you. I love you. You gave me everything you had to give. I'll never forget you. All the banalities that had a wealth of significance. Because they comforted.

She wouldn't leave it too late with her father. Maybe by being here in Roancarrick with him, she was saying them already.

Venus found herself charged with emotion as she drove along the dual carriageway. Rain splattered against her windscreen and she switched on the wipers, wincing at the main beam of an oncoming car which forgot to dim its lights. It seemed to her that she'd been given a second chance. Maybe that's what the sky-writing had meant – not searching out her mother, launching a quest, but learning to appreciate what lay under her nose.

Try Finding Not Sacrificing Yourself.

Still in ruminative mode as she turned off the main road and dipped towards the village, she thought of Conor Landers. Birdie had described him as a runaway. Did Venus want to become involved with someone like that? She knew more about him than she felt at ease with and, despite wavering that night by the gate when he'd touched her cheek, she did care that he'd been involved in a case of euthanasia. Of course there were mitigating circumstances – but mercy killing still meant someone lost their life. Where was the mercy in that? Venus didn't know if she and Conor could be friends, let alone lovers.

Then again, sometimes you didn't choose your friends and lovers. They chose you.

She parked her car in the main street and looked at the shops under threat. There had been strangers in pinstriped suits with briefcases in their hands on the seafront earlier that day. The village was buzzing with theory and counter-theory and whispers about a luxury hotel complex were only the tip of the speculative iceberg. A Hollywood movie set was the favoured version, parts as extras for one and all and a chance to watch the antics of those notoriously strange film folk. Venus knew the pinstriped strangers were the money men who would bring Senan his Ferrari. She should have done something to prevent it – but she couldn't uncover the past, let alone shape the future.

Nora Brennan's black and white frontage had lost its daytime aura of neglect and lights trumpeted from it. A couple of taxis were parked outside, ready for business when the pub shut. At the far end of the street Mrs O'Dea was still open, plastic cone on the pavement – she could give the Asian family in London, who used to stock Venus's Kimberley biscuits, a run for their money on the 24-hour trading front.

Venus could just discern Kathleen Magee's head bobbing about in the flat above her restaurant, with no notion of the danger to her business. She was probably doing some last-minute packing, for she was off to Boston the next day and her somewhat lugubrious face had been transformed with excitement. Venus had lent her a soft leather holdall and had received a whispered confidence: Kathleen had been emailing a second generation Irish-American who had dined in Seascape during the summer. He was a police officer, divorced with two daughters, and he'd shown Kathleen his silver badge over dessert. A meeting was now arranged in Boston, precipitating a ruthless search and discard operation in Kathleen's wardrobe. The selection process seemed to be in train still, despite tomorrow's five a.m. alarm call.

Venus stepped out of her car and inhaled the tart salt air.

It flooded her lungs, invigorating her. It had been that tang, so corporeal she always imagined she could stretch out a hand and grasp it, which she'd missed during her years in London. However often she'd told herself there was nothing of value in Roancarrick apart from her parents, she'd yearned for the sea. Sometimes she'd catch a train to Hastings or Brighton and stand outside the station – intent less on seeing the sea than sensing it.

The rain drizzled off, leaving damp air in its wake, and she watched the moon, full for the second night, sail in stately fashion through a cloudbank. Venus walked a few paces towards the pier, to see the moon follow her like a dog on a leash. She broke into a trot, to tempt the moon likewise to quicken its pace. As a child she had marvelled at its ability to keep step with her, neither falling behind nor overtaking, trailing her in whichever direction she would lead. It had seemed nothing short of enchantment.

'Slowly, silently, now the moon, Walks the night in her silver shoon,' Venus quoted.

She felt absurdly delighted with her powers of recall: perhaps her father wasn't the only Macken who could dredge up a few lines of poetry from schooldays.

The pub door opened and a cheerful draught of light and noise tumbled out the English couple who ran the fishing-tackle shop by the harbour wall, and who'd adapted so readily to life in Roancarrick. They called to Venus and crossed the street. Jenny, a vivacious brunette from Stockton-on-Tees, suggested Venus should stop in for a glass of wine at the weekend.

'It's busy during the summer, but we have to make our own fun in the winter,' she said. 'Bring that nice painter chap I've seen you out walking with.'

Her bearded partner, Graham, draped an arm across Jenny's shoulders and mentioned he'd been taking *bodhrán* lessons. 'Some of the gang from my class are dropping by for a session on Sunday week. You may as well come and listen to us – the whole village will be able to hear us beating away on our drums anyway.'

Even just a month ago, Venus would have been furious that people had noticed she was friendly with Conor Landers. But Roancarrick was moulding her – she accepted that the locals observed what their fellows did. It didn't mean they were forever crouched behind squinting windows, simply that they took an interest in their neighbours.

She accepted the invitation on her own behalf, but said she couldn't speak for Conor. A whisper of sorrow fluttered inside her – if only he'd given her a chance to get to know him properly before spilling out his euthanasia confession. His honesty was commendable – but his story had put Venus on her guard against him.

She waved at Jenny and Graham and drove uphill towards home – no deviating to pass the captain's house. Her father, initially concerned that she was late – he'd been watching the clock and fretting in case she'd had an accident – was delighted with her job news.

'I knew today would be a lucky day,' he hooted. 'I found your mother's Tara brooch that I bought her on honeymoon and we thought was lost. I've left it on your dressing-table – I thought you might wear it for her sake. It had slipped down the back of the sofa. Then I had the winner in the two-thirty at Fairyhouse, on the nose at five to one. This is the third stroke of luck.'

'How much did you win, Dad?'

'Twenty-five euro, lass.'

Hardly much to crow about, she thought. Then again, it was all down to perspective. If somebody had told her this time last year that she'd be celebrating the offer of a maternity block at Sligo Tech, her powers of credulity would have been stretched.

'So are you up or down money this year on the horses, Dad?'

He batted a mischievous look. 'Surely you know by now there's no winners in gambling, only losers and liars.'

Later that night, Venus sat on her bed, her gaze circumnavigating the uneven-shaped room where she'd spent her childhood and adolescence. Superimposed on it was the detritus of her London life: the marble washstand, the cinema posters, the laptop. But more prominent were the trappings of her youth. The dark wood dressing-table with its semicircles of woodworm near the base, inherited from her mother and father's room when they'd invested in a new suite some twenty years ago. The framed 'Highly Commended' certificate she'd won at the annual *feis*, aged eleven, for a song about a woman who killed herself rather than marry her father's choice of husband. An unconventional song for the organisers to impose on competitors in the under-twelve category, all the parents had agreed. But they'd packed in to applaud anyway. Venus touched the rug her mother had crocheted, folded over the back of a cane peacock chair. Her *Mayfair* chair, Teresa O'Dea used to call it, because she'd seen one like it in the magazine with a nude model straddling it. Venus fingered the rediscovered Tara brooch, bought in Lisdoonvarna and worn every week of her marriage by Maura Macken on her Sunday going-to-Mass coat. Venus couldn't see herself wearing it, for all that it connected her with her mother. It would lie in a drawer of her jewellery box, the silver darkening with disuse.

She looked in the dressing-table mirror and saw herself aged fifteen or sixteen, plotting to leave Roancarrick. She'd managed it, too. Except fate had stolen the last laugh. The dream-catcher fluttered, taunting her – life is what happens to you when you're making other plans.

Then her eye landed on Conor's eloquently understated tree in its new frame, propped against the dressing-table mirror. For some reason that she couldn't quite fathom, Venus felt less despondent.

Chapter Thirty-two

The next day's post brought a reply from the Adoption Board. She saw its stamp on the envelope and a vibration shook her: a name, at least, if nothing more. Just give her the name of her mother. Let her have contacted the board and left a message for that red-haired baby daughter she'd forsaken more than three decades ago. In her anxiety, Venus ripped a corner of the paper as she opened it. A momentary pang – 'You're still my Mam,' she murmured to Maura – and then she had the sheet out of the envelope and in her hands.

It was an apologetic letter, with the sender admitting there was no further information on record other than that listed on the birth certificate in her possession. The board had a voluntary contact register, the letter advised, and it would be happy to add her details, following her authorisation. This allowed people who'd given up their children for adoption and those who'd been adopted to get in touch with one another, by mutual consent.

Venus felt cheated. Her mother eluded her at every twist and turn. She stuffed the letter in her pocket and flung on her coat. She'd pay a visit to the garda station in Bundoran – there was a sergeant coming up for retirement who'd spent all his working life in the town's barracks. He might remember something of her case.

'You're in a bit of a lather,' remarked her father, as she almost collided with him on the back step as she flounced out.

'Haven't I every reason to be?' snorted Venus. 'I'm a non-person.'

Dan lifted his trilby and scratched his head. There was no accounting for women's moods; she'd been in sunny form when he was leaving the house only half an hour earlier.

A whistling Conor came upon her, fumbling to open the car.

'You have the look of a woman in a hurry,' he greeted Venus.

'I haven't been in enough of a hurry – I've let myself be fobbed off. But I'm away to do something about it.'

'Need any company?'

She might as well let him come with her. 'What is that tune you seem to spend your life whistling?' She leaned across to unlock the passenger door.

'I don't know what you mean – I don't whistle.' He was mystified.

'Of course you do, you're forever whistling.'

His blue-green eyes gazed at Venus, trying to fathom why she was teasing him.

As they pulled out onto the main road Conor enquired their destination.

'Barracks, Bundoran.' She was terse.

He sat in silence for a few minutes. 'Any particular reason?'

'Detective work. There's an old guard there who might know something about the circumstances of my birth. I'm planning to bring him to the interrogation room and squeeze him until he squeaks.'

'Do you know, I think a few of your winning smiles might achieve faster results.' His tone was conversational. 'You're a goddess, after all – sure what mortal man could withstand you? Oops, sorry, you don't like being reminded of your divine status, do you?'

She shot him a warning flash.

'Oh well,' Conor was unperturbed, 'if you're really set on slapping about an old fellow in uniform, don't let me stop you. They say it can be therapeutic. Sometimes even addictive.'

He was at it again, jabbing her temper tantrums. Against her will, Venus smiled.

'Much better,' Conor approved. 'I could tell you that you're magnificent when your dander's up. But frankly, I prefer to see you relaxed and happy.'

'I'm feeling sorely tried,' admitted Venus, parking near the garda station.

'Tell me all about it before we go inside, my bundle. Then we can decide the best way to tackle this guard.'

The tattered remnants of Venus's ill humour melted. 'What did you say "my bundle" stood for again?' she checked.

'Of gorgeousness.'

Her eyes danced.

Then she remembered his euthanasia confession and steadied herself. This was just flirtation, it couldn't go

339

anywhere. Tamsin's harmless endorphins theory: no expectations raised, no promises to keep.

* * *

Sergeant Logan was on a meal break when they walked into the station, a hiatus for which Venus was unprepared. Conor brought her for a cup of coffee to pass the time until he'd be back on duty. They sat alongside one another in a booth in the disused church, just down from the amusement arcade, where they'd whiled away her birthday afternoon. Venus felt the heat from his body reach out to her. She turned away from its siren reassurance and watched the seagulls outside: they appeared to be operating some kind of queuing system for a chimney-pot on the roof of the gift shop opposite, for as soon as one flew off another landed in its place.

She withdrew her gaze from the gulls and turned to Conor. 'How do you manage financially? I know that sounds impertinent, but I'm puzzled – you don't seem to work regularly.'

'I sell a few drawings. I had an exhibition in the spring which attracted some attention and I'm hoping I'll have enough material for another one next year. I can raise some ready cash by teaching classes from time to time, mostly summer schools and the odd week-long course at an adult learning centre such as my friend's in Omagh. The big plus is that I live rent-free.' His leg nudged Venus's under the table. 'Not exactly a catch, am I? It's a spartan life, but it suits me. I've given myself until I'm forty and if I haven't made a name for myself by then, I'll do like my mentor Donal Flynn and become an art teacher in a school, sidelining the drawing to a hobby.'

Venus stiffened. Donal Flynn was the man he'd helped to take his own life. She checked her watch. 'Sergeant Logan should be back at the front desk by now.'

The garda had the look of a farmer and, indeed, he had a small-holding which he devoted himself to when he was off-duty – and sometimes when he was meant to be on, for harvests paid no heed to the station rota. His hands were gnarled, soil under the nails, and he had a shock of silver hair above his veined face.

Venus introduced herself and explained her business.

'Dan Macken's daughter from Roancarrick way,' said the sergeant, who was only a few months off retirement. 'Didn't you go off to London to work?'

'I did, but I'm back in Roancarrick now.'

'I believe I might have had a daughter a year behind you in school. Do you remember Colette Logan?' He leaned on the counter, buttons straining across his blue shirt.

'Certainly, I do.' Venus was impatient but realised she had to allow him his leisurely introduction. 'Whatever happened to her?'

'She did very well for himself.' The sergeant smacked his lips. 'She married a man with a farm of land down Meath way. Fine land, they have there, not begrudging like ours at all. She works part-time at the social work, doing a job-share. But sure Colette has her hands full, with a couple of children and that farm foreby.'

'Won't you remember me to her? Now, the reason I dropped in to see you –'

'And what about Dan?' Sergeant Logan cut across her. 'Is the leg still giving him gip?'

It took composure, prodding, and a certain amount of lip-biting during an interruption when someone reported a missing dog and wanted to put up a poster in the window of the garda station, but finally Venus had the sergeant on the subject closest to her heart.

To be sure, he remembered the circumstances in which Dan and Maura Macken had found that tiny scrap of a baby. In all his forty-five years in the Garda Siochana, and he'd seen some sights in those decades, God knows he had, he'd never heard tell of anything to match that mite being abandoned by the seal's rock at the heel end of the year. It's a wonder she hadn't frozen to death. But at least she'd been taken into a good home – Dan and Maura Macken were as decent a pair as you'd tramp the country to meet, and hadn't they troubles of their own with those grand boys washed out to sea. A big funeral, it was. He'd been on duty that day and had gone along in an official capacity. It was important to show that the gardaí were part of the community.

Venus listened and sighed and intervened again. Did he know who the baby's mother was? Sergeant Logan scratched at that sumptuous thatch of hair and couldn't recall. Then he called to 'young Quigley' to hold the fort at the front desk while he took a look in the files. 'It's 1970 I'm looking up, is that right?'

'October 31, 1969,' corrected Venus. 'But it might have been November 1 before they reported it to you.'

Venus and Conor hunched on a bench, waiting for the garda's return. Conor gripped her hand, sensing her churning anticipation without needing to read it in her pearl-pale face. She saw the ink-stains mapped on his long artist's fingers as she laced her own fingers through them.

Sergeant Logan had a handwritten file and was still leafing through it, returning to his station. 'And not a stitch of clothes on the baby,' he marvelled. 'Nothing to identify her. But the doctor's report said she was a healthy infant, born without difficulty so far as he could see, maybe a day and at most two days earlier.'

'Is my mother's name there?' Venus wrenched her hand away from Conor and dashed to the counter, trying to read the file upside-down.

'I can't see it anywhere. I compiled the report – this is my own handwriting here. Your parents made efforts to find the mother but nobody claimed you. I see they ran ads in the *Donegal Democrat,* the *Sligo Champion,* and other papers further down the country as well as one of the Belfast papers. But it was a dead end.' He pulled off his reading glasses and nodded at Venus, sympathetic to her distress. 'Like as not it was some poor lass that had nobody to look out for her. She must have been at her wits' end to do what she did. Times were harder then for girls who got themselves in the family way. You just be grateful, Venus Macken, that decent folk took you in – your story could have had a different ending.'

Her story had no ending at all. Nor a beginning either. Venus, barely able to bank down the disappointment fermenting within her, mumbled her thanks to the sergeant and trailed outside.

Conor touched her shoulder. 'You still have options. Have you tried the social services or the hospitals?'

'Had no joy at the hospitals. Social services put me in touch with the Adoption Board which knew no more than I do already.'

'There's always Barnardo's.' His fawn-fair curls rustled in the wind and she wondered if they flattened against the pillow at night. 'I hope you don't mind, I asked my mother how adopted people trace their relatives. Obviously I didn't mention your name. She said Barnardo's do great work. You might consider an approach to them.'

Venus opened the car door, slumping in the driver's seat. 'This is such an uphill struggle. It's almost as though nobody wants me to find out who I am and where I come from. Maybe I should just admit defeat.'

Chapter Thirty-three

'Don't lose your spirit,' urged Conor. 'It's one of the first things I noticed about you. You strike me as a person who can bounce back after any setback.'

He seemed genuinely concerned, and Venus hesitated. She wanted a wallow, she needed a wallow, she deserved a wallow, but she couldn't cave into one with Conor calling her spirited. It made her feel like a wasp-waisted Southern belle – he'd be addressing her as Mizz Venus if he kept this up. 'All right then,' she agreed weakly.

Conor turned businesslike as he suggested she tell him every avenue she'd tried in her search for her identity. She took him through it comprehensively, even including her sky-writing epiphany – which sounded less cogent repeated to an audience. However, he made no comment but listened intently.

'Birdie's the key to unlocking your puzzle,' he announced. 'All roads lead to her. She was there just before your father went off and found you, and she came back again almost as soon as he brought you in. She backed your mother to the hilt when she insisted on keeping you. Most significant of all, she persuaded Dan to take the coast road when he was inclined to walk another way.'

'I've tried Birdie.' In her agitation, Venus started unravelling her braid, then plaiting it again, fingers moving restlessly. 'That woman couldn't lie straight in bed, let alone give a straight answer. "Give me a clue, Birdie," you say to her, and she tosses you one of those enigmatic glances of hers and trots out some jargon like, "We must learn to decipher our hearts before we can decipher clues".' Venus snorted. 'All very soulful, but it doesn't progress my position the tiniest iota.'

'Maybe I'll try her for you.' Conor was contemplative. 'I could pay her a social visit. I'd love to inspect that serpent mirror you described, apart from anything else. Mirrors could be my next theme.'

If Conor Landers spent as much time drawing as he did thinking about themes, he might actually be earning his living as an artist, Venus reflected. But she shouldn't mention it – it was never a good idea to alienate your allies. Especially when you didn't have many.

* * *

Dan waved to her from the kitchen window as she pulled up, indicating a certain urgency. 'That friend of yours from Dublin is on the phone in a desperate state altogether.'

Senan had a nerve ringing her after the news he'd carried with him last time, harbinger of doom that he was. Unless it was to tell her the deal was off and they'd found some other village to vandalise in the name of de-stress weekends for overpaid suits. Venus quickened her pace: she could use some good news to offset this trying day.

'Karim's left me,' came a despairing wail. 'You have to help me win him back.'

It was Lily, not Senan. And from the sound of her there wasn't going to be any good news. Venus was sorely tempted to start biting her nails again.

Between Lily's sobs, Venus elicited the information that Karim had vanished from Lily's apartment, leaving only a farewell note. Lily insisted on reading it aloud, sniffing as he called her his angel, which he did an excessive three times, according to Venus's calculations.

'Here's the sweetest part, Venus. It says: *I can no longer allow you to make this sacrifice – it is too much to ask that you undertake a marriage of convenience with me. I will never forget you, my angel sent from heaven. This one favour I ask of you and I know in your generosity you will grant it. Forget me, my Guardian Angel. Let my image ripple gently from your memory, as a leaf dropping onto water disturbs the pond's surface only fleetingly.* Oh Venus, it's so poetic.'

Oh Lily, it's so cringe-worthy, thought Venus. Bad enough if he copied that from a book, but if he pored over it himself . . .

Lily was bawling incoherent sentences about how she realised she loved Karim now that he was gone.

'But it's obvious you love him – you've been infatuated with the man from the start,' said Venus.

It halted the tears. 'I have?'

'Certainly you have.' Madly in love and convinced she was engaged on a humanitarian relief mission, tacked on one of Venus's thought-waves. But she held her peace.

There was a tremulous silence from Lily, followed by a renewed bout of squalling.

'Why don't you come to Roancarrick and forget about him?'

'I don't want to f-f-forget about him. And I don't like the c-c-country.'

'Shall I come to Dublin then?'

'Yes, you can help me look for him,' quavered Lily.

Venus rolled her eyes. The last thing she wanted to do was trace Karim. As far as she was concerned, he'd shown a belated spark of decency by vacating Lily's apartment and her life. It wasn't as if he'd be homeless – the State had an obligation to house him and she was certain that his application for asylum would be treated fairly. Venus heard Karim's deep-pitched voice tell her, as he had at their first meeting: 'I'm still waiting for my application to be processed. But I suspect it will be rejected – you don't have an open-door policy. Just a fraction of supplicants are allowed to stay.' She tried to ignore the suspicion he'd be turfed out before you could say *céad míle fáilte*, but the doubt lingered.

This was the limit: now she felt guilty about Karim.

'I have a class tomorrow night, but I'll drive down on Wednesday morning,' Venus promised. 'Maybe I can try and make contact with Karim through the social services for you, just to establish if he's all right.'

'Venus, I'd be so grateful. I can't take this in – it feels as though the sky has fallen on top of me. Did I tell you we'd set our wedding date? We decided it would be Christmas Eve. I was going to wake up on Christmas morning as Mrs Karim Azarbayev. I'd even gone to the trouble of learning how to spell it.'

* * *

Lily was in purdah. She crouched in pyjamas which hadn't been off her back for forty-eight hours on the counterpane, picking at her toenail polish, the blue of Our Lady's sash in statues the length and breadth of Ireland. Her hair had been released from its topknot and flopped in rats' tails on her

348

shoulders. It was this unprecedented lapse in grooming which shocked Venus into agreeing to anything Lily wanted. Including having the farewell missive read aloud by Venus while Lily mouthed along, word perfect.

Venus recoiled, yet again, at Karim's exhortation to let his memory ripple away. Raw emotion only sang to the two people involved in a relationship. And sometimes one of them was tone-deaf. But she kept her expression deadpan because Lily was suffering.

'Have you told anyone else about this?' Venus joined Lily on the bed.

'Only Senan.' Lily moped. 'I thought I'd try for the male perspective. I didn't tell him about the passport business or anything – I just said we'd planned to marry but now it was all off. He was worse than useless. He said: "Love is like oxygen – full of nasty lumps you have to filter out." What in God's name is that supposed to mean?'

'Lily, Senan's twenty. He probably stole it subconsciously from a pop lyric and thinks he invented it. Anyway, credit where credit is due, at least he didn't tell you there were plenty more fish in the sea.'

They lapsed into silence, Lily trying to make sense of Karim's disappearance and Venus thinking that it proved the 'no good deed goes unpunished principle' – but not quite insensitive enough to voice it.

'I think it was a panic attack that sent him diving for cover,' Lily mumbled, after a time.

Venus looked at Lily's neat size-three feet with their polished blue toes and envied them. She stretched out a hand and cradled one. 'You hear of it happening to people in the run-up to a marriage,' she agreed.

'No, that's pre-wedding jitters. Karim's panic attack was

because he couldn't bear the thought of being chained to me for four years until we could apply for a divorce. He was horrified when he heard how long it takes here – his face turned ashen under the tan. He thought I was joking at first.' Lily's facial tic kicked in and she began floundering once again.

Venus stroked Lily's caramel hair, which knotted between her fingers.

'So Karim didn't realise you'd have to be separated for four years before you could start divorce proceedings.' Venus was contemplative. 'Perhaps he wasn't running away from you – he might have been trying to save you from wasting four years on him. Maybe he did it for you.'

Lily raised swimming eyes. 'I never thought of that.' She reeked of gratitude.

Still on the trail of Karim's motives, Venus asked, 'Did the two of you ever speak of love?'

Lily shook her head.

'So you don't know how he feels about you?'

Lily shook her head again, utterly miserable.

'Does he know you love him?'

Lily was panicked. 'No. I was afraid he'd feel under an obligation to me if I said anything. The circumstances were hardly the usual boy-meets-girl ones. There's no way he knows that I regard him as anything other than a friend.'

Venus felt a little exasperated at Lily's blindness. It was obvious her friend had been smitten with Karim from the outset – she hadn't been able to tear her eyes away from his face. And nobody set about learning a language like Russian because it made a change from tuning in to *Fair City*, or they wanted to read *Anna Karenina* in the original.

'Lily,' she protested, 'I don't mean to pry but I was under

the impression you and Karim were sleeping together. I wasn't eavesdropping, but the bedroom walls are thin and the last time I visited – well, I heard you.'

Lily reddened. 'It only happened that one time. Karim doesn't usually drink, but he had quite a lot of vodka that night and after you'd gone to bed he became upset. He's not exactly having a wonderful time in Ireland. He was a doctor in Moscow – he's a number here. A number who'll probably end up among the deportation statistics unless we reach him. Anyway, I tried to comfort him and we wound up in my bed – it was a bit of a drunken fumble, to be honest, but I don't regret it. Karim, on the other hand, was mortified and insisted it must never happen again. He said he'd trespassed on my hospitality. He was so formal, you know how he gets, and so regretful that I didn't have the courage to tell him he could lash away and trespass as often as he liked. It might have sounded –' her blush intensified, '– sluttish.'

'So what is it exactly you'd like me to do?' asked Venus.

'Find Karim.' Lily was eager. 'Tell him I'm still willing to go through with the wedding but he'd be under no obligation to me. He could walk out of the register office and not see me again until four years later in the divorce court. He doesn't have to live here in Adelphi Court. Once he has citizenship he'll be allowed to work. I know he'll be studying so it won't be easy, but he could afford a bed-sit. Maybe I'll be able to help him find a cheap one – we have a letting division in the agency.'

'But Lily, what if you meet someone in the next few years and want to marry them?'

Lily grew sombre. 'I'm forty years of age, Venus. In the twenty-four years I've been going out with men, or sometimes they've been boys, I've clocked up one broken engagement and a failed living-together experiment. No-one has ever been in a hurry to marry me and there's no-one I feel a sense of "if only" about. So there's no point in hanging on to my single status on the off-chance. The bolt of lightning's not going to happen to me – not a bolt where two of us are struck by the same shockwave, anyway. I may as well see to it that Karim has a fighting chance.'

Venus swallowed. It all sounded impossibly noble – but it was typical of Lily too. She was just behaving according to her nature and natures weren't exchangeable, like a wrong size shirt from Marks & Spencer. 'I envy you, Lily,' she admitted.

Lily's tear-blotched face reflected her astonishment. 'Why?'

'You're doing something selfless because you love somebody.'

'You moved home to look after your father – that was selfless too.'

'I owed him,' Venus contradicted her. 'He took me in and raised me. You owe Karim nothing.'

'But I love him.' Lily's candid blue eyes met Venus's searching hazel ones.

'And love is the answer?'

'It's not even the question, Venus. It has a will of its own that transcends everything.'

Venus marvelled at her certainty. She thought of Conor Landers: there was no doubt she was extremely interested in him, was possibly on the brink of falling in love with him, and yet a barrier existed. Except the hurdle was only in place because she allowed it to be so. He had told her about helping someone to die, honest from the outset; suffering, too, as he had reprised the event, and she had acknowledged his decency before hurtling, screaming, for the exit. Venus drooped. She wanted perfection – it was one of her failings. Lily had challenged her about it before.

'What are you looking for, Venus?' Lily had lost none of her ability to discern her friend's thoughts.

'I don't know,' she admitted. 'I only seem to know what it is I don't want.'

'I'll tell you what you ought to want. Someone who's willing to lift floorboards for you.'

Venus waited.

'One of my favourite earrings fell into a crack – the little turquoise drops,' Lily expanded. 'I was distraught, but Karim never hesitated. He fetched the toolbox and prised up the floorboards to find it for me. That's when I knew beyond a doubt that I loved him.'

Venus dragged her teeth across her lower lip, frowning. Perhaps she didn't need to fret over Conor's moral sensibilities – life wasn't black and white, no matter how convenient it might be. Maybe all she needed to concentrate on was an answer to the question: would he take up floorboards for her?

In the meantime she should do what she could for Lily. Venus climbed off the bed and laced on her boots. 'Write down the address of the last bed and breakfast Karim stayed in. Even if he isn't there, someone may know where I can find him. There can't be many Chechens in Dublin.'

'I'll drive you,' offered Lily.

'You won't. You'll have a bath and a rest and maybe tackle your hair if you feel up to it. And don't even think about cooking – I'll bring us back a takeaway. As well as news of Karim, with any luck.'

Chapter Thirty-four

The bed and breakfast was in Stoneybatter, not far from the law courts. It was in a cul de sac and appeared to be two terraced houses recently knocked into one, because it still had both front doors. Only one was equipped with a bell so Venus rang it, then knocked when no answer came.

The door was opened by a boy with his thumb in his mouth who didn't look tall enough to reach the latch. He regarded Venus with a blank-eyed lack of curiosity.

'Is your mammy in?'

He extricated his thumb from his mouth and gave an exaggerated blink.

Venus assumed this meant yes. 'Would you tell her I'm here?'

He blinked again but didn't move.

'Who is it, Darren?' a mistrustful voice travelled down the darkened hallway.

The boy turned and scampered up the hall, leaving the door ajar. A young woman in a puce suit and three sets of heavy gold hoops in her ears came to the door. 'Are you from the social services?' she asked Venus. Her cheeks were hollow as she dragged on a cigarette.

'No, I'm looking for a friend.'

'What makes you think he's here?' The woman was wary rather than actively hostile. She sucked on her cigarette again, and a finger of ash trembled on its tip.

'This is his last known address. His name is Karim – he's an asylum seeker. He's about my height, very dark. He comes from Chechnya.'

'I've never heard of no Chechnya.' The woman watched Venus from under her frizzed fringe.

'He might have told you Russia. He's a doctor.'

That seemed to register with the woman, but she didn't volunteer any information.

'Look,' said Venus, 'this isn't going to cause trouble for him. I'm here on behalf of someone who wants to help him.'

'He did stay with us for a while,' the woman admitted grudgingly. The ash from her cigarette landed on her sleeve, but she ignored it. 'He came back a few days ago asking if I had a room, but the house is bursting at the seams. I had to turn him away.'

'Did he say where he was going?'

'I can't remember.'

'Please try, it could help him stay in Ireland.'

'Well,' the woman twiddled one of her Creole earrings, 'he did patch up Darren when he caught his finger in the sash window and screamed fit to wake the dead. Saved me having to take him to the doctor's at our busy time, with all the breakfasts on the go. You could try Annie Fisher's house in Dunroe Close, that's down the hill, left at the lights, then take the second right. She's the house with the frog in the front garden.'

The frog turned out to be a fountain, water spouting from a pump under its lolling tongue. Annie Fisher's eyes kept darting admiringly towards it, as she directed Venus to the Refugee Applications Commissioner in Lower Mount Street.

'What time did he go?' asked Venus, in case he might no longer be there.

'After breakfast.' The woman was older than the first, but with as many heavy gold hoops in her ears. 'The refugees spend all day there sometimes, between queuing and waiting and queuing some more. They do be calling in about their dates and papers and the like. Many's the time their teeth are chattering with the cold when they come back to me. Of course they aren't used to our climate – they all come from sunny places.'

Not all of them, thought Venus, pointing her crocodile-green Polo in the direction of Lower Mount Street.

Feeding a meter in Merrion Square, Venus spied a solo magpie. One for sorrow. To avert the misfortune, she saluted it. Then she laughed. Roancarrick customs were engrained in her, however sophisticated she imagined herself, but somehow she didn't mind.

Asylum seekers were milling outside the nondescript 1970's office block a few minutes' walk away. Dignified African women with multicoloured turbans or beaded plaits caught the eye, alongside their men in western clothes with thinly-soled shoes and no socks. Milling among them were Rumanian gypsies with soulful eyes and coloured petticoats or ankle-length leather coats. The noise levels were deafening by Irish standards as people conversed in a variety of tongues, voice pitched above voice in the babble. And everywhere the eye fell it was met by babies, strapped on backs or carried in arms or dandled by older children.

How to find Karim amid this horde? Venus shrank at the prospect. Just then the cauldron of bodies parted and out stepped a stocky man with a jet of hair and jutting cheekbones. He stopped short when he saw Venus. His eyes flickered behind her, looking for someone else, then he advanced towards her reluctantly but took her outstretched hand with his habitual courtesy and bowed over it.

'Good day, lady.'

'Can I buy you a coffee, Karim?'

He shrugged. 'I am not permitted to return to number thirty-three Dunroe Close until six o'clock. Coffee would be most agreeable.'

They walked in silence, ending up at the Kilkenny shop, and Karim simply nodded when she pointed him to a table on the first floor with its low, pipe-networked ceiling. It overlooked the pottery department and he became engrossed by the shoppers browsing there.

Venus ordered vegetable broth and brown bread for both of them, along with coffee. She wasn't hungry but didn't want Karim to feel he was a charity case. He looked pinched around the mouth and she didn't know what arrangements were in place at his bed and breakfast regarding evening meals. Some fed the asylum seekers and others allowed them access to a cooker.

He ate hungrily and didn't protest when she pushed her own untouched bowl of soup over to him too.

'My social worker expects my case to be heard any day now.' He mopped at the dregs with bread.

'What are your chances?'

'Slight. At least I have until after the appeal before deportation. Or I could try and cross to England and apply again there.' His voice had developed a shadow.

'Isn't an application for asylum meant to be lodged in the first port of entry?' Venus watched him, head on one side.

'Yes. I would be committing an illegal act.' His still bruised eyes held hers. 'But I would not be abusing the good nature of one who has shown me nothing but kindness.'

'Karim.' Venus was hesitant, fidgeting with the vase containing a single carnation bud on their table. Some shoppers rustling carrier-bags overran the table next to theirs, loudly discussing a wrought-iron candelabra one of the women was debating whether to buy. She lowered her voice. 'Karim, what happened to change your mind? Lily told me you'd been given a wedding date and everything was settled.'

His eyes were hooded. 'It seemed wrong to allow one such as Lily, so trusting and wholesome, to make this sacrifice.'

'It wasn't wrong last month – why is it suddenly wrong this month?'

He looked away, over the railing, at a shelf stacked with lampshades for the pottery lamps alongside it. 'Last month I liked her, I respected her and felt grateful to her,' he whispered. 'This month, I am in love with Lily. That changes everything.'

Venus decided it was time to interfere again – she'd misjudged Karim and she should make amends. 'Tell her,' she encouraged him.

'It would be unfair.'

'How can telling someone you love them be unfair?'

Karim's brown fingers with their square-cut buffed nails drummed on the table. She sensed he was irresolute.

'Tell her.'

He looked at her, wanting to be persuaded.

'It would help her understand why you left so precipitately,' Venus pressed him. 'It hurt her. I don't think you intended that.'

'Why would I want to hurt my most precious angel, my Guardian Angel, my angel sent from heaven?' He was outraged now, eyebrows meeting in a black rod of condemnation. 'Nothing and no-one should be allowed to harm my sweet Lily.'

Venus gathered him up and led him to her car. He waited outside the door of the apartment while she went in to Lily. The topknot was in place and all was well with Lily's world. Or was about to become so. Lily grabbed Venus, demanding news of Karim.

'First things first,' insisted Venus. 'The bad news is, I haven't brought a takeaway.'

'Food.' Lily was disgusted. Who could think of food at a time like this?

'You haven't asked me for the good news,' Venus hinted.

Lily's eyes opened wide and she held her breath. Venus decided the suspense had lasted long enough and caught Lily by the shoulders, guiding her to the front door. 'There's somebody standing out there who's very keen to see you.'

And then, because Lily appeared rooted to the spot, Venus opened the door and Karim stepped inside.

'I'll go for a walk around the block,' said Venus.

Nobody responded.

She peeked over her shoulder as she left and saw Karim lift hands shaking with tenderness to take Lily's radiant, freckled face between them.

Chapter Thirty-five

Venus stood looking at the Viking ship moored close to Adelphi Court, on the far side of the Liffey. She could distinguish its outline by the floodlights attached to it, for darkness had fallen already since she'd delivered Karim to Lily. Home and dry. Maybe home and a little moist – his eyes had been watering as he'd crossed the threshold for his reunion with Lily.

A channel of cold air whistled up the sleeves of her coat and she shivered as she leaned on railings under a brass streetlight, peering at the Viking vessel. It struck her as unfeasibly small, and it occurred to Venus that there must have been a lot of testosterone crammed into that limited amount of space. Pumped up for pillaging. A Danish teacher had spent a year at Bridges Across The World and he had been the least machismo-ridden man on the staff – too gentle for teaching, even. Perhaps the Vikings had used up all their testosterone a thousand years ago and the current generation were husks.

She dug her hands in her pockets and found a piece of

paper. It had Conor's mobile number written on it, given to her just before she'd left Roancarrick.

'Ring me. I'm never sure when I'll see you again, you're such a will o' the wisp,' he'd joked.

He could talk, she'd thought.

But his fingers had felt familiar, almost as familiar as her own, as they'd pressed the scrap of paper into her hand.

Venus stroked the paper now, considering. Would he lift floorboards for her? She knew beyond a shadow of doubt that he would. In which case, there could be only one course of action open to her.

And yet she hesitated. An impish voice inside her asked what John Óg O'Dea would do, in her situation. She rattled out a gold coin from her purse and tossed it. Then she flipped it for the best of three until it gave her the answer she wanted. She looked left and right along the quays and decided her chances of finding a phone-box would be improved nearer to the O'Connell Street intersection.

She punched in a string of numbers, and an automated voice invited a message. Was there ever a more deflationary gadget in the history of innovation? Answerphones were giant needles designed to prick a caller's resolve. She swallowed and forced herself to leave a message. 'This is Venus.' *Say something witty.* 'I'm busy straightening out the universe – the work of a goddess is never done.' *Call that witty?* 'I'll be home tomorrow, perhaps we could meet.' *You can do better than that, Venus – this is the man you want to spend his life taking up floorboards for you.* 'I'm really looking forward to seeing you, Conor, I've missed you.'

She was hopeless; a schoolgirl with braces on her teeth could sound more alluring. She replaced the phone and checked her watch: too soon to go back to Lily's apartment.

Although she'd been joking about tweaking the universe's glitches, it gave her an idea. She might be able to catch Senan before he left the office.

Venus rang Lily's work number and was transferred to Senan, who agreed to meet her for a pint in Neary's in half an hour. She dawdled along Grafton Street and was still early. Reluctant to go in, she hovered beneath the sculpture of an outstretched arm holding a light on the exterior wall. It always reminded her of King Arthur and the Lady of the Lake. Last year some of her Japanese students had gone to Tintagel for the weekend in seach of Camelot. They had returned to class, dejected, because the Cornish ruin roosting on a clifftop had not fitted their Hollywood-incited preconceptions. There had been no round table in a banqueting hall, no Excalibur in a museum.

'You never struck me as a woman who'd be afraid of sitting in a pub on her own.' It was Senan, bristling with young executive panache in a herringbone suit with cufflinks but no tie.

'I was admiring the architecture,' Venus lied.

With that confidence which often characterises the very young or the very dense, he swept her into Neary's. It was still reasonably quiet, since it was early on a midweek night. She had a Ritz to keep him company, which disconcerted him because he enjoyed the barman's inevitable uncertainty about which drink belonged to whom.

'I wanted to talk to you about Roancarrick.' She tasted the mixture of white wine and fruit juice and shuddered. Oh, for a gin and tonic. Anything grown-up, with a slice of lemon in it.

He became cagey, tapping his green glass bottle against the ashtray on the table.

'I know it's confidential,' she continued, adopting the solicitous voice with which she'd settled problems at Bridges Across The World. 'I'm not asking you about business. But it's been on my conscience that I was unfair to you when you visited. I snapped at you and you didn't deserve it, especially after selling me the Polo at such a fair price, and your being a friend of Lily's and everything. She speaks very highly of you – she says you're going places.'

Senan relaxed, raising the bottle to his lips.

'So I wanted to buy you a drink and apologise.' Venus tossed her red hair. 'You took me by surprise when you came to Roancarrick and I reacted aggressively – it's my home and I didn't want it changed. But perhaps a hotel would be good for the village. Like you said, it would create employment. Change is healthy.'

'My client is only in preliminary discussions with another party – nothing's been agreed,' said Senan.

'Naturally not,' Venus soothed, 'and of course I wouldn't want to know the details. But a multinational with deep pockets coming into Roancarrick would be a blessing. For starters there'd be money to take care of the flooding on the main street. The businesses at that side of the village all keep sandbags along their walls for three or four months every year. It's a notoriously exposed part of the coastline.' She pretended not to notice the alarm chase across Senan's face. 'Maybe your client could build some kind of fire wall, although the local council is opposed to anything that might obscure the sea view. It's a terrible worry – all you need is a wet spell and an incoming tide and the ocean crashes across the road. The main street was impassable for a week last year – we had to use the back road in and out of the village. Insurance premiums went sky high after so many claims. Have you time for another Ritz, Senan?'

Senan wasn't in the mood for drinking Ritz. 'The other party didn't mention anything about flooding during negotiations.'

'Would you, if you were trying to sell?'

Senan resumed tapping his bottle against the ashtray and the air of urgency with which Venus associated him became accentuated. 'Listen, Venus, I'm pushed for time tonight, I have to be moving on. Maybe we could do dinner tomorrow night? I could give you a bell if you like.'

'Senan.' She trickled so much regret into her voice she was nearly afraid of overkill. 'Tomorrow night I'll be teaching an intermediate Spanish class at Sligo Tech. As you can imagine I'd infinitely prefer to be wined and dined by you – sure what woman in her right mind wouldn't? But I'm a working girl. Maybe when you're back in Roancarrick on business?'

His mouth set in a grim line. 'I'm not sure if I'll be in that neck of the woods in the foreseeable future.'

'I'll just have to hold you to that meal the next time I'm in Dublin.' She was reckless now, scenting victory.

'It's an open invitation, doll. I've always been partial to the older woman. She knows what she wants and she goes for it. Plus she has a more interesting collection of underwear, in my experience.' His face closed in on hers and a perspiration-popping flash of insight warned Venus of his intention to kiss her on the mouth. She turned her head and his lips landed on her ear.

Cheeky strap. She stood, clattering her chair. 'Lily is expecting me.'

'And I have calls to make. See you around, Venus.'

The trouble with men, she thought, making her way back to Lily's apartment, is they never kiss you when they're supposed to. The wrong ones are up for it and the right ones back off.

Cutting past The Screen cinema with its stubby doorman statue, she checked the listings, just in case it would be still a case of three's a crowd back at Adelphi Court. Couples were sitting in the window of a restaurant she passed and Venus fantasised about a romantic dinner for two. Although not if Senan were the other half of the two, discussing her frillies with the nonchalance of someone who could tell a chemise from a camisole. As if. No, her idea of a candlelit meal involved someone with long artist's fingers twined around the stem of his glass. Maybe with an ink-blot on them which she could tease him about.

Venus whistled unconsciously as she walked.

She pressed the buzzer for Lily's flat and said quickly, 'I can go to the pictures if I'm in the way here – there's a slushy one I've been meaning to see that's due to start in fifteen minutes.'

'Of course you're not in the way,' Lily sang down the intercom. 'We're both longing to see you. We have a fabulous surprise for you.'

Chapter Thirty-six

The fabulous surprise turned out to be surprising only to Lily and Karim, who sat hand in hand on the sofa. They were intending to marry after all, on Christmas Eve as originally planned. Venus had to promise she'd be there with them, even if it meant disappointing students panting to be drilled on the subtleties of when to use the familiar as opposed to the formal address in Spanish. Venus didn't bother telling them she wouldn't have any classes on December 24 – they were swaddled in their own construction of the universe.

'My other angel,' breathed Karim.

'Lily is your angel.' Venus was firm. 'One angel should be enough for any man.'

Naturally she pledged she'd be with them come hell or high water, as her father would say. Which reminded her, she'd have to drag Dan with her because she wasn't leaving him on his own in Roancarrick on Christmas Eve. There'd be war; cities were anathema to her father. Still, she could bribe him with the prospect of a new audience for his stories: he'd be bringing rural folklore to the poor city ignoramuses.

Then Venus remembered she had an early wedding gift for Lily in her overnight bag. She'd slipped it into a side pocket for luck, although not convinced an opportunity to present it would offer itself. 'This is for you.' She reached a small bag with a ribbon drawstring to Lily, who tried to look inside one-handed so she wouldn't have to drop Karim's hand.

'Lace,' breathed Lily, losing all compunction about letting go of Karim while she spread out its spider's-web coils.

'I don't suppose you'll be going in for the meringue dress,' said Venus. 'Well, of course you can if you want to – pay no attention to me,' she amended, as Lily looked hurt and muttered something about never being too old for bridal frills. 'You'd look divine in duchesse satin,' Venus rushed on. 'I thought this could be your something new – you could stitch it onto a petticoat or something. Apparently it was made by Belgian nuns, a claim which I'm inclined to take with a pillar of salt. I bought it in Sligo because it reminded me of the lace on my First Holy Communion dress, and that came off my mother's wedding dress.'

Lily's impetuous hug brought Venus's rambling explanation to a halt.

'I didn't think I'd be able to give it to you. I packed it as a lucky charm really,' Venus admitted. 'In case the seahorse needed some back-up.'

'You and your lucky charms,' laughed Lily. 'I love the lace. And I love you. I love Karim. I love everybody.' She opened her arms to include Karim in a tri-partite hug.

Group hugs. Venus swallowed. Still, it was Lily's day – she was entitled to exuberance. It wasn't every day your marriage of convenience became something altogether less convenient and infinitely more promising.

They ordered pizza and opened a bottle of wine, most of which Venus consumed because the other pair were too enraptured with one another to do anything as pedestrian as eat or drink. Venus, by comparison, was at the stage where she'd raffle off her grandmother for a shot of alcohol. Lily announced she'd be serving beef at her wedding reception, because there were so many other health scares that people might just as well start eating it again. Venus tuned out from wedding-reception discussions, hoping her father had cooked the sausages, eggs and rashers she'd left in the fridge for him. He was well able to handle fries, but she was concerned in case he hadn't bothered and had made do with a sausage sandwich. At least Birdie would call in to see him. She'd promised to keep an eye on him.

A need to make contact with him swept her. 'Would you mind if I rang my father?'

Lily nodded, engrossed in compiling a seating plan for her wedding reception on the inside of the pizza cardboard. 'We can't put my brother next to Dad because the pair of them will welly into the whiskey and Mum will get upset with Dad, who has no tolerance for the hard stuff any more, and then . . .' she was explaining to Karim, who exuded compassion and understanding.

As Venus dialled, she wondered where couples stored their brains until after the wedding plans were finalised. Trivia seemed to obsess them.

Dan was in fine form, pleased to hear she'd be back the following afternoon but more interested in telling her about a court case in the *Donegal Democrat*. It involved someone related to him on his mother's side who was fined for having an illegal still. Dan was engrossed in excited speculation about whether the cousin had the same recipe for poitín as himself. Venus smiled as she listened to her father's creamy burr.

Her excavations may not have turned up the identity of her real mother, or her father for that matter, but she had unearthed a treasure she'd forgotten to appreciate in Dan Macken.

He was still pondering his cousin's recipe, jealous in case it was superior, when she arrived in Roancarrick the next day. And then he remembered an important gobbet of news. 'That artist fellow of yours called in yesterday evening.'

Venus tensed. 'Why?'

'To see if I needed any messages run – he knew you were away in Dublin-town. It was civil of the lad. He sat and had a cup of tea with me and then Birdie called and the three of us had a grand chat.'

'Did my name crop up in conversation at all?' Venus affected indifference but she was on tenterhooks.

'It did. Conor asked if you found Roancarrick dull after city life and whether I thought you could settle here. I told him it was your home, of course you were happy here. "She's too old for London-town," I told him. "Places like that are for the young and carefree." And besides, I said, you were never able to come across a man to your taste there so maybe you'd find richer pickings on home ground.'

Venus groaned.

She managed a quick walk before she had to drive in to Sligo for that night's class. Hopeful that Conor might see her and join her, she lingered by the shoreline, watching the seagulls swoop near the harbour end. The cold water never seemed to bother them. A man approached, calling her name. It was John Óg O'Dea.

'How's it going?' she asked listlessly. She meant it in general terms, but John Óg imagined Venus was referring to his love life.

'Couldn't be better,' he enthused. 'I see young Wendy Toner from reception on Tuesdays and Fridays and Una McAteer, that's the woman from the Ulster Bank, on Mondays and Wednesdays.'

'What about the weekend?'

'At the weekend,' he was bursting with importance, 'I meet Mrs Evans – Megan.' He slapped his upper lip against his lower as he said her Christian name.

Venus couldn't resist. 'Who's Megan, John Óg?'

He tapped the side of the nose. 'She's leading the field at the moment. A Welsh widow lady, she's dripping with class. I'm handling her affairs – she has a dress shop in Sligo and I'm going through the books straightening them out for her.'

'There can't be much time for visiting the Mammy at this rate.'

'True,' conceded John Óg, 'but I've told her what I'm doing and she's right behind me. She's especially keen on Megan, although the two haven't met. She thinks a ritzy frock shop is exactly what Roancarrick needs.'

Venus didn't know how she managed to keep a straight face at that. Roancarrick needed a frock shop even less than it needed his earlier suggestion of a delicatessen. She wished him well, and said it sounded as though he wouldn't need to buy weighing scales for any more women of his acquaintance, which was bad news for Dunnes Stores but good news for him.

As they parted, John Óg gave her the class of a look that her mother would have called old-fashioned. 'I know you think I'm dry as a bone and not husband material at all, Venus Macken, but any woman I take to wife will want for nothing. I'll treat her with consideration too – there's many's a woman would sell her soul for a small bit of respect.'

Venus felt the smart of shame as she went home to gather up her books for the Spanish class – she was too quick to judge, she chided herself. Then she forgot about John Óg in the disappointing realisation that she wouldn't be running into Conor Landers that evening. She could always ring him and tell him she was back – perhaps after the lesson.

Venus wasn't able to lose herself in teaching, as she usually did. The intermediate students sensed her distraction and there was a corresponding slackening in effort in their discussion of *Chronicle Of A Death Foretold*. Some of the students hadn't bothered to read the Spanish version, cheating with the English translation. Still, they were entitled to be lethargic, she reminded herself. Most of them had completed a day's work before going back out again on an inclement night.

Her father had taken out his teeth and was preparing for bed when she returned. 'Birdie's for Belfast-town again tomorrow,' Dan lisped. 'She called in with another of her ginger cakes. That woman has a light hand with cake batter – there's many's a man would have chanced his luck with her on the strength of it. I think she was hoping to see you – she'd forgotten this was one of your teaching nights. I had the impression she was anxious to speak to you about something.'

371

Venus contemplated calling next door, but decided against it. Birdie always promised more than she delivered. She probably just wanted to tell her to buy herself a pair of ruby slippers and click the heels three times to find her way home. But Venus had had enough of whimsy tricked out as folk wisdom.

'Did nobody else call?' she asked.

'You mean Conor Landers?' Her father's eyes twinkled with a merriment that shaved decades from his age.

'Maybe.'

'He phoned. Said he'd seen you down by the harbour with John Óg O'Dea and you were so engrossed in conversation that he hadn't liked to intrude. But he'll be sketching by the seal's rock tomorrow morning if you're free.'

* * *

'I think I've discovered something about how you came to be left here as a baby.' Conor didn't bother with preliminaries.

He had been leaning against the rock, focused on the horizon, when Venus came upon him. She had admired his profile for a moment, smiling at the snub nose which sabotaged its angularity, and at the tuneless whistle which floated back to her on the breeze. But as soon as she touched his arm he spun around and launched into enflamed speech.

'Tell me.' Her pulse speeded up and colour welled along her neck and breastbone.

'It happened the other night, when I was in your kitchen and Birdie dropped by.' Conor steadied himself with both hands on her shoulders as the words continued to tumble out. 'I seized my chance and started your father talking about the day he'd found you, right here by the seal's rock, because there was something about the story that struck a false note. Remember how we realised that Birdie was integral to the entire enterprise? And how she made sure your father went by the route she wanted him to take, so he'd pass above the mermaid's cave?'

'So you think Birdie might have seen me lying there' – Venus spoke haltingly, realigning this story as familiar to her as her name, and yet now undergoing modification – 'and sent Dad out for me?'

'No.' Conor was impatient, blue-green eyes lambent. 'She placed you there.'

'But she's already denied to my face that she's my mother. I don't think she'd lie about it, not to me. Not point blank.'

'Maybe she did it on behalf of someone else. You have to tax her about it, insist that you know she left you there and demand an explanation. Don't let yourself be fobbed off, Venus, she's covering something up. I can smell it. And she realises I suspect her involvement. Whenever I looked at her, her eyes kept skimming away. Dan was as innocent as a child – he prattled on about seeing a patch of white by the rock pools and wrapping you up and bringing you home to his wife. But Birdie was restless when I pressed him about why he took the cliff path with a gale blowing. Birdie left you by the seal's rock, Venus, I know she did.'

Venus's mind was reeling. 'You'd imagine anyone in their right minds would have left a baby somewhere more obvious than the seal's rock. I thought church steps were supposed to be traditional.'

'Birdie Ross doesn't strike me as a woman for whom the obvious is at all obvious.' Conor folded his arms and watched her, sympathetic to the tumult in her emotions.

Venus pursed her lips. 'I'll go and see her at once.'

'Would you like me to come with you?'

Preoccupied though she was, the offer warmed her. But she declined it without hesitation. 'This last part is something I have to do on my own, Conor. But I can't thank you enough for your help. I've been hearing my story so long, I'd stopped listening to it.'

His disappointment percolated through to her and she lingered, not wanting him to feel rejected.

'I've been invited to a *céilí* next week. It's the couple with the fishing-tackle shop. She's called Jenny Barton, I can't remember his name. It's something tweedy. Anyway they're having a bit of a session – I said I might drop in. We could go together if you like.'

His gap-toothed smile flashed. 'I'd like that very much. Will you do me one favour, Venus? Will you come and see me as soon as you've spoken to Birdie? I'm nearly as anxious to know how it turns out as you must be.'

She nodded automatically, senses heightened. Her instincts told her she was about to learn answers to questions that had haunted her all her life.

Chapter Thirty-seven

Fired up to confront Birdie, Venus suffered an anti-climax. The half-door always kept open at the back of the house was closed and there was nobody home – then she remembered that Birdie was in Belfast. Quarrying the past was proving to be a halting process.

She simmered with impatience for the rest of the day, but it was the following afternoon before Birdie returned. Venus heard the distinctive whine of the Bundoran firm's diesel taxi chug uphill. She gave Birdie half an hour to settle in and then arrived on her doorstep.

'I was expecting you,' said Birdie. Her expression was its usual impassive mask, but her eyes had sunken into tired folds and her thin mouth sagged.

There was neither jazz music playing nor the computer's motor running and it struck Venus that Birdie was cloaked in loneliness. Even the red ribbon holding back her mass of dark hair straggled.

'You know, Venus, I've discovered something.' Birdie's

habitual rasp was sorrowful. 'The only thing you can be sure of gaining with years in wrinkles – wisdom isn't guaranteed.'

Venus stood in the doorway, wrong-footed by this melancholic version of her neighbour. Then she advanced, for her business could no longer be postponed.

'I know why you're here,' said Birdie. 'As soon as that boyfriend of yours began interrogating me, I realised it was only a matter of time.'

Venus looked around the room. Birdie hadn't lit the fire yet and there were no lamps or candles gleaming, although the afternoon was gloomy. Birdie had been sitting in the dark for the past thirty minutes.

'I'll put on the kettle while you set a match to the fire,' suggested Venus.

Soon it was cheerier, although Birdie still wore a woebegone aura and shivered as she sipped at her tea. Venus waited, eyes resting on the spot on the hearth where Jude used to toast himself.

After a time Birdie roused herself. 'How much do you know, Venus?'

'I know that you left me there by the seal's rock, and that you engineered it so my father would find me.'

Birdie's deep-set eyes sparked. 'But you don't know who your mother was.' It was a statement, not a question.

'No.'

Birdie heaved a whispering sigh and went to the kitchen table, opening the cutlery drawer. As she did so, Venus suddenly recalled how her neighbour had seemed to stare at the drawer that time she'd challenged Birdie, convinced she was her mother.

She produced an envelope, removed a photograph and studied it for a moment. Then she passed it to Venus. A girl with hair as red as Venus's and eyes equally tawny looked out. She was laughing into the camera, head thrown back, leaning on a bicycle that was almost as large as her and which appeared too heavy for her slight weight to hold. With a certainty that was dazzling, Venus knew she was looking at her mother.

'Yesterday was her birthday,' said Birdie.

Venus kept her eyes on the photograph as she spoke.

'I went to Belfast to visit her grave. I brought her hothouse sunflowers, because she loved them, and a pot of rosemary for her name's sake. Her name was Rosemary – for remembrance, you see, although there's no danger I could ever forget her.' Her tone grew fierce. 'She was the dearest child, and I wasn't there for her when she needed me most – I'll never forgive myself for that.' The swell of emotion exhausted her and she hunkered in towards the fire. 'Rosemary ran away to Belfast with a pop group when she was barely sixteen. They were only boys themselves, convinced they'd set the world alight. She lived with them in a squat with another girlfriend. Such a golden creature Rosemary was, always singing. She had a radiance about her. The Troubles were just beginning then and Belfast was becoming a city to avoid, but nothing seemed able to penetrate the lustre of Rosemary's world. I hoped it would always be that way for her.' Birdie pushed her slipping ribbon back towards the base of her neck and brooded. 'One of the musicians was your father, but I don't know which – Rosemary never told me, and I never saw her with any particular one of them. She became pregnant almost at once, and had you at home, shortly before her seventeenth birthday. I hadn't seen her for a couple of months and didn't know she was expecting a baby. I had no way of contacting her – she rang me sometimes, but I had no address or phone number for her. I used to send her what money I could spare to the shop where she worked, selling shoes, and once she agreed to meet me in the self-service restaurant of a chain store in Belfast. Littlewoods, it was. It's not there any more. I was horrified by how bedraggled she had become, wrung out at such a young age. I begged her to come away with me, but she insisted she was happy and said it was the life she'd chosen – she didn't want to be part of the mainstream. What did she know of choices at that stage of her life? But I was only a few years older and I didn't argue with her, more's the pity.'

Birdie leaned forward to throw another sod of turf on the fire. As she settled back her glance browsed across the photograph in Venus's hand. 'It's the only one I have of her. But it captures her spirit, the laughter and the optimism. It was taken a few weeks before she ran off.'

'Why didn't she keep me? Was she too young to mind a baby?'

'She was only a child.' Birdie's eyes reflected two miniature banks of flames. 'I can't imagine how she must have suffered. She decided to have you at home rather than go into hospital, something to do with this daft decision to drop out from the system, and the other girlfriend in the squat helped her when she went into labour. The lads were off gigging somewhere. Little Rosemary was filled with brandy to dull the pain. The friend, although she was no true friend or she'd have called an ambulance, rang in a panic to say she was crying my name. By the time I reached her you were already born. And Rosemary was dead.'

Birdie fell silent, searching the glowing fireplace, and Venus scrutinised the photograph of the girl with a bicycle, a scaled-down version of herself. Confidence shone from her eyes, as though the future was a wonderful adventure beckoning her to join it.

A sod of turf crackled onto the hearth and Birdie roused herself. 'The post mortem said she died of an amniotic fluid embolism – a bubble crossed into her bloodstream during labour. It's a rare condition but death is almost always instantaneous. I couldn't go to the post mortem – I read about it in the paper. You see, I knew it would also show up that she'd just had a baby and there would be a police enquiry.' She pressed the heels of her palms against her eyes, trying to erase a memory. Or nudge one to the surface. 'Rosemary held you before she died, that I do know. The silly friend who panicked during Rosemary's labour told me that much. She said Rosemary was sorry you were a girl, for she felt a son would have lifted her out of the chasm she'd fallen into – I think poor, sweet Rosemary had realised life in a Belfast squat was no great adventure after all. But I never paid any heed to that business of her wanting a son – it was just the pain and the misery tumbling out of her. She'd have done her best for you if she'd lived, I know that as surely as I'm sitting here.' Birdie, whose voice had grown heated, bit down on a thumb-knuckle and subsided into a quieter tone. 'I didn't know what to do so I brought you back to Roancarrick with me, and at first I thought to raise you myself. But Maura and Dan had lost their boys and needed a child to love – they were folk you could trust with your life, and I knew they could give you a more stable home than I could manage. I was only starting out and barely scraping together a living. At least I'd be able to watch over you if they took you in.'

Birdie dragged both hands across her scalp, wrenching at her dark hair, while Venus listened, saucer-eyed.

'I meant to offer you to them openly, that's why I called in.

To test the water. I left you in my cottage and I went next-door, intending to raise it with them. But Maura had a headache and Dan was going to O'Dea's shop for tablets, and it occurred to me that I could make sure he found you on his way. Finding a baby forces someone to become responsible for it, don't you see? It makes it seem as though they were meant for you and you for them.' Her eyes implored Venus to understand. 'All of a sudden it came to me that I should leave you by the seal's rock. I suppose I could have set you down somewhere more obvious, but I couldn't take the risk of being spotted. The seal's rock just seemed the right place to do it. So I grasped my opportunity with both hands and I raced back to the cottage, knowing Dan was slow on his feet. I'd have a few seconds' grace. I snatched you up, Venus, and I dashed ahead of him, then I laid you down in the most sheltered place I could find, where you'd be protected from the wind. I took off your little jumpsuit and the blanket wrapped around you, because I wanted it to look as though you'd just washed ashore. Dan came along a moment later. I threw pebbles to attract his attention – I was terrified in case he'd pass by without noticing you, especially as you were burbling away and not crying at all. God help me, I pinched your little toes to make you cry, Venus, because there's nothing like a child's wail for slicing through the wind. Then I hid in the mermaid's cave and watched him lift you up in his arms. I don't know if what I did was right, but I did what I could. I was half-deranged with grief for Rosemary and I wasn't much more than a girl myself – not yet twenty.'

'Why did you care for her so deeply?' asked Venus, heart pounding as she waited for the reply.

Birdie raised her pain-clenched face and locked eyes with Venus. 'She was my sister.'

Chapter Thirty-eight

So Birdie was her aunt. Venus was numb, neither shocked nor dismayed nor even stimulated at finding a blood relative. It was as if she had first to hear everything Birdie could tell her and then she would attempt to digest it.

Birdie, who had seemed indifferent to her presence while she spoke of Rosemary, watched Venus attentively now. 'That means I gave away my own flesh and blood.' Her demeanour was challenging as she pre-empted what Venus might be thinking.

Venus didn't react.

'I admit I was frightened of the responsibility and I didn't know how I'd be able to earn enough to feed and clothe us both,' said Birdie. 'But that's not why I handed you over to Maura and Dan. I saw that you could revive Maura, who had all but given up the ghost after her twin sons were taken from her. And I knew Dan would be a doting father on a little girl. He'd nurse her and cosset her and stretch out his hand and reach her the moon if she asked for it. He did, didn't he?'

Venus nodded. After a pause, she asked, 'What made you tell me now, after so many years?'

'You knew half the story. You may as well know the other half. And I had a longing yesterday, as I stood by my sister's grave – Protestants on one side, Catholics on the other, with the Republican plot at the back, divisions, divisions everywhere. I had an impulse to bring Rosemary's daughter there. To show you your mother's headstone amid that jumble of marble and stone. If you wanted to see it. I was sitting here thinking about it and then in you walked, with your eyes blazing exactly like Rosemary's, and you challenged me and I answered you.' She rested her cheek against her hand and dwindled into herself. 'When Maura was alive it seemed wrong to tell you – it would have been as though I was trying to claw you back for myself. I was blood kin and she wasn't. She was sensitive about that, Venus. After Maura died, it felt disloyal to speak of it. She was a true friend to me these years I've spent in Roancarrick – I couldn't trample on her memory. I arrived here knowing nobody after renting this cottage' – her gaze riffled the room – 'and on the first day she turned up on my back stoop with fresh eggs from those hens she used to keep and a cake of her soda bread. She persuaded the owner to sell the house privately to me, too, when he had a mind to put it on the open market and invite bidders. That was before I came into any money of my own and times were tight. So you see, I owed Maura on my own account, and I'll always owe her for what she did for you, Venus. That's why I maintained the fiction of knowing nothing about your origins until you forced my hand. Or maybe Rosemary forced it. All I know is that yesterday's visit to her graveside at Milltown Cemetery changed my mind and I couldn't tell you why it should have happened then and not a minute earlier.'

Venus had always imagined she would feel complete when her mother's identity was revealed; instead a void was yawning within her. She wanted to be outdoors. Still holding the photograph, she stumbled for the door.

Her feet took her to the mermaid's cave and she perched on the seal's rock, waiting for the sea to soothe her, as it usually did. She thought only of a girl almost half her age having a baby in a squat in Belfast, brandy ladled into her but failing to allay the pain and terror.

Venus held her knees locked tight against her chest and rocked herself on the rock under which her aunt had left her thirty-three years ago. Sea spray, carried on the breeze, prickled her right cheek and along the side of her neck. Peace didn't drape her in its comfort blanket, however, for the truth, now that she knew it at last, seemed too overwhelming to assimilate. Suddenly, she wanted nothing more than to see her father. Venus scrambled back uphill, towards home.

'What's that in your hand, lass?' Dan nodded towards the photograph she was still clutching.

'It's my mother.'

'That's not Maura,' he began, then ground to a halt. Comprehension dawned.

She told him the story recounted to her by Birdie and he listened, transfixed. When she'd finished, he said, 'Of course, your eyes are the spit of Birdie's.'

Birdie's face swam into Venus's mind. She'd never noticed, until this moment, that they both had identical sherry-gold eyes. Deep-set and watchful.

'Birdie's always felt like family – now she is,' Dan continued. 'This is a weight off my mind, Venus, for you won't be alone when I'm gone. Not that I'm planning on going anywhere, although there's no denying I've more hot dinners behind me than ahead of me.' From habit he smacked his lips, preparing to indulge in some bogus resignation, but caught sight of Venus's expression – midway between exasperated and emotional – and hurried on. 'I'm going nowhere yet, lass. Mickey Joe would only claim I was trying to avoid letting him win back some of the money's he lost to me, on all those donkeys he thinks are racehorses. And we wouldn't want to give him the satisfaction, would we?'

'No, Dad.' She hugged him. He was still her father, whatever else changed. 'You know,' she addressed the crown of his head, 'I always believed you knew who my mother was but held off for fear of upsetting Mam.'

'It's true your mother was sensitive about it.' His eyes strayed to the photograph of the twins on the dresser. 'But she couldn't have loved you any more if you'd been fashioned from a rib taken from her side.' Dan surfaced from her embrace; the lass was holding him so tightly she was choking him – she didn't know her own strength. 'Maura always worried that another woman would turn up one day and claim you. That's why she preferred not to discuss how you came to us and from where. It was just her way, as though talking about it might make the evil deed happen. I suppose I picked up the habit from her, of discouraging you when you asked questions.'

'It's odd you weren't more curious about my origins.'

'Well, lass, I'm a bit of a man for the horses – Mickey Joe can vouch for that. If I've learned one thing, I've learned this. Never look a gift horse in the mouth.'

Venus laughed and stroked his age-freckled scalp. The skin felt vibrant against her palm.

Dan reached down the side of his armchair, produced a

bottle of cough mixture and took a swig. Then he hauled himself to his feet, holding on to each arm of the chair. 'We'll go across and see Birdie, now. Reach me down my hat, Venus. No, not the greeney-coloured one – that's for wet days. Give me the grey fellow.'

'Why are we going to Birdie's?' Venus felt ambivalent towards their neighbour.

'She'll be in a bit of a state, God love her – sure Birdie's as soft as butter.'

* * *

Birdie was crouched by the fire when they walked in. She jumped up and began to approach Venus, but backed off when she saw the younger woman was studiously not meeting her gaze. Birdie transferred her attention to Dan.

'It's been a fair while since you set foot across my threshold, Dan Macken.' She pattered towards a cupboard and reached for a bottle of whiskey. 'A rarity like that needs marking – you'll take a drop.'

He pantomimed reluctance, out of manners, and then accepted when she poured it anyway. 'Sure it'd be a shame to waste it,' he said. ' Especially since we're celebrating.'

'We are?' Birdie hopped from one leg to the other, uncertain.

'We are?' Venus plucked at the lint on her clothes, uncertain.

'We are.' Dan was determined. 'Venus has found her blood family. Maura loved you like a sister, Birdie. I know she's watching us now, sharing my pleasure that you've made yourself known to Venus. So pour yourself and the lass a drop of that yellow hooch you brew up, Birdie Ross, because I want to propose a toast.'

He waited while an uncharacteristically flustered Birdie did as she was bid.

'To the two mothers who loved Venus,' said Dan.

They went to clink glasses, but he raised his hand to stay them.

'And to Birdie, the causeway between both,' he concluded.

Birdie looked at Venus with eyes afraid to hope, waiting for her reaction.

Venus lifted her glass and chimed it against Birdie's. Then she smiled into eyes that were replicas of her own – and swallowed its honeyed contents.

* * *

'And that's how it happened. I've neither added nor subtracted,' concluded Venus, nestling within the circle of Conor's arms.

'But there's something missing,' he complained, propped against the mouth of the mermaid's cave.

'There is?'

'Nobody found out what Birdie does for a living.'

Venus slapped a hand to her forehead. 'Dad asked. After we'd all had a couple of drinks he started ribbing Birdie about her secretive nature, and he said she might as well come clean about everything in one fell swoop. She couldn't have been going up to Belfast all these years just to tend to my mother's – my *other* mother's – grave. He wanted to know if they were business trips as well. She admitted they were and then he hounded her until Birdie confessed the nature of her business.'

'It must be something illegal. Or pornographic. Or both,' guessed Conor, as the wind ransacked his fawn-fair curls.

She dug her elbow into his ribs in mock-indignation. 'I'll have you know that's my aunt you're slandering. She was seeing her agent. Birdie Ross is none other than Penelope Power, the romantic novelist with the Midas touch, a writer who makes Barbara Cartland look like a cynic. Her novels have been translated into fifty-eight languages, eleven have been given the mini-series treatment and they've even named a street after her in some little town in Brazil. Chaste yet paradoxically spirited young women and dissolute barons just waiting to be redeemed are her stock in trade. Poor Birdie is mortified now in case her cover is blown – only her agent knows her identity. She prizes her privacy – she's petrified of fans trekking around Roancarrick on Penelope Power pilgrimages.'

'I'll carry her secret to the grave,' said Conor, 'provided she pays me a weekly gratuity. Or at least lets me taste that mead she brews up. I'm sorry I wasn't there to share in your toasts – did you have stacks of them?'

'Scores,' agreed Venus, 'but Birdie's mead never gives you a hangover. Dad turned a little maudlin and confessed he'd saved a few of Mam's ashes to have her buried with him after all, among his people. Typical of him to start talking about funerals in the middle of a celebration,' she added fondly.

By and by, Conor caught her by the hand and pulled her to her feet, guiding her the couple of paces to the seal's rock.

'Where are we going?'

'We're there already.' He reached down to the hollow at the base of the rock, where a plastic bag lay tucked away. Inside was an oblong wrapped in brown paper and secured with string, and Conor handed it to Venus.

'*Brown-paper packages tied up with strings, these are a few of my favourite things,*' she quoted.

'*Sound of Music* junkie.' He nuzzled her neck.

'You seem to make a habit of giving me presents.' She grappled with the knot, while he rested his elbow on the rock and breathed in the salt air, watching her. 'It was only the other day I had a drawing from you.'

'Offerings for the goddess,' he teased. 'I always understood deities were a temperamental lot and needed humouring. Propitiation, isn't that what they called it?'

Venus didn't answer, too beguiled by what was revealed beneath the paper. Its wood was walnut, its brass was polished, its dials read *set fair, fair, change, rain* and *stormy*: on her lap lay the barometer from the captain's house that she'd hankered after as a child. Venus gazed at it in wonder.

'I found it in an antiques' shop in Bundoran. It is the right one, isn't it?' he checked, anxious at her continuing silence.

She looked up at him and her expression was a benediction. Carefully, tenderly, Venus set down the barometer on the rock's flat surface and answered him with a kiss – a kiss that melted, solidified and melted again.

After a while, she remembered her barometer. She touched it, where the needle was lodged between '*change*' and '*rain*'. 'Is it broken?' she asked.

One of Conor's hands covered hers, squeezing reassurance, and with the middle finger of the other he tapped the dial. The needle sprang to life and quivered, seeking its position.

Then, with a dart that brought a smile to Venus's face, it came to rest on '*set fair*'.

The End